To

Mary, Josh and Alysha.
Still my Universe.

Also by Scott K Bywater

Genesis Makers
eVOLUTION
Emissary

eVOLUTION 2

Induction

by
Scott K Bywater

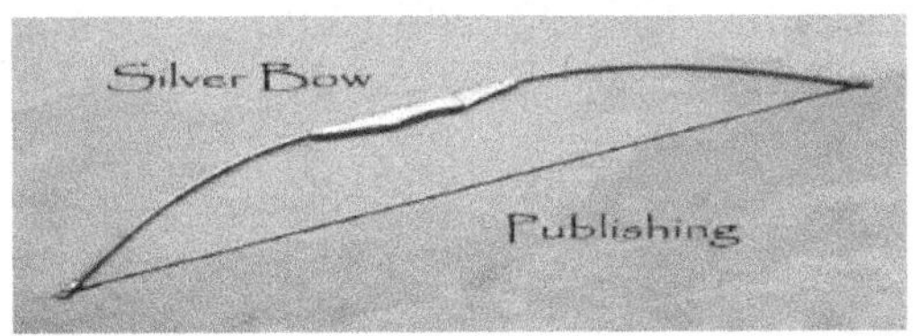

720 Sixth Street, Unit # 5
New Westminster, BC V3L 3C5
CANADA

Title: eVOLUTION 2 - Induction
Author: Scott K. Bywtater
Cover Art: "Portals" painting by Candice James
Layout and Design: Candice James
Editing: Candice James

ISBN 9781774032237 (softcover)
ISBN 9781774032244 (e-book)
© 2022 Silver Bow Publishing

Library and Archives Canada Cataloguing in Publication

Title: Evolution. 2, Induction / by Scott K. Bywater.
Names: Bywater, Scott K., 1962- author.
Identifiers: Canadiana (print) 20220467919 | Canadiana (ebook) 20220467951 | ISBN 9781774032237
   (softcover) | ISBN 9781774032244 (Kindle)
Classification: LCC PR9619.4.B99 I53 2022 | DDC 823/.92—dc23

Chapters

Prologue – Nowhere / 7

6

Prologue

Nowhere
"Imagination is the highest form of Research."
– Albert Einstein

Becker opened his eyes and swivelled his head as far as it would go, all he could see were stars, suspended in a colourful but mainly black expanse.

In the background were stars, colourful dust and the blackness of space, in the foreground was his visor and helmet and all he could hear, within his suit, was his own raspy breathing that went up a notch.

He knew where he was, although "being in space" hardly hammered down his location. Becker knew why he was here, it was at Minan's whim, he thought. *The boy*, it had to be. Was he better, or worse off than where he used to be, that was the question? Becker assumed he was better off, he had to be, but looking around, he wasn't so sure.

'Where was Connie for fuck's sake,' Becker wondered? He looked left and right, turned his head and looked behind himself and in front, his heartbeat increasing a bit.

She had to be close by - there was a white spot in the distance, he hoped that was her but he really didn't know, not with his dodgy eyesight. Becker didn't have his glasses on so, everything at a distance was a blurred mess. The visor of his helmet itself was hardly prescription, although it should be. For short-sighted astronauts, he thought, trying to push the panic further down his throat.

Becker looked at his personal-RCS, which was little more than carbon in an aerosol can, mounted in his backpack and on the front of his suit, and on his arms, with the important stats splashed on his visor like colourful graffiti. It was below twenty-five percent. In other words, he had fuck-all propellant left.

There were only three, maybe four decent spurts left. Becker knew he'd need one decent spray to get going and two sprays to slow down. One, if things went perfectly. And two to get back. Hopefully, he could piggy-back off Connie. If it wasn't Connie in the distance, he could be in deep trouble. If it wasn't her, *WTF*, he reckoned?

Becker gave himself one full burn which sent him forward, *fast*, but as he thought, he'd miss her to the port side by a fair margin. By using the RCS to burn to the starboard or opposite side, Becker moved toward what he assumed was Connie. The remaining spurts were used from the front of the suit to null his inertia and momentum through space.

Becker was glad to see Connie's face through the visor, although she seemed to be yelling something at him but he couldn't hear a thing. The helmet was set to "non-comm", so he couldn't hear a thing from anyone. Becker didn't even know there was such a setting. Otherwise, he would have used it before. He pressed the external button with his glove before he thought about it further.

'I'm, uh...*here*,' Becker said, rotating around Connie and trying desperately to look her in the eyes. He pulled her in and held her tight and tried to stop their rotation which continued unabated.

'I can see that...I *said* I would come to you, my RCS is nearly full,' Connie said gruffly.

'Well, I'm here now, don't worry about it...oh, and, um, you're welcome,' Becker said, with a wide grin, obvious through the visor.

'Okay, thanks,' she replied uncertainly. He honestly thought he was a hero. Flying through space to "save her" and all.

Becker and Connie were now both tumbling and falling through space. Every now and then he'd see her face. It was there and then it wasn't. Up, down, forward, back, they were together and rotating through space, and every now and then, he'd spy her face. Becker sort of wished he hadn't seen it.

She looked horrified. Her mouth was open and moving but there was no voice or meaningful sound, apart from rasping and ragged breaths he could hear coming through the comms. If circumstances were different, it would have been quite funny.

But things were indeed dire. Previously, before Becker's wild goose-chase into the southern wilds, they'd been in Sydney, Australia having a great time, enjoying the fruits of a very successful company. Now they were spinning through space. *Go figure, right?*

How in the name of God did they get to this unenviable point in time and space? Becker yelled to himself, not necessarily in those words. From where they were, to here – it sounded impossible, at the very least, implausible. From Antarctica to space was quite the journey and it was very unlikely, no matter what perspective you had.

He knew the answer to his quandary, even before he asked it. It was Minan, no doubt about it. It was that little shit's doing, he'd engineered the whole lot of it. He made the goddamned Universe,

Becker thought, while he tumbled, it had to be him. Nothing, *no-one* else could or would have done it. No wonder he didn't like him. Becker grudgingly admitted that Minan may have saved him – but that didn't make up for everything else he'd done.

The kid was never, *ever*, positive. Never did anything that, to them, was for the greater good. Becker had to admit the formulation of his algorithm which led to the Universe and to *them*, was to their benefit. But everything since then, hadn't been good for humans. Becker scratched his helmet and cleared his throat - he wasn't quite sure why he and Connie were here...wherever *"here"* was exactly. He assumed that was to his benefit but he wasn't sure.

Why the kid did what he was doing, he had no idea whatsoever, and especially why they were in space, he had even less idea about, if that was possible. In short, Becker had no idea how or why *anything* was happening. He was just bereft of any decent ideas at all. Becker just wanted he and Connie to stay alive. That had to be his only focus. And hers hopefully.

Then she disappeared. Not slowly, piece by piece, but just *gone*, in front of his eyes. She was there and then she wasn't. Now, it was just Becker floating in space...alone.

Now he was really scared – alone, somewhere, *nowhere*, in space. Becker had no idea where he was. Nothing looked familiar. None of the stars, none of the nebula, the dust clouds, nothing at all. It was all totally, thoroughly alien and he didn't like any of it.

His oxygen gauge that flashed over the visor of his helmet said he had fifteen minutes before it ran out of oxygen completely and he was left in the vacuum with no pressure at all. Just a dead suit. Becker started breathing in shallow, rapid gasps as he contemplated what might be in front of him.

Fuck, he thought, thinking about his demise and the agony of running out of air, that probably lay in front of him. 'Shit, *shit...fuck*,' Becker screamed. There was no help, anywhere. He swung his head around violently - he didn't want to expire in this horrible, unfamiliar place...alone. But that's what was on the horizon. He was a long way from help, he could see that. That's about all he did know – that any help was probably light years away at best.

Becker gawked at the countdown on his visor as the seconds sloughed away, not as sure he'd be assisted, as he was before. He assumed Connie had been helped by the kid, who had clearly taken a shine to her, but now he wasn't sure about that either. Becker wasn't sure about anything. Perhaps she just disappeared and went nowhere. Maybe his eyesight was way worse than he thought. He tilted his head around as much as he could. She was still nowhere to be seen. It was just space, everywhere.

By the time two minutes had rolled passed he was sure in his own mind he wouldn't be helped. Numbers maintained their inexorable downward slide, and he could feel a weird pressure in his chest and knew what it was...it was backpressure, the prelude to asphyxiation and an awful death. Becker watched the numbers approach zero and he began to feel serious nausea. The numbers were at ten seconds and the pain got worse, his breathing was shallower and the intake of air louder, and more urgent. His eyes were moving around rapidly, looking everywhere. But there was no help to be seen anywhere.

All he could hear was his own tight, raspy breathing and the hollow thump of his heart which was getting louder. '*Fuck, it hurts*,' he yelled to no one. The last thing he saw, was his own spittle hitting the inside of his visor, as he thought morosely, 'This isn't fair'.

He felt the panic rise in his throat. Becker's heart was now racing, beating strangely, he sensed a tightness across his chest and felt dizzy to the point of feeling crippled and knew if he was in gravity, he would have collapsed to the ground. The cold sweat dripped down his back. Becker felt like he was dying or going mad, or something. Both probably.

At minus four seconds, he disappeared from space. One second, he was there, then he wasn't. Becker had disappeared from the Universe, not as quickly as Connie but he'd gone all the same.

Neither of them were left in space. There were only a couple of hydrogen atoms, a bit of dark energy and a spray of dark matter. Apart from that, space was empty of anything baryonic, for light decades in any direction.

*   *   *

The first thing he saw was...er, *Christ,* what were they, he exclaimed to himself, sleepers, wooden, but standing upright? He struggled to work it out, all he knew for sure, was that he was alive and somehow had plenty of oxygen to breathe. The data on his visor confirmed it. Where the air to breathe came from, he had no idea. It was incredibly illogical but – he could only think of Minan. Even though he had a great imagination, he could think of nothing else.

Where the hell was he? Not in space, obviously, Becker knew he'd shifted – and he was relieved and thankful for it, but where the fuck had he gone? Shards of blackness and whiteness whirled around him, overwhelming him with nausea and faintness.

What was this place and more importantly, where the hell *could* he be? And where the Goddamn was Connie? That was the most important thing of all. Becker hated being alone. He whipped his head around - she was nowhere to be seen. He gawked into the distance and could see her nowhere. If he'd gone to a different place, he was alone again – a prospect that didn't thrill him at all.

She was the first thing he hoped to see, but it wasn't to be. *Where the fuck was she?* Had they gone to different, distant places? He refused to consider the other, more odious option. Becker continued to jerk his head around anxiously. He couldn't see her anywhere. Maybe, she really wasn't here, he thought grimly. Which meant he was still alone - in whatever this place was. Becker gaped around and took an immediate dislike to his current locale.

Underfoot, were large tiles and bricks, and on the walls and roof were wooden pylons seemingly keeping a slightly yellowish rock strata back that looked hard and stable. There were no broken pieces of it on the ground, that he could see anyway, which was unusual in his experience. Normally, there'd be chunks and tiny pieces scattered everywhere.

Becker seemed to be in a tunnel of some sort that went in both directions. '*Well fuck me,*' he said loudly, raising his eyebrows as high as they would go, staggering back a few steps and looking around at the far reaches of the tunnel. He noticed an echo that brought his words back a few times. Very odd, he thought. This place was very unlike space...which was good, he reckoned, but why did he come to a *tunnel?*

Connie *was* here. She was in a heap almost under Becker, right beside him really, unconscious, but definitely, unquestionably alive. She was breathing and looked asleep, which, in itself, seemed very strange indeed. To see her like that was a first, she was normally, in fact, she was always the *up-and-at-em* type. Something had clearly gotten to her. He couldn't stop thinking about Minan's role of in all this.

Becker was ecstatic Connie was there and alive. It meant he didn't have to face this place alone. Whatever this place was. Nothing looked familiar so far. Becker was focussed on "why". Why had they been plucked from space to end up here? What was this place? This place looked so unlikely to be a destination for anyone. Both areas were total unknowns...space and now a dim tunnel. Very odd indeed.

Connie was making strange gurgling noises and moving her arms and legs jerkily, suggesting she was coming-too from whatever state she was in. Becker bent down and flicked Connie's cheeks with his thumb and forefinger. She was breathing quite noisily, almost snoring. Becker stood up - confident she was okay. All she had to do was open her damn eyes. Everything else seemed to be working fine.

'You're breathing and moving...*so wake the fuck up*,' he yelled, bending down again, only a few centimetres from her nose. He could see her battling for consciousness and was sure she'd be up and around soon enough. Behind the visor, she looked like someone waking from a good night's sleep.

Becker was thrilled to be alive and out of space but had absolutely zero idea where he was now. He looked around and saw nothing but more of the same. Wood, rock and tiles with a few bricks down the centre. The gravity felt normal, but he had no idea if it was or not. Proof was in the eating, he supposed. If it felt normal, it was normal.

Connie had her back against a pylon and was attempting to stand, wobbling and swaying at the same time. '*Whoa*,' Becker yelled, 'easy tiger...just take it easy.' He held her as she attempted to get up. She was very shaky, but quickly regained her land-legs. Unsteadiness soon became surety.

'I'm fine Becker, thanks,' she pushed his hand away, 'worry about yourself.' She was breathing in tight, angry gasps. 'Fine, I tell you.' Pushing him away, she was awake and annoyed with him already.

He stood back and watched her quizzically. 'Excuse me for trying to help,' he said. '*Jesus Christ*,' Becker stood back, still grimacing at her. 'Next time I won't bother,' he snapped quietly. Becker watched Connie from a short distance. He pulled at an ear lobe and took a step backward, relieved she was here, and not lost or something worse. *Christ*, she was hard work though, he groaned to himself.

'Relax Becker, we're both fine.' Connie's breathing was finally under control. 'We've gone from a boardroom, to space, and now here, wherever *here* is,' she said, peering at Becker dimly and then gazing around her, grimacing and groaning as she did so. Like Becker, she had no idea what this place was. It was better than floating in space though, *that* she knew.

Nothing looked familiar to her, but it had Minan written all over it. Had to be him. If it wasn't, how on Earth did they get here, and out of space? She thought about it and had no answer.

'Yeah, quite a trip,' he said, into his helmet mic, also looking around, and up and into the distance. Silence descended on them as they gave their current environment more attention.

'Where in the good fuck are we?' Connie said, swallowing hard and listening carefully for any sound, over and above her own breathing. The tunnel closed to darkness in front of and behind them.

'...Could be anywhere,' Becker said, 'nothing looks familiar...at all. I mean I don't think I've ever seen anywhere like this. Is this the uh...the afterlife? He couldn't help but grin at her dumbly after that comment. Connie was doing the same, staring at him like he'd grown a third leg. She'd expected stupid comments from Becker and had gotten precisely that. He could be daft sometimes. That sort of stuff was better kept internally or right on the down-low. Connie had warned him about that - many times.

'You complete twat, is that really what you really think?' Connie moved back and lowered her head, staring him in the eye.

Becker was only bullshitting - he wasn't really serious. But he remained quiet, Becker said nothing more to Connie. She continued to glare at him though, shaking her head, thinking he was a right goose.

'I've told you about airing those crazy ideas.' Connie wasn't happy. 'Actually, this place is as real as it gets Becker, let's explore the damned thing and see if we can find out what it is, where we are – um, things like that,' she said, trailing off.

'This way,' she said, pointing with a hand. Connie trying to sound authoritative sounded anything but. She had no clue where they were, or what they should do. Connie just followed her instincts. Walking this way was simply the first thing she thought of. What were they walking into though? She had no idea.

'Sounds good to me...lead on.' Becker gestured forward with his gloved hand. He wasn't tremendously happy to be walking but realised there was little choice.

The two of them, fully suited for space, headed off, travelling what they assumed to be due west in what was a flattish floored tunnel, timbered every ten feet or so with heavy planks of wood on the roof and walls, between which were islands of yellowish rock with grey bits here and there. It all looked very un-Earthly. Becker assumed the bolsters were wood – it sure looked like it.

They walked further onward, which was really hard work in a spacesuit. If they were weightless, things would have been very different. But they weren't in space and weightless and it wasn't easy. So, they walked on, stymied by gravity, which seemed very Earth like or, unsettlingly, could match numerous exo-planets, he reckoned.

Becker could feel the hunger as though his gut was trying to eat itself. Connie frequently said he had a huge *napetite* – referring to his strong desire both for food and for sleeping. He was just like a fucking cat, she thought cheerlessly.

'I wonder what the atmosphere's like in here?' Connie asked, watching Becker closely. The twit probably reckons it's like Earth. Connie cautiously admitted the gravity felt similar to home, and there was definitely atmosphere in here. She tested for pressure the same way they did at Primary School, which thankfully, she still remembered. Using the paper from one pocket, normally reserved for writing notes on, she placed it on her stomach, and it stayed there. So, there was pressure in an atmosphere of sorts. What she didn't know, was what was in this atmosphere? In a vacuum, the paper will slide off, no matter how fast you move.

'It's probably okay, the gravity feels close to Earth-like, so maybe we're on Earth,' Becker hoped, peering around blindly as he ambled forward. As an astronaut, Becker made an excellent miner.

Connie looked carefully at him - nothing had changed. 'We could be spinning through space or possibly standing in a complete vacuum, despite the test,' Connie said, her voice husky with despair, thinking Becker was still a fool. Or was that a tool, she thought lightly? Definitely one or the other. 'Realistically, it could be anything – we should take nothing for granted. Forget the paper test Becker.'

He shook his head vehemently. 'I'll, uh...lift my lid a bit and see what it's like,' Becker said, in a strained voice.

'Yeah, you do that and we'll see allright...*oh*, if you start foaming at the mouth, do put the lid down again.' Connie gave him a slow, sarcastic smile and a wink.

He stopped and turned around to find Connie also stopped behind him, hands on hips, tapping one foot, watching him intently.

'Tell me you're kidding Becker, one breath or the absence of it, could be enough you know. Surely, you know better than that.' She studied him closely and for quite a while. He has no idea, she decided. Every time she'd thought or said, "he should know better", he didn't.

'Oh, *whatever* Con, I reckon it will be fine, besides I'm not wearing this heavy, suit any longer if I don't need to.' His face didn't convey the same optimism as his voice did. Becker couldn't help a sense of doom and ruin setting in. He felt like shaking his head to get rid of it. He needed something to go his way, and Becker reckoned it would start with air they could breathe. The suit and helmet were slowly crushing him.

Without further debate, he pressed the red button on the joist of his helmet which, unless overridden by a further two presses within twenty seconds, would unlock the visor, and allow "manual adjustment". He'd be able to move it just by pushing it. If his suit started decompressing or filling with something unpleasant, he'd still have time to take immediate action.

'Here goes nothing,' Becker said, his eyes swelling to look more like golf balls than normal eyes. He pushed the visor up enough to take a small breath. He fairly sipped what was all around him. Becker could immediately tell there was pressure around him.

'*Jesus, well I'll be...n-not b-bad,*' he said tentatively. 'It's obviously not vacuum, pressure seems about right, oxygen is good, it even smells okay, a little woody and musty...but pretty fucking good. I even taste chocolate and a hint of strawberry or raspberry. Becker had a smile like a Cheshire cat and had the visor fully down now and was breathing lungfuls of the atmosphere. It tasted very good indeed - full of everything they needed, including pressure. Becker inhaled deeply.

'*Told you Con*, it's fine,' he said, smiling and holding his thumbs up. It's taken on the flavour of the stuff that's in here, but it's fine. He took a huge, raspy intake of breath.

'You're a fucker Becker, *know that*,' Connie whispered under her breath. Her visor was down nearly all the way, given Becker's observations and tastings.

Off came Becker's suit, helmet first and right down to the cooling garment. He was standing there in jocks and a t-shirt, breathing deeply, peering at Connie, gesticulating for her to do the same thing. Becker was completely unashamed. '*Lucky it's warm,*' he yelled.

'Oh Jesus...quite the look Becker, I reckon it might be better to leave it on, hides all the *yuck* bits. Anyway, whatever ... I suppose,' Connie said, gawking at Becker and moving her hands to her helmet. With that, off some of it came. Connie left the suit on but removed the helmet. She'd learned enough simply by looking at Becker. Seriously, he looked like a fat oaf. She refused to follow suit but did take some of it off.

Walking continued and the view was more of the same. It was like they were in space and kept looking at the same galaxy and stars. The wooden pylons and islands of rock seemed never-ending and the view never seemed to get any closer, or even change.

'What if something pops out of nowhere Becker?' Connie looked horrified and was visibly trembling. She wondered if that was really possible and quickly realised, of course it was. 'Don't tell me it's not possible Becker, because it is, most anything is.' *Anything* was possible, she knew that.

'You'll be the first to know Con,' Becker said, surveying her grimly. 'Seriously, do you think this is some sort of alien holding station?' He nodded and chuckled at her.

'Well, it could be...it could be a-anything I -suppose, right? We'll have no idea until something ... *anything* bares itself.' Connie snapped her head about, looking in every direction she could. She wondered what was behind her in the shadows.

'It's rather dim in here but it's not pitch black,' she said, 'which it probably should be...shouldn't it?' She was questioning herself, not asking Becker, he wouldn't know.

'Pitch black...yeah, I guess it should be,' Becker, scratched the top of his head.

Case closed then, she reckoned, smiling at Becker. 'Where is the light coming from though,' again she was talking to herself. Connie twisted her head looking everywhere but couldn't find the source of the ambient lighting. '*Fuck knows,*' was her considered opinion. Her brain was fairly spinning as she gazed around. There were questions everywhere. Connie tried to place a brake on her mind by curling her toes hard inside her boots.

She was still peering around. 'Perhaps we shouldn't guess at all until we know something as a fact. Nothing good will come of it.' Connie knew that wouldn't happen, especially with Becker around. He wasn't called Mr. Question Mark by his ex-peers at Becker Resources NL for nothing. He'd ask something just to hear the sound of his own bloody voice. Connie figured Mr. Frustrating would have been a good name too.

Ahead, the tunnel appeared to come to an end. Becker wasn't exactly sure, his eyesight at a distance was shit, but he was fairly sure it came to a rather abrupt termination, courtesy of a solid-looking wall.

He listened carefully for any sound that wasn't them. As he got closer to the wall, he was more certain. Connie too was convinced there was something behind the wall they couldn't get to. It definitely ended in a sheer wall, but he wasn't sure if that was good news or bad. By the look of Connie, who he watched intently, something about the wall and what was behind it, was not necessarily good news.

She ran to the end of the tunnel and started knocking on the wall, standing close to the rock, seemingly listening to it. Then she put her ear right on it. Right on the yellow rock and really listened.

'I can hear -water,' Connie said, '...a lot of it.' She removed her ear from the wall and eyed Becker. 'I could hear it whooshing and swooshing against the rock, on the other side,' she said, with widened eyes. I don't know what it means...but it definitely sounds like water.

'I can't hear a Goddamn thing,' Becker said, with his ear firmly on the rock. All he could hear was ringing caused by long periods spent way too close to rock borers. For noises that were low volume, he was essentially deaf. Blind, at long distances and deaf for anything low in volume, *great*, he thought, what an asset. Connie should be thankful. Becker shook his head drearily. '*Christ*,' he whispered bitterly to himself.

'Believe me, that noise is real,' Connie said, theatrically squealing. 'Trust me, it's there.'

'I don't trust anyone, but I accept that it's not a way out,' Becker said, giving a strong, decisive nod. They still didn't know what this object was that they were in. It could've been *anything*, and they could have been *anywhere*. After all, they'd somehow been "put" there direct from space. They could still be in space, in some pressurised receptacle. She knew from experience how deceiving looks can be from the inside. If this thing was hurtling through the void, where did the atmosphere come from? The mystery deepened, for Connie anyway. For Becker it was just that monkey banging away on a Tambourine.

A decision was made, actually there was no other option, to walk the other way and hope like hell it too didn't culminate in a dead-end. If it did, well...things wouldn't be looking good. They'd be trapped. Connie had the same thought. 'What if this thing ends in a frigging wall like it did the other way they had just come from;' Connie pointed toward the wall, asking the obvious, unanswerable question.

'You know the answer to that one, we'll be caught in this tunnel or whatever it is, with no exit. In other words, we'll be completely and absolutely *fucked*,' Becker spat the words and again his voice echoed, which he didn't like. To him, it meant the area was totally enclosed. *Fuck*, he thought to himself. In that case, it meant no way out.

They began their journey, with the aim of finding out if this thing they were walking through spelled hope or a slow death. If it was open to the East, they had some hope of surviving. If it was closed, well, *fuck knew*, he thought grimly. They'd essentially be trapped in some sort of strange, dim tunnel of unknown location.

Whatever, he was sure they were barely better off here than in space. The only benefit here was they had available atmosphere to breathe, rather than air they had to take with them, which was easily extinguishable. Apart from that, they might as well be floating in the great wide open.

*   *   *

'Well, this is about where we started the first time,' Connie said, peering at the spot on the ground where they'd first appeared in this crazy place. Before that, they were in space, floating about like so much discarded rubbish. They sort of realised that Minan had to be responsible for that...and probably this. It appeared his powers were pretty much unlimited. Whatever he wanted, he got. To us, it was magic. To him, no doubt, it was just tinkering with physical laws.

They walked past "the spot", which didn't seem to be anything special, and kept going, without paying too much attention to it. The tunnel took a slight bend up ahead and they both hoped to God it didn't end in a sheer wall like the other end did.

They ambled along the centre of the dim tunnel slowly and reluctantly along the single line of bricks, that were laid at ninety degrees to their direction of travel, craning their necks and gazing closely at their tunnel-like surrounds. Everything around them seemed so banal. It was just a hole in the ground – the unknown was where that "hole" was. Connie made a mental note to look closer at these "bricks" later. See if they were like the Earth kind. From where she was, the bricks and the mortar sure looked like it.

'W-What the hell is this p-place?' Connie said again, for the umpteenth time, looking around to establish perspective and then eyeing Becker, this time expecting an answer. Connie had eyes like a frightened puppy. She really needed to know where she was.

Of course, any answer he gave would be bullshit, but it would still be an answer. Talking in this environment was good. This place made her church at prayer-time seem rowdy.

'Haven't we been down this...er, path before?' Becker said. 'We have no idea what this place is, right? Alien holding room, inside an asteroid like Oumuamua, or...maybe ending up in this place is a totally random event. Perhaps we're just tumbling through space, not as an asteroid, but as we see it from the inside, a long room of sorts, full of this shit,' he pointed around himself to make his point. 'Remember, there's atmosphere and gravity ... that doesn't come from nothing. There has to be a source.'

She looked at Becker and his empty stare. Connie shouldn't have asked him a pointed question and put him on the spot. She realised he didn't know a fucking thing.

Connie couldn't believe he used the word "remember" in a sentence. Looking at him again, she may as well have addressed the wall. He had the worst memory of anyone she knew. Now, he was grinning at her. She looked at him long and hard. The man that stood before her with the grainy memory had the temerity to believe he was hilarious. Trouble was, Becker was about as funny as a bathroom stool. She would never tell him as much, but the man was genuinely un-funny. Stupid perhaps...but not funny per se. The good, *funny*, comedians had a *need*, an obsession, to display their "wares" on stage in front of an audience. Unfortunately for Becker, the only obsession he had was to do nothing. And that wasn't an "obsession", it was called being lazy. Connie would never tell Becker that either because he'd mope and pout and generally be unbearable for days.

'Let's just keep walking, Becker.' She'd heard quite enough.

Becker turned his head wonderingly, this way and that, having barely heard Connie at all. '*Who-fucking-knows where we are?*' Becker emphasised all three words and articulated every syllable slowly and kept repeating it. The old buggar didn't have a clue and was rambling like a nutter. She'd asked him that question ages ago.

'What I do know,' Becker said, 'is we should be thankful to Minan. I mean, who else could have engineered all this?' Becker was laughing...and chuckling. 'Saved by a little shit in black clothes...so, he did like us after all. *Amazing*,' Becker said, shaking his head and glancing at Connie, grinning. 'The little fucker *liked* us. He actually liked us. Well, you mostly.' Becker broke into a fit of laughter, unable to stop. It welled up and came out automatically and uproariously. He literally couldn't help it. '*Fancy that,*' Becker laughed. He laughed and laughed. And then laughed a bit more, throwing back his head. The whole thing had a strong air of incredulity.

Connie reckoned Minan "liked us" less, per se, and was more befuddled and curious with our highly anomalous behaviour. He probably wanted to know *why* we were like we were. After all, we were the first species to go "outside its algorithm".

'It's not that funny Becker, look around you,' Connie said grimly.

'Ohhh, lighten up would you ... Mr. Black, no emotion, actually taking a shine to us ... it's a little bit funny.' He elbowed Connie and she looked at him and smiled faintly.

'Okay Becker, it's a little bit funny, you happy now? All I know is this place is a whole lot better than floating around in space counting down to zero and then suffocating. Excuse me if I don't find oblivion, funny or fulfilling.'

'Jeez...if you put it like that, yeah, you're right. Space sucks, sometimes, right?'

'Thanks funnyman – now let's go. Hopefully, going this way will give us some answers.' Connie's distant expression suggested she didn't think the odds were in their favour. Still, she knew being positive was one of the few things they had control of, and they needed to do it...or they were genuinely in trouble. State-of-mind was important, she knew it and also knew she had a lot of improvements to do in that area. She eyed Becker and gulped.

Connie looked ahead and swallowed hard again. There was something odd she could see in the distance – lying against the wall...rubbish maybe. It was something very different, apart from the seemingly endless stream of wooden supports and rock. From here it looked like opened, empty cans and rags. It looked very different from the wood and rock which they had gotten used to.

Becker had his glasses folded up and hanging from his shirt, so there was no point asking him. He could barely see that far, let alone focus. Becker squinted but it still was barely a smudge in the distance. Connie elbowed Becker and pointed ahead with a sharp flourish of her head, indicating she wanted him to follow her. She set off at a good pace and left Becker in her wake. God he was so bloody slow, she turned around briefly to see him leisurely pottering along behind her.

Looking ahead, the "rubbish" slowly came into sharper focus. It wasn't rubbish at all. The scene that presented itself was the most atrocious, odorous thing she'd ever seen. It was surely a horrible murder scene, but then seeing the bites and the deep claw marks, she was unsure.

There was another party involved here that wasn't even close to a human. Connie was happy because the poor bugger that was dead *was* human. Being human was good, being dead and partially eaten was bad. So, taken together, it was bad for him and sort of good for them. Connie knew she shouldn't feel happiness because the poor bastard had clearly died in the worst of circumstances. Connie should feel lousy and sad, which she surely felt, but there was definite joy in there too. He was a *person* from Earth, or at least what was left of him looked like a human being. That was at least a reason to be hopeful, although the way he died was most unfortunate. It meant...she wasn't sure what it meant, but it wasn't *all* negative.

The murder weapon was not a gun or a knife though, or anything like it...it was *teeth*, much like a vicious, violent shark attack but on land. The victim's head was completely gone, as were both legs, bitten off raggedly at thigh level. There were jagged, deep bite marks on the poor sod's thigh that looked horrible. Dried blackish blood was everywhere around him. He'd clearly died in great pain, with the infliction of enormous violence.

Given that there were no body parts around or anywhere near the mauled body, Connie assumed the missing bits were eaten. Blood pooled around the decimated body in horrible dark, almost black puddles, that looked dried. The person subject to whatever happened, was wearing a black puffer jacket with a bit of red on the front. All of it was savagely and viciously ripped.

'Jesus...*fuck*,' Connie whispered, checking out the bite marks. 'What the hell did this? A bear perhaps...a big cat? I mean, he's a human...so it makes sense, right?' She looked behind them and to the front, there was nothing there. Her eyes told the story, they were swollen with fear and dread. She wondered what was lurking around the corner here and over there in the shadows.

She was now terrified by this place and gawked everywhere to make sure they weren't being stalked by something, whatever it might turn out to be.

Something was definitely in here with them. That was good because it meant this place was bigger than they thought, and was probably connected to something else, or the outside, or ... maybe. Her thoughts drifted to what might be "outside" and she tried her best not to think about it. Connie's heart started beating in her mouth. Of course, whatever had done this might have entered the same way we did. Surely, this thing wasn't sent here … but then she thought of Becker and her. We were sent here. It just didn't make sense. Murphy's Law was high in her mind but she rejected it. Connie screwed up her face and rubbed her chin. She didn't know what to think.

The situation with this dead person was very bad because it meant their lives were in serious danger. This thing in front of them, was presumably, just like them. A human being walking around, complete with legs and a head.

Whatever the creature was, that inflicted the horrible injuries, it was obviously a people-eater and extremely vicious. One look at the dead body without a head and legs and with vicious bites to nearly all of his body, was enough to hammer that home.

Becker made his way up to Connie with his hand cupped over his nose. '*Shit, poor fucker*, he smells like bags of wet penny's,' he said, with an audible intake of breath. 'What the *fuck* happened to him?' Becker said, getting as close as he dared, still with a hand over his nose. Poor guy stunk of a violent death.

Connie waved an arm at the unfortunate visitor and stood to the side and allowed a closer inspection by Becker. It should be obvious, she thought, even to Becker, that he'd been attacked by a wild animal or animals of some sort. She looked at the deep bite marks and exposed tissue and felt dizzy and faint. No-one would want to go like that.

Becker gestured her nearer to him, not wanting to get any closer to the partly eaten corpse. He was already too close. Looking left and right, he saw nothing but barren tunnels. Connie did the same and saw nothing and no movement, although it was rather dim.

Whatever had done this was thankfully nowhere to be seen. They both knew there were blind tunnels that headed off the main tunnel – and they couldn't see what was in them, which made them both nervous as hell.

'The guy that ended up dead…he got in somewhere,' Becker said, swivelling his eyes to Connie, 'however he got in, is the way we get out.'

'That's fine Becker, but how did *we* get in?'

Becker grunted and *hmmphed* a few times, scratched his chin, then said, 'good point. Still, we should search for a way out. Maybe we'll stumble over it, you know, find out how he got into this place.'

'Sure, *whatever* Becker, but we need to stay frosty – that's a reasonably fresh kill.' Connie said grimly, looking down and taking a few steps backward.

'No shit,' he replied, gawking, revolted at the blood and guts.

Connie turned and eyed Becker front on and really focussed on him. 'What if there is no "outside"?

*   *   *

They began walking over the same large square tiles and line of side-on bricks laid down the centre of the tunnel. They just hoped they didn't meet up with the bear or huge cat or whatever it was that lurked around here. Dispatching unknowing explorers, it seemed.

She'd heard of crocodiles in sewer systems, but that inferred an earthly origin as did a bear or a cat, which was a fair stretch. The injuries could quite easily be related to a croc attack when they grab and shake. Gross ripping of limbs and huge, deep bite marks were common, Connie knew that. And they were really quick over short distances, so catching prey, *'people'*, was very possible.

Basically, it could've been anything, known or unknown. She didn't think or even talk about *alien* creatures, but it was in the back of her mind somewhere. Connie didn't want to give the thought any oxygen. It wouldn't do Becker or her mindset any good at all. But it increased the type of possible creatures geometrically. *Now* it could literally be anything.

'I know I keep repeating it, but what is this place then?' Connie restated the same question again as she watched more of the same come into view as they ambled forward. It was like Groundhog Day down here. Apart from the dead guy, everything about this tunnel looked the same so far, doesn't matter where you were looking from.

Connie scrutinised everything around her. 'I reckon we're on a planet...like...um,' she didn't know any with an atmosphere which included oxygen, 'an exoplanet, location unknown,' she said, 'underground perhaps. At least we can breathe and walk on a solid surface.

'What do you think Becker?' Connie said, peering up at the nether reaches of the tunnel that were shrouded in darkness. She thought about what she'd just said and realised what a bunch of unqualified crap it was. And she'd just asked Becker an open question – that was inviting trouble.

'You're asking *me* for an opinion? Let me think about it ... I would go with, *who fucking knows?* It's what we know for sure, which is nothing, and it may be all we ever know about this place, *it all looks the fucking same*,' Becker said loudly - predictably making little sense.

They were clearly struggling, both with their locale and the lack of answers to anything. They were essentially groping in the dark. Blind as blind gets.

*   *   *

The poor old bugger was clearly way more nervous than usual. He was blowing out a series of short puffs, trying to get himself under control. Connie was pointing in every direction, taking deep, steadying breaths as she went. Where, who, why or what? Everything about their location was an out-and-out guess. *As for definitives, they had zero.*

'Why wouldn't Minan put us back on Earth...in Antarctica, and be done with it,' Becker said, turning and staring at Connie full in the eye. 'At least we'd know where we were.'

'Brilliant Becker. Only thing is, Earth and Antarctica were probably gone, as was the Universe. We saw it deflate to virtually zero, remember?' Connie started walking past Becker, who eventually started following her. 'That's the question, isn't it?' Connie was looking everywhere, her back facing him as she spoke. 'If everything just went, disappeared, then, where in God's name would we be? The question is a good one Becker.'

'I guess it is,' Becker said slowly, hearing Connie gurgling with laughter. 'What's so damn funny?' He said crossly. Becker watched Connie and frowned with irritation - pretty sure she was laughing at him. She continued to burble and warble with mirth.

'I was about to say, "stop overthinking it.' She was grinning sarcastically, 'You need to think first...before you can *over*think.'

'Very bloody funny,' Becker said, looking around himself and agreeing with Connie that everything looked the same. Same wooden supports, same rock. Same everything.

*   *   *

'How long does this damn thing go on for?' Connie said, breathing in rib-stretching gasps. It seemed to go on forever. The stupid tunnel seemed never-ending in this direction. They'd walked and walked, but still, it went on and on. Connie watched it squeeze to a dark nothing in the far distance. Thankfully, it was just a visual anomaly, a bit like a mirage in the desert.

Time to rest,' Becker said loudly. That wasn't a question. He flopped down with his back against a piece of wood which went up to the ceiling, breathing in long, shuddering breaths. He'd walked a long way, both of them had, but Becker was in worse condition. Connie shook her head at him, making various, quietly disparaging comments.

As far as Connie was concerned, he'd hardly walked at all. But once the fool had made up his mind, like now, any words and arguments, no matter how loud or cogent, were simply words in a windstorm. *Useless*. He didn't hear them. So, she didn't bother to argue, just sat down herself, and fronted him, without saying anything or listening to his breathing or his moaning which went on unabated.

Better to save her energy. She *knew* his knees hurt. He'd told her at least a dozen times, to which she'd been most concerned, saying "poor baby", or similar, on the last few occasions. Becker was such a drama queen - Connie didn't know where to start if she were to describe him. The man could be so embarrassing, she thought quite seriously. He should never, under any circumstances, be taken out in public. Connie knew only too well what horrors lay in that direction.

Becker looked upward and saw similar islands of rock to the sides of the tunnel, just less intrusive. Were they in a fucking mining drive, he wondered? If so, what was the goddamn ore? All he'd seen so far were yellowish sandstone-like rocks rich in silica. Becker was almost positive it couldn't be that. Who mined sandstone for silica?

He knew silica was mined, but only really high-grade stuff not this stuff. Becker could tell just by looking that this rock was low-grade. Anyway, he hadn't seen anything like a stope. So that left...*what*? He really didn't know. It couldn't be a mining drive, he decided.

No way it could be silica. Of course, he conceded, this could be a world poor in silica...and maybe the place they were in was evidence of that. Becker got up, with various muffled grunts and groans, and plodded on toward what, he didn't know? The exit maybe...or something different than they'd already seen perhaps. Anything different would be welcome, or so he believed. *Different* could be bad, but he hadn't considered that.

Up ahead was something *very* different. Becker's wish was apparently granted. Maybe fifty metres ahead was something that fit the bill perfectly. On one of the rock faces was human graffiti, it was probably why the dead guy was here. But they didn't find any spraying implements with him which was odd. *Go figure*, was Becker's considered impression. They'd gone through all his pockets looking for ID and found nothing in his pockets at all. They were all empty.

The graffiti on the dark rocks was quite beautiful with a brilliant red heart surrounded by black paint with black letters spelling "bad" in steep calligraphy across the red heart. *Someone* got in to paint it, whether it was the dead guy or somebody else.

The implication was inspiring to say the least, although the graffiti itself wasn't. It sure looked Earthly and human, and the word was in English, but she didn't want to make any judgements. How did whatever made this graffiti get in? The whole scenario was very intriguing indeed. Becker reckoned this had to be Earth.

Connie calmly stood and watched Becker slowly get up and start ambling forward. She was gobsmacked, Connie expected Becker to be on his arse for ages. He appeared totally spent, at least that's what she thought. When Becker was tired like that, he was normally down for hours. Once again...*go figure?*

Now, he was up, walking, or at least staggering. She raced up to him, that was the least she could do for the old clod, Connie reckoned, seeing him weave and lurch, but standing on two legs. He seemed okay though. Tired, but moving forward.

Here we go again,' he said, looking directly ahead, and carefully putting one foot in front of the other, *more walking...great*. Becker realised it had to be done. He was keen to get out of this place – but into what, he didn't know. He hadn't thought that far ahead. Nor had Connie.

'Yup,' Connie said, staring at Becker's dusty brown shoes. She didn't want to degrade his walking mood so she said nothing, just started moving forward with, and soon past, him.

They walked, walked more, and kept walking until Becker was almost on his knees.

'I've got to rest Con...I'm completely fucking done.' He sat down and groaned all the way until his bum hit the ground. With his back against the wooden supports, he tried to relax his screaming back muscles hurt a little less than his hamstrings which begged him to stop. *Demanded* it really.

Becker was gasping for breath and shivering violently. His knees – forget it. They were a complete write-off, according to Becker.

Connie knew this time he was done, at least for a decent while. There was no exaggeration in his movement whatsoever, a good

Becker tell-sign for faked exhaustion. He was truly done. The poor sod was huffing, coughing and rasping, and rubbing his legs, trying desperately to get some feeling back in the lower part of his body. He gave up and leant back, sighing deeply and looking back at the empty dim tunnel.

Becker continued to peer up the tunnel and could barely open his eyes - he had expended every bit of energy he had. Even his eyelids were tired. Becker squinted at Connie, she seemed okay and was still on her legs, making him look fat and unfit, which he guessed he was.

'*Whatever*,' Becker said to himself. It was what it was, and would be what it would be, he reckoned, totally confusing himself. He wasn't sure what that even meant – his mind was spinning. Thank God, he kept it to himself. Connie would have a field-day with it. *Goddamnit it*, he was better than that. He grinned faintly and snorted quietly – he wasn't with Connie just to make her look smarter. He'd show her, somehow.

*   *   *

Looking up at the farther regions of the tunnel, it seemed to go on forever, shaded by the mists of his rotten distance vision where it narrowed to zero. Something was different with this picture though.

That's what they sought...something *different* to what had become very boring and very "the same" architecture of wood, rock and tiles. Apart from the graffiti – preference was not to see that again; that wouldn't help them in any material way. They also didn't want to see a sheer wall at the end. That would likely spell doom for their little expedition.

Becker looked forward and saw within the mists of distance, a brightness up high, that he thought was directing a beam of brightness to the ground. He grabbed his glasses from his shirt and put them on as he struggled to his feet. With his glasses on, the view suddenly took on an incredible new clarity. He could actually *see* with focus.

A ladder of sorts extended from a wooden sleeper on the rear of the wall to a roundish opening up top. To Becker, it looked like a regulation manhole up there, it was circular anyway. The ladder was huge and spanned the entire distance between the floor and the roof and was firmly wedged in. It would have been a major engineering feat just to get it up there and down here. That led Becker to wonder how it happened? It'd be hard enough to get the fucker down here, let alone getting it up there and wedging it in. His brain was spinning as he thought about it.

'*What the fuck*,' Becker spouted, gawking at Connie and then back at the ladder and the hole it led to. What is it?' He glanced at Connie uncertainly. It was good news, wasn't it? Possibly, it was a way out. They both wondered ... a way out to where and what?

'Where the hell does the ladder go?' Becker asked tentatively, ping ponging his eyes from the ladder to Connie, 'I mean where will it take us?' Becker was wide-eyed and totally dumbfounded by its sudden appearance, moving his head and gawking at the bright hole above. He could hear a loud noise coming from it, he was sure he could hear the wail of an ambulance piercing the air. And see clouds of something that looked like smoke and smelt acrid and unpleasant...but strangely familiar.

It was pretty obvious where the ladder went. What wasn't as obvious was, what was "up there", because whatever was *up there*, would probably tell them where they were. There was no decompression, so whatever was up there was pretty much the same pressure that was down here. Becker took that as a major positive. They could try and move as they were, without a suit.

The soreness had gone and he fairly sprang to his legs and moved quickly forward to inspect the ladder. It was very stiff and wooden, as he suspected. Hopefully, it would support his weight if he chose to climb it. If it didn't, and it broke and he fell to the ground, it'd be horribly embarrassing, not to mention, very serious, medically. '*Fuck*,' he thought, pushing and prodding the ladder. He realised he'd have to suck it up, try it and *hope*. It looked okay. At least it passed that test.

'It's a ladder, right?' Connie said, standing next to Becker and angling her head back to look at the light streaming into their space.

'Yeah, apparently, a pretty good one, wooden but firm...let's go Con.' He gave the ladder a good "twang" to see how stable it was. It seemed to pass the first test. 'Con, what do you see at the top?'

No way he was admitting quite yet that he needed help with his vision, especially to her. He couldn't bear the personal jibes about his vision at a distance. The truth was, Becker couldn't see a thing up there, it was way too blurry. He thought he could see some movement, but he wasn't sure.

'Okay blindy, can't see a thing at a distance, right? Obviously, can't wear your glasses. Well, there's sunlight punching through from above somewhere,' Connie pointed upwards with her whole hand, 'so I think, um, I *hope*, that's our way out.' The bright light washed out any detail above. All they could do was look at the glare.

She held her chin high and gaped directly at Becker. 'To be honest...*God knows* where the ladder will take us,' she said, glancing nervously at it. She could've done without the mental images that were flitting through her mind - all death and destruction. Another mental image of falling onto the hard, dusty ground after the ladder bends then snaps under Becker's weight. Connie tried desperately to visualise something positive. Or at least something different to that.

Becker scrutinised the ladder again. It seemed new and quite tight, but was it made of wood of some kind? It sure seemed to be. More importantly, he wondered, would it hold his weight ... that was the real question? He reckoned yes - Connie wasn't sure.

Connie was gawking at the hole. She could hear noise beyond it that sounded mechanical. It sounded like a continual roar and rumble – no doubt, there was definitely something up there.

Becker felt obliged to try the ladder first How the hell did the damned thing get here? Apart from throwing "Minan" at everything that didn't make sense, he had nothing. And by nothing, he truly meant *nothing*. No idea at all. The ladder seemed like a gift from God, a golden parachute as it were, a very lucky find indeed – call it what you like. It was there and they would use it. Whatever was outside this tunnel was up there – so, they had to use the ladder.

Becker climbed the ladder slowly and carefully, Who knew how old this thing was? Becker went very slowly higher and higher, rung to rung, looking and listening carefully, until he was silhouetted by the light from above. For Connie it was like watching an eclipse of the Sun. But instead of the Moon, it was him.

Becker stopped in the light for a second before he went on. The creaking and the squeaking of the ladder continued, but Becker took solace from the fact there was no snapping or cracking. He stood near the top and stuck his head out of the hole.
'*You are definitely not going to believe this Con,*' Becker said gleefully, gawking down at Connie from his position near the ceiling of the tunnel. Then he penetrated the apron of light and was gone. It wasn't a pretty sight from below, so she wasn't sorry when the bane of her existence had departed from view, leaving only the bright hole and the ladder. Becker had literally disappeared, leaving her in the tunnel alone and she was immediately worried he'd gone somewhere hostile.

Despite being generally very stupid, and a fucker to boot, most of the time - she did care for the big lug. He was her mate. Connie didn't like the idea of going or being anywhere alone, especially at the moment. She climbed up the ladder, confident it would hold her okay, after all, it held Becker who was at least double her weight. Connie wondered what the bloody hell had happened to Becker.

She went slowly at first, but then quicker when she heard that noise again – it was louder and way more distinct and was clearly coming from the tunnel itself – from the darkness. She stopped completely, about half-way up and really listened and looked for the source. It sounded like long toenails scraping on something hard. Like fingernails on a blackboard. The footfalls were heavy and fairly slow, which probably meant only one thing. Whatever it was, was big and probably heavy.

Connie squinted into the tunnel but could see little, thanks to the glare and the bright light let in by the open hole. It looked way darker than it really was. There was definitely movement and footsteps, hard and heavy, to go along with the scraping toenails. Connie didn't like this sound at all. Whatever this thing was, she could hear hissing breaths to go along with the scraping toenails.

Something was getting bigger in the darkness, and she could see numerous eyes flashing in the light as it moved. It was walking toward her. Whatever it was looked monstrous - she hoped it was only her imagination in the dark, but immediately knew it wasn't. Whatever she saw was very real.

She scooted up the ladder, hand over hand and saw Becker on his hands and knees not far away. She gaped and Connie too, saw what was above. She was just trying to get over what was below. Both views were truly beyond belief. To think, they were under *this* place all the time.

Looking down, she saw the base of the ladder and *it*, not far away. A monstrous beast that looked up hungrily at her with eight spidery eyes focussed on her, shark-like teeth and massive gnarly arms, replete with multiple sharp, bony scimitars on each. It was the beast she'd come into contact with on blue Mars, which posed several unanswerable questions in itself.

Somehow, that creature, from that planet was summoned here, unless it existed on more than one world. It didn't really matter because it wasn't indigenous to Earth, both of them knew that. It was bad news for them, the fact that it was here at all. Looking at the beast's legs, it's feet and likely overall weight, it wouldn't stand a chance of following them on the ladder. It probably wouldn't know what to do with it, anyway.

Becker reckoned the real "and only" question was how the hell did that ugly thing get in there? But Connie knew it wasn't a matter of *how* it got into the tunnel. It was, how did the fucker get off its home world, assuming it had, and why? *Why was the damn thing here at all?* That was the obvious first and most important question. It quite simply didn't belong down there. Fancy that thing popping out of a toilet rather than a croc. The whole thing beggared belief.

It had to be Minan. The second question was way harder. No one had an answer to that. Apart from throwing Minan at it as well. But *why* would he do it? Nothing made any sense. Connie was completely lost - Becker was confused by a myriad of thoughts that summed up to nothing much at all. Just that monkey and a Tamborine, going hell bent for leather.

1

Above

"Reality is merely an illusion, albeit a very persistent one."
– *Albert Einstein*

Becker recognised the place that was above the tunnel as *home*...Sydney, in Australia. On *Earth*. He popped out of a manhole near the side of what he later found out was Bridge Street and he was surrounded on all sides by bumper-to-bumper traffic. He had pushed off the manhole cover right off with his shoulder, and fortunately, the manhole itself was near the gutter, so the honking cars and the manhole cover itself didn't immediately kill him. That was good, he thought. Dressed in a singlet and jocks, he quickly ran to the side of the road amid a lot of beeping and braking to avoid him. He was lucky to be in Australia - in America they aimed for you.

Looking like that people would probably think he was an escapee from a local nuthouse, Becker guessed. Connie, dressed in a spacesuit with no helmet, wasn't much better, and quickly joined Becker on the side of the road, dodging cars as she went. What a couple, he thought. Apparently, they were both nuts. They'd certainly look like it to anyone on that part of Bridge Street, that day.

Traffic had pretty much come to a halt where they were on Bridge Street. She heard a lot of beeping, they probably thought she was an escapee, too, dressed like she was. Connie looked like a complete loon, dressed in half a spacesuit in downtown Sydney. Not what most people expected to see on their way to work. Still, they'd probably seen worse.

Standing together on the footpath of Bridge Street, near mid-town Sydney, they were surrounded by tall buildings, shops, people, cross-roads and a lot of motor vehicles. It smelt like a city, dirty with exhaust fumes, dripping oil and it was very bloody loud. There were cars everywhere and it was really hot and humid. It was the complete opposite of where they were underground, silent, dim and cool.

They were on the doorstep of a menswear shop thankfully, so Becker was taken care of, and Connie was amazingly, happy the way she was – pressure suit and all. Dressed okay, or so she thought, they walked and walked along the footpath, dodging adults, kids and a hell of a lot of nervous stares. After a bit more walking and many traffic lights, they ended up on Macquarie Street, near the Opera House.

Becker and Connie were in the immediate foreground of the imposing Opera House, languishing on tan-coloured steps that led to the strange sail-shaped shell structure itself. Becker was still visibly puffing after the journey to simply get there and collapsed on the bricks like he'd been shot. He was sprawled over the steps like something the tide had left behind.

'*Well fuck me*,' Becker piped and puffed, turning his head and focussing on his surrounds, 'who would've thought? We were under Sydney all the time.' He scraped a hand through his thinning hair. 'Absolutely Goddamn incredible,' he said, swivelling his head to take in the entire view of Sydney and the bridge itself. Becker reckoned the view from where they were was fucking amazing. They were looking directly at the Harbour Bridge and Sydney itself with the beautiful blue sky everywhere. And it was warm.

Connie looked at him sideways, 'if you're trying to assert your domination by manspreading, consider it done Becker.' Connie looked away, toward the bridge. 'There's plenty of room around here, so it's completely unnecessary.' She gawked at him and shook her head, grinning in the sunshine.

He immediately straightened up. 'Oh...yeah, right. How's that?'

'Better,' Connie retorted, grinning and giggling at such quick action.

'So, what now? Becker asked. He spoke while he was gawking at a group of Japanese tourists, all carrying the same pamphlet, presumably of Sydney and pointing and sniggering incessantly. 'Stupid tourists,' he said, looking curiously at them.

It was a beautiful day in Sydney, the Sun was beating down with only a couple of stratus clouds high in the sky. The sight of the Sun over the Bridge was stunning. Connie lay back and enjoyed the heat of the Sun on her face. It beat the hell out of space or being underground, especially with that monster thing running around. How they'd managed to avoid it, she had no idea. Recalling visions of the individual who clearly had come face-to-face with it, Connie was very glad they had avoided it. '*Jesus Christ*,' she said to herself. The images in her head were ugly to say the least. After a period of horrid introspection about what could have been, she repeated Becker's inane question.

'What now?' She said, 'I assume the question you posed was rhetorical Becker, but you have an opinion, right?' It was scary how well she knew the old bugger sometimes. Connie had no doubt he would have a firm opinion on their next move. Might be bullshit, but he'd still have an opinion.

Her mind was still spinning in bewilderment. The last few weeks had been ridiculous. And the *piece de resistance* was Minan and the simulated Universe. And then the return to Earth. It really had been quite a month. Ridiculous, stupid, illogical, any of those words would fit, perhaps all of them, she reckoned. And be very, *very* appropriate. It truly had been a crazy month.

'What um,' Becker eyed Connie front on, '...did you see when you went up the ladder?' He asked her seriously. Becker realised she had seen something that had affected her deeply. 'It was enough to scare the hell out of you...right?' Becker looked at Connie, really focussing his eyes on her. He could see she was terrified just thinking about it. Her eyes were massive...owl-like as she recalled it.

'I don't know what I saw, but I think...I think it was a creature...of sorts.' Connie was pale and tried to speak more, but there was no voice there. She croaked a bit and decided to stop trying.

A creature...that's not very specific,' Becker said, smiling faintly. Just looking at Connie's face, he could see it was a serious subject. Poor thing looked terrified just thinking about it.

Connie eyes were swollen and with a quick shake of her head, she said, 'well, actually, it looked like the predator from blue Mars...you know, the one that sniffed me and didn't like it.'

'Yeah, the one that didn't like what it smelt,' Becker said, giving a slow grin, which quickly gave way to a more serious face. 'What's that thing doing in the tunnel, *with us*, for fuck's sake, although it answers the question to the injuries sustained by that guy out there,' Becker said pensively, eyes still fixed on Connie who looked seriously unsure and perturbed to say the least.

'You sure it wasn't just a Lion or a Croc, the light *was* dim,' Becker said, and immediately wished he hadn't spoken.

Connie raised her eyes and looked at him scornfully and said nothing, sighing loudly. Eventually she dragged in a chestful of air and spoke, narrowing her eyes.

I'd recognise that ugly fucker anywhere Becker. On blue Mars it smelt DNA chirality, you know that, don't act like you're completely dumb...and who knows *what* it's doing here, but to think we shared a tunnel with that thing is enough to give me serious anxiety.'

Connie rubbed her arms and looked around nervously. 'What role Minan played in all this – *who knows?*' Connie said, frowning and scratching her chin, losing herself in thought. "Why" was high in her mind.

'No doubt Minan had some involvement...no doubt at all.' Despite the words, or maybe because of them, Connie looked seriously confused, blinking feverishly. None of it made sense. The creature, Minan and the tunnel – everything was a nonsense.

*   *   *

'I want to check out my old building,' Becker said, smiling broadly. 'It was fairly close to where we were on Bridge Street.'

'*Great* – thanks, good idea – why not,' Connie said, sighing heavily. The question from Connie was obvious indeed. 'Why didn't we do it earlier, when we were a hell of a lot closer,' Connie asked Becker sceptically. God, she thought, he was such an arse. We were just *there*, for God's sake.

Apparently, he used to jog from his building to the Opera House with some regularity, so he knew the route well. Connie found it hard to believe Becker jogged anywhere, but fair enough, if he said so, Connie would accept it at face value. After all, he was talking about the past. If it was now – forget it. The goose could barely walk.

Both of them got to their feet and eventually ambled down Macquarie Street and turned right into Bridge Street.

They arrived at the site of the building and it was just a park, there was no development or improvements on it at all. There was only grass, a statue, an old anchor and an even older cannon. Certainly, there was no building and no works to start a building. It was virgin territory, as far as his building was concerned. Nothing close to it existed, much to Becker's chagrin.

'Where the hell is my stupid building? Becker yelled, glaring at the undeveloped park with burning, flinty eyes. He walked across the park, pointing and yelling something unintelligible. Hopefully, nobody was aware she knew him. It didn't look good for anyone.

The Park was full of people. Kids were mucking around with the cannon, pretending to fire it. He looked and sounded like a complete nutter, waving his arms around and talking loudly to no-one. He came across as someone to be avoided at all costs.

The park was very serene and then there was Becker, yelling and pointing like a two-bob nutjob. Luckily, they were used to that around there. No-one called the Police. Most took Becker in their stride, others just moved them and theirs away, staring at him suspiciously - peering sideways at him like he might do anything, any time.

Abruptly, he stopped pointing and stomped toward Connie, and then past her, walking across the empty road and straight into a florist shop. Connie very much doubted he was there buying her flowers or chocolates.

After about five minutes, he came back to her, not looking any happier. In fact, he looked downright grim. He came back, eyes bulging and breathing like a steam train. Becker shook his head in denial.

'Well fuck me if that doesn't beat all,' Becker said loudly, after returning from the florist shop. 'That girl has worked in that shop for nearly twenty years and she's never seen anything but a park...*ever*. No building...no people wanting to build anything, no Government or environment types - *ever*.'

What is the answer, he wondered, scratching his chin, gawking at the park. No building. That's how the park used to look before his Company rocked up.

Connie was watching him closely. 'Careful, you might blow something, if you think too much I mean. You're not used to it.' Connie's mouth pulled into a sour grin.

'Oh...very good indeed, but seriously, look around yourself, what a headfuck. The girl in the shop showed me the Telegraph, you know, the newspaper,' he said, '...and it was July 22, 2014, a year and a bit before it was even built.'

Becker shook his head and Connie could see he was at a loss for words. *Him*...at a loss for words, she never thought she'd see the day. It was quite incredible. Becker stood in the park and literally said nothing, he just stared at the old cannon like a fully blown looney-tune, his brain doing back-flips.

'So, we've been sent back to an Earth younger than we left it.' Connie said, looking gravely at Becker. 'We sort of expected that, right?'

clearly hadn't thought about it at all. That tambourine player in his head must have really been going for it. He was stunned, but on thinking about it, felt lucky to be on an Earth so close in history to the one they left. They could've come back to the middle-ages or the 1800's. Then they'd really be fucked.

'No doubt it's Minan, he had to have done it.' She said, wondering why he brought them back here. Of all places, Becker thought, although this *was* their home city. Connie had no immediate idea why Minan did anything. No one knows how an advanced alien thinks, she thought, especially one as advanced as he was. Connie guessed they had to come back to a time before Becker's trip down south – when the Universe was whole. Otherwise, it became very complicated indeed.

'Why though...*why* the hell would he do it to them?' Becker questioned, having a similar thought process to Connie. Neither of them had any real idea why he would bother with them. Surely, he had bigger fish to fry. It was all guesswork. Probing Minan's behaviour was like questioning a Wombat or a Mongoose, quite sure they'd get nothing useful in return.

'We won't know until we're told in language or something we can understand, or until we're shown. Minan is clearly running his own private project. All we can do is guess about it, or keep quiet, I suppose,' Connie said, trailing off. 'And guessing is useless, so I suppose we shouldn't bother to question anything.'

'We need to worry about ourselves now, not the trials and tribulations of that black suited little shit,' Becker spat, swaying his head back and forth.

'*Firstly,*' Connie said loudly, suggesting that anything they'd just spoken about was nothing more than window-dressing, 'where are we going to sleep tonight? Food, drink, I mean *come on,*' she saw Becker nodding vigorously,' leaning on my family is not an option, and yours are in what, Perth? That's a long, long way away. *Jesus Christ, talk about screwed up.* So, the upshot of all that is, forget family, they're either too far away or too fucked up.' They both took a sharp intake of breath and surveyed each other closely. Becker let out a hard sigh and closed his eyes.

He smacked one fist into another. 'We couldn't be more isolated if we tried. 'Well...we could be, but you know what I mean,' Becker grunted and griped as he walked away slowly. He was frustrated, clenching his jaw until his teeth hurt.

'We used to put short-stayers up at the Establishment Hotel,' Becker said, 'it's not far from here on Bridge Lane...we could stay there I suppose.' He looked away and stepped back, reconnecting with Connie and taking a deep, audible breath.

Becker swivelled his head and eyed the end of the road, calculating, or trying to, how far he'd have to walk to the hotel. He decided that it wasn't very far away. Becker prayed they had a room for two. Separate single rooms hopefully.

'What about cash...remember... *money* Becker?' Connie said, feeling like knocking on his forehead. Sure, as shit, she didn't have any, nor did Becker as far as she knew. How the hell could he? Which meant they couldn't pay for a room or do shit in this city. Connie stared blank-eyed at Becker. It took a while, but it eventually sank in. Neither of them had a thing to pay for anything. They were both totally broke.

'I have this key though,' Becker dragged it out of his shirt pocket for all to see, 'it should open my Safety Deposit box,' Becker said, biting his lip as he spoke and his eyes clouded a bit. He reckoned the box had an emergency stash of money in it, although he struggled to remember much about it. He couldn't remember anything about it actually. In other words, he was lying through his teeth.

Connie almost did a double take. 'But...hang on...those clothes are new to you, are you saying you put the key into a pocket? That you even had a key?' Connie eyeballed Becker and waited for him to confirm the impossible. Becker...prepared? No way. Her bet would've been that Becker had no security deposit box at all. But where did the key come from? He didn't prepare for anything. Never did, never had. Never will. The whole key-thing sounded very unlikely indeed, where had the damn thing been during all their explorations? To end up in his top pocket was way too much to believe.

'Actually...no,' he said.' There was a long pause. 'I just found the key there and assumed it was mine.'

*   *   *

'Okay Becker...whichever way it got there, you are going to need to identify yourself before you can use the key. Remember, like I said, the bank will have a key and you'll have a key. But they'll want photo I.D. big guy, which you don't have.' Connie said, crossing her arms roughly. *Fuck*, she thought. If he didn't know that ... God help us. Did he expect to just waltz in and use the key? He was worse off than she thought.

Connie gazed at him and started to feel very nervous. 'Their only route to money that didn't involve face-to-face crime was gone.

38

Unless he had photo identification, he, *they*, were fucked. And her strong bet was he did not have photo identification or anything like it.

Becker walked forward, then back to Connie again. 'I, uh...have an idea.'

'*Oh Christ*,' Connie whaled. 'Tell me it's not true.'

'Wait, just wait,' he said, holding a palm up. 'There's a guy who works at the Commonwealth Bank here on Bridge Street, who knows me well, pretty sure that extended back well past 2014. He hopefully won't need any I.D.,' Becker thought, grinning cautiously.

He reckoned that could work. Becker would say he forgot it, left it at home or something and hopefully, Luke wouldn't require it and wouldn't check names, and he'd be welcomed into the Securities Room for the branch to supply one of two keys to the box. That would be the plan anyway. He'd see how it went. If he came running out like a criminal, she wouldn't be surprised. But it was the only way so Connie agreed...sort of.

The Bank was on the high side of the street, full of colour and people. Becker went in, and an hour later, he came back with cash and plastic.

'Easy as,' he said with a huge, shameless Becker smile. 'He couldn't do enough for me, including waving the need for I.D. Luke took me straight in to the Safety Deposit room and I did the rest. I've got pocketfuls of cash and new cards that'll keep us going for a *long* time. I paid a heap of money into my everyday account.'

'That's one of many problems solved.' Connie said, again trailing off, as she considered how many problems still existed. 'Good work Becker,' If she didn't say that he'd mope and sulk, and generally be unbearable for hours. He acted like a big puppy dog sometimes. Being positive to the big sucker was important when he deserved it. Connie equated it to a handful of doggy treats. Made him sit up and take notice.

Becker went to the ATM and withdrew even more cash, as if to make a point, having the PIN which was scrawled on a piece of paper inside the Box. So, he had wads of cash in his pockets and even more in his own account in the Bank. He made a mental note to pick up a new wallet. Now, he could afford a good one...made of leather!

The Establishment Hotel only had one room left to let, so he grabbed it for a month and paid a sizeable deposit in cash and gave up an imprint of his credit card. So, Connie and Becker were set for accommodation, and they had access to plenty of money. But what about the world? Would the thing under the ice down south have a say in its future?

*   *   *

Was there a use-by date on Earth, and the Universe, or was that now null and void given that Becker's investigations under the ice probably wouldn't happen.

Who the hell knew how the future would play out? He hadn't and *wouldn't* activate the damnable object beneath the ice, so presumably everything would just continue as it was now. The status quo would be safe, he thought, meaning the Earth and the Universe would presumably also be safe, from that object anyway. But that also meant, Minan and his GC wouldn't know about Earth – yet they clearly did. These were the vagaries of time-travel, Becker supposed. Memories of by-gone events might or might not be remembered.

In their case, there would be no Program Close, instant transmission or shrinkage of the Universe. Things would just progress as "normal" here on Earth. The dark side of Murphy's Law would not be unleashed on the Universe. That's what Connie and Becker believed anyway. If they and anyone else didn't go drilling in Marie Byrd Land, Antarctica, they would let sleeping dogs lie.

But that still left *the* big fat question. *Why oh why* was Minan involved, and why was that creature from blue Mars back to hunt, if they didn't activate the sphere yet? They'd both returned to Earth well before all that happened. Connie tried like hell to think it through, but nothing about this place made sense. Occam's Razor said things should be very different...but they weren't. Minan was somehow aware of this planet and this Universe. And he was doing things they didn't understand.

They came back to a younger Earth, there was absolutely no doubt about it. Then, why was it that Minan continued to "play" with them and Earth? How on Earth did he stand outside this time movement? They were the questions that haunted both of them...all of them completely counter intuitive. All things being equal, Minan shouldn't even know about Earth. The "simplest explanation" no longer applied to any of this.

2

Voyage
'I love to travel, but I hate to arrive.'
– Albert Einstein

He yelled to Connie. *'What do I do about my orebody...my deposit?'* Becker moaned loudly, from his bed in the room adjacent to Connie. 'Y'know, the IPO...the company...the money.' He had a seriously pained expression on his face and sighed loudly, throwing his newspaper on the floor in a heap.

'Forget about it, that's the best course of action Becker,' Connie said, hearing a very maudlin Becker. He looked like he was about to cry. She felt like prodding him more, but Connie held onto it. Becker gawked upward and shook his head grimly.

'It doesn't even exist, I mean the deposit does, but my mine is non-existent.' His voice was barely audible. *'Fucking gone,'* he said.
'I used to hit rocks with the CEO of the mob that owns Prominent Hill, which isn't that far away from my deposit. In fact, I'm surprised they haven't found the fucker by now, with the gravity analyses that must be going on. Shows how good that tech is, I suppose.' There was a long silence and at the end of it, Becker's eyes had started to gleam and glimmer. 'I could give him the GPS coordinates of my deposit for a say, five percent finder's fee, based on a valuation of course.

'Or you could do it all yourself, engage a company to drill there...and keep it all.' Connie fed his ego, or at least that's what she thought she was doing. Connie sat on Becker's bed and pulled the covers over her legs.

'I can't go through all that shit again. Raising funds, licking the arses of so many people, listing on the ASX and NYSE, the risks, accidents, *no*, I can't go through all that shit again. I won't...I *can't*.'

Connie's face was ashen at the thought, almost as white as her teeth. God, she'd somehow woken a sleeping giant inside her. Last time, she'd done most of the leg work – never again. And she knew Becker was super-stressed too, just at the thought of all that work happening again.

Becker looked genuinely horrified - his mouth was frozen open as he contemplated the true awfulness of doing it all over again. He definitely didn't want to do it. The rewards were great, no doubt about it, but it would be a fucking nightmare, he knew in great detail what would be ahead of him.

Becker said, 'the whole horrible episode would hopefully *never* be repeated.'

'Okay, I get it,' Connie said, 'I get it...just calm down. Best you give him the GPS, take your five percent and run. That's still a whole lot of money.'

Becker, surprisingly, seemed more off-put than her at having to go through it all again. It was a huge no-way, all around. Neither of them wanted to do it again. Once was too much. Twice...*forget it.* He looked at her and gave a long, slow grin.

'Okay, I'll ring him and we'll see what happens, I guess.' Hope he still has the same number, Becker thought. He was nervous already as he contemplated how he would frame it. What the fuck would he say...I was out walking one day and happened upon it? Becker didn't think so, after all, the damn thing didn't outcrop on the surface. It was only found after a lengthy remote sensing programme and drilling. Still, they missed most of it – well, the best parts anyway.

Connie left his bedroom and allowed the old bugger some privacy to ring his mate who now occupied an executive role with a medium-sized mineral producer. 'Good luck,' were Connie's final words, before leaving him alone. In reality, she was really worried about what cock-and-bull story he'd devised in his mind. She felt certain he'd find a way to fuck it up.

Connie wondered what he'd say when asked, and he surely would have wondered the same thing. "I thought" or "I believed" just wouldn't do the job. He was going to have to come up with something way better than that. Something credible and believable. God knows what he'd go with. Although he was thick as a brick outside his field, on occasion, he could baffle with bullshit. She hoped like hell this was one of those times.

After about fifteen minutes, Becker came looking for her and he eventually returned to the bedroom and sat on her bed this time. 'So...they'll pay me five percent on formal valuation of whatever's found, after a decision is made to mine it. They'll send a contract to that end tomorrow. If I'm happy, I sign and return it.' Becker wore a huge grin.

Connie smiled. 'How the hell did you say it was found? That you kicked over a rock and found it to be pure spun silver, or maybe a wombat hole showed you the way.' Connie tried desperately not to laugh in his face, Becker wasn't making it easy. His general confidence and wide-open stance really pissed her off. He must have come up with some bullshit story.

The real surprise was that they took him seriously. She thought the CEO would simply hang up on him. Assume he was just another prospector who'd gotten too much sun. Clearly, he knew Becker not only as a friend, but from a geological perspective as well. Back then, she wondered what credentials he could have possibly had?

Becker grinned proudly. 'I'm *not* telling you what I said...but whatever I did and what I alleged, it worked a treat. That's all you need to know. The only risk is whether the orebody is still there. I mean, it should be, right? The only variable here is Minan. Christ only knows what he's done, I mean he can do whatever he wants I guess,' Becker said, stony-faced, staring at the monastery through the window.

Minan's tech would be akin to magic in its purest form, that he knew.

The last thing Becker said on the subject, and he repeated it throughout the afternoon was, 'it should be there, right?' Connie assured him, "*it should be*", several times, hoping against hope that he'd shut it - she'd heard quite enough. The big lug didn't look as confident as he had a few minutes ago.

*   *   *

After a week of drinking way too much scotch, he knew things had to change. Connie was of similar mind. They hadn't seen the so-called contract yet, but that would hopefully change his thinking. If she had to watch him drink himself into oblivion one more time, she'd quite literally go mad. Old rummy was seriously an octopus when he got drunk. *Very* touchy-feely, but she put that down to the alcohol.

So, for her, it was off on yet another walk, down Bridge and Macquarie Streets and back again, collecting a paper and a long black coffee along the way at Gerard's Cafe. Becker could please himself. She didn't care or check what he was up to. Last time she looked, he was snoring, loudly. It was like living with a large dog. All he did was eat, drink and sleep...oh, and go to the toilet, she thought, snuffling with laughter.

Connie went to the nearby AMP Tower to sit down on one of the benches and read the newspaper. She glanced at page 2, focussing on the main story. The headline for the story caught her eye.

'*Jesus, holy...fuck,*' Connie whispered to herself, reading every word that was splashed over the second page of the newspaper. '*About fucking time,*' she said, pumping her fist and hitting the paper with her hand. '*Good...good,* she repeated emphatically, reading the words, getting up and walking back to whence she came. Connie could barely hide the massive smile on her face. *About bloody time*, she reckoned.

*   *   *

'Check out page 2,' she said, gaping at Becker, as she threw the newspaper onto the small, round table.

'No worries boss.' Becker saluted casually, picking up the paper, and putting his glasses on, then reading page 2, amid various grunts and murmurs, that she couldn't distinguish as any language she knew. He read a bit and gawked at Connie, smiling.

'Are you suggesting what I think you are?' Becker said, ping ponging his gaze between the newspaper and Connie.

'No, I am not suggesting that...or anything, actually. I knew you'd be interested in reading it, *that is all,*' she said, frowning and blinking rapidly. 'Although I'd be happy if you went...by yourself. Then I could steam-clean your room and use it myself.' Connie wrinkled her nose and curled her lip, then smiled and chuckled to herself.

'Ho, ho, ho,' he said. 'Very good. They say it'll take twelve years to get there, presumably at thirty percent of the speed of light. They are using fusion propulsion and they want a hundred people, half male, half female. Six chefs and the rest of them are spending twenty years on the planet as colonists. *Twenty years!*' Becker *hmphed* loudly. 'They want a hundred guinea-pigs to go.' He *hmphed* again.

Connie read from the paper, 'they will take all the infrastructure with them, to be inflated when they get there. And after twenty years, they will receive an influx of eight hundred additional colonists from Earth, "all things going to plan". Whatever that fucking means,' he said, breathing and groaning loudly. Connie knew what it meant – it meant the original colonists would probably never leave Proxima B.

'And the initial one hundred people will then come home to Earth after serving their dues as colonists. Assuming the larger ship actually gets there and back to Earth. It's a long, *long* way. Multiple journeys to orbit will be required by the sojourn craft that will detach from the mothership and then re-attach. Of course, some colonists won't want to leave Proxima B, and that will be fine, apparently.'

'They will help coordinate and teach the new arrivals it says. Everything has been accounted for, they also say. Of course, the initial one hundred colonists will have likely swollen to at least three hundred people, so multiple orbital trips would be needed to ferry them home – also, no problem.' What a load of promotional crap, Becker thought, assuming things a long way in the future. *Nup*, can't be done, he reckoned.

'NASA are in for a rude shock, predicting the future. How do they know the mind-set of the original colonists, and the birth rates? They don't and they can't.' He rolled his eyes and sneered. 'Of course, there is modelling but if the initial parameters are wrong...so too will be what it spits out. I hate to say it, but NASA are wrong or at least, off the mark.'

Connie ignored him and said, 'Breakthrough has been past the planet, and has imaged it. It has an atmosphere of similar vertical dimension to Earth. Most thought that the star would have blown it all to hell, but Breakthrough sensed a lot of charged particles and significant magnetism coming from the planet. So, it can protect itself from its star. Seemingly and quite incredibly, the planet had a magnetosphere or bubble of protective particles, like Earth, which probably means that the planet has a solid and partially liquid core to produce the required magnetism,'

Connie swallowed and took a deep breath. 'Or the planet has a *lot* of the right minerals.'

Connie briefly closed her eyes. 'Vegetation is er...they don't know,' she said, 'and there is an ocean of water or ice, but again, they're not sure. There is both hopefully. Life itself or animal life - multi-cellular, they don't know, none was seen or detected, apparently.'

Becker continued reading, 'There was nothing on any image despite a lot of scientists poring over them for a lot of time. Significant questions about the planet still abound, even NASA acknowledged that. They had little choice than to admit that the planet was still largely an unknown quantity. But they do say it is definitely tidally locked in its orbit around the star and has most of the characteristics of an eyeball world – in other words, time is a place, rather than timing the motion of a sun in the sky. On the surface, the star remains motionless...wherever it is, it stays there.'

Connie's eyes widened, then relaxed. It sounded quite fascinating, but that was only because it was different to Earth. Eyeball life would soon get very boring indeed.

'On the far side of the planet, the star is never seen,' she said, 'similar to Earth's Moon, there is an orbital resonance that keeps the same face of the planet always pointing toward the star. The destination for the crewed capsule was the eyeball, where temperatures *should* be around fifteen degrees C, but again they're not sure. NASA weren't overly sure of anything. Breakthrough Starshot was a fizzer. Apart from visualising Proxima D and discovering Proxima E, which are both, even closer to the host star than our planet, it didn't achieve a lot. Many of the questions about Proxima B were expected to be answered *before* they sent humans. But they clearly weren't. Some were answered, but not all of the important one's as they hoped. *Fuck me, Becker*, how did we miss this story?' She was grimacing and frowning, clearly thinking deeply.

Connie was thinking about NASA and shaking her head. 'Is there anything important they *do* know about the planet? She said angrily, grinding her teeth. '*Shit*, I mean, are they desperate to send a crewed capsule there or what? Sending people, knowing so little, is amazing and as far as I'm concerned very reckless.'

Becker scratched his jaw, looking at her seriously and couldn't believe her comment. He was *always* on NASA's side and she should know that.

'Given that it imaged the planet at close range, there's still an awful lot of unknowns,' Becker said, with a flat gaze. He guessed that was what Connie was referring to. Not much they could do with the level of data they had. Most of the tiny sensors didn't make it all the way to Proxima B. They were taken out by impacts along the way. Not much they could do about that, either.

She continued to roll her eyes and shake her head, strongly suggesting she wasn't impressed with any of it. 'The detected a bit of nitrogen, helium, oxygen and methane, the actual composition of the atmosphere...if you look through the bullshit...is a mystery. There are way too many maybes and guesses,' Connie said, swallowing hard. 'We'd know more if the next space telescope could help, but the James Webb isn't ready to deploy, and won't be for years.' Connie looked forlornly at the ground.

'A lot of the Breakthrough cameras were destroyed or damaged in transit, and those that did survive intact, unfortunately didn't do a very good job. Forget the Collective and the GD, this is all still amazing stuff Becker,' Connie's eyes were as wide as they could go, 'the Fermi Paradox, we, or more to the point, Earth, can finally put that to bed if there is life. I know it's a big "if", but just imagine the reaction back home if there is.'

Connie's eyes were gleaming. 'Remember, they know nothing of Minan, the Collective or the GD. So, as far as Earth is concerned it's still very much an active paradox.' Connie took several steps backward and then forward, becoming suddenly still.

'*We* know other life exists, you and me Becker, but Earth generally, doesn't have a clue,' Connie looked at Becker and surveyed him closely. 'Like simulation, we know it, but nobody else on Earth does. You have to see it from Earth's perspective. We've suspected, guessed, assumed, and hoped that we weren't the only example of life...and now we'll know for sure if it's there. Imagine if other life exists on Proxima – boy it will be close, which means only one thing Becker.' Connie gulped and it looked like it was hard to get the words out. Eventually, they came.

'It means that life is everywhere Becker.' Connie's eyes were huge and trance-like, as she scratched at one of her arms. Occam's Razor says that because Earth hasn't found alien intelligence, despite looking hard, it doesn't exist. *Have we got news for them!'*

'Despite what *we* know about the Universe, life itself would have to be common if we find any evidence at all...even bacteria. Two examples so close, three if we include the pseudomorphs on Mars, means it *has* to be everywhere through the Universe. We know it exists because of Minan and his cohorts, but no one else does.'

Becker could tell Connie was getting worked up, so all he could do was wait her out. Trying to interrupt her, would only make her go longer - and longer and then longer. This was almost her favourite subject.

'We just need to locate where it's reached a complexity to be self-aware and conscious,' Connie said, with an over-bright, almost fanatical shine in her eyes. She knew "just" had no right to be in that sentence.

'*Anyway*, that's why NASA wants to get there so badly, have a look for any life, alive or dead, and establish a human colony. Just like Mars. In case we wear Earth out – we have a back-up.'

Connie was grappling with an ethical issue and decided there was no answer. She wasn't going to say anything, but what the hell?

'What if something is in the process of evolving on Proxima B and humanity goes and plonks itself down in the middle of the planet. Does that impact evolution? In the longer term, probably *yes*.' She asked Becker and immediately wished she hadn't. He started droning on about "tough love" and "who cares" and all that interventionist and don't-give-a-shit crap.

Becker was such a typical male sometimes. Connie was sure they had to take the idea seriously. In a few billion years, maybe something that could genuinely *think* might evolve on Proxima B, but if some group of aliens got in the way, maybe it wouldn't.

What if aliens had come to Earth before Apes split species into the first humans? Things could have been very different, if the newcomers made enough noise, which meant *interference* with natural processes. Humanity may never have come into being.

So, the colonists would need to tread very carefully indeed, Connie was sure of that. That was the answer to her question, she supposed. NASA and their people would be the exact opposite of careful. They would do whatever was necessary to survive – goodnight indigenous evolution. *Perhaps forever.*

Humans would eventually change everything on, or about the planet. It would rapidly become a human planet. All other evolution would either stop or become irrelevant in the face of what would become an unstoppable human avalanche.

Those from Earth would charge in, *gung-ho* style, and it would be goodbye to any progression that was happening across the globe of Proxima B. One thing was fairly sure, if there was vegetation, there was evolution.

Plants and trees that were large enough to be seen on photographs started as embryonic spores, and evolved DNA, Connie knew. It was evolution *en evidence*. If humans came, all that would likely be gone, certainly altered, probably for the worse, especially in the longer term.

Connie felt like crying, trying to imagine what *wouldn't* have been moulded within an environment, if evolution was interfered with by a third party, an intelligent, imperialistic one.

None of their own babies would have been born. Connie contemplated all the human babies that *wouldn't* have been born had it been only slightly different on Earth. She very nearly lost the contents of her stomach, thinking about the lost human children. The lost human adults. Humanity period.

Fortuitous evolution had a lot to be thanked for. Any small environmental factor could have put a stop to humanity. Instead of a new intelligent species arising, it could well have been "just" another great ape from Africa.

Connie's breathing was quick and shallow, she was almost hyperventilating as she considered the billions *gone before it started*. Her final thought on the issue, was that this so-called colony shouldn't go to Proxima B...humanity should leave well enough alone.

'Well, what do you reckon Becker?' Connie said, thinking, *this'll be good*. The goose did his best to pretend he was smart. She sat back to enjoy the show. Her main job was not to laugh in his pious face.

Whenever she sought his opinion, he felt quite proud and Connie found it rather humorous, as Becker hummed and hawed and tried his best to sound smart and well read.

'I think, they'll go, despite what you think. In fact, I'm sure NASA could care less what you think. No offence.'

'Oh, none taken,' Connie said. 'I'm sure you're right though. The colonists will go and make a home on the planet...and change its future forever. Goodbye natural evolution.' She looked at Becker and nodded confidently, making the point emphatically, or so she thought. Connie gave a strong wink to Becker and straight-away wished she hadn't.

'There's only one way you can help them,' Becker said, smiling and thinking about it. He regarded her quizzically, then winked strongly back at Connie.

'Talk to them, right? I don't think so,' she said, feeling suddenly uncomfortable. Connie drew away and shook her head at Becker. 'No...no. They won't listen. They could care less what I've got to say.'

Becker said loudly, *'then*...your only option is to volunteer and go on the journey. Persuade them over time. You know...massage their thinking.'

'Is that seriously your answer? "Massage NASA's thinking?"' Connie peered at Becker with wide eyes, like he'd suddenly sprung another limb. She was genuinely horrified by his stupid response. 'Even for him, it was totally and utterly ridiculous.

'You fucking oaf...I don't want to go.' Connie was being totally honest. She could think of nothing worse.

'Twelve years just to get there, *Jesus*, and they use EPR on 95 percent of everybody onboard, it's a bloody long time, *too long*, to play dead.' Connie glared at Becker, shaking her head and giving him a pained look. She was stunned by his raw idiocy. Connie swallowed hard and pinched her lips closed. Nothing had changed with him, she thought, not that she'd expected it too. Becker remained very slow on the uptake.

He looked at her critically. 'You have no choice, you said they won't listen to you here. Either go on the trip or shut up about it. There's no other way,' Becker said, with bulging eyes. 'You can't do jack from here, you said it yourself.'

'Do something about it or shut it? Geez, thanks for the advice, Becker. *By the way I'm being sarcastic,*' she barked.

Becker tried to ignore her entirely. After a while, he said, 'Well...what's it going to be *smart-arse?*'

'What about you Becker, the same applies, right? Would you be put to sleep for twelve years while that thing hurtles through space?' Connie's face was reddening, and a sheen of sweat broke out on her forehead as she contemplated EPR. 'Doesn't sound like an indulgence of spirit to me. *Well?*' she glared directly and expectantly at Becker. '*How's it sound to you?*' Connie spat.

'Me, well, ah...I'd have to think about it, long and hard. It's a, big commitment. And a long way.' Becker coughed and cleared his throat, glancing episodically at Connie. 'There's nothing to keep us here, though. Not a thing.' Becker glanced around uneasily and finished with a hard, obvious swallow, a huge tell-sign for Connie.

'So basically, it's a no, don't be shy, you can say it Becker,'

He eyed Connie seriously, and a little annoyed. 'It's not a no, or a yes, it's an I have no fucking idea. He averted his gaze, basically he didn't know, *period.* That was the God's honest truth. He had no idea what he wanted to do. Going had some appeal...so did not going. He'd have to think about it. Recent events made it easier, he supposed.

That night, neither of them slept well, kept awake by thoughts and dreams, some horrible, of joining the Proxima journey. Connie had odd nightmares of going on the journey but dying on the ascent to space in a catastrophic explosion and free-fall from the stratosphere. When she hit the ground, she "woke" into the darkness of her room.

Connie felt like she'd had the horrible vision several times over, finally waking to a sweat filled bed. Walking slowly into Becker's room, she found the big lug asleep and seemingly very happy on his stomach, snoring quietly. She ambled back to her own bed, got under the covers, and after a lot of thinking, she slipped off to sleep and woke soon after. Her brain wasn't finished with her yet.

*   *   *

'I want to go,' Connie blurted, the next morning, she'd been thinking most of the night, building a case for both going and staying in her mind and then starting all over again. Go...don't go, it was a tough decision either way. She continued to stew over it most of the night and really didn't come to a decision, either way.

'I have to go, I have to try,' Connie said more urgently, talking overly quickly, like a machine-gun. 'What about you...how do you feel about it?' She gazed at Becker, needing to get the spotlight off her for a while. Her anxiety levels were through the roof, her heart was beating so hard her mouth hurt. Count to fucking ten or something. It was way too early for a drink but she had to relax a bit. Connie smoothed her hair and closed her eyes, willing herself to calm down a bit. She could feel the vascular pumping in her wrist.

'I've been thinking about it quite a bit as well,' Becker said, rubbing his eyes. In actuality, he'd kept himself up most of the night, weighing it up, like Connie had. It was half yes, same amount, no. He still had no idea what was best. The fact that Connie wanted to go, pushed him a little. He was teetering on the edge of a decision, just like Connie.

Going to Proxima B as the colonising force from planet Earth, could be either the best or the worst thing he'd, *they'd*, ever done. Anyway, the likelihood is that they would apply, if that's what he and Connie decided, and not be accepted. They would simply be turned down by NASA and its cohorts.

The main problem was – there was no return trip. It was strictly a one-*way* journey, despite the official line and the rhetoric that was mostly lip-service. They said that a ship or ships would come again in twenty years as wave #2 of colinisation. It would drop off new colonists and pick up original colonists and their families. That was the NASA spin and plan.

NASA and its affiliates had no intention of picking anyone up, whether they wanted to go or not, it's just that no-one would admit it, certainly in writing. In any event, who could effectively forecast what would happen in the next twenty years? What state would the world be in – no one knew. They could cite any reason they liked for not going.

Effective, real-time comms to or from the colony was physically impossible. Best to go into this thing with your eyes fully open. It was a one-way trip. Forget the bullshit NASA drivel. They only said that to make the voyage more attractive. To bolster the number of people who would apply.

Presumably, those with younger children wouldn't apply for the trip, nor would those people with strong and healthy caring roles in the community.

Most people suffered to a lesser or larger degree with Astraphobia, a chronic fear of space. Many of those who actually worked in the space industry were irrationally scared of the vacuum and would never, *ever*, apply to be a colonist. For most, it was the very last thing they would consider doing. Yet, they worked in the industry.

'They'll attract a lot of criminals and ex-prisoners, those people wanting to escape something or perhaps someone,' Becker said. He hoped NASA's questions would weed out that element. He could've done without his mental images of cons with guns aboard a spaceship. Becker was sure the questions would eliminate that element, but it was concerning. Connie told him the UNSC and NSA were involved in assessing the applications, so this type of oversight gave Becker some comfort.

'*Firstly*, where are the Goddamn interviews held? Connie asked, eyeing Becker closely. 'In America, right?' She was deadly serious and glared at Becker, tapping her foot, expecting this whole exercise to be very US-centric which it shouldn't be.

'Well, they spoke about world locations for interviews,' Becker said, 'Houston, London and Sydney, Madrid and lots of others, no nationality is barred apparently. It's the person that's important. Apparently, it will be a UN effort to the last. I think they would prefer a hodgepodge of colonists from various nations barrelling through the ether. Interviewees are to bring ID and that's all that's required. The interview itself is secret of course, but you can probably guess what the questions are.' He stared at Connie knowingly and she looked at him, nodding, seemingly surprised that democracy and equality extended into space. Especially the way the world is today, she thought sombrely.

'Why don't we just apply,' Connie said tentatively, 'we can always say no later on *if* we get selected. I mean, they can't send us if we don't want to go, right?' Connie's voice lacked any strength and tapered off as she spoke. She just stood there, dead still, presumably thinking about what she'd just said. Could they *make* you go...compel someone because they applied, she seriously doubted it, but wasn't completely sure.

'I suppose we could apply...,' he said, 'but what if we need to go into quarantine straight away. *Hang on,*' Becker was thinking and speaking at the same time which, for him, was especially difficult.

'We'll, er…need time to tie things up, and they'll need time to do their due-diligence checks on whatever we say, so any decisions they make, won't be immediate…they'll take time, right? The applications will need to through the UNSC and NSA as well.' It sounded about right, Becker reckoned. All this was way beyond his regular sphere of experience.

'Look at you Becker, most of what you said made sense. Well *done*. I agree with everything. What sort of people will this mission attract, that's one of the major issues here, right?' Connie surveyed him grimly. 'No doubt NASA must be wondering the same thing. If they're not, they should be. Let's be honest Becker, leaving the planet - who's that going to appeal to?' Connie stared at Becker, biting her lip and gripping her hands into fists. She was visualising the losers who would apply – and it wasn't pretty. As far as she was concerned, the way she felt at the moment, going to Proxima B was a one-way ticket to hell. And she was going to apply to go. It sounded like insanity.

Becker glared back at Connie, '…seriously though, who the hell would want to go? It's a one-way trip at best. Most will be playing dead, and some may never recover, *and* it'll take the best part of thirteen years to get there. It's hardly something to get excited about.' Becker buzzed his lips and shook his head. 'Maybe it'll appeal to space-nuts and adventurists, but the appeal to criminals and ex-cons can't be ignored,' he said.

'I'm sure NASA and everybody in charge or doing oversight, including various government security units, are all over it Becker,' Connie said, gazing at the ground. At least she hoped they were.

'They'd better be,' Becker dragged a hand through his hair.
'And once you get there,' he said, 'the real work begins. I mean, the infrastructure is mainly inflatable, but there will be a hell of a lot of digging, hammering and moving stuff required, and then there's mixing untold amounts of concrete for footings and tending to food and plants. And don't forget all the setting up, putting together and mechanical work. There's also shifting, using and replenishing the huge 3-D printer and the blower, to pump everything up.

Connie looked at Becker seriously. 'We also need to form a hierarchical command system which will eventually become a sort of rough democracy I suppose, once they get more people on the planet. This is detailed in the manual Becker – best you read it.'

Becker clenched his jaw so hard - he almost broke a tooth. He nodded uncomfortably to Connie and mouthed "okay". Reading wasn't his thing.

'It won't be a south-pacific holiday Becker – there's no point looking at this shit with tri-coloured glasses, it will get really ugly. Starting with the people who will likely apply and certainly extend to the planet. We'll be expected to live in blow-up domes which will be inflated by a half-dozen machines and live with questionable people we've never met before.' Connie looked as though she'd been chewing on a lemon. She admitted, the whole scenario was quite appalling. The only "interesting" bit was Proxima B itself. 'God only knows what the atmosphere's like, we might be confined to the bubble-dome, with suits to be worn outside – hopefully only breathers.'

Connie continued. 'Food and drink will be of the NASA space variety and generally, be very boring indeed. You will need to prepare yourself.' Connie gawked at Becker, and watched his face, 'no more rib-eye and scotch if you go to Proxima.'

'*You're kidding me,*' Becker exclaimed, 'I refuse to go, *period*. I want *steak*,' he found it impossible not to laugh out loud at that. Becker recovered himself and stared at Connie with narrowed eyes. 'At the risk of repeating myself...who do you reckon will want to go?' He already knew her answer. It pretty much equated with his biggest fear. He wasn't great with people. In fact, he was downright unsociable.

'You're right, we've *already* discussed it...listen hard brainiac, it could be anyone with clean histories, credit or criminals or ex-cons who've been in gaol. Anyone who wants to start over, anyone who's done the wrong thing and has never been caught. There won't be too many families or family *people* wanting to go – remember there's no kids allowed, and no possibility, ever, of a return. Even pets left at home will be gone forever. Everything – *gone forever*. Forget the company line that you will return. That is just hot air and bullshit.'

'*Jesus H Christ*, if you put it like that...*fuck,* what a nightmare.'

'Some "normals" will apply for the journey Becker, don't panic yet,' Connie said, trying desperately to appear calm, giving Becker a shaky smile. 'Let's just apply and see what happens.'

Becker looked sceptically at Connie. 'And, if we happen to be successful? What then...oh grand seer of the future?'

'Then, we've got a lot of hard thinking to do Becker.' Connie rubbed her chin, hard thinking what a hopeless understatement that was. Becker and hard thinking – *Jesus* – what was she thinking.

*　　　*　　　*

Mr Becker and Ms. Lennox, please come through,' said a painfully pale and thin individual with very dark lips and very white skin. He was so pale as to be almost blue – he definitely had a blue tinge to his skin. If this bloke told them he loved the night, and slept upside down in a closet, Becker wouldn't have been the least bit surprised.

They both followed him cautiously into a room with a heavy oak table fronted by two similar chairs. They were clearly a set. On the wall was a painting of a young man with the picture having a wooden frame which seemed to also be of a very similar wood to the table and chairs. Becker couldn't help checking out the canines on the thin guy. Always good to know what you're up against, he thought. The other guy was big and round with a ruddy face, eyes full of expectation and hope, almost the exact opposite of the thin bloke, who looked tired and ready to collapse.

'So, who do we have here?' Thin guy was smiling like a lunatic, waiting for them to speak. He knew damn well who he "had here". He clearly preferred not to show his teeth, his hand was always close to his mouth. Thin guy looked as though he had something to hide.

'Becker and Connie,' he said, glancing at her as she was about to speak.

'Here's our I.D. to prove it's us,' Connie said, with the slightest whiff of sarcasm. Thin guy sat back on his chair and watched them closely. Every move they made, he watched very closely. Becker was fairly sure that, among other things, thin guy was the body language expert.

'Why do you want to go on the journey to Proxima B?' ruddy guy asked.

The expected first question, Connie thought. She dug her shoe into Becker, but he spoke anyway, getting the sign from Connie all wrong - no real surprise there. Connie had followed what they had agreed to, but the goose just ignored her poke and took over anyway. She glared at him and he stopped mid-sentence.

'Uh, yeah, over to you Con, we are a team,' he said proudly, seemingly chuffed at his sense of timing. Connie shook her head and sighed sharply, making various disparaging comments to Becker under her breath.

'Okay, well we want to explore the local cosmos,' Connie said, 'confirm what Starshot has shown us, that there are habitable planets beyond the solar system. And that there might be life beyond the solar system. That will be our main job, apart from performing our regular duties and establishing a permanent presence on Proxima B, to investigate the planet.' Connie was pretty sure they'd like all that. After all, they were NASA's aims, wouldn't hurt to be aligned with those.

'Okay, very good,' thin man said, smiling widely, setting Connie's teeth on edge. Just why he was smiling and his teeth gleaming so brightly, Connie and Becker didn't know. He liked their response presumably. But the teeth – no idea.

'What personal skills would you bring? Like say, forklift driver, bricklayer and so forth. You know, technical and personal skills and abilities that would be needed for everyday stuff like using industrial tools, reading and using blueprints, having manual dexterity and tolerating potentially dangerous, noisy, or unpleasant working conditions.'

Becker said, '*Jesus,* sound's wonderful,' he coughed and wiped his face, and they all grinned. 'I'm a geologist from Flinders Uni. and experienced mineral hunter.' Thin man was scrawling notes as Becker spoke. And I'm partial to a good scotch and a rare steak, he thought, but didn't say it.

Connie broke in because she didn't want Becker speaking for her. 'I did a double major at the Uni. Of New England. History and Geography,' she said, trailing off a bit, looking a tad sheepish. That didn't really answer his question, but still, that was her. Thin man was still writing.

A nurse entered the room wearing a white coat with a "nurse" band around her upper arm, in case you couldn't tell she was a nurse. She was there primarily to take blood which would be tested for everything - blood type, infections, organ function, cholesterol and genetic disorders. They would get the results from a government lab in a few days, Connie was told.

The name of the lab wasn't shared with her. She hoped it was a decent one, not just the cheapest. If it was the latter, they were all in serious trouble, none of them could hide from - her sample would likely come back with genetic diseases and disorders she couldn't even pronounce. And most would be false positives. That's how cheap labs rolled.

God knows how Becker would go with the test, she wondered grimly, with his drinking and meat-eating, he was like his own methane plant. In-short, Connie had serious doubts about his blood test, no matter who did the testing. She'd be very surprised if those that were charged with blood analytics didn't find something wrong with it.

'Current employment?' Thin man asked, staring straight at Connie and then Becker. He could see that both of them were struggling for an answer. 'This is not an exercise in judgement, thin man said, making strong eye contact with both of them. Just be honest with us. Just be straight up.'

Becker gestured with his arm and smiled broadly, suggesting strongly that Connie should field the question. 'Gee, thanks, at the moment, we're both unemployed,' she said, smiling churlishly at Becker and shifting in her seat. His mouth fell open at what she didn't mention. But he thought about it more and wasn't surprised that she didn't mention where they'd been.

Both of them would sound like delusional nutters if they conveyed their first meetings with Minan, and they'd be the last people they'd want running around as part of an isolated planetary colony. It would result in instant rejection. Their card would be marked in indelible ink, "Declined". Any notes would clearly detail "insanity" or "delusional disorder" as the reason for the decision. They wouldn't even need a formal diagnosis.

Thin man was winding up for another question. He *definitely* looked like a vampire. If he had an Austrian accent, thin man would have been a perfect copy. 'Tell us about your family,' he said, staring with what appeared to be a sexual appetite at Connie. Becker wondered who the hell this guy was, where in God's name did they find him?

'Family?' Thin man gawked at Connie, looking her up and down and apparently liking what he saw. His smile was very off-putting indeed.

'Neither of us really see our parents,' Connie said, 'all of them are overseas, or a long way away. We don't have kids or spouses, essentially, it's just us. Becker and me, friends.'

'You're not married or de facto? Thin man sort of waved at them both as he spoke. Sorry...I just assumed, there's nothing on your card. He'd been warned about that before. Thin man should never assume a thing.

'It's okay, but no, *no*,' Becker said, laughing heartily and feeling slightly self-conscious. 'Just joined by circumstances too bizarre to believe. Now, at the moment, we're together, but nothing like that...just friends.' Thin man smiled faintly at Connie, displaying his well-developed canine teeth. Christ knows what they took from that little exchange.

Thin man stepped up from behind the desk. 'A bit about us. The journey, the vessel, the Company called Proxima B is eighty percent owned by NASA and the rest is split between two other aerospace companies, one American and one Russian.' He looked at Becker and then his gaze lingered on Connie once again.

Thin man continued. 'So, the best craft and the most up-to-date propulsion system is guaranteed, funded mainly by the US Government through NASA. The prop system fuses helium-3, an isotope of helium, gathered from the lunar mines near Copernicus. The helium-3 is fused with Deuterium, an isotope of hydrogen, to produce huge amounts of energy and thrust. As a result, the vessel will travel at thirty percent of the speed of light. The rest – you know. Now, a bit about your role,' Thin man sat down behind the desk before he spoke. He adjusted his chair silently. He spoke very slowly and deliberately.

'Colonists will live in cramped quarters and spend most of their time on monotonous tasks like cultivating vegetables and maintaining and cleaning equipment and the living structure. Scientists and administrators will conduct experiments and use 3-D printers to make things that will help you all survive. You will assist all scientists and administrators, he said, looking deeply into Connie's eyes, occasionally glancing at Becker. Perhaps to gauge their reactions, or maybe just to be professional, or there could have been other reasons which Connie refused to entertain.

'This is an opportunity for people who like adventure,' thin man said, with a fine spray of spittle and a decisive nod. 'There will be groups that depart and return each day and some will take 3-4 "days" to return. They will be expeditionary groups into the planet that will be headed by one of our scientists who you will all assist.'

Thin guy really believed what he was saying. As far as both of them were concerned, this guy really had no idea. Most of what he said came straight out of the manual. Anyone could have done it, probably a lot better. The man sounded like a fool. He droned on and on. Hardly what NASA would want from someone in that position, Connie was certain.

It will be an "opportunity" alright, mainly for criminals, she couldn't help thinking, *not* for adventure. Most people wouldn't see the journey to Proxima B as adventurous and wouldn't give a flying toss about possible "adventure" once they got there. Although on paper, it was probably the most adventurous opportunity ever offered.

Thin man glanced at ruddy man, narrowed his eyes and eyed Becker. 'What about sociability, you'll live closely with others, so it's an important attribute,' he said, clearing his throat.

Connie tried desperately not to laugh. Becker was about as sociable as a pit-bull, so she couldn't wait to see how he answered that one. She smiled and nodded at him. Connie knew this situation was serious, but looking at Becker's face, and talking about sociability was hilarious. Connie almost broke her toes, tensing herself and stifling laughter.

'I have a bit to learn about that, but I'm willing to do that,' Becker said with a straight face, strong eye contact and a set jaw. Connie snorted and chuckled a bit, she couldn't stop herself, despite the toe clenching. Sociability for Becker was one thing, and was ridiculous in itself, but using the word "learn" was abjectly insane. Becker was easily the most impatient and unchangeable person she had ever met, *ever*.

Ruddy man wrote notes feverishly, looking up every now and then as though coming up for air. Thin man continued talking, 'so, how would you get someone to do something they refused to do, but which was necessary for the greater good?'

I'd tell 'em to do it or else,' Becker started, looking and sounding aggressive. Connie elbowed him gently. 'I'll field this one Becker, you just relax, you answered the last question,' Connie broke in, 'so let me take this one.' Becker looked suitably chastened.

'*Fine – it's all yours*,' Becker said, throwing a hand in the air, pretending to look annoyed that he couldn't answer the question. In actuality, he had finished.

'Uh, I...*we,*' she gave Becker an icy stare, 'would provide the person or persons with the pros and cons of inaction and help them see sense,' she said, still staring at Becker and shrugging her shoulders. Better than Becker's "or else" approach, she was sure. Ruddy man madly took notes as she spoke. He was sweating and looked seriously hot. Connie couldn't imagine him doing this sixty or seventy times.

'How do you feel about leaving Earth, knowing that you won't see it again for two decades,' Thin man said theatrically. Becker was sure he saw an extended canine tooth. He looked just like a vampire, Becker reckoned, maybe he should follow him, see where he sleeps...in what position.

I'll also talk to this one,' Connie whispered, elbowing Becker lightly in the side again. She blinked several times, focussing on thin man in front of her. 'We've known for some time that we are exhausting our planet, and that Earth's limited resources cannot sustain our increasing population. Carbon is a major problem and it's only going to get worse, despite or because of the poor targets taken by world leaders. Sea levels will continue to rise as will temperatures, ice will melt, weather will be wilder, more wildlife will become extinct, and there will be more wildfires. Then, there is the toothless, useless United Nations. It's a real fuck-up.' She stopped talking on that subject, she'd gotten way too fired up, smiling at Becker who nodded his understanding in return.

'So, this is a first step, I guess. Leaving our planet permanently is part of that...finding a new planet and treating it *right*,' Connie said, awkwardly, clearing her throat. She was sure she went too far. But still, it had to be said. Probably not the right forum though. Oh well, she reckoned. Way too late to take anything back.

Ruddy man stepped in with a question of his own this time. Thin man took up the writing duties. He got to his feet, a little like Becker, grunting and groaning all the way – it was seemingly a major effort just to stand. Connie wondered if she should go to his aid as he visibly wobbled on the spot. Walking or standing clearly wasn't his thing, a bit like Becker.

'What would you consider to be a major achievement on Proxima B? Ruddy man said, somehow still standing and still swaying. Speaking while standing was clearly a big effort too. He looked at thin man and grinned, as if to say, "I'm okay".

Connie made eye contact with Becker, giving him a clear message that this one too, was hers.

Connie cleared her throat with two tiny coughs. 'Finding life that is definitively different to Earth's life-event would exceed our hope,' Connie said, 'but that's the main hope. Even single-celled life, anything, that will put the Fermi Paradox to bed. My take on the Paradox is that humans were just early – the populations are coming I think, maybe...*just maybe* on Proxima. You know, with evolution and the like.' Connie moved her eyes over Becker and onto thin man and his NASA cohort.

Connie lengthened her gaze and ogled both of them, raising her eyebrows. 'Perhaps this planet is destined to be similar to Earth. Of course, if there is microbial life, we need to ensure that its evolution continues. It needs to be protected - we need to treat the planet very carefully. That will be difficult given that NASA plans to ultimately fill any truly habitable planet with a load of human beings.' Connie glanced at Becker and shrugged her shoulders.

Connie continued. 'This would be coupled with building a sustainable and minimally invasive habitat on the planet. And of course, a decent justice system, a sort of precursor to formal Government I suppose.' She glanced at Becker and offered a nervous smile.

Thin man was still taking notes like a crazy man. Connie watched him writing, long after she'd finished talking. Why they didn't use a recorder, to save them the grief of taking notes under pressure, she would never know.

It was thin man's time to talk again. Clearly, he'd had enough of this writing stuff. He handed the pen to ruddy man who glared at him murderously, in fact Connie thought thin man was going to stab him with the pen. All ended nicely enough though. Thin man stood again and said, 'tell me about a project that wasn't going to meet its deadline and how you confronted it.'

Becker gawked at Connie, and felt like yelling *"what?"* or *"shit"*. By his body language, it was up to Connie to answer and thankfully she picked it up. Becker looked at Connie with an intense stare, expecting her to field the question.

'In one case of a deadline probably not being met, I took the venture over myself, didn't sleep for three days and finished it myself, to the point of being ready. And at Uni, I finished most assignments in the last couple of days, working all day and night to finish, the same would apply on Proxima B – show them what you mean by example, by doing it yourself if required.'

Very nice, he said, smiling unnervingly. Ruddy man was writing furiously this time. 'Was there ever a time when you had to learn something you weren't familiar with very quickly?' Thin man looked at Connie hopefully. Becker too, looked at Connie expectantly. He didn't have a hope of answering the question. If he tried to respond, it would be one hundred percent bullshit. And they would both see through him easily and quickly. He eyed Connie hopefully until she started speaking. Then, he smiled proudly.

'It was a project, covering mine design and planning operations and we had to learn the details of orebody modelling very quickly. Otherwise, the orebody couldn't be valued in the time we had available.

The modelling turned out to be a complete success and a Competent Person signed it off, quite quickly. The mine commenced and proved to be very successful indeed, *and* we made all ASX and NYSE deadlines for reporting.'

Thin man grinned again after she'd finished talking. Ruddy man kept scratching at the paper but was soon enough finished. He too, smiled at them widely. Relativity of the various applications were never discussed, for obvious reasons, so they had no idea where they sat in the bigger scheme of things. And would probably never know.

Other questions were asked around using microwave ovens and making bread, gardening, fishing and knitting, as well as putting out a fire in Earth-like gravity and rendering first-aid. Becker and Connie had done all the courses and had the basics, and everything was a hearty yes for all of those skills.

The fact that Becker knew how to knit, got an almighty look of surprise from Connie. Thin man and ruddy man seemed to take it in their stride. After all, men can knit, right?

Thin man looked Becker full in the eye while still seated. Connie held her breath. 'Is there anything else we should know?' He asked. 'Anything at all?'

'I'm not sure how to broach this question,' Connie started, eyeing thin man closely, 'so I'll just come out and say it. What about guns? There could be life on Proxima B that doesn't take kindly to a bunch of new arrivals...hell, it might even see us as food. It's not likely, but it's got to be a possibility, right?' Being totally unprepared for such an unlikely eventuality didn't appeal to her at all.

Thin man stood and held his hands loosely behind his back and smiled at Connie. 'There is a locked cabinet full of hand-guns, rifles and grenades...so be assured, the colonists will be well protected, in times of need.' Thin man stood there with a gleam in his eye, smiling confidently. 'Is there anything else you'd like to add?'

Becker so wanted to tell them about Minan. About the simulated Universe, and about his algorithms, the GD, and the Collective itself. Even the object under the ice. The whole lot would make their heads spin. But he stayed quiet, and so did Connie. If he came out with that, they would think them a couple of hard-core loonie-tunes. No way they'd want to take us anywhere, least of all into space. Thin man and ruddy man would react minimally, but mark them permanently and immediately with a big, fat "declined".

'No...nothing else to add,' Becker said. Connie...uh, anything else? Becker asked.

She shook her head. 'No...nothing,' Connie said, offering a weak thumbs up. As soon as she did it, Connie realised it was a Beckerism she'd somehow picked up. Connie was horrified.

Well...that's it then, interview is over.' Thin man stood up from his chair, meaning they were expected to leave the room. 'If you'll just sign the privacy waiver to allow us to receive your blood test results, and provide your best contact number, that's all we need. You can telephone my office this time tomorrow, hopefully for the results of the blood tests.'

'We'll be in touch. In the meantime, take this questionnaire with you, ensuring each question has an answer. And deliver it back to this office within 24 hours.'

The broad-spectrum questionnaire would allow Security to weed out any undesirable personality traits. Assuming, of course, it was answered honestly.

Connie looked at the pages and wondered quite seriously if Becker would even pass the test. She wasn't sure if he had the personality to help colonise a new world. If they were all like Becker, God help the planet, she thought seriously.

Would he be what NASA sought? Connie doubted it. In fact, she suspected he'd be declined outright. Maybe they'd be approved as a team, least she'd have someone else to blame if things went sideways.

*   *   *

'*Fuck me, that was quick,*' Becker reckoned, as he trotted down the steps to the Bridge Street footpath.

'Quick but intense,' Connie replied. 'So, now we just wait until they call, I guess? She gazed at Becker. It was more of a statement than a question.

'Yep,' Becker said, 'it'll only be a couple of days - give us some time to make proper sense of the interview and decide if that's what we really want. If they come back with a no, it doesn't matter much, does it?' Becker scrutinized her face closely. She looked gloomy and confused. Connie was rubbing her chin and thinking deeply. Presumably she was already contemplating the trip. Did she actually want to go, or didn't she? The question remained.

The thought of going filled her with such wonder-terror. She wasn't sure which emotion was stronger. Probably the terror part, Connie thought, struggling to get passed EPR and the horrors of extended "sleep" and the possibility of never waking up.

Connie felt a bit off physically, everything important in her body seemed to ache and throb, unsure if that was because of the possibility of NASA's cohorts saying no, or the looming decision Becker and she had to make, if NASA's answer was yes. Either way it would be tough. It was definitely one or the other, she knew. She recognised that EPR was the main problem.

If the answer was no, it was easy, she thought. If it was yes, it became a whole lot harder. Did they go or didn't they go? Not an easy choice to make. To somehow tolerate EPR and likely never return to Earth. It was an exceedingly difficult decision to make. It was too hard even to contemplate, most times, because each answer had laundry list of pros and cons. Mainly cons.

If they did go, it would take twelve years to get there, even though they would undergo EPR and only age six months, compared to those on Earth...or so NASA said. That really didn't make a lot of sense because they wouldn't be going fast enough to be truly relativistic. Still, it would be twelve years playing stone dead. Totally blood free. Quite the fucking journey really. They wouldn't experience a damn thing. What a waste of years. And the worst thing – there was apparently no prospect of a return to Earth.

Our lovely blue planet would become a just a memory, as they established a colony on a brand-new world, but what if the atmosphere on the planet wasn't breathable? It's not like they could turn around and come home – there wasn't enough food for a start. Starshot was no help in defining most of that. It was yet another responsibility for the colonists. Making the best of things was fine, but there was a point that could not be crossed. If it proved too much for them, what the fuck were they supposed to do? No-one, not even NASA, had an answer to that one. "Make the best of it" was the best anyone could come up with.

From over four light-years away, that really wasn't good enough. Yet, there were lines of people applying. *Truly go figure.*

*   *   *

There were at least a dozen ways that uninhabitability might arise. Breakthrough Starshot had ruled many out, but a lot would also have to wait for human visitors. If the worst did eventuate, they would have to learn to survive in an inflated dome. They would have no help from anyone. Everything they did, they would do alone. The colonists were it. Connie looked at Becker and gave a huge sigh. If there were too many like him, then they were well and truly fucked.

What was needed were three out of four attributes. Young, agile, strong or robust people that were motivated and driven ...basically the opposite of Becker. That wasn't fair, Connie knew. He could be highly motivated, obsessed with driving toward success, but *only* when personal gain was at stake. Unfortunately, the big oaf didn't have a selfless bone in his body. That didn't bode well for their chances of success on Proxima B.

*   *   *

Eventually, all the breathable ether and food they brought with them, would run out and be gone. They had been assured that Earth air was very similar, according to the orbiting AEON telescope. There was more argon and no krypton, but it was, NASA said, *thought*, eminently breathable. But again, what if it *wasn't?*

NASA reckoned it was okay, but they didn't know for sure. The atmosphere hadn't been analysed directly because they just didn't have the technology. They could only assess it indirectly, and it looked good, apparently. Meaning there was an atmosphere, with depth similar to Earth. The exact componentry was unknown though.

NASA believed they sighted purple cyanobacteria on parts of the daylight side of the planet. It didn't extend to the eyeball itself but they think mats of it are growing in the waterways that ring it. It's not in the eyeball itself, maybe because it's too warm and or too dry.

If it is cyanobacteria, that means there is firstly life, and secondly, there is probably oxygen in the atmosphere. They believe there is both. Proof was in the eating though. They are assuming the bacteria is like Earth and expels oxygen in exchange for carbon dioxide. If it really was present, who knows what its fundamentals were?

But - what if they go all that way and they can't do anything with the planet? What was the contingency for *that*? There wasn't one because it didn't exist. If the planet proved to be uninhabitable, they were all dead. It was that simple.

So, it wasn't going to be easy, in fact, it would be damn hard work, no matter what the environmental conditions were. There were horticulturalists aboard who would direct the planting and cultivation of veggies, the success of which were about as good as a guarantee got on Proxima B. Of course, the plants and soil were brought from Earth. Fully sterilised and guaranteed decontaminated, apparently.

*   *   *

They were close to the steps that led to the foyer of their hotel. Becker hadn't done this much walking in his life. It was fairly standard for Connie, who took amusement from how much Becker huffed and puffed from the mere act of ambulation. She found his misery with walking, quite entertaining. He was so out of shape - it was quite amazing. Too much drinking red wine and eating meat, not enough aerobic activity. *That*, she was sure of.

'Glad someone finds this torture funny,' Becker said, hunched over, looking at Connie sideways with the slightest of grins.

Connie ran up the steps to the foyer of their hotel, leaving Becker on the footpath, fighting for breath. Fighting for life, really. He was really stuffed.

*   *   *

'Hmmm...a letter from NASA. 'I thought they'd text...how the hell did they know our address?' Becker asked, eyeing Connie who was keenly aware of his scrutiny. He was waiting for a sarcastic response...and he got what he expected.

'*Der...Jesus, Becker*, by our address on the form they gave us to fill out,' Connie said, '*remember?*' She fired a pretend gun into her temple, using her thumb and forefinger. Becker was used to her treating him like a fool. One day, he'd show Connie just how smart he really was. That's what he thought anyway.

'Oh *yeah*, okay,' Becker replied. 'You open the letter,' he said feeling duly chastened.

'You can't read?' Connie said, offering a sudden, quite arresting smile.

'Just read the damned thing,' Becker snapped, losing patience with his flat mate.

With a flurry of hands-on paper, Connie opened the letter. She unfolded it and the first line said, they were "pleased" to welcome us on-board, our application to join the interstellar voyage had been "successful". *Fuck*, she immediately thought. *Holy shit*, that'd be right, was her second thought. A myriad of ugly images passed through her mind.

Now, they really had to decide. And really, *truly* had to contemplate it. *Go/no-go*, she thought, immediately overwhelmed at the prospect, and frightened to death by the decisioning that they had to do.

Turned out it was way too hard to consider. Connie had already tried and developed a severe headache really fast. There were plenty of reasons to go but there was an equal number of bigger questions that summed up to not going. The strongest negative was the "getting there" part, that scared her silly.

The most amazing thing was that Becker had somehow passed his blood test. He was clearly more robust than an African Rhino. Another *impossible* somehow scrambled over. Now that NASA and their cohorts had said yes, she was really, *really* worried.

'*Holy shit*, they actually said *yes* Becker, they said *yes*.' *Christ*, she thought, blinking like mad - she couldn't tear her mind away from "twelve years" and "one-way trip". What a fucking, horrible nightmare. Now, she was thinking about the genuine horror of EPR...in fact, the horror of the whole thing.

'I thought for sure they would say no. I replayed the scenario in my mind at least a thousand times and came up with "no" each time. I'd talked myself into it. *Holy fuck*, and now they give us the nod.' Connie seriously couldn't believe it, she openly stared at Becker with huge eyes and no voice. '*Holy fuck*,' she eventually repeated. Connie struggled to believe it. She slowly backed away from him, toward the wall. Connie was at a total loss to explain their decision. And at a total loss as to what to do next.

'They liked *something*, about us,' Becker said, smiling broadly. 'Good old thin-man, right?' Becker thought strongly that there was no way he'd have been chosen without Connie. After all, she answered most of the questions. He was sure they'd been chosen as a *team*. By himself, he would've had no chance. Becker had no decent answers to a lot of those questions. He had answers – but not good ones.

Connie looked deeply troubled. She pressed a fist against her lips and thought deeply. A percentage of people would die from unspecified medical events along the way and twelve years was a *really long time* to be medicated to the point of unconsciousness. It was too long, surely.

Although these drugs were apparently "different" when taken in tandem, twelve years in a medically induced coma at home, usually meant death or at the very least, permanent incapacitation.

Now, they could cool you down and administer certain drugs in certain amounts that would keep someone in hibernation for years. And as long as muscles were periodically worked, no harmful effects should be experienced. That was the spin from NASA anyway. She refused to believe it. NASA and its affiliates were full of shit.

Connie preferred not to think about it. All the guarantees by men in white coats fell on very deaf ears. The whole idea still scared her. They drained your body of blood. As far as she was concerned, it was very nasty business indeed.

'NASA probably weren't inundated with applications to go,' Becker said. 'I mean, given the nature of the trip and all that. Being the first to land on the planet and after all the hoopla and ballyhoo that went with it. Once that was over, their life wouldn't be pretty, none of it. Maybe that's why we were chosen – the lack of options.'

Connie surveyed Becker closely and wondered if the big lug really understood the nature of the journey. Looking at him, and listening to him, she doubted it. He knew where the craft was going, but that's about it. The rest, including the colonisation, was just some nebulous whimsy, well beyond the scope of his mind, even though he'd been told several times and in great detail.

Connie squinted at Becker and said, '*well*...do we go or do we stay? *We both have to want to go*,' she said with a blank look. Silence lingered. Eventually, Connie glared straight at him and grunted questioningly. 'You're not speaking Becker.'

'You'll just argue the other way,' Becker didn't look at her.

You need to be able to explain your decision, whatever it is,' Connie said, trying her best not to grin and remain serious. She had a mental image of a monkey with a pointer and a slideshow. It'd be like expecting a dog to show you the way home – it wasn't gonna happen.

'*Yes, I want to go*,' he said dramatically. 'We have nothing to keep us here, certainly no family. All are far away, and none are keen on visiting. Nor are we keen or invited to visit them. The whole relationship with family for you and for me is a complete shmozzle. Even my stupid building isn't there and I've leased my orebody. There is *nothing* on this planet left for me.' Becker looked ready to cry with his head bowed, and a slack expression, then he gawked at Connie and eyed her closely.

'We have friends but they'll be fine,' Becker said. 'We are perfectly positioned to go. My answer is definitely yes,' he said, his jaw set firmly, waiting impatiently for Connie's words. He knew she was very uncertain indeed, but he believed she'd finally made her mind up. She'd weighed everything up, considered all the pros and cons, thought about family, contemplated the time-shift, the GC, and Minan, and came to a resolution, of sorts. Connie still ummed and ahhed though

'Um, ah...I'm not sure,' Connie said, blinking rapidly and giving Becker a nervous smile. She got up, walked a few steps and swore loudly. Then Connie walked back and sat down, pulling a hand through her hair. She repeated the sentiment not quite as loudly and sighed deeply. She was totally unable to make a decision. She was still grappling with the pros and cons. There were so may cons it wasn't funny. Any sensible individual would say no outright, but there were incredible strengths in the pros.

Connie's own ambivalence about the journey was really annoying her. Being unsure about something normally meant the answer should be "no". *Period*. But this wasn't like that. It was yes *and* no. That was the problem.

Becker seemed so sure. He wanted to go – unreservedly. Which left only *her*. She wasn't sure she could do it. They would drain her body of every drop of blood and stop her heart, introducing cold saline water into her circulatory system...for twelve Goddamn *years*. Apparently, it was "proven" tech. But it had never been proven to be viable for a dozen years without a break. She was fairly sure that twelve years would be quite long enough to kill her and Becker and probably everyone on board. But, according to NASA and its cohorts, the tech had been proven.

'NASA surely wouldn't want their most precious cargo to be dead, when they arrived at Proxima B,' Becker said. 'Or unable to engage in heavy labour. That's not logical. Anyway, they were NASA for God's sake. So, maybe we just have to harden up and trust in the tech and trust in NASA. I've said yes Connie.' He hoped she took that all onboard.

Connie looked hopefully at Becker - she didn't give a damn if he'd said yes but was a little reassured by his calm words. 'The trip is so fucking *long* though,' Connie whispered, 'and it's totally one-way.'

'*Jesus Christ,*' she whispered to herself, thinking how horribly risky and perilous it would be.

Becker gazed at Connie speculatively. 'Um, they've asked us to come to another interview tomorrow...to congratulate us no doubt.' Becker had a huge grin on his face. Connie was smiling nervously, tucking hair behind an ear as she grinned. Becker slapped her softly on the shoulder.

'Thanks,' she said. Connie was terrified. She took a deep breath and signed 'Okay...I'll go,' she said weakly. Connie surprised herself by agreeing to what she reckoned was akin to hitching a ride in a torture chamber. She had huge reservations, but somehow, she said "yes". A tentative one was as good as a strong one. Yes, still meant yes. Doesn't matter how it's said, right?

Connie had said yes, albeit tentatively, to becoming one of the colonists of a new planet. It was definitely not something she *ever* expected would happen. A number of extraordinary, if not totally ridiculous, circumstances led to it.

*   *   *

'Here we go again,' Becker said cheerfully, slapping Connie softly on the back, walking up Bridge Street toward Macquarie Street and into the huge InterContinental hotel, where the initial interviews were held. They'd been asked back again for what Becker assumed was a confirmatory and essentially pre-flight interview. Becker expected to be congratulated for being selected to go to Proxima B. He walked into the hotel with a skip in his step and a gleam in his eye. On his face was a clear, knowing grin.

'Good to see you again,' said a guy on the door they'd never seen before. He handed another unknown man their ID and he made some notations on his laptop. 'Go on through,' the unknown man said, whereupon they were met by another guy they'd never met before. They were led into a room which was pretty much identical to the room they met in the first time.

'I'll leave you with them, the unknown man said, with a smile that cut his mouth in half. He was wearing a name tag, but neither of them caught his name. He walked very quickly.

'Welcome and congratulations Carson and Connie. This time there was a lady seated behind the oak desk with yet another unidentified man. 'I'm Magda, that's Paul, she said, 'nice to meet you,' she sat back down. Paul nodded at them and smiled creepily.

Becker wondered where they got these people from. That was probably just his take on things, he knew it, they were all probably "normal" – every minor imperfection was noticed and exaggerated to abnormal proportions. There seemed to be a lot of imperfections though.

'There are a few things we need to tell you,' Magda said seriously, jutting her chin at them. 'No doubt you have a lot of questions, this should answer some of them. The first one is congratulations, which we have already passed on, and secondly, for you to fill out this consumption form – to advise of any special dietary needs. NASA's own research has provided a lot of detail, but some of the finer stuff, only you can provide, from your own brains. NASA, believe they know almost everything – trust me, they don't,' she whispered, chuckling.

Becker glared at her. He disliked anyone who used the term "trust me", made them sound like a politician or a car salesman. Didn't matter how apt it was.

Magda continued, 'there will be pilots, technicians and the general population. You are part of the GP and will be responsible for following orders from the other two categories of travellers, inflating the protective habitat, and establishing and maintaining the very important indoor gardens where food and other plants will be grown in our soil and water first, and then the topsoil of Proxima B, which we are confident exists, and with the addition of Earthly fertilizers and soil, should result in a reasonable growing medium.

'So, we're fucking gardeners now,' Becker whispered, glaring mortified at Connie.

'You knew that Becker, *start low*, re-fucking-member?' Connie spat back, low and hard.

'Correct,' the unknown man said, 'that's how we start, from there – who knows? Like any organisation, work hard, develop a good reputation and well, hopefully, the sky's the limit.'

Connie eyed Becker and thought fat chance of that happening. If it relied on reputation, he'd probably go backwards, poor old bugger. She desperately tried to put a cork in it, fighting to stifle the explosion of laughter that was building inside her chest. Reputation indeed!

Looking at him and knowing him, he had little hope of being a success. He was far better suited to stumbling over an incredibly rich orebody and bathing in money for the rest of his life. Definitely not working for it.

*   *   *

Connie was impatiently waiting for EPR to be discussed, but she was sure it had been skipped over, hoping the poor victims of the procedure wouldn't notice. She refused to be silent, even if it did her "reputation" no good.

'Um, what about EPR,' she said, sounding like she'd swallowed a good quantity of helium, to which Becker prodded Connie, looking sideways at her, seeing her eyes bulging and goggling which betrayed her feelings perfectly. Connie was shit-scared of EPR, or even talking about it. Connie cleared her throat with a loud *uuheem.*

'That's fine,' Paul said, 'it was next on the list anyway. All but one of the GP's and a third of the technicians will be placed in a metabolic-baseline state for virtually the entire voyage. This includes all the GP.' He looked straight at Connie and Becker and nodded crisply.

'With EPR,' Paul said, 'the patient is cooled rapidly by replacing their blood with ice-cold saline - the heart stops beating and brain activity almost completely comes to a stop. At normal body temperatures, cells need a constant supply of oxygen to remain alive, but the cold temperature slows or stops the chemical reactions in cells, which need almost no oxygen as a result.' Paul gulped and stopped, having apparently run out of air. After a gusty sigh, he continued, taking small coughs. His reaction didn't help his credibility one little bit.

'Um...er, initially, it was seen as a continuation of sleep, but physiologically it is very different because your metabolism is totally stopped. Your body is regulated using software that also exercises the muscles.' There was a long silence and they all glanced at each other. 'Is that it,' Connie said loudly. Her eyes narrowed with irritation. 'You didn't mention the drugs you're going to use.' Anger flashed in her eyes. She stared at both of them directly and could feel her heat rising. She was sure they were trying to hide a lot of things.

Connie whispered to Becker behind her hand. 'These guys just want us to trust them and assume everything is cutting-edge and to our benefit.'

'If you want to know the details, no problems whatsoever. We have nothing to hide Connie,' Magda said, looking at Connie full in the eyes and understanding that she was a "details" person. 'We are here to help you, to give you information,' she said. Connie and Becker briefly exchanged bemused looks.

'Each of you will have individual pods, that will be cooled to about ten degrees with all blood removed and the circulatory system filled with cold saline and a few goodies. Brain activity is zeroed and the heart stops.'

'*Shit...holy fuck*,' Becker spat, that sounds horrible. He looked truly mortified. Becker grimaced as though he had no idea what EPR was, which he probably didn't, although Connie had told him several times. His eyes were bulging and Connie could hear him breathing like a fucking gorilla that had just climbed a tree, getting more and more audible. She felt like slapping him or hitting him or something.

'Are you serious Becker? What did you think EPR was?'

Not *that*. I thought it was just lowering body temperature.'

'Well, it is that, but not *just* that. That's a walk in the park, compared to full EPR.' Connie turned back to face forward and tried to ignore him. Becker was such a dunce sometimes. She'd told him about EPR over and over ad nauseum. He couldn't plead ignorance. But of course, he did. That's exactly what he did.

Magda was reading one of the many newspapers strewn across her desk. From the drawer to her name plate, the desk was totally disorganised and messy, a bit like you'd picture an old-time editor's desk. Like Jimmy Olsen's editor-in-chief at the Daily Planet maybe.

Magda looked at them seriously, pushing her glasses up until they were snug on the bridge of her nose. 'So, you will travel to the Baikonur Cosmodrome in Kazakhstan.' She seemed keen to change the negative tone of the conversation. 'From there, you will be taken by a specially modified SLS NASA craft to Luna, where the *Exo*, awaits, and is ready to go. The vessel and the reactor have been built over the last five years, with the morphology of the craft and the nature of its propulsion system changed several times.'

'*Oh great*,' Becker said, getting an elbow in the ribs from Connie, making him shut it and listen. He didn't have any air in his lungs anyway.

Magda saw it all and smiled, saying, 'be assured though, the craft is Earth's best, put together by Earth's finest and brightest techs.' Magda took a breath of air and looked closely at Connie, who looked back at her and the only thing she could see was a large wart on the bridge of her nose. Connie smiled tentatively and looked at the ground, which seemed to be the safest thing to do. Otherwise, she'd give the game away.

Magda continued, 'Each person is able to take five kg of belongings only. *Exo* is complete, including its reactors which have been tested many times, and it is ready to go. You will board fairly soon. I trust you both have said your goodbyes.' This wasn't a question. They didn't have a lot of goodbyes to make, in fact they had a grand total of none. No-one knew they were going.

Both of them were, in essence from the future, and all their close relationships were yet to be entrenched. In fact, they would never happen, because the future, for them, was very different now.

Becker stroked his chin, 'wow, a *whole five kg*.' He regarded Connie carefully and there was no grin, not even the feeblest. She was stony-faced and could be extremely fiery if he said the wrong thing which he reckoned he was on the verge of doing. Becker watched her and knew he needed to be vigilant. Walk on fucking eggshells, he really meant. Connie was clearly confused about what to do next. She tilted her head and pursed her lips, making various incongruous noises that summed to nothing much at all.

'Anyway,' Paul went on, 'what other questions do you have? I might add that all the participants in the Proxima mission will receive a detailed compendium together with a glossary and lengthy Q and A on the mission. This includes the spacecraft, propulsion system and what is expected on Proxima B itself. Prepared by our friends at NASA, for and on behalf of NASA, for you especially, of course.' Paul's eyes sparkled with positive energy.

They assumed both of them wanted to go, which was reasonable, given that they'd applied and then rolled up here. It was up to her to break into a narrative and tell them that she was having misgivings, chiefly about EPR. But Connie couldn't and didn't.

That must mean she wanted to go, and she did. She knew it. But EPR and the length of the voyage, two of the main parts of the journey, put her off. Connie wanted to go and equally didn't want to go. Half yes and half no didn't do anyone any good. Connie had applied for it and been accepted. That was basically it. According to NASA, she was going to Proxima B as part of the General Population of Phase 1 of the colonisation of the planet. Connie knew it, but wasn't excited at all, she felt locked into something awful and probably life-ending.

Becker, it seemed, had his heart and everything else set on it. Somehow, for him, it was a dream come true. Becker held his chin high and smiled widely. He was proud to go and be part of the initial colonisation effort. The fool would be impressed with damn near anything. If someone reputable and well known signed it off, like NASA, it was correct in terms of its claims and undertakings and thoroughly reliable with appropriate safeguards according to Becker. Irrespective of the data and information to support it, or even if there wasn't any. What a hopeless joke. Poor fellow. Connie thought his picture should be in the dictionary under "fool". He was the archetype.

Connie had heard enough spin from this bloke. She just wanted to get the hell out of there, to give her some extended think time. She needed back to the apartment. Becker, well fuck knows what he wanted. To have a scotch probably.

*   *   *

They landed with a thump at Baikonur Krayniy airport in a 737 aircraft using every metre of the short and rough landing strip. From here, Connie could see a huge smoking NASA SLS vehicle which would take them into orbit, and then, onto the Moon. *Hopefully*, that is, if the damned thing didn't explode getting into orbit.

Then, they would hook up with the *Exo* craft, which would take them to Proxima B, using friggin' EPR on near everyone.

Every time she looked at an SLS rocket, she was overcome with a sense of doom and despair, born from seeing too many explosions on her laptop, phone and TV. SLS rockets frequently crashed during or soon after take-off. That was probably an overstatement, but they were awfully unreliable, at least the ones she'd seen. Apparently, the modified Block 1 types were very good indeed. Connie was glad that was the craft taking them to the Moon.

The group of people in front of them looked tall and young and all Becker could see were tattoos, nose rings and shaved heads. Why youth would choose to go, he had no idea. In reality, they were only a small proportion of those going. Most were over fifty years old and single, but they weren't too old to have kids, and they were encouraged to have them with similarly minded females - if they bothered to read the Proxima compendium, which he knew, was rather ironic coming from him.

It was a point which would no doubt be further emphasised once they got a lot closer to Proxima B. Once they woke up, of course, and felt like they could absorb something.

The plan was to disembark and file straight into the *Exo* craft. The fewer stops the better, they thought. Get 'em on, get 'em going, was the theory. NASA apparently had it all organised, all they needed were the people.

It was considered to be the most efficient and effective way of onboarding personnel for a mission like this. Cambridge, Cornell and MIT Universities all agreed. No twelve-month camp for this mob. Any training required would be done on site once they got there. All they needed were the right people with the right mind-set. Long term training was not required, apparently. It would be detrimental rather than being a benefit to the group, so it was vetoed.

Becker walked with the group, having a backpack on his back and Connie carried a very small suitcase well under her weight limit. She had no idea what to take with her. Leaving her phone home seemed wrong, but it would be useless where they were going. Still, it gave her a sense of comfort so in it went along with chocolates, lollies, photos and lots of active-wear clothing. Connie wondered what Becker was taking. All that really mattered was plenty of comfortable clothes. The rest, he could decide. The only help she gave was to share the contents of her bag. Apart from the clothes, she hated to think what Becker brought with him. As long as he didn't breach the weight limit, he could do what he liked.

Becker reckoned her suitcase looked "more like a fucking purse" than a suitcase. Authorities assessed it and thought it was okay. Connie's luggage was well under the limit and Becker's take-with weighed in at precisely the limit. He was tempted to use Connie's available weight, until she told him to "fuck off" because it might stop the "damn rocket" taking off.

She didn't see anyone outed with luggage that was too heavy. That bided well for those who were on the ship, she supposed. Connie trusted that they were being tough enough though – the 5kg rule was there for a good reason, presumably. There were a *lot* of future colonists aboard - any additional weight would soon add up. Exploding soon after take-off was something they both wanted to avoid.

'I'll be fine Becker, don't worry about me.' Connie watched the fucker high-five some toothy young guy nearby. She watched him stop and gawk back at her. 'It's okay...*continue.*' She waved him on. It's starting, she thought. Boys will be boys, she reckoned grimly to herself. She walked along, toward the ship, totally alone, watching Becker ham it up with a group of colonists that looked more like homeless people in spacesuits.

Becker came back to Connie. 'I'm not your fucking wife Becker, but we are a team, right?' She stared at him quizzically.

Yes, yes, of course we are.' Becker rubbed the back of his neck with one hand and tugged the back of his hair with the other. He felt completely off-balance. He hadn't expected that "clingy" reaction from Connie. Becker realised they were doing this as a team. But that didn't mean he'd ignore other people. Everyone being friends was really important, it was part of the deal, wasn't it?

They walked together, slowly and deliberately, surrounded by a crowd of people, toward the smoking and primed Block 1 NASA SLS rocket. The vessel looked huge, it was almost four hundred feet tall amid the railway tracks and the dirt and dust of the dry Russian countryside.

Connie had the feeling they were taking off from some clandestine desert location. Everything looked totally unfamiliar. The strange gantry mechanisms looked bizarre to say the least – the whole area had an odd, industrial feel. It was very, very strange. Nothing like a regulation space-centre if there was such a thing.

Looking away from the cosmodrome, Connie couldn't see one tree, and the area was as flat as a plank of wood. Overall, the place was very unwelcoming indeed. Baikonur Krayniy was currently the world's go-to spaceport for human launches and was the largest space launch facility in the world. The spaceport lay in the desert steppes of Russia and was by far the driest, hottest and dustiest spaceport anywhere.

Both Sputnik 1, the world's first satellite, and Vostok 1, were launched from Baikonur. The launch pad used for both missions was renamed Gagarin's Start, in honour of Russian Soviet cosmonaut Yuri Gagarin, pilot of Vostok 1 and the first human in space. Dry it may have been, but it wasn't short on history.

In any event, they were in very good company indeed.

*   *   *

There was only one entrance to the beast, which was at its base. A line of metal stairs led to the ship's interior, and there were numerous personal pods aboard, Becker reckoned around fifteen on the first level, and it turned out that there were seven levels of pods with the two pilots above that, the pods themselves were not unlike the ones he'd seen in BA first-class. The bed folded up and was also a seat and was quite soft and luxurious, had seatbelts and a high surround, which encased each pod entirely in transparent Perspex.

There was another ship slated for a later interstellar journey to another exoplanet, further away than Proxima, if this journey was successful, to Teegarden's Star or perhaps Gliese. The craft was different, *better* than *Exo*, and it departed from Earth direct. "Better" she thought, *then*, why weren't *they* using it. Taking off from Earth direct would be a whole lot easier.

Timing presumably. But why tell them it was "better". Something seemed off with such an odd strategy. "Honesty" was the best policy, Connie assumed. *Yeah, right*, she scoffed. When it suits.

*   *   *

Becker saw a lot of people milling around, all sorts of different people from young to old, all in a single file, like going to the cinema – they eventually made it inside and then found their level. 4/51 and 52 they turned out to be. The pods even had their names on them, stencilled on the side. She hoped *Exo* was as impressive.

Connie shivered at the sight of the button which had the word "blood" on it. There was a rolled-up tube, narrow and clear, which was near it and that made her tremble more. No doubt the other craft, the one that would take them on their long journey, would be the same. Except it would have needles too. It seemed that this vessel was very similar to the one they'd be travelling on to the target planet, well beyond the solar system.

The suited people around them had badges that read "All Assistance". Fair enough, Becker thought. They didn't need to show him how to sit down. To harness into the pod for take-off was a bit more problematic, but he worked that out too, without asking for help. *What a hero,* he thought with a shameless grin, as a lot of those near him asked for help.

With everyone strapped in, wearing partial pressure suits and holding their helmets, pods closed and their seats inclined to seventy degrees, the rocket was free of anyone not travelling. It seemed they were finally ready to go.

The fire beneath them changed from blue to white in colour and each of the passengers could feel their own heaviness magnify as gravity increased geometrically. Becker's eyes were owl-like and his fingers fairly dug into the armrests. He would've killed for a scotch or even a beer, anything to take the edge off.

When the main engines ignited six seconds before lift-off, the entire craft rattled and shuddered as they took over and became the main driver. A deep rumble shook Becker as the main engines came up to full thrust. He was sure the vessel was falling apart - it was shaking so much. At T-minus-zero, the solid rocket boosters ignited fully, giving him a massive kick in the back as they blasted the ship off the pad.

The pounding exhaust from the twin boosters shook them continually as the vessel accelerated at two and a half G's, ripping through the lower atmosphere with seven million pounds of thrust. Both of them were pushed downward under very serious gravity as the craft pushed upward through the thick atmosphere, on a perfect geometric trajectory.

The vehicle orbited Earth twice in low orbit, slightly deeper than ISS and then throttled up to be cut free of Earth's hold altogether, entering the translunar corridor. By using the Helium 3 and deuterium fusion process, they could travel at nine hundred K's per second, and would arrive at Luna in five hours give or take.

'Time to sleep I guess, or at least rest,' Becker said, stretching out, putting the helmet down realising they were now fully ex-atmosphere.

'How in God's name can you sleep, with so much in front of us? So much to think about...to worry about.' She was taking deep, audible breaths to try and calm herself, sighing loudly and wondering seriously about Becker's state-of-mind. Everything took on horrendous proportions, she wasn't sure how she'd relax, or even if she could relax. Connie was certain all the future colonists were probably feeling the same. Very, very uncertain. It was the first time, so fair enough, she supposed.

Becker was unbelievable, she wished she could relax like him. His ability to unwind under pressure was nothing short of extraordinary. He acted like someone about to jet off on a Bali holiday, all he needed was a bintang in his hand and a tank top to replace the shirt.

In reality, he was as nervous as hell, he just pretended to look relaxed. Someone had to set the example, he reckoned.

'I'm tired, he said, that's *how* I can do it,' Becker stretched out, manspreading over the entire bed, making all sorts of strange noises. He was still harnessed, although it was loosened to the point of not doing anything at all. He was completely asleep soon enough, leaving Connie shaking her head in disbelief. She honestly couldn't believe him sometimes. Here she was stressed to the max and there he was, like he was at his favourite diner. *Situation normal*, she supposed.

*   *   *

The craft landed perfectly, fins first on Sinus Iridum and they could see Moonbase 1 shining like a star, directly ahead on the edge of Mare Imbrium. Archimedes crater was close by, on the edge of the scarily short horizon.

They'd already been shown lecture-style how to put on the pressure suits and how to check and fill the air-bottles. They were now shown by someone experienced, how to inflate their pressure suits and fill empty oxygen cylinders until they were full of life gasses, using their own pods.

There was a button for everything. Nitrogy-Oxygen cannisters were carried on the back and connected to wrist-meters and numbers on their helmet-visors so they could be effectively monitored.

Everyone had to fit their helmet and show a thumb-up before being let out of their pod. That was confirmation they were ready and properly protected from the vacuum. If they weren't ready and they entered vacuum, they were told in no uncertain words that they were dead. Beware the vacuum. *Always prepare properly. Always beware the vacuum.* These warnings were hammered into everybody by continual repetition. If you didn't know that by now, you had no business being here. *The vacuum could kill you.* Messaging was blunt but accurate. It was designed to save the lives of impatient people.

Becker told Connie he didn't think a lot of them had the smarts to do it right. Good coming from him, she couldn't help thinking, but she was sure they would all be fine. After all, it was made as easy as possible. It wasn't difficult to protect yourself from the vacuum, it just took a slow, methodical and most-of-all a careful approach. That had been drummed into them time after time after time.

All of them ventured out of their pods, the few who weren't entirely sure they were ready, were removed from the group for an equipment check and a little help.

80

'Next step is the *Exo*, I suppose,' Becker said, impressed with the 1 G of gravity they had managed to obtain in the rotating habitat. Walking up to Connie, his eyes shifted from one person to another. He already recognised some of the people and wondered if he would get close to any of them once the colony got up and running. Assuming things went to plan of course. He was taking nothing for granted. By that, he clearly meant two major things – that they actually got to Proxima and it was somewhere they could live and establish a working colony.

'Yep,' Connie said, 'it's enter the *Exo*, and hello to my pod for the next dozen years...and EP and fucking R.' She looked haunted and put shaking fingers over her open mouth. None of the journey was anything, and she meant *anything*, to look forward to. Being a corpse for twelve years was nothing to celebrate. And what came afterward was none to flash either. None of it was anything to look forward to.

Connie hadn't even agreed to it, well she had, but didn't *really* mean it. Anyway, here she was, in the midst of it – she was one of the fucking colonists. Connie was mainly in this position to support Becker, the big lug seemed determined to go, and possibly would have gone on his own. There was no talking him out of it once his mind was set – *forget it.* Talking was just piss in the wind. Even negative talk was of no value – he either wouldn't listen or he'd manicure it, making a negative a near-positive in his mind. NASA was a major backer of this trip too and Becker loved NASA. There was absolutely *no* talking him down.

*   *   *

of them stood in a group and walked in a large single line across dusty Mare Imbrium to the *Exo* craft which seemed eager and ready to take-off from the Mare's northern edge. Earth was very evident in the blackness above, and Connie was sure the damn planet was following her – a blue and white marble of dazzling lustre set in a pure black background.

That's where everyone she knew and loved, *lived*, surrounded by the grand vastness and supreme silence of space. It gave an emphasis to what they were trying to do, even if it wasn't really the Earth she knew. She and Becker had information that gave its very nature a vastly different light. And they weren't telling anyone...yet.

Their first glimpse of the craft didn't fail to impress...Becker said it must have been a big-arsed craft, and it *was*, the thing looked huge, much bigger than the craft they were currently in, sitting on its small, metal legs resting on the lunar talcum, atop the KREEP and basalt of Mare Imbrium. It was massively long and an odd shape...although it all seemed logical enough - to engage in interstellar flight, with gravity onboard in selected locations.

'*Fuck me,*' Becker said, through his suit-comms to Connie. 'It's, humungous ... Jesus ...where do *we* fit in this damn thing?' Becker was truly overwhelmed by its size, to him it looked like a gigantic rifle, sitting atop the Moon's surface, waiting for some poor sod to happen along.

Hard to miss was the frontal shielding, a metre-thick barrier of titanium and beryllium which extended two metres beyond the walls of the ship proper. Given that the ship would encounter the equivalent of a bucket of sand each year and say ten or twelve pea-sized rocks, the need for frontal shielding was essential. If they didn't have it, they'd be like Swiss cheese after a couple of years.

Connie was similarly taken aback. '*Holy fuck*, have a look at the goddamn thing. It's q-quite i-incredible,' her skin was tinging inside her suit as she gawked at it. 'We go inside that barrel thingy Becker,' Connie said, pointing straight ahead with a gloved hand, which was no help to anyone. 'No...*there*,' she said with more urgency, stabbing the air. God knows where Becker was looking.

The whole thing was well over a kilometre long and presumably, all the humans would be held within several levels of the gigantic cylinder that was mid-ships and apparently would rotate six times a minute. This provided gravity very similar to Earth for as long as it rotated at that speed and didn't break-down or otherwise stop its centrifugal motion. For that length of time, asleep or whatever, gravity was essential for the human body.

Even though they'd be effectively dead for the entire voyage, it was easier on the body apparently if they "*played dead*" in Earth gravity. A software program was set to periodically to exercise or pulse their large and important muscles.

So, the theory went, that they'd wake up fairly much ready to go. A bit like a toy suddenly gifted battery power, Connie had said over and over to Becker, so much so, that it was now a running joke between the two of them. She was the Energiser bunny. He was the opposite. He'd frequently wondered what the opposite was – but never reached a satisfactory conclusion. Perhaps an oversized sheep that had a bad hair day - that would be about right, she reckoned, but didn't tell him that.

The administrator of the mission, Albert Johanssen, was about to speak to them all through their suit comms. Hopefully, it'd be more edifying than the last time she'd heard him speak. Hopefully his words would actually mean something this time, rather than the regular UN blather they'd all heard before. Becker doubted it. This guy, Albert Johanssen, could talk underwater, and most of it would be UN spin.

'I can see that this journey has suddenly become very real for most of you.' He paused and coughed gently, away from his helmet mic. 'There will be medicos on each floor to get you set with EPR, and then it is up to you...each of you will be alive, but asleep, ready for your voyage and then your landing on Proxima B.'

Albert Johanssen then walked off, back toward the lunar spaceport, in a trail of fine dust, without making any further comment. All of them just stood there.

'Is that it?' Connie asked, gaping at the rest of them. What a load of simplistic crap, Connie thought, gawking at Becker who was about to say something. He was definitely winding up for something. Words of wisdom no doubt. Her small, tentative smile gave her thoughts away.

'It's only twelve years Con, it'll go like *that*,' Becker enthused, clicking his fingers inside his gloves.

'Yeah, it'll be quick alright...*more stitch-me-up bullshit*,' she said. 'Especially as we'll be totally and utterly lifeless for all that time.' She crossed her arms and sneered at Becker. 'Real fucking quick,' Connie reckoned, whispering her words grimly at Becker. '*Fuck*,' she emphatically finished on, putting her head in her hands. She really couldn't believe she was here...about to be hit with blood loss and EPR. The exact culprit she'd always been terrified of, was only minutes away. Connie didn't want to do it, no Goddamn way, but what choice did she have? The rest of them were doing it. Connie also didn't want to be awake for twelve years while they travelled endlessly through space to Proxima B. She was in a colossal dilemma. Wherever she looked there were negatives and horrors.

They had nothing on Earth to keep them there. Becker hadn't formed his company yet. They were both at loose ends and *family* – Becker disliked his and she had major issues with hers, so being away, they wouldn't even notice.

All scenarios, family on Earth or being in this craft, were totally objectionable. So as far as Becker was concerned, the craft was the perfect place for them. Family could suit themselves...friends, well, most of the close relationships were made in the future, so onward and upward, they could go into space without too much regret.

Connie looked through the portside window at, or at least near, Alpha Centauri, which was quite bright in the night sky, even though she knew it was the combination of Alpha Centauri A and B that made it so bright. Proxima Centauri wasn't even visible, it was so small and dim. It was almost as far away as Alpha, off the portside slightly, to their direction of travel.

Their destination, including its star, was entirely invisible to the eye. That worried Connie although she didn't know why. She knew how big it was and how far away it was. As they got closer, they would eventually see it come into view. Well, she wouldn't see it because she, and in fact all the colonists. would be under EPR. It would be there, a very dull reddish star. In fact, none of them would see anything until they got really close to Proxima. Then, it would be there, in all is crimson beauty.

The little red star held a small family of four planets - among them, their target world. The planet was slightly bigger than Earth and was a *lot* closer to its star. As a result of the star being tiny, Proxima B only received about the same solar energy as Earth, despite being a lot closer to its sun.

Starshot told them it was definitely tidally locked and an eyeball planet, *believed* to be relatively warm and ice-free only where it faced its star. And it had a thick atmosphere, Hubble told them, although its constituents weren't well known. Had the next space telescope they really needed, been in place, they would probably know more about the atmosphere, but it wasn't and they didn't.

It really made her think deeply about the journey and where she was at. They would be travelling toward a planet, whose star was so small and so dim, they couldn't even see the damned thing. It seemed incredibly incongruous.

Of course, it *was* there, she said, they'd even sent unmanned probes passed it. Connie had seen Breakthrough's images of both the planet and Proxima Centauri itself. Connie hardly needed a Liberato direction to conclude that the star and its planet were real.

Still, she wondered. Disputing established facts was a Lennox trait unfortunately – she knew that and would have to get over it. The first step in the elimination of a problem is to acknowledge there is an issue...she'd gotten that far at least. But no further.

Connie had always joked to her "old friend" Joe that she'd need a truckload of drugs to make her sleep properly, such was her penchant to take work home and deal with it straight away. Now, it seemed, she was about to get her wish.

The medico stuck the short Bevel needle into her arm as gently as he could and gave her a low dose of NMDA Ketamine and a few other goodies in specific quantities including thiopentone, etomidate, estrogen and urea, having already given Connie some benzodiazepine a few minutes before. The doc ensured that the pod was closed, the temperature was cold and lighting was very dim indeed.

Connie was given a very low dose of hydrogen sulphide to breathe, which seriously stank. The doc set up the short holder and the drip, and soon enough, she was thoroughly under, and the pod was cold and rapidly getting colder.

Connie's body temperature, normally at thirty-seven degrees was quickly reduced to only twelve degrees. Her heart was stopped by automation, by electric shock, and she would have cold saline instead of warm blood running through her circulatory system. It had all gone to plan so far, but still, the whole process was very ugly indeed. Her blood, all five litres of it, was refrigerated with preservatives, ready for re-infusion back into her body, when the time was right.

Further injections of drugs would be provided to every colonist at years 4,6,8 and 10, plus a wake-up procedure when they entered the orbit of Proxima B.

The drugs would induce a chemogenetic torpor that was very similar to hibernation, by activating so-called Q neurons in the brain – quiescence inducing neurons. Connie and the others would then enter an extended nap from which, tests and research told them, would not cause organ or any other damage. The Doctor then moved on to someone else on Level 4 of the craft.

By the time he was finished, all the travellers on Level 4 were asleep and fully under. Blood removal and replacement with cold medicated saline would occur episodically between Earth and Neptune.

By the time they left the solar system, the ship would have one hundred essentially dead people aboard, who were, apparently, primed to be resurrected just before they landed on Proxima B. If the colonists were awake, and ready to go before they landed, there'd be high-fives all around. Very few of them expected this journey to end well. There appeared to be a well-entrenched pessimism amongst the colonists. Definitely no surprise there.

Next stop was indeed Proxima Centauri B, unless there was an emergency, severe enough that required them to be on deck and fully conscious. Everything else was mostly automated. Some pilots, techs and doctors would remain at their posts for the entire trip to monitor and attend to certain people and critical componentry, mainly the reactor.

The travellers just had to trust that they would be looked after medically on the long journey. Trust was a five-letter word that needed facts and a good prior history to back it up. And here there was none of that. They all hoped like hell they'd be okay when the time came to wake up. Few of them entertained much positivity.

There were two pilots who would remain awake for the entire voyage and keep an eye on things. Someone had to remain conscious while the vessel proceeded, to keep an eye on the reactor, and make sure everything was going as it was designed and planned to do. They'd earn a fortune from NASA but that was little recompense, unless they returned to Earth, which they knew was very unlikely.

Also, medical officers were there to monitor the health of their greatest asset – the colonists. NASA was fairly certain that no external manual adjustments to the reactor or the course would be needed. A-I monitored performance every second and it would hopefully provide ample warning of any looming catastrophe.

The course was manicured to the centimetre by NASA specialists and the computer watched it to make sure it complied with the required velocity. If it didn't, A-I told the pilots about it in no uncertain terms. So, there were multiple fail-safes to make sure they went where and when they were supposed to.

The Fusion-driven rocket was a revolutionary approach to fusion propulsion where the power source was deuterium and lunar-sourced helium-3, a relatively low temperature but very effective approach to fusion. It released its energy directly into the propellant, not requiring any conversion to electricity to obtain thrust. The propellant was rapidly heated and accelerated to high exhaust velocity and it had no substantial physical interaction with the spacecraft, avoiding damage to the rocket and limiting the thermal heat load to the spacecraft itself.

So, hydrogen and helium-4 were released from the ship in copious quantities as thrust from the fusion of helium-3 and deuterium. It would send the craft hurtling through the void at an amazing speed of 100,000 kilometres per second when fully primed.

At the front of the rifle shaped craft was a huge shield which bent over the primary structure and was composed of steel, lithium hydride and beryllium. Even the humble hydrogen atom would pose a problem at the stunning speeds that were planned by the vessel, let alone anything that was bigger. They would not be going fast enough so that relativism became a problem. In other words, travelling into the future would be kept to a few hours.

If they were travelling closer to the speed of light, the ship would appear quite short and they would travel years, perhaps centuries, into Earth's future. That wouldn't be the case.

With such a huge protective "umbrella" at the front of the craft, their safe journey through space was apparently assured. Nothing short of a decent asteroid would represent a problem, and the chances of meeting one of those along their direction of travel, especially in "empty" interstellar space, were considered astronomical.

The reactor pressure obtained from the release of hydrogen and helium-4 provided a very fast and relatively safe way to travel in space, despite the very high temperatures and ultra-strong magnetics. That's what NASA and ITER said anyway.

The demand for, and price paid for Helium-3 encouraged lunar mining, and provided an extremely energy-dense propellant, and fused at a relatively low temperature. It was definitely the way to go. As long as the reactor and the magnetics kept the temperatures properly confined and away from the hull of the vessel that is. Explosive decompression wouldn't be good for anyone. Especially in deep space, a long, *long* way from Earth.

*   *   *

Connie awoke into a hellscape. There were people running around everywhere. She saw some people trip over others, in their haste to get moving and get to where they were going, wherever that was. Connie herself was unable to move. The harder she tried to move, the heavier she felt. Everything Waas don in hier mind's eye.

Somehow, she knew the pilots of the ship were AQAP fighters that intended to reverse the direction of travel of the vessel, return it to Earth and detonate the vessel in a nuclear fireball above New York City in America. Poor old New York, she thought dismally, AQAP certainly didn't like it. They hated America and all it stood for. New York was considered, rightly or wrongly, to be the capital of America.

Eighty percent of the people onboard apparently belonged to AQAP. How the fuck did they get past NASA and UNSC? Connie wondered, distantly and vaguely. It didn't seem possible. Surely, they'd all be looking out for imposters of those approved for travel...wouldn't they? Somehow, they had been the subject of a massive ruse.

In any event, the reactor was supposed to be very safe and would not lead to a nuclear chain reaction no matter what happened. They must have re-worked it or managed to fundamentally alter it so it would produce a huge atomic blast.

Connie thought about it, long and hard - that didn't make any sense whatsoever. She somehow watched herself rubbing her chin. The reactor was how they propelled themselves. That was spectacularly senseless. Connie tried to guess how that could be, but all she could do was scratch her head and wonder.

So, the vessel was taken by AQAP, and before most blood was removed from the colonists pre-Jupiter, with its direction of travel reversed, it started a journey back to Earth. The question remained though, how did so many terrorists get passed NASA, UNSC and the NSA, and why weren't they alerted to a problem by the CIA or DoD who were monitoring the selection process? Everything seemed very strange indeed.

Whatever, Connie thought, feeling tired and dreamy, putting it down to the anaesthetic. She just wanted to sleep, what would be, would be, she thought without any panic. Connie wondered briefly why she couldn't move. She lay in her pod totally sessile.

The vessel was now arrowing back toward Earth. A nuclear missile with a beryllium and steel tip, and Earth didn't even know it was in trouble.

Earth would assume something had gone wrong with the vessel and all comms were off-line. They would realise the ruse way too late. New York and surrounds would be obliterated when the reactor exploded in a huge nuclear detonation.

Connie felt heavy and still couldn't move no matter how hard she tried. It was like she was nailed down or held a very heavy weight which seemed to centre on her legs. Why she knew all that, about AQAP and the reactor, didn't occur to her.

The dream ended and Connie continued in crio-biosis.

3

Meteor
"A clever person solves a problem. A wise person avoids it."
– *Albert Einstein*

Connie woke properly, this time, to see someone standing above her with a drip in her arm putting, she assumed, her blood back into her body. Sixty percent blood equalled consciousness and ninety percent was mobility, she was told, by who, she couldn't remember. Connie remained deeply tired and felt thoroughly drained, and was perhaps at best, marginally conscious.

She thought she had heavy weights all over herself, especially on her legs. Connie was way beyond knackered. She was sapped of all energy and unsurprisingly, had never felt as fatigued in all her life. Having received all her blood back and now fully warmed up, she felt a tad better. She avoided vomiting, but others around her clearly weren't as well off. The sounds of many people reeching and vomiting water was unpleasant in the extreme. The smell wasn't too flash either.

After twenty minutes, the brightly-suited figure moved away from her and onto the next poor sap. There was a loud whooping sound which Connie took to be an emergency of some kind. Becker was perched on the side of his bed, having already been seen to by the tech, drinking something from a long cup.

He'd been disconnected from everything. Both of them were tired, hazy and very woozy – welcome to *Suspension*. NASA and its affiliates were very careful to avoid the name "animation" when talking about their own version of EPR. Wake up from the long "sleep" was slow but was accelerated by giving Ritalin and other drugs.

Connie also heard the words hyperventilation and hypertension as well as nausea yelled by someone, above the loud klaxon that was wailing. Connie felt desperately like going back to sleep, she was so tired, she felt like she was severely drugged which, she dreamily supposed she was.

The tech told her to drink the entire bottle of red liquid he'd left for her, but it tasted like hell. She remembered her nightmare in a moment of sudden recall, and she nearly lost her balance entirely, wobbling and rickety, she just managed to stay upright. '*Jesus Christ,*' she muttered to herself as the details came back to her. *Shit*, she thought.

Connie tried to put it to one side but was upset by the experience, even though it happened many years ago. It still felt unpleasantly fresh in her mind.

Connie forced a bit of the red fluid down. It tasted like something steeply alcoholic that Becker had once made her try. She was certain this stuff wasn't alcoholic but still, it tasted like shit. *Never again*, she'd said to him. Connie had broken that promise, at the behest of absolute necessity, she told herself. Both tasted the same – *yuck.*

Becker and Connie gawked beyond the panelled window and then eyed each other, trying desperately to remain seated upright. They both wondered what the *fuck* was going on. Was this normal? It sure didn't seem like it. The "whoop whoop" blare and yellow strobe had stopped, thankfully. But there were people still running everywhere. It reminded Connie of her dream.

They were told firmly by the same tech, to *"find a fucking evac ship"*. The air to breathe apparently wouldn't last. Becker could tell that the pressure had already reduced. His ears had just popped and his head hurt like hell.

'*What about everyone else?*' Connie screamed, pointing and wondering what would become of the people the Doc wouldn't get to? Connie looked at him, then glanced at Becker and the people who would remain bloodless. There was no response to any of her questions. The poor bloke was too busy running around, doing short sprints, to answer any questions.

'I thought this was *"no risk"* travel,' Becker bellowed. He even made quotation marks with his fingers. He really meant – what the fuck happened? They were both too stunned to take it any further.

'*Find the closest evac ship and get aboard.*' Tech guy boomed, turning his back with a needle in hand, making it clear that there would be no explanations or further discussion. He was too busy and probably didn't know the details anyway. He just knew they had to get off the fucking ship. Apparently, the ship had been fatally wounded somehow.

Becker felt exhausted, bewildered and totally confused. He pulled his fingers hard through his hair and blinked rapidly, '*What the fuck?*' He muddled, shaking his head and blowing out his cheeks. '*What in shit is happening?*' His mind was racing and doing backflips, searching for answers. He had nothing. This ship was meant to be virtually impenetrable, so what in God's name had happened? Why was it like it was. Both of them could barely stand up. The entire floor was rolling and shaking like the surface of a stormy sea. The words yelled by Tech guy meant nothing to him, Becker was still tired and very confused, staring expectantly and blankly at Connie, massaging his forehead with fingers from one hand. Nothing made any sense to him.

Connie poked Becker and pointed backward with a thumb to the egress steps which led to the equipment bay. She was saying they'd better go. Do what their manager said and find an evac ship and get in the damned thing before they ran out of air to breathe. Connie was dizzy and woozy and she wondered how Becker felt. He seemed to be walking oddly.

She'd ask him later, but right now there was a job to do. *They had to get moving,* the ship had been damaged. Terminally, she assumed – you don't get told to abandon ship if a chair leg breaks. Only when something truly disastrous happens. In space this probably meant only two things. They may have been struck by an asteroid, but with the amount of frontal shielding, that was highly unlikely...but, depending on the size, and its attitude in space, it wasn't impossible. So essentially it came down to Murphy's Law. The second option was problems with the ship itself. ITER claimed the reactor was foolproof. But perhaps it wasn't – nothing ever was totally foolproof.

There was still gravity, so the passenger-zone continued to rotate, that had to be a good sign, Connie was reasonably sure. They weren't floating everywhere which they easily could be. The throaty *whoop-whoop* of the emergency siren started again, as did the blinding yellow strobe light to indicate an emergency.

'*We fucking know already,*' Becker yelled at the noise. 'I thought they'd stopped that shit,' he said, looking Connie straight in the eye. The damn thing kept re-starting.

She too, could feel the reduction in air-pressure between her ears. '*Jesus, hurry Becker, let's go,*' Connie squealed, looking through the triangular portions of the window at black, unfriendly space. God only knows where they were. Were they nearing Proxima or were they somewhere along the way, she had no idea, they may still be within their own solar system, Connie thought about it grimly.

Their location was a total unknown, at this stage. She looked at the closed evac pods which to date, hadn't been opened and wondered how the other levels were going? Hopefully, they were all in the process of escaping, although the lack of numbers at the beginning of the stairs was concerning. The "whoop whoop" stopped for a fourth time.

'Come the fuck on,' Becker growled at Connie, pushing her toward the steps that led to the escape pods. *'Let's do as we we're told,'* he yelled. *'Let's go,'* he bellowed. He didn't give a stuff about anyone else - he didn't have time for it. All he could do was worry about himself and Connie. He was sure the others were of a similar mindset to him. *Self-centred and narcissistic.*

Both of them ran down four levels of stairs, despite having no energy, ending at the bottom level of the NASA craft, near where the Emergency Vehicles were stored – that were ready to go when in need. And they were needed *right now*.

The craft they were about to jump into was a "go anywhere, fly anytime, evacuation vehicle and planetary lander". We'd see, Connie thought, looking sceptically at it. It looked very small. All of the pods were lined up together, there must have been dozens of them, she couldn't see the end. There weren't any other people though, which was strange in times of emergency.

Two other people were sent in with Becker and Connie and they too, found empty seats and sat down. Tech guy strapped them in military style and passed an eye over Becker and Connie and made sure they were in their seats right. She could see no-one outside, clambering for help to get into the craft. All things being equal, there should be. Neither could she see people getting in other crafts, through the portside window, which was also odd, and very concerning. Where was everybody?

Becker was gasping for breath and shaking violently against the tight restraints. He was damn sure he didn't sign up for this type of shit. Connie looked ready to die. She was white as a sheet and drew a quick intake of breath and gawked out the window of the pod. Her eyes blinked quickly, trying to clear away the fog in her mind which was still making her see spots – her fingers were restless and she was visibly sweating. Connie had just awoken from a decades long sleep, been reintroduced to her own blood, warmed from freezing, and been in receipt of truckloads of drugs...and now *this*.

The space-tech closed the hatch from the ship side, pulled the abort lever up, rotated the yoke clockwise until it clicked, then thumped until it locked with a clunk. He then sent the pod on its way. Away from the gigantic *Exo* vessel, to the relative safety of open space.

Becker looked around at their new hopefully temporary home and grimaced, already very red in the face. The evac ship was built for ten people, based on the number of seats...so where were they all? There was only four people in here including him and Connie, spread across the entire vessel. And he saw no other people at all and nor had Connie. He thought he knew what that meant – and it wasn't good. The rest of the people were still aboard a doomed vessel. Presumably they were all dead or incapacitated and couldn't get to the E-pods in time to evacuate.

But the main question had to be about the *Exo* vehicle itself, what the hell had happened to the damn thing, to force its passengers to awaken and then flee the bloody thing? Well...a few of them anyway. Given the condition of the passengers, it was the last thing anybody wanted or expected. Evacuating the craft was planned for, but definitely not expected to happen.

There were only a few things that could've gotten them, but any largish object above a centimetre in size should've been detected by their phased array radar system which again, should've given them plenty of time to react. The radar was designed to detect anything that size or larger along their line of trajectory for half a light year.

There was nothing detected, so, whatever did the damage must have been rare and very unexpected indeed. In other words, they were damn unlucky, and probably hit by something small, hard, and in the wrong spot. "Hard" meant iron or nickel...at the very least, *metal*.

Becker looked directly at Connie and saw her staring morosely into space. The damaged and limping *Exo* was in the distance and they were slowly drifting away from it, on the cosmic tide if you will.

'What happened to the bloody thing?' Becker said, having little idea, but wondering out loud. Hit by *something* he thought...he assumed something *big*. Unless something happened to the reactor, maybe hit by the same thing, he thought. Becker knew fuck-all about it but assumed that being hit with something at speed was really bad. The front of the craft was protected with such bulbous material though. Becker assumed rightly that everything had its limits.

Whatever it was, it was major...and very unexpected. And here they were in an evacuation pod, having not even made it to Proxima B. Hardly on-plan, he reckoned.

Becker abruptly felt sorry for the human race as a whole. We only wanted to get to our nearest planet...but were seemingly defeated by our impatience to get there. NASA and its friends wanted to get to

Proxima B but realised it would cost more, the longer they waited. Soon, it would be totally out of their reach, so they just did it, before all the required information was made fact. Mind you, an unexpected asteroid, which he assumed, did the damage, would probably still have gotten them.

*   *   *

The two new people glanced at each other apprehensively. Both were making nervous gestures with their hands. Neither knew the other, or anyone else in the pod for that matter. Connie looked at the floor, scared out of her wits, not keen to make anyone's acquaintance. She was in an escape pod, trillions of kays from home, with two people she didn't know and the main vessel was disabled and probably doomed by means unknown. *Great*. Thank God Becker was here to dilute the bullshit and hopefully help deal with the two newcomers who seemed mega-anxious, which was fair enough. Silence enveloped the pod. All they could hear was the whir of the oxygen-circulators. Someone had to break the ice.

The two people he had no idea about looked up and surveyed Becker briefly and then glanced quickly at Connie. Neither made any attempt to talk. They eyed the *Exo* through the window, then resumed their floorward gaze. Both were clearly very nervous and unsure.

'He-llo?' Becker said, urgently. No one was saying anything. He was expecting something from someone. The pod was dead silent but he could hear something hitting the pod, episodically. It sounded like someone knocking loudly to get in.

Becker gently pushed Connie in the shoulder. She looked asleep with her eyes open.

'Uh...oh, yes, *what?* Connie squeaked, eyeing him dimly. She felt dizzy and woozy and felt like going back to sleep. The last thing she needed was to be berated by Becker, especially since she just came too and was *so* fucking tired and woozy.

'*Oh Jesus, forget it,*' Becker snapped. He'd talk to the newcomers himself, Connie appeared way too tired to open her mouth and make proper sense.

'*Who the hell are you*?' He gawked at the two unknowns, who stared back, not keen to say anything to anyone. Becker really meant it though, *who were they?* They just sat there, staring at the floor of the craft. He felt like bashing their heads together, that'd make 'em speak...wouldn't it? He knew it would, but it'd be a rotten way to start a relationship.

The man cleared his throat. 'I am...' He cleared his throat again, a deep, guttural burst, '...Dimitri Sulanov, he said with a heavy Slavic accent. 'From Obninsk, near Moscow in Russia.' Everyone stared and raised their eyebrows at her. '*Well?*' Becker asked, staring right at her. Everyone had their eyes fixed on the other one, a girl.

'*Jesus Christ*, alright already, I get it, it's my turn, right? I am Emma Sewell, thirty-five years old, from Chelsea in England. I'm a goddamn limey okay...satisfied?' She looked directly at Becker who held her stare until she looked away and back at the floor. Becker immediately took her to be an entitled Brit, who assumed everyone knew of her importance.

Becker was great at making snap judgements about people, normally negative. He thought Obama was a one-term loser after hearing part of one speech on TV. No doubt it was the reason he had virtually no friends. Becker was almost always wrong about people, his intuition about people lousy indeed. His judgement of human nature was so lacking that no doubt he would've thought Ted Bundy was a great guy.

NASA had made sure all the evac pods were the equal of the bigger craft, which meant they all had fusion drives as propellant. So, getting somewhere quickly was hopefully not a problem. Connie wondered what they would do if their evac pod developed a major problem. That one was easy – they'd be genuinely fucked if that happened. They were currently occupying the single and only back- up. If something serious happened to it, they were gone.

Dimitri might have been from Moscow, but he looked a lot like Nolan Steyn, a South African chap Becker had done business with to supply specially prefabricated tracks for his Antarctic expedition. He'd agreed to use him at the quoted price. Steyn had promptly told him to "go fuck a cow" in perfect Afrikaans and then gone about his business of installing the tracks. Strange, odd fellow. Hopefully, Dimitri was not like his doppelganger, even though the South African did good work.

'So, what do you reckon happened to the *Exo*,' Becker said, watching the goliath of a vessel in the upper corner of the viewing port. All of a sudden, as if on cue, it *exploded*, the reactor and bits of the craft itself, going in all directions, some of it hitting and rocking their tiny ship. There was nothing left but a strange, colourful nebula, the blast wave had already gone over them and was on its way into deeper space.

Initially, pieces were on fire, but were quickly doused by the vacuum of space. Now there was only a depressing nothingness in its place, everything the ship was, had been snuffed out by space itself. Their home through light-years of space was gone - it was just them. They were totally alone in space. Apart from the bits of their ship that were rapidly receding into space.

Dimitri said, 'I am no astro-whatever, but we're between home and the planets that orbit Proxima Centauri.' That was clearly the no-brainer part.

Becker scoffed. 'Thankyou Mr fucking Einstein,' he piped, 'that's exactly the problem, *where* are we along that line?' Becker couldn't help thinking the whole thing was an unmitigated balls-up. Their ship was a burnt wreck and essentially gone. It had exploded and disappeared in front of their eyes. It didn't get much worse than that.

'Well, you've got that telescope over there, best you start star-gazing Mr Becker, find out where we are and do please let us know.' He could tell already, he didn't especially like Becker, he'd seen and dealt with his type before. And more often than not, it hadn't ended well for either party.

Connie could similarly tell she would like Dimitri as long as he continued to give the big goose a hard time and didn't take what Becker said too seriously or that he knew what he was talking about. She watched the star ahead but it seemed too bright. *Red and dim indeed.*

They must have been very close because, when she really focussed on it, the star actually *was* cool and dim, compared to stars like the Sun. And up close it was clearer, and they see its disc, which probably only meant one thing. They were really close to it.
There was something indistinct, and small just ahead which she focussed on instead of the star. Were they that far advanced in the journey? It seemed impossible. Whatever it was, was quite dark. *Twelve years...surely not.* It seemed unlikely, to say the least. *Impossible surely.* Had they spent that long in EPR? Almost getting to Proxima B and then getting mowed down just before the final hurdle. Just before landing on the target planet. It was Murphy's law at its worst.

Up ahead of their craft was an icy world and she could see it quite well, despite the dimness. It was quite reflective and either had a very transparent atmosphere or it was like the Moon, having a very anaemic atmosphere, or maybe no biosphere at all. Any atmosphere may have been frozen and collapsed and gone.

Connie stared carefully and closely. It was definitely a planet, she thought to herself. What the hell does that say? Connie cogitated hard but her brain was still hazy and foggy from the drugs. It sure didn't seem like twelve years had passed. Were they in the star system of Proxima Centauri already?

'*Jesus Christ Almighty*, are we that far...is it really possible?' Connie said, looking Becker full in the eye for a moment and she thought about it. 'Surely, we can't be...not yet.' She put her eye back on the scope and gawked again. 'That *"whatever* it is", is venting something to space. At the end of the scope it looks like Proxima Centauri C – *it has to be*. Jesus, we've been asleep for a long, *long* time.'

They were clearly in the star system of Proxima Centauri, having apparently travelled for well in excess of a decade, ship time. A very long time to be lifeless. *Too long*, Connie still reckoned. But they were living and moving and had gotten barely any older. Almost as though those years had been skipped. Some experts said there were minimal relativistic effects, some said there were very significant effects. NASA and its affiliates said it wasn't relativism that would impact them, but simply going very fast. Those in the ship were assured that they'd only age six months in the twelve years it took to get to Proxima B because of the effects of extreme speed.

They couldn't really tell who was right – if we weren't happy – who the hell were we supposed to complain to? She was pretty sure there was no Fair Work or Ombudsman services out here.

Connie's intake of breath was heard by all, it was hard to miss. She was gasping and rasping, breathing like she was about to pass out or at the very least, hyper-ventilating, as she properly considered how long they'd all been under. It felt like a bad dream, but this time she was certain of full wakefulness. All this was really happening. Incredibly, she and Becker had been in EPR for about a dozen years. And, more incredibly, they'd come out of it conscious and intact.

'*Fuck me*,' Emma said, looking at Becker with wild eyes, 'so, we've been a-asleep for almost twelve years, right? *We're almost there*,' she said loudly, gazing blankly through the dome at very black space outside. Emma turned and stared at Connie with huge brown eyes clearly thinking hard. Emma continued to look at Connie wordlessly, her heart pounding, as she considered their position in space, what had just happened and how close they were to the target planet. Everything was flashing over Emma's brain, leaving her exhausted and terrified. She struggled to believe any of it had really happened.

'Yep...almost there, and you're spot on...we've been asleep for a very long time indeed,' Connie smiled faintly, feeling a tad more alert than she had before. The drugs had dissipated a bit, which was good. She almost felt like a human being again.

From what was visible to her, the planet was big, like Neptune, but it wasn't a gas giant, it looked rocky but made of mostly ice, through which, dark mountains emerged, not unlike Antarctica, underneath the ice, who knows?

Maybe, in places, bodies of saline water existed like Europa or Enceladus in their own family of planets? It was visibly an ice-giant, probably including its atmosphere which was probably frozen and collapsed.

*　　　*　　　*

Becker had no right being where he was, he knew that, but he was sitting in the pilot's seat ogling the control panel all the same. He had tired of all the talking and was ready to go...*somewhere*. The "on" button loomed luminous yellow for Becker. All he had to do was press it and the reactor would start cooking. The craft was ready to go in front of him but he didn't do anything. This pod was their last shot at doing something positive. He knew it wouldn't get them home, but hopefully it could get them *somewhere*.

'Don't touch a thing Becker,' Connie said slowly, looking at him and cocking an eyebrow while she spoke. Becker was officially on notice not to touch anything, she genuinely feared for their lives with him getting anywhere near the controls. 'No doubt you were thinking about a stiff drink and peering out the window during the tutorial on flying this thing,' she said, grinning tentatively.

One wrong move by Becker could spell disaster, and Connie well knew it. It was difficult to do any harm to this craft, but she was sure Becker would find a way. He could fuck the most unfuckable things up.

Connie ogled the control panel, and it was overwhelmingly daunting and intimidating looking at all of it, filled with buttons, actuators, high-speed readouts, rotational and translational hand controllers, toggles, cc-tv's and AVU'S, knobs, switches and dials. It was just as well it had "PWR" and "ON" as well, she thought, together with a throttle and steering wheel.

Also, it was really good that she was paying attention during the "How to" sessions. Hopefully, the other two did as well, but she doubted it. She knew Becker's eyes would have glazed over as soon as the session started. Learning something new wasn't his thing.

'So, what happened to the *Exo...*the ship?' Becker said, gazing at Connie with focus. 'The damn thing exploded, and I don't know about you, but I didn't see many of these pods floating around. Which means a lot went wrong with the ship...*really fucking quickly,'* Becker, sighed dejectedly and looked miserably through the window at the spot he thought it all happened. *'What a fuck up,'* he said.

'They never had a chance to wake up,' Dimitri said, staring off at nothing. 'They all just died where they lay, I suppose.' He looked despondent and dejected, trailing off as he spoke.

'Not fair,' Emma said, looking mortified and hanging her head. 'They were promised Proxima B, and instead they got fairly much instant *death,'* Emma jerked her head around and settled her bulging eyes on the window. *'Jesus Christ*...they received EPR, and then that was it. They died in their sleep.'

Connie spoke up, 'What happened to that *Goddamn* fucking craft, it looked so tough...and large and-capable,' she said, still with wide eyes. She was stunned that it had happened at all. She asked again, louder than the first time, 'What the hell happened to that piece-of-shit ship? We were nearly there - look how close we were, almost in its own system for *fuck's* sake.' Connie took a hissing breath and immediately continued talking.

'They were nearly ready to turn and slow the vessel for orbit around the target.' She scratched her jaw hard and watched the small star through the portside window. *'Fuck,'* she spat again, staring at space.

Emma watched through the window and with restless, steely eyes, thought NASA was somehow to blame for the debacle that played out with the *Exo.*

'Lateral meteor,' Connie said, after thinking hard about it...'had to be. Not all pieces of rock and metal and ice came from straight ahead, some come at us from the side, as this one, presumably, has. It is extremely unlikely and is never factored into space travel, but it seems that this one got us good.' She gaped at Emma and shrugged her shoulders with a *"hmmph"* expression.

'The only thing we can take from it,' Connie continued, 'is that it's very unlikely to happen...very rare,' she emphasised, looking a bit sheepish as she stopped talking. She realised how bad this all was for everyone, and saying it was "unlucky" didn't help. It *had* happened. It truly was what it was. Murphy's law got them good.

The lateral meteor was actually an asteroid that was orbiting Proxima Centauri, well beyond the ice-planet. It acted sort of like a small moon and it was made of chondrite almost exclusively. It struck the vessel at fifty kilometres a second, an instant explosion of the entire ship was only just avoided. Had the asteroid struck the reactor directly, that's precisely what would've happened – instant death to all onboard.

'Well, very unlikely or not, it did get us, and here we are, in the middle of nowhere, sitting in this old clunker and our vessel is no *more*,' Emma fired at Connie, giving her a brutal stare.

Connie glared back at Emma with cold and flinty eyes. How dare you, she immediately thought. 'This "old clunker" is all we've got Emma, and clearly you don't realise it but this old clunker is a fusion driven, atmospheric-entry ether-producing spaceship that can reach the primary destination and save your *fucking life,*' Connie said loudly, getting way more worked up than she'd intended. Old clunker *indeed*. That really riled her. For them, for everybody onboard, it was the difference between life and death.

She peered at Emma and immediately felt sorry for getting so heated. Emma looked as though Connie had shot her with a large calibre gun. Poor girl, Connie thought. Emma sat with her head in her hands and appeared quite distraught.

Emma suddenly looked up, and piped, 'so, what do you reckon happened...you know, to our ship...was it actually a meteor?' Having asked the question, she put her head back in her hands and appeared to continue to mope. Strange girl.

'It's only a theory, but it seems about right,' Connie said, 'answers all the questions...meteors or asteroids come at the craft from all angles, but the beryllium shield stops them from impacting the ship. Those from angles beyond the shield that will impact the ship are almost non-existent. Our math tells us that we could travel across the observable Universe and not be struck.' Connie had a sour look on her face and ended up sneering at the horrible luck they'd suffered.

She shook her head and stopped talking, snorting long and hard at the dumb luck that befell them. Connie stared out the window and was completely still, apart from her head that was still shaking. Damn the frigging bad luck, she thought grimly, also knowing that dwelling on their misfortune helped their situation not one iota.

'So, we've been unlucky, right?' Emma said.

'Very, *very* unlucky.' Dimitri barked and Emma nodded at him profusely, as if to strongly agree.

'*Jesus*...have you lot finished? *Christ, woe is me...I've got no hope*...it's all I fucking hear,' Becker trumpeted, 'we're here, just deal with it. We're *lucky* to be sitting here...plenty aren't. We're the only emergency ship that made it off the *Exo*, the rest...just gone.' Becker looked daggers at Dimitri. Connie watched Becker with a smile in her eyes.

'There's no point debating what's already happened, it was rare but it happened.' He was breathing like a steam train, saying "get on with it", and do what we can.' Becker was tiring of all the negativity. Even though he sounded nervous, Connie was impressed by the speech – shame it was all a load of crap. Becker might have said it, but there was no way he'd do any of the "getting on with it". The big guy was all hot wind and bluster.

'And what do *you* suggest?' Dimitri asked Becker, drumming his fingers on the seat. Emma glanced at him and nodded furiously, egging him on. Dimitri narrowed his eyes and glared at Becker. For whatever reason, they all looked to Connie for answers and direction. Nothing more was coming from Becker, and they realised by now that anything coming from his mouth would be absolute palaver. They all relied heavily on Connie.

As far as they were concerned, she was the captain of the ship. The leader. All their eyes were now plastered on her. Waiting for directions.

'If Proxima C is out there, which it is because we saw it, let's fire this thing up and head toward the primary destination, see what's there.' Becker said and gave a crisp nod and a goofy smile, satisfied with his response.

'So...head toward Proxima B, that's all you have to say?' Emma snapped, her expression one of wild frustration.

Connie saw him – he may as well have put his thumbs above his head and waved them around. What an idiot, she thought quite seriously. He acted so daft but what he said was about right.

'Actually, that makes perfect sense, we should go to Proxima B and follow up on Breakthrough's photos.' Connie looked at Becker and flashed a sudden grin. 'Be nice to tread on solid ground for a while...wouldn't it?' He thought about it and couldn't agree more. Becker's face broke into a weary smile as he remembered the glorious feeling of hard ground.

'Yeah, hard ground,' Becker mused. He never thought he'd be excited by the thought of hard ground, but there you go.

'This craft is a planetary lander after all, if the planet looks remotely hospitable, we land, right?' Becker ogled Connie hopefully.

All of them stared back at him wordlessly. All of them desperately wanted the feeling of walking on a solid planet again. They'd all had quite enough of this spaceship stuff.

'Well, we can't stay up here forever and do nothing. We know roughly where it is, its inclination, distance from the star and from Proxima C...so I say we head there.' Connie paused and then said, 'to check it out I mean. We all need to agree though, although I don't know if we have a decent alternative.'

'There is no alternative, either we go back home, which we can't,' Becker said, 'or we try for Proxima B. That's it. There aren't any other options. Becker stared at Emma and Dimitri with an expectant, knowing face.

4

Planet
"All generalizations are false, including this one."
– Albert Einstein

'Agree,' Dimitri said, 'it's the only thing we can do.'

'Yup,' Emma replied, 'I'm in.'

'Okay then,' Connie said, gawking at the unnerving control panel. She'd been trained to use the fusion drive, but the entire exercise had only taken two hours – and it was all theory. She'd never used the real thing.

Actually, using this machine, all their experience summed to zero hours. In deep space, light years from home, that was bad. Experience in the pilot's seat was everything. She'd keep her inexperience to herself, although they probably already realised her greenness. Still, they looked on her as "captain".

Connie approached the control panel confidently and sat down with Becker taking the seat next to her. There was a huge number of strange dials, buttons and switches on the console between them, showing amongst other things, Atomic Mass vs Binding Energy and Phase vs Poloidal Angle, which she made sure not to touch. None of them meant anything to any of them anyway. She couldn't remember even being taught about them, so on that basis, those knobs and dials were a no-go zone. Connie would just assume they were set correctly. The small graphs looked very unfriendly indeed. The data they showed was meaningless – and she was attempting to fly the damn thing. She was confident the ship was set right and would operate correctly. If it wasn't, they were all in huge trouble and she guessed, they would soon know it if that was the cases. Connie doubted whether anyone could set the fine tunings of the reactor. Only ITER or Tokamak personnel could do that.

Becker looked morbidly at the instruments and the displays in front of him, seeing numerous VDUs that were showing a variety of things. He wished like hell he'd concentrated when he'd had classes about this stupid craft. Thank God Connie had been paying attention. Still, it did have an "on" button ... he got that one okay.

Connie made sure everyone was properly belted into their seats, Emma had a few problems but eventually got it. All of them were set to go. Connie pressed "power" and waited the required sixty seconds while the reactor with its hyper-strong magnetics, woke itself up and the plasma rapidly heated to working conditions. That meant really fucking *hot*.

The reactor used solid helium as a propellant, under extreme magnetism so there was no significant mass, or interaction with the craft, and there was no electricity required at all, apparently. The ship was designed with the average person in mind, so it was supposed to be as simple as possible to use. It was designed as a decent emergency craft for astronauts, who were not necessarily schooled in piloting a craft such as this.

Trying desperately to recall her tutorial on flying this ship, Connie eyed the main screen. Thermal and Pressure were in the green so they were essentially ready to go. She grabbed the flight control stick that looked like a modified steering wheel with switches on the top as well as on its body. Connie had no idea what they were for and kept well away from them.

Pushing the half-wheel forward slightly, Connie felt the extra G's from acceleration, which she guessed was good. She quickly glanced at everyone else, they too were pushed back in their seats, bulging eyes and all. The harder she pushed, the faster they went. Their current velocity was seventy kilometres per second, the suggested "normal" speed.

Around her, eyes stared forward in silent horror. They realised who was flying the vessel – someone with zero experience, either with the spacecraft itself or its fusion propellant. Connie understood the craft and attended all the classes, but actual practice in such a vessel was zero. Not surprisingly, no one took any comfort from that. Every one of them hoped like hell that things would turn out okay. Connie crossed herself, Emma and Dimitri did similarly. Becker was an atheist, but he hoped "the powers that be" were looking in their direction as they arrowed toward the planet's location.

Ahead was Proxima Centauri C, a huge snowball of a planet, as expected. It was further away from its tiny star than the Earth was from the Sun, and the star was only an eighth as big and nowhere near as hot.

So, it was hardly surprising that this planet was cold and looked a bit like Saturn with a huge variegated system of rings which dominated a gas and ice world of pure white, at least twice, maybe three times the size of Earth. The world didn't look unlike an oversized

Europa, with huge cracked and discoloured ice-sheets, which begged the question, was there a hidden sub-ice ocean here too? This world was smaller than they thought, but everything else, Earth seemed to get right.

Even though Breakthrough Starshot failed to image it, the planet was here where it was predicted to be, and it was mainly an ice ball – as foretold by those in the know. All of it augured well for Proxima B, even though it had already been imaged, although not as well as they hoped, so they basically knew what they were in for. They didn't know exactly what was in the atmosphere, constituents including radiation, or pressure. They'd have to wait to get there for that.

This planet in the Proxima system was supposed to be the size of Neptune, but no way it was that big, although it did have rather dense rings. The world clearly rotated, and did so quite quickly, the imperfection on the planet's surface had shifted slightly in a clockwise fashion, Connie was absolutely certain.

Breakthrough told them that the stellar system probably contained four planets, the imagers got photographs of three, because the larger, deeper world was probably on the far side of its star at the time. There were three near its star, but only one was in the Goldilox zone – Proxima B.

The frozen outer planet paid little mind to the new visitors arriving at these lands, and onward they went toward, they assumed, Proxima B which very closely hugged its star, along with the smaller, hotter inner planets of Proxima D and E.

The last alien entry to this part of space were a few ultra-light laser-driven spacecraft sent by Earth to photograph the nearby exoplanets. This time there were *people* from the same world, sent to follow up on the photos and set up camp on one of its planets.

Earth was really ramping up its efforts to colonise the innermost planet of the closest star. It had great fears for the longevity of its home planet. That hadn't gone to plan at all,

Of course, the UN and its research arms wouldn't tell anyone that. It didn't matter what humans did or didn't do now - it had privately reached a fatal tipping point. The only thing to do, and not many realised it, was to find a new home, and do things right, from the beginning.

Which meant, sending nothing into the atmosphere which would have a detrimental effect on the planet...like human-produced carbon, methane and nitrous oxide on Earth. The new population could send nothing at all into the air that was anything like that. It was banned by legislation on Earth.

The red star itself was only slightly bigger than Jupiter and, ironically, very white to the eye, and sat almost directly ahead, trying desperately to heat the parcel of space around it, but generally failing. It was so small. It orbited the other Centaurian stars at a distance, and it took its own good time doing so.

*   *   *

Connie ogled space and so far, could see the inner planet nowhere. She knew it was so close to its star that it whipped around it and did a complete transit in eleven and a bit days. So, any flares from its star would get it good.

But she couldn't see the planet anywhere. It must have been *behind* Proxima, she reasoned, because all things being equal, it should be shining in the light from the star. They knew it was there, they'd seen the images from Breakthrough, and even though they couldn't really see what was on it, the world itself was unquestionably where it should have been. They'd seen it with their own eyes thanks to Breakthrough.

The Russian turned his head quickly, he saw something in the corner of his eye, '*shit... behind you,*' Dimitri barked, in heavy Slavic, pointing at a dim and occasionally shining something to the side of them. No doubt it was a world of sorts that wasn't far from their craft.

Connie moved her head and could see a dim planet to the side and back of them. They could see it was moving around its star quite quickly. The planet's atmosphere was only a few thousand kays away.

'*Fuck*...it shouldn't be that far away from its star,' Connie muttered, almost hyperventilating, at best breathing very quickly and audibly, referring herself to a book or manual of some sort. 'We're, um...twelve million clicks from that star...not seven.' She knew exactly how far away it should have been. Connie even checked to make sure. But it *wasn't* there...it was *here.*

There was no planet where Proxima B should have been, but there was a planet where it shouldn't have been. Well, according to science-types on Earth who "knew" its distance and Breakthrough confirmed it. They couldn't all be wrong.

So, she wondered, where the hell that left them. *Fuck*, she thought to herself, shaking her head. What the hell was going on? It didn't make sense that there was no planet at that distance because all things being equal, there should be. Starshot had imaged it.

Connie flew the craft in for a closer look at the planet. The math just didn't stack up. She checked the stats again to make sure she wasn't going bonkers, and sure enough – the planet definitely wasn't supposed to be here...fairly much at arm's length, a full twelve million kays from Proxima Centauri.

What the fuck was this planet? Perhaps it was yet another new one and simply looked like Proxima B. It was certainly nothing she knew about, nor did anyone on Earth, which seemed very odd indeed. Checking what they could with the onboard telescope and waiting the time for part of an orbit to complete, they determined that they were actually looking at Proxima B not a new planet. *Somehow, it had moved in space.*

'Breakthrough put the fucker at seven million kilometres from the star, like NASA had told them, so everything lined up - *why the hell was it now at twelve million?*' Everyone eyed the planet suspiciously but there was nothing but silence on deck. Connie didn't expect an answer, and didn't get one, it was more aimed at herself. The question was real, but rhetorical. Nevertheless, it echoed around the ship. Everyone looked out the window again at the newly positioned planet and wondered why and how? At this stage, none of them could even hazard a guess. It seemed incredibly ironic that it would move now.

Dimitri scratched his head and floated over to the window to get a better look. Emma was simply staring and Becker who was man-spread on his seat, wondered what all the fuss was about. He was listening to the tambourine go nuts in his head.

The Breakthrough light-sails had imaged a tidally locked planet that was largely protected from its star by charged protons and electrons they detected near the planet. There was only ice and a few dark rocks on the night side, no habitability there because it was clearly too cold - but it looked pretty good on the star-facing side where dunes and water seemed to exist in the middle of the planet...and *maybe* there was vegetation, and warmth. The pictures taken by Breakthrough were distant and ambiguous. The greatest minds on Earth disagreed on what existed and didn't exist. *Big surprise.*

That was one of the fundamental aims of the mission. To quantify what was and wasn't on the intriguing planet known as Proxima B. The more detailed analyses could come later.

Science bods on Earth were looking for any signs of life. NASA wanted badly to kill off the Fermi Paradox and justify the huge expense of sending a craft with people, to a distant planet. Finding life, be it oceanic or land-based would be huge. The Fermi Paradox was *the* most important cosmic mystery for humans, more significant than even finding dark matter or dark energy, as important as they were.

With fossilised Mars life regarded as probable Earth-life, possibly seeded by meteorites which made it to the red planet, and in the absence of Earth knowing about Minan, the Paradox remained strong, perhaps stronger than ever. So, solving it was the number one priority for the mission to Proxima.

Although a Government Utility, NASA still craved good reviews on Earth and wasn't immune to the value of good publicity anywhere. Their funding by the US Government, to a level they were happy with, depended on it. Solving the Paradox would assure their funding for decades.

*   *   *

Looking at Proxima B, it just didn't seem right. Up close, it was a frozen and bitterly cold world, it was now just outside the habitable zone of the star. But water was still a liquid on its surface, where it faced its star anyway.

Proxima B was totally different to Proxima C, which was a long way from its star and as a result was frozen solid everywhere. Even its tenuous nitrogen atmosphere was a collapsed, frozen solid on the surface, it was so cold. And it rotated freely, not gravitationally bound, like its smaller and much-closer-to-its-star sibling.

Proxima B was covered with thick ice as well, and only right in the middle of the "eyeball" facing the star, was Proxima Centauri free of ice, and water was a liquid and not solid and frozen and very bloody hard. On the night-side, the ice was as hard as steel at the surface.

'What the *fuck* happened to this planet that *was* in the friendly zone of its star...with decent ion protection?' Becker asked, glancing from the frozen world to Connie, and back again, expecting answers but getting nothing but more questions and raised eyebrows. No one could offer anything useful. Why the planet had decided to migrate was an out-and-out mystery.

'I mean...can this Goddamn mission get any worse?' Becker was angry and frustrated, tapping his fingers in time with his words.

'First, we have to evacuate, and then this shit...*what happened for Christ's sake?*' he spat. He gawked at Connie, before turning his back on the lot of them. '*What a complete debacle,*' he said loudly, while his back was turned. Becker continued to mumble and grumble in a display of despair.

'Well, we have no idea why the planet's here...but we can guess and surmise I suppose,' Connie said, as calmly as she could – she could feel the heat from three sets of eyes. 'The gravity of planet C and hell, maybe there's more planets, who knows. *Earth* may have shifted a few times in its history as well, we don't know. Same with Jupiter, which used to be an inner planet, apparently.

So, Proxima B has moved as well, no huge surprise really although the timing...is odd, to say the least.' She lowered her head and rubbed her chin, contemplating the probable movement of the planet since Breakthrough went past.

Connie continued to think hard, trying to recall old memories. 'The gravitational interplay and movement of Saturn might have pulled our own home world and been responsible for some of the ancient climate changes. It's possible, likely even, that Proxima B was on the move when Starshot took its happy snaps,' Connie said, sighing heavily and looking from one to the other of them, waiting for some sort of reaction. None was forthcoming so she continued.

'The planet probably started to more widely freeze up as soon as it got far enough away from its star. Hopefully, it's now in some sort of resonance with the gravitational field around here.' Connie crossed her arms and sat back down in the pilot's seat. Becker grabbed her hand and nodded. That was the best she could do and Becker agreed with her. *Great.*

Given the strange goings-on with the planet, she really felt like they were in a lot of trouble. Connie looked at the floor of the vessel, giving a long, low sigh. Becker watched Connie closely, seeing her demeanour. She was fairly sure they had nowhere to go that was life supporting.

'Um, why don't we go closer to B and have a gander at it, we might find out something useful about it - something we don't already know?' Dimitri said. 'Might be worth it.' There was stuff all else they could do, he thought.

All they could do from here is ask meaningless and empty questions and maintain the status quo and eventually expire in an alien cosmos. Or they could take proactive action. Seemed to Dimitri that it was a no-brainer to proceed onward and have a look at the planet that had most of Earth intrigued. It was the closest exoplanet after all.

Connie turned around and smiled ruefully at Dimitri, 'Emma, are you okay with that? She didn't seem happy with much at all. Every time someone spoke, she made incoherent, disparaging noises, grunts mainly, of various pitch. Unhappy and annoyed, summed it up nicely.

Who could really blame her though – there wasn't much to be happy about, apart from being alive and breathing. That had to be a plus.

That said though, Emma needed to make the best of what she had. She needed to get with the program and suck it the fuck up, like everybody else, Becker reckoned. He looked at her with a touch of sadness and a lot of frustration, shaking his head hard.

He had no idea what to do with her. He felt like picking her up and shaking her. She was a very frustrating person, never positive...never uttered anything that was remotely optimistic.

'Do we have any choice other than doing what Dimitri suggested?' Emma remarked, in her posh English accent. She sounded quite put out to have to speak. Everyone was gawking at her closely, wondering what was to come, and then glancing at the Russian who was also looking curiously at Emma. 'Do it if you want to, I really don't care,' Emma snarled, and looked down. Her mouth trembled as she spoke, her sad eyes resting on Dimitri. A sense of "giving up" was felt by all as she spoke.

'I'll take that as a firm yes, and I've made the decision for you Becker, so you don't need to worry about it.' Connie adamantly stated.

'Well thanks, I guess,' Becker said, peering at Connie dimly. He realised there wasn't much else they could do. Staying here was out of the question. One look at Emma was enough – she clearly needed something else to think about. Emma looked terrified, staring with wide eyes in nothing less than frightened despair. She was breathing audibly and looked ashen, the colour continuing to drain from her face as she contemplated what it all meant.

*   *   *

Connie turned away from Becker and grabbed the control yoke, and commenced flying by sight toward Proxima B, using RCS spurts to yaw in the planet's direction. Everyone was strapped in tight.

She used both RCS engines to slow the craft to 10.2 kilometres per second, considered by the eggheads on Earth, mainly at NASA, to be the correct velocity to enter a circular, low planetary orbit above Proxima B.

They all gaped at the planet, and all they could see was ice. Ice, ice and more ice. Time was no longer a regular part of the day, it was a *place* on Proxima, one stationery, huge star filled the sky no matter where you were and there was no day or night, just eternal sameness, the position of the star dependant on what part of the planet you were on. It was truly an eyeball planet and it was only in the pupil of that eye that the ice had melted, although at that distance from its small, cool star, it was probably still cool. They wouldn't know for sure about anything until they landed.

The planet actually did rotate but the resonance with its sun kept the same side of the planet always pointing toward the star. It had a perfect resonance with Proxima Centauri and despite it now being further away from its star, it remained tidally locked and behaved like Earth's Moon back home.

The same side of the planet was always getting warmed by its star. The rest was frozen and ice-covered. Winds were insufficient to share the warmth with the other side. The other side of the planet was truly dark and very cold indeed.

'At least we can we land in this thing,' Dimitri said hopefully. He was blinking rapidly, taking in quick spurts of the atmosphere inside the ship. He had a mental image of the pod crashing on the surface, or exploding in space, close to the planet. Dimitri was trying desperately to remain positive, but the thoughts in his head weren't helpful at all, he was losing the battle. The way he was going, he'd soon end up like Emma.

We can go...but we *all* have to agree to it,' Connie said, 'because there's no taking off again.' She looked at each of them and shrugged her shoulders. 'No chance, okay. Remember that.' Connie surveyed the group grimly. 'All of us, right?'

'Anywhere but here,' Emma said. The rest of them nodded. Even Becker acquiesced by showing thumbs reluctantly. They could never take off again. Leaving the planet would be akin to getting this ship off Earth's surface. It wasn't going to happen. *Ever.* Not in this thing, it'll go down, but no way it would ever go up again. It would need an external rocket strapped to it like the space shuttle. It simply didn't have the power to exit the atmosphere. *Period.*

There's no choice, right? I mean, we can't stay up here forever, and we can't get back home, so, we obviously go,' Becker said, staring fixedly at Emma.

'Um...I agree, Emma said, but what about the atmosphere?'

We, ah...don't really know,' Connie said, 'but the planet probably has water vapour and nitrogen in its atmosphere and it might have oxygen and other Earth gasses – it certainly has decent pressure. But just how "decent" the pressure and the atmosphere are, we'll have to wait until we get there. We know there are charged particles that protect the planet from some EMAR nasties thrown out by the flares of its very close star but again, we'll have to wait until we get there to check on them. It might be safe, but equally it might be very harmful, maybe lethal, to humans.' She shrugged at Emma and took a deep breath.

Connie looked at them all squarely in the eyes, one by one, and thought now was the time for more truth bombs to drop. 'The air could also be entirely poisonous,' she said, 'and the planet itself, could be devoid of anything organic at all.' That was the most likely story, but she'd keep that part to herself.

'Until we unfold Stellar, we won't know much at all,' Connie continued, swallowing sharply before speaking. The atmosphere on Proxima B was believed to be rich in nitrogen and quite thick, with the pressure being somewhat like Earth, but when it came down to it, there were a hell of a lot of unknowns. Starshot gave them some details but *couldn't* sample the atmosphere, so it remained mostly, a mystery.

The Stellar was a small, portable device carried in each E-Pod, which allowed the user to dissect an atmosphere, including pressure and ionising radiation, to a relatively fine level of quantitative detail. They would know whether to de-suit or not to de-suit.

If the answer was "no", they were in a world of trouble. The air they took with them to breathe would run out quickly, as would the atmosphere generators and batteries on the craft. Was there ionising radiation that would kill them? Even too much oxygen would kill them. Over a period of time, it would be harmful and dangerous, and possibly, ultimately fatal.

The potential for an atmosphere to be a killer was huge. Too much of this, not enough of that and so on. Clearly, humans evolved on Earth to match Earth conditions. Hopefully, and they all hoped against hope...the atmosphere on this particular planet would turn out to be breathable.

Orbiting above a dirty ice-sheet, Connie was waiting for the eyeball of the world to come into view. Very slowly, it emerged from underneath the planet as they moved around it.

Connie had to admit it looked pretty amazing. An oasis of relative warmth amid ice and severe cold on the dark side, away from the star that looked white, not red. Apart from the eyeball part of the planet, the other side of Proxima B only received the ice-cold vacuum of space. It never, ever felt the heat and the light from its star. Warmth of the star and winds of the planet were insufficient to warm it, so it was composed of hard ice, broken in places by dark upthrusts of rock. Becker eyed the planet through the front window.

'*Shit...*is that what we've been searching for,' Becker said, wrinkling his nose, 'how fucking underwhelming,' he sneered, shifting slightly in his chair to get a better view and sniffing loudly. Connie looked at Becker, briefly frowning in his direction, shaking her head and making gruff, incoherent sounds.

'So, you are underwhelmed...*by that?*' Connie was incredulous pointing at the eyeball of Proxima B. 'What the hell were you expecting? They told us it was likely an eyeball planet, on several occasions, and it was described as such in our reference material.' Connie eyed him like a naughty child, furling and unfurling her fingers, almost daring him to repeat it.

'So, what in the good fuck did you expect? Maybe a butler to show you around the planet or point out the highlights.' Connie was dumbfounded by Becker's embarrassing ignorance. What a complete goose, she thought quite seriously. Of course, that was how it was, Breakthrough had shown them as much, images of the eyeball were very obvious from orbit.

'Very good Con. No, no, I mean underwhelmed by the fact that life wasn't evident, on *looking,* and there's certainly nothing we can see from orbit.' Becker seemed satisfied with what he said, puffing out his chest and steepling his fingers in front of his nose. 'That was one of our main objectives, right? *Find life, or evidence of life.*'

Connie hadn't changed her stance and her eyes were still flinty. 'Tell me you know how rare animal life is likely to be...Becker. *Jesus Christ,* if you were underwhelmed each time, you didn't see it...*shit*, get used to it.' Once again, Connie was stunned by his sheer ignorance of the most basic concepts.

'It's likely, Becker, that multi-cellular life on land might happen on one planet in a trillion. Maybe the odds are much higher. No doubt though - it's very, *very* rare Becker.

'*Jesus...shit*, no wonder then.'

'Now you know,' Connie replied. 'Just remember it. Write it down or something.'

'Yes, Sir Connie,' he felt like goose-stepping or marching on-the-spot and saluting.

Dimitri and Emma stared at Proxima B in silence, listening to the to's and fro's of Connie and Becker. Both were rich in thought and hopes about what the eyeball and the atmosphere held.

Into view came ice, and a lot of it with a few dark outcropping rocks. The eyeball itself looked very distinct and it seemed very small, ice covering everything but a small roughly circular central part that was brown or tan in colour and faced directly toward its star. It looked hot and sandy to Connie, but she reckoned that was probably wrong on both counts. No way it could be hot out there and she reckoned it was mainly rock in the eyeball, not sand.

'For an eyeball...it makes a great *misty*,' Becker said, 'which is a marble I used to on own,' he added, seeing the blank faces around him, 'with a tiny eyeball thingy right in the middle.' His face-splitting smile was aimed directly at Connie.

'Truly, words of wisdom,' Connie grinned benignly back at him. Fucking idiot, she really meant. Comparing Proxima B to a marble. *Enough said*, she reckoned. That was Becker in a nutshell. Reducing everything to a joke.

There was a large river or at least a waterway that went around the edge of the ice in a rough circular fashion before the brown-ness of what they took as sandy or rocky desert, maybe with dunes began. The river was presumably fed by the melting ice from glaciers that stretched across the far side of the planet.

It looked a lot like Antarctica, with the cleaving glaciers falling into the water beyond. The glaciers were episodically melting, and Connie wondered how long that would continue for, given the new location...the deeper location, of the planet. Presumably this whole area would get a lot colder.

We'll land in what I reckon is desert or small dunes or something like the plains on Mars and see what happens,' Connie said, with a flourish of her shoulders and a pained expression. 'I mean...what the hell else do we do?' She said, with owlish eyes, feeling very anxious.

Visions of crashed, broken technology on Proxima B didn't help her confidence any.

'We have little choice other than to try it...like the *Exo*, we can't land on fucking ice.' She glared at Becker who just sat there, unsure what they should do. No one disputed what she said or offered any other suggestions.

They were all relying on Connie to land their vessel safely. The *Exo* had air brakes and reverse thrust, this had nothing like that, just a footbrake that was basically useless. But they had to put the craft down. There was no choice. They couldn't stay where they were.

Yikes, she thought, wondering how the hell she was going to do it, she had about as much experience as them. Well, perhaps a little more in space, but not much more in terms of this vessel itself. She tried her best to expunge those negative thoughts from her mind. No pressure, she said to herself silently.

'It sort of looks like Mars in that one small spot,' Emma said poshly, gawking below their craft at the broken clouds. Becker gazed at her and decided against making any comment, he wanted to thank her for the strikingly obvious, but resisted.

He'd wait till he knew her a little better before using trademark sarcasm. Hopefully there would be time for that to happen later, Becker thought to himself grimly. The way it was going so far, it didn't look good. They were about to land on a planet that looked barren, and assuming they did land, their E-craft was totally unable to take-off again.

'Can you take this thing in and bring it down on that brownish piece of land in between the ice?' Becker's outstretched arm was pointing while he was speaking. He was deadly serious, eyeing Connie dramatically. As far as he was concerned, that was their only chance to live.

'Sure Becker, perhaps you would like to land...right...*there*.' Connie put her finger on the canopy glass. 'This thing will come down like the space shuttle, you do remember, *right*?'

Clearly, he didn't remember a thing about it. This craft would fly a lot like the shuttle when it entered the atmosphere. Connie was thinking "flying brick".

She eyed everyone and didn't like what she saw, realising they knew nothing about the craft. They thought the damn thing was like a light rubber-tyred aircraft and could land wherever it wanted to. *Were they in for a surprise!*

Connie gaped at them and said, 'I'm sorry to say, we have no atmospheric engines. No RCS *or* OMS that will work in air, it will in essence be a flying brick...there's no turning around and coming in again. We have to land where and when we come in, there's no turning around to have another go – one way or the other, for better or worse, we land.'

Connie rubbed the back of her neck and stared at them until she was satisfied that they understood, *actually got*, the tenuous nature of their situation. She then turned her focus to the control panel and tried to block everything else out.

'The pod has a heat shield but that's it, no return engines, *at all*. It's strictly a one-way trip for us, everyone needs to understand that, if you didn't already know it. *Christ*,' she yelled at herself.

"Just enter and land", she thought and kept repeating it in her mind. Both events filled her with dread. Connie knew everything had to be done just right.

She cleared her throat and held her shaking arm with the other hand, to try and stop the damned thing moving of its own accord. She knew it was a decision for her to make as well. A big decision. But the answer was obvious. They definitely couldn't stay static as they were now.

'We can't stay up here,' Dimitri said firmly, and returned to his window to ogle the planet. 'I say do it.' He swallowed hard and squared his shoulders. His mouth was gaping and his eyes bulging.

Master of the bloody obvious, Becker thought, cracking his knuckles and staring at Dimitri's back. 'Obvious it is, but he's right, we can't stay here.' Becker was staring at Emma now, who was nodding feverishly, although she looked drop-dead terrified, having squeezed her eyes shut. When she opened them, Becker had never seen such big eyes. Except on his dog, but he guessed that didn't count. He made a mental note never to say that out loud.

'Okay, in we go then,' Connie burbled nervously. Becker briefly rubbed the hollow of Connie's shoulders and felt her neck muscles which were like piano wires. *Shit*, he thought, wondering what she'd be like once they entered the atmosphere. And worse after, *if* we landed. Becker realised everyone expected her to be invincible, but she wasn't. She was just an ordinary person that had been thrust into a leadership role, that she didn't ask for. Connie felt as much stress, probably more, than he or anyone else did. She had to do things and make decisions that determined whether people lived or died. Becker rightly reckoned he should remember that. Connie was just a regular person.

Understanding what was next, she used RCS to spurt some gas and re-orient the craft in space to ensure the thermal tiles on the underbelly were exposed to their direction of travel. She set their velocity and angle of descent into the astrogation computer. If they entered too fast, the heat would overwhelm the tiles and they would probably burn up. That would be very bad.

Too shallow and they would bounce off the Karman line like a rock skipping off a pond. Both outcomes were equally bad and both had to be avoided at all costs. This far from Earth, any assistance was a long, long way away. If a mistake was made out here, it was more than likely going to be fatal.

The science bods on Earth reckoned they should approach Proxima B at thirty-five degrees and six kilometres per second, which would keep them safe, supposedly. There was a large manual on atmospheric entry, which the experts went through with them page by page on Earth. Connie had paid close attention while Becker seemed to ignore it. He would be worse than useless in this situation. She needed to focus on what she was doing, and Becker couldn't assist in that area at all.

Connie believed that the movement of the planet away from its star would make no difference to the entry parameters of the world. It should be exactly the same. Hopefully, she was right. They'd soon know if she was wrong. If they started to burn up or got flung away from the planet, she'd be the first to know.

Connie surveyed all of them, their granite eyes were locked on her and studying her carefully in return. She held their fate in her hands, she guessed, so fair enough. Staring and hoping was expected. Even Becker looked alert and watched her every movement which was unusual but under the circumstances "understandable".

'Here we g-go,' Connie said without much authority in her voice as into the bizarre-looking violet atmosphere they went. She could see a broken bank of slightly grey clouds way below them.

She slowed the craft down with a burn from the front OMS which could be rotated in need, for fine directional movement, but she had them straight forward to slow the craft without any movement, either to Port, Starboard or Yawing up or down. There were also OMS engines at the back. Of course, both would be little help once they got into the atmosphere.

Connie glanced at Becker, if he wasn't asleep, he was doing a damn good job of looking like it. For whatever reason, he had decided not to watch the proceedings and looked a lot like he was dozing. He was either tired and fatigued or really trusted Connie to do a good job. Or he was just lazy and disinterested. It was probably the latter, she reckoned. The other two were paying very close attention to what was happening, ping-ponging their gaze between the front and side windows, presumably making sure they knew where the craft was, relative to the planet.

Connie thought Becker had the right approach, after all, *what would be would be*, there was fuck all anyone could do about it now. They'd either land or they wouldn't. She hadn't forgotten "brick", in fact, Connie couldn't get the term out of her mind. Wherever it was pointed, that's pretty much where it would come down. There was minimal "flying" involved. Most of it was to avoid crashing in a calamitous heap. She had to bring the craft down very carefully indeed. The astrogation computer took them directly through the Karman line, whipping the molecules of Proxima's atmosphere into a burning frenzy which they could see through the main window of their vessel. After about seven minutes, the fiery plasma soup abated and they were into clear air at about 80,000 feet. Connie wondered if they were the first conscious *anythings* to view this sight.

All anyone could see anywhere below them was ice...there was so much fucking ice. It must be what Antarctica looked like from the air. That was good because it probably meant they were on course, Connie hoped. They were moving forward toward the planet anyway. That was also good.

Below were grey cirrus clouds that floated in the atmosphere and looked just like Earth, even if the landscape and the colour of the atmosphere didn't. This clearly wasn't their planet. Nothing about this place was Earth-like, apart from the clouds.

huge waterway or maybe a large river came into view as Connie did S-turns and wide C-turns to get rid of heat and speed. Most of the rivers and streams on Earth emptied into oceans but this one seemed to go around the edges of the ice, in a pseudo-circle. That was a huge difference already.

She held the manual in one hand and the heavy half-steering wheel in the other, and then dropped the manual and fought to keep the craft level, quickly wiping wet hair from her eyes. Her eyes were bulging, followed by rapid blinking.

The computer would search for the best landing area and then bring the craft down until it was stationery on the ground.

If the IT of the ship failed to find somewhere it could land, the vessel would require a manual landing. It looked sort of okay though, from here - where the ice ended but they were still high in the sky, so smaller boulders that might cause problems with landing couldn't be distinguished yet.

Connie didn't fancy landing herself but had a nagging feeling that this was how it was destined to be. If it couldn't find an appropriate landing site, it would "hand-over" to someone on-board. The astrogation computer boasted autonomous decision-making and that was good and bad.

Setting down, as she thought, *was* a major problem for the astrogation computer and the "manual" warning was flashing which, according to the manual, would go for thirty seconds and then it would simply yield. It would just give-over to someone or no-one, and if it crashed, it crashed.

There would be no further A-I intervention after it yielded. There was an assumption by the A-I that there was at least one pilot on board, which was fair enough. If there wasn't anyone on-board to fly the vessel, it would be very tough going indeed.

Connie thumped the button and she had total control of the craft. There wasn't much altitude to play with and the steering wheel itself felt really heavy. The A-I built into the craft said "too hard" but Connie herself didn't have that luxury. She had to somehow save the vessel and the humans on board and land the fucker safely - based on a single tutorial. No one had ever actually piloted the vehicle in space or in the atmosphere. That was bad.

She knew the pod would come down hard. But what if the surface was too soft or too hard and angular for the nitrogy-tyres?

Wasn't a hell of a lot she could do about it. Connie's breathing was getting louder and raspier as they fell from the sky like a huge block of metal with wings. The ground was getting closer.

She saw the altimeter - two thousand one hundred feet, so she hauled back the heavy control yoke slightly, having already deployed the wheels that dutifully locked into place. Even the Ziesel "tank-inspired" tyres would be harshly tested by this rough landscape. If they crashed and decompressed, God help them all. They'd decided not to wear their pressure suits as a sign of faith, both in the tech itself, and in Connie's ability to bring the pod down safely. Hopefully, they wouldn't regret that decision. Gawking at the ground, and A-I's decision not to be involved in the "landing", Connie wasn't sure if the surface was hard or soft but it was totally academic, because they were a brick on the way down.

Becker and the rest of them were tightly strapped in, watching Connie feverishly as she flew the craft with one hand and again had the manual hanging out of the other, until she dropped it, and had both hands tightly on the steering wheel. It was even heavier than it was before if that was possible. Connie thought she knew enough to fly the fucker, but a few years of experience would have been nice.

The vessel was skimming two hundred feet above the surface of Proxima B. She couldn't help wondering what would happen when they touched the planet – would it skid along the surface or stick fast in deep sand? She'd find out soon enough.

From here, it looked more rocky, not sandy. The tyres were good, great even, but even they had their limits. If it landed in deep sand, Connie knew they were in massive trouble. It would explode or break apart or something bad. Even the best tyres would sink in sand, this pod was extremely heavy.

'Okay...here we go,' Connie barked without warning. She pushed on the yoke and started a relatively steep descent to the ground - it was now or never, she thought. She needed to get this thing on the ground, as soon as possible. It was inevitable, so it may as well be now. The terrain here was as good as it was going to get.

This low though, she could see that the ground was hard and rough. *Very rough* in places. Connie would have to try to avoid those areas entirely which wasn't going to be easy. There were rocks everywhere, most were flat lying like water-borne Mars-strata, but some rocks stood above ground to varying heights. It was those that she needed to be wary of. Small rocks would be okay, but higher or larger ones would need to be avoided at all costs. Thankfully, she'd have some control over the craft once it hit the ground. Not much, but a semblance, slightly more than the old STS shuttles. This was better technology. She fought with the ponderous steering wheel to rise above a series of rocks but hitting the ground was inevitable.

The E-Pod struck Proxima B not far from the waterway on the eyeball of the planet and the first touch was very hard, almost a collision, eliciting profanities from Becker and Dimitri who looked closely at Connie, expecting her to scream, followed quickly by complete demolition and depressurisation of the ship.

Thankfully, that wasn't the case. Everything around them rattled a lot but seemed to stay intact, despite the shaking and screaming of metal around them.

Becker was relieved to see the picture stay the same...the ship somehow stayed in one piece. It bucked and shuddered, slid in the dirt and gradually lost momentum until it eventually slowed, surrounded by a cloud of dust which formed behind them, in the near Earth-like gravity that prevailed outside.

Wind was almost absent entirely, which meant the cloud of dust enveloped the craft and just stayed with them, reaching all the way back to their landing spot.

Connie had already used the airbrakes which were useless as she expected and now used the foot brakes by depressing them as hard as she could with both feet. The vessel slowly came to a complete standstill, some distance from the ice and the adjacent flow of water in the river, that seemed to form one giant watery ring around the circular edge of the glaciers which appeared to cover the rest of the planet. Her racing pulse gradually subsided a bit as did her raspy breathing. She gaped straight ahead and looked at the landscape of Proxima B though the bull's-eye window of the craft. It looked amazing, Connie was ecstatic that they had stopped without any explosion or destruction of the craft, and having no one die, and have the three wheels of the E-pod still attached. It was quite incredible. The tyres were probably cactus, but that was of no concern at all. They wouldn't be needed again - they'd done their job.

* * *

Becker eyed the dusty and rocky landscape from where he stood. He stared at it apprehensively, chewing the inside of his cheek. He was glad they'd landed without major incident, they all were, but he wondered, what the hell now? Where had they landed...he knew where they were, but he repeated the question to himself, louder, as he gazed beyond the forward window at the rock and water and ice that dominated the planet.

'As they thought back home, it's a tidally locked eyeball planet,' Becker stuttered, gazing at the fairly close ice cliffs and confirming what everyone could see. Some of the glaciers were melting and creating icebergs in the water below. He could see one, two...no...three, areas of the waterway where a "blackish" something was growing in the water and had crept onto land. It seemed to grow in large mats in the water and on land, that appeared quite dense from here, and probably formed a ring around the entire eyeball, like the waterway did, if it kept going.

To get to it and have a close look would be difficult, it seemed to be restricted to the opposite side of the waterway including growing in the waterway itself. It was apparently too warm and dry on the eyeball for this stuff to exist. There was little doubt though, it was *life*. Very basic though, and this was probably all that existed on the planet. Connie told them it was probably similar or even the same as cyanobacteria on Earth which was a bluey-green colour – here it was black or grey, no doubt, it took all the colours of light or energy from its rather dull star. Still, it was life. It showed that biochemistry could spontaneously arise from plain old geochemistry almost everywhere, as long as water was a liquid and could act as a solvent. Connie didn't reckon life was restricted to what we term "habitable", but those conditions were "proven" to be friendly to life.

They were on the edge of a decent piece of a shallow-sand, land that wasn't unlike the Mojave Desert in the US, although everything appeared a little flatter. What they could see from where they were, apart from the black-stuff, was vegetation-free by the look of it, and permanently faced the small star that was large in the sky, at least two or three times the size of the Sun. It was almost directly overhead and a brilliant white in colour.

Plenty of ice had sheared off the massive glaciers and were now melting in the river, much like he'd seen it do in Antarctica back home. He gawked at the enormous icebergs floating and melting in the river or waterway or whatever it was. They were very Antarctic-like and cleaved in a very similar way to Earth. When the glacier started melting, it weakened and eventually, bits fell off – icebergs, and they slowly melted in the waterway. And the mighty river went right around the zone of melting – they'd seen it from orbit.

And we're right in the pupil,' Becker blurted. Proxima Centauri, the home star, was really big above them – the size of at least two Suns, even if the star itself was tiny. Distance *ruled*, in space. Small could look big...if you were close enough.

'Is there an atmosphere out t-there?' Dimitri asked tentatively, in his deeply Slavic English, staring at the odd landscape beyond the craft. 'Is it air or atmosphere or er, ah...*something*?' He wasn't sure how he should say it in English. He wondered what was out there outside the confines of the ship. Dimitri stared down at his hands, unsure if he should follow up with something else. He found silence in the pod to be very uncomfortable indeed.

'There's *something* out there,' Connie said, I flew through it, and it's thick and resistant like Earth, but we're not gonna know until we unfurl the Stellar,' she said. This planet is slightly bigger than Earth, in size and mass, so it has the gravity to hold onto gasses...but for now, that's all we know. The rest is little more than guesswork.' She blew out her cheeks and released her breath without much noise at all.

'The really significant question is, will whatever be out there allow us to breathe?' They all variously raised their eyebrows or shrugged their shoulders. Until it was analysed, no one knew. It could be anything. Had the James Webb Telescope been in orbit at L2, they, they may already know. But it wasn't and they didn't. NASA said there was nitrogen and some oxygen in the air but pressure and ionising radiation levels were an unknown. They would be the Guinea pigs to find out. NASA and its affiliates had detected charged particles and magnetism near the planet, so, they held high hopes. Becker in particular, was unimpressed. *High hopes* indeed, he repeated to Connie when she told him. The administrators of this mission seemed to be acting like politicians – treating them and their lives with utter disdain.

The *Exo* had protection in its hull in the form of reticulated lead and the pressure suits were similarly endowed as was the plastic dome. The E-pod though, had nothing. So, it was literally finger-crossing time. *High fucking hopes*, he repeated to himself. Becker found it hard to believe. '*Holy shit*,' he exclaimed. They were apparently sent here by a bunch of gamblers and the worst thing of all was their okay to it all. All of them had only themselves to blame.

*   *   *

Connie was mentally exhausted, and grateful that the ship and all of them had survived such a non-regulation landing on Proxima B. "Landing" was probably over-selling it a bit, she reckoned. "Flopped" was a more apt description.

'Becker, into your suit,' Connie said sternly. He felt like saluting again, or at the least replying with a "yes sir". He was being ordered, no doubt. Becker remained silent and did as she suggested. He went briskly to put it on, arms and legs everywhere, it was like putting jeans on that were way too small. If he was going outside, at least he'd be properly protected from whatever was out there. It was just that it took a while to get the damn thing on.

'What about me?' Dimitri said, gazing at Connie like a sick puppy. She was apparently the inferred captain of the ship, even though none of them was the official leader. Everyone, Becker included, looked to her to make decisions as the pseudo-captain.

"Go get suited up too Dimitri." Connie had never been the leader of anything, but there you go, she said to herself, raising her eyebrows and breathing out in a rush. She supposed she effectively ran Becker's company and ordered Joe around, but that was about it. And now here she was. Captain and leader of an interstellar voyage, even though the circumstances genuinely sucked. *Go figure.*

Connie looked at Emma and watched her blinking fast and massaging the back of her neck. She was worried or at least anxious about something. Being here probably. Or going outside. No doubt, a combination of everything. Connie agreed that there was a hell of a lot to be anxious about.

'I am more than happy to stay in here by myself,' Emma said quietly. She swept a shaky hand across her forehead to get rid of cold sweat. Anywhere outside of the ship terrified her. Despite her signing up willingly to be a Proxima B colonist, now that she was here, the planet, not to mention space itself, or *anywhere* outside a ship, was a house of horrors for her. Emma believed she would revel in space, but she was wrong.

On Earth, space equated to freedom and massive scientific potential, but up here, it was very different. Space, *vacuum*, was really, *positively* terrifying.

Becker and Dimitri both went hell-bent for-leather to put their suits on. Becker was none too keen to go outside either, but he had to keep up with Dimitri so he really went for it. He wouldn't be beaten to the punch by a Russian. Becker was a real fucker sometimes. He'd compete with most everyone about most anything, and normally get beaten. But he still kept doing it. On this occasion, he beat the Russian, but had a fair head-start so it probably didn't count.

The Lower Torso Assembly went on and soon after came the Hard Upper Torso and Arms and gloves following the cooling garment. Connie herself only needed the helmet properly fitted and she was ready for the airlock.

She had the Stellar in her velcro'd hip pocket and was ready to attack the atmosphere and finally find out what the hell was in it.

Dimitri didn't want to go outside the craft either, but he thought he may as well. It'd come sooner or later...the writing was splashed on the wall. And he wanted to keep up with Becker as well, who acted like a King, but did fuck all to deserve the standing. In fact, it appeared, he did very little, but moan and groan. Apparently, he acted like he did because he could do it and get away with it. Dimitri reckoned it was like travelling with an oversized child.

They were never going home again, or even back into orbit, so that made this place, whatever the hell it was, *home*. Dimitri felt dejected and miserable and looked out over the part of the planet they could see. It was obviously people-free and looked like a desert hell out there - the entire place might as well have been called the Sahara, although it probably wasn't as hot. In fact, now, it was probably quite cool.

It had a desert-dune look to it, there was ice on the far side, surrounded by a broad, long river, with hard strata leading up to it, and on top, a sandy, dune-like interior on the nearside. Basically, the whole area facing the star was flat with a few rocky rises here and there. On the far side, it was cold and dark with glaciers and the occasional outcropping of dark strata. The planet was *very* different from Earth. The sun staying in one position was really strange. Very hard to get used to.

Emma nervously watched them all enter the airlock after Connie thumped the "open door" button. Emma felt guilty for not going, but she wouldn't go now, even if given another chance. She'd rather stay where she was and feel guilty. Better the devil she knew, she reckoned. And she knew a few.

The outside of the craft, especially on this odd, distant planet, scared her senseless. They didn't even know what the air was like. To her, going outside was like hanging off a cliff – the whole thing was panic inducing.

It was a strange reaction, Emma reckoned, given that she was supposed to be part of a colonising team, and had willingly agreed to go. Good on the rest of them for going out. That was all she had to say. Emma watched them go, happy to stay within the inferred safety of the ship. Outside, with its ice, water, rock and sand dunes and unknown atmosphere and radiation was horrifying. They could have it. Clearly, the death of the large vessel had affected her badly. The E-pod was way too small for her. It didn't seem to affect the others though. To that, Emma had no answer. She didn't even have a decent theory. Maybe they were tougher than she was? That was a no-brainer.

*   *   *

Connie was the first onto Proxima B and she stumbled a bit, after alighting from their pod. She was a bit surprised by how hard the surface was. She realised this was as poignant a moment as Neil Armstrong walking on the Moon, in fact much more so, because instead of stumbling around on a stillborn seed of Earth, they were walking on a brand-new planet in a brand-new solar system. Yet, she had nothing to say. Too many had died getting there to worry about inanities like that.

And looking at the others, through their visors, they had nothing either. They were all terrified, not knowing what they might encounter on this odd planet.

It was fairly close to how she thought it would be. Arid and orange, like Mars, with thousands of small grey and brown rocks strewn everywhere. It could have been way worse than that. It looked a lot like certain parts of Earth, certainly a lot like Mars, Chryse Planitia maybe. Very rocky, very orange, although the sky was a first. Very different *indeed*.

Connie turned around and the view changed entirely. Apart from Becker and Dimitri standing in front of the E-Pod, she saw mountains of ice, a huge waterway and melting icebergs in the river. She might have thought it was an ocean except they'd seen it from space, so they knew. There were also mats of blackness that on occasion grew from the water and lay next to the waterway and disappeared over the icy hill. None of the black growth extended to their side of the river. This was pre-evolutionary life. Connie was glad it was hard to get to.

In front of her was a hard, rocky and in places, sandy landscape that seemed to end in mountains of ice some twenty or so kilometres hence, maybe more, and behind her was the same. The contrast in the landscape was stark. To see ice and sand in one view was very unusual indeed.

The horizon was far away, like Earth, and the extremities of the river behind them were shrouded by the mists of distance and then, the curve of the horizon kicked in. In front of them the distance with a tan desert-like panorama was full of tiny rocks leading up to it. The landscape was littered with dunes of sand or small rocks but apart from that it was as flat as. a pancake.

Dimitri peered down and, on his haunches, picked up some soil and tiny rocks in his hand. It was very dry, probably with no organic matter at all. There were narrow and long rivulets everywhere, presumably made of coarse sand and tiny rocks. Clearly, weathering and erosion were active on this world but weren't as harsh and emphatic as Earth.

Becker and Dimitri joined Connie to stare shamelessly at the landscape. Their internal comms system comprised a wireless mic near their mouth and was set to work between all of the astronauts.

One of the first objectives of their little sojourn was to determine the makeup of the atmosphere and the pressure at ground level, together with the amount of harmful radiation. All of them stared at Connie, hoping to find out what was around them. Would it kill them? That was the first question. The rest would come later. If, they could breathe what was around them, it would make a huge difference to all of them.

She had the equipment in her pocket which would hopefully tell that story. With luck, they hoped the story was a good one. If the ether was breathable, it would make life sustainable and so much easier.

They tried to approach it with an open mind. Whatever the result was, it had probably been that way for millions of years although the recent movement of the planet showed that recent events had occurred on this world. The atmosphere itself was probably unaffected though.

'Okay, okay.' She ripped open her pocket and retrieved the Stellar, bending the tech open for five seconds and then closing it. The device would soon proffer its determination on the composition, pressure and safeness of whatever was around them.

She already knew the gravity was Earth like – no surprise there. Connie had already flown a vessel through it, gravitational field *and* atmosphere. From deep orbit all the way to the ground. She knew the answers to the broader issues already. Now, it was time for the finer ones.

Connie waited for the numbers to populate, Becker looked over her shoulder, tapping his foot indiscriminately. He was impatient at the best of times. Even waiting for the Stellar, he found it difficult to pause whatever he was doing. Connie eyed him with raised eyebrows.

'*Jesus...just wait Becker.*' He was so infuriating, she thought, grinding her back teeth and shaking her head. She glanced at the Stellar and could not have been more surprised. Elbowing Becker, he too, looked closely at the tech while his eyebrows retreated far upward, colliding with his moist fringe.

'*Fuck,-shit,*' he cried, his eyes widened and his lips parted as he gaped at data on the Stellar.

'*You are joking...well, there you go,*' Connie piped, reading the figures. It took a while for the numbers and letters to sink in as real.

'*Holy shit,*' she yelled as the words and percentages tickled her cortex.

Nitrogen 44%
Helium 31%
Oxygen 20%
Neon 4%
Air Pressure 1,058 hPA
Ionising Radiation 3.88 mSv

Connie gawked at the numbers and thought about them hard, doing her best to ignore Becker who was waving his arms around and making a variety of annoying noises, none of them helpful.

'*This air...I think...is breathable,*' Connie eventually spoke, 'helium is a huge part of the atmosphere, here...and it won't h-harm you and the levels of xenon are okay...I reckon,' she vented eagerly, with eyes that sparkled and gleamed. 'We've come all this way, and we come across...*this*. Apart from the helium, it's sort of like Earth, and I think we can tolerate the helium okay.'

You *think*,' Becker repeated. '*Jesus.* I for one am not going to take a breath based on an "I think".'

'Helium is okay to breathe, it'll be like fucking nitrogen you goose...although it will make your voice sound a tad higher - because of its effect on your vocal cords. She refused to giggle or even smile...yet. She was too busy thinking.

'*A tad higher?* At thirty odd percent it'll make me sound like a fucking cartoon character,' Becker whined, looking at Connie like he was scrutinising a wine label.

Connie glared at Becker and raised an eyebrow, 'how fucking appropriate,' she quipped. 'Anyway, it shouldn't be that bad Becker, it's mixed with nitrogen, you know, so it's impact will be diluted a bit, at least it's breathable, and I don't think it will cause a heap of nasty side-effects.' She scratched her chin, then the side of her head. 'But what replenishes the helium in the atmosphere?'

Connie tilted her head and scratched the top of her head this time. 'Don't tell me something so light doesn't escape to space, maybe cryo-volcanoes and uranium reloads it,' Connie said, hunching over and examining a rock closely. It looked like mainly basalt with inclusions of finely vesicled pumice, both very Earthly examples of volcanic rocks, according to Connie.

'*Crio-what*?' Becker said, having no idea what she was talking about. What the hell was a crio-volcano? There was only one sort he'd heard of and it wasn't "crio".

'You didn't read any of the papers or brochures they gave us, did you?' Connie said firmly, more than asked, looking right at him with bulging eyes and sighing heavily. She already knew the answer. He never did anything he was supposed to. He'd signed off to say it had been done, but he hadn't done it. Typical Becker.

'Well... no, actually, I ran out of time,' Becker said, when confronted, swallowing and starting to feel hot. He already knew he should have read them, and a lot more. Clearly, Connie had. Trying to read the documents he was given to read, Becker kept falling asleep and, in the end, he'd given up and admitted defeat. He signed to say he'd read and absorbed them. He was seriously his own worst enemy sometimes. And he knew it. So did Connie.

'*Anyway,*' she said,' shaking her head, 'I'll test the air, we now know what's in it and we know the pressure and radiation are similar to Earth. We already know gravity is about the same.' She eyed everyone. 'So, I'll lift the lid and see what it's like.'

'You make it sound so easy,' Becker said, 'if you turn green, we'll know I suppose.' He gave a shaky laugh.

Connie's mouth was dry and her heart was beating hard beneath her spacesuit. It sounded so easy but it wasn't. She pressed the directional switch to the left which broke the visor seal. The air from Proxima B seeped in. Connie pushed the visor up and took a decent breath. The constituents and the pressure were known so the breath was less of a risk, it was more of a mental trial.

It felt heavier and thicker than the air on Earth, but it was fine, she thought. There was no dizziness or wooziness that she noticed, yet. She hesitated to talk, but decided, the hell with it, and reported to Becker. The atmosphere was full of balloon-ready helium and it was reflected in her voice.

'The air seems fine, I've taken deep breaths and there's no dizziness or faintness, so, I don't think I'm affected,' Connie said. She realised how she sounded, all that remained was their reaction.

Becker nodded while chuckling and glanced at Dimitri, a wave of hysterical laughter sweeping through him. He tried to supress it, to no avail.

You're laughing with me, right?' Connie said, staring deadpan at Becker, who nodded and chuckled at her voice. She sounded like a child's character come to life from a book. Thankfully, the laughing and everything else was hardly audible, enclosed as they were in spacesuits with the audio turned off.

'Of course...*with* you, of course.' Becker said loudly, feeling the laughter welling up inside him. He struggled to keep it down. Gritting his teeth helped.

'Whatever Becker, it'll be your time soon enough, and you too Dimitri. Both of them stopped chuckling when they heard their names spoken. They were quiet and stared at each other and then Connie who dropped her helmet on the rocky ground and took a few steps forward. Connie knew they'd have to talk, sooner or later. She couldn't wait for that to happen. There'd be no holding back - she'd laugh in their faces if given the chance.

Looking up and out, she felt free for the first time in ages, and for the first time, she truly eyed the planet, seeing its violet skies and grey cumulus clouds, not unlike the ones back home. She was happy to see the water in the river was blue in colour, it was like a piece of home, here on Proxima B. Very welcome indeed. It was like the blue of a south-Pacific Island and she wondered why.

Connie wondered why the water wasn't violet like the sky. She knew the water absorbed the reds and oranges, but there must be some reflection of the sky, surely. *Go figure*, was her only response with a shoulder-shrug. It didn't affect them, so it was curiosity only. Someone else could work that one out.

Connie gawked at a huge white star – it had to be three times as big as the Sun and almost as bright, she reckoned, with two other very bright stars to the East. The brightest one may have been a red squib of a star, but they were so damn close it looked anything but red and small.

Time was not time as humans would define it, on this world - it was a place. Here it was permanently about 1PM.

*   *   *

All of them exited the craft this time, even Emma, who forced herself out, to have a gander at the place that was now their permanent home. The ship was where they lived and the planet was their back as well as front-yard. It wouldn't last though – they all knew that. Unless there was something organic to eat, sooner or later, they were all doomed. Food on the ship wouldn't last forever...nor would the batteries and reclaimed water. Eventually, they would have no food. No one had any good ideas what they would live on once the onboard food ended. There was no point in rationing food because they had no idea what they would eat after it did finish. Ration until when? There was absolutely no end date.

No rationing would occur, until or *if* they found a permanent supply of food. They voted to eat what they did have, normally. A supply of food would either be found or it wouldn't. Rationing wouldn't help any. That was their decision anyway.

All they did was make sure they didn't overeat, which, for Becker wasn't easy. He desperately craved meat, but that wasn't going to happen. Not here. They would continue to scour the planet for anything organic, be it food or something interesting.

Currently, they ate food and drank fluid and went to the "sucking toilet" on the pod, but again, none of that would last. They currently lived on dehydrated macaroni-cheese, which after water was added, made a reasonably nutritious and decent meal. Taking vitamins helped too. Water was produced using the "closed loop" water system which was basically electrolysis of all waste-water in the craft. Drinking water would go on for a long time...but again not forever. When the batteries on the craft went, so would water production.

So, it was food that would get them first and they all knew it. Connie was certain that finding food outside the craft would eventually be the difference between life and death. If they didn't find it, they were all done and gone. They needed some sort of calorie intake to keep the human body humming along. It needed 100 watts to keep functioning and that had to come from somewhere. Otherwise, the body would consume itself and, on another planet, where there was no possible help, that was bad.

With no food and no vitamin supplements, they would get thinner and thinner and ultimately die of malnutrition. Going blind before death was probably on offer too. Eating the dead was also one of the less palatable options. In her mind's eye, Connie could see Becker biting down on Dimitri...and enjoying it. She'd keep that one to herself. Anyway, she hoped this'd all be sorted out well before then.

She supposed the food quandary would be answered by their expeditions into the wilderness and their ability to find some sort of multi-cellular life, be it mobile or not. If that or some other sort of edible, nutritious vegetation wasn't to be found, Connie had little idea what they would do. Die, probably. Whatever would be, would be, she thought grimly. Cyanobacterial mats would likely kill them if they tried to eat its toxin-rich filaments.

Becker had joked about it being a bloody long way for Uber Eats to come, and she'd laughed uproariously. Uber would probably get struck by a meteor too or come up with some other half-arsed excuse. Now it was no joke though – it was very serious indeed. They *needed* to find some source of nutrition. The entire group was fed up with instant noodles, no matter how tasty they were. But seriously, what was the fucking alternative?

They would travel and by "travel" Connie meant walk, *north* by compass, which she held in her palm. It proved this rock had a strong magnetic field, meaning the core of the planet was probably iron, partially solid and the rest probably liquid. That was the only scenario that made any sense to her. Hence, the charged particles that Breakthrough detected, in the presence of magnetism from the planet, formed a defence that shielded this world from dangerous high energy particles coming from the star. It was, after all, a flare star, of considerable peril to the planet's environment.

Without the magnetosphere, the atmosphere probably wouldn't exist. It'd be much like the Moon around here. But it begged the question – where was the vegetation? Or maybe the insects? To take advantage of the air. So far, there was nothing, apart from primitive cyanobacteria, which was probably full of toxins. Was this the only example of biochemistry? Hopefully not, but time would tell.

'Well...let's go then,' Connie said, and started ambling along in a straight line, with Emma at the back, the two men next and Connie at the front, compass in hand, leading onward by example.

Becker was at it again behind her...already. He was puffing and wheezing like an old locomotive and they'd only gone a few steps. Seriously, what was wrong with him? Apart from Becker, they were all ready for a long walk, if that's what it took. Emma and Dimitri were determined to walk and find food, Becker was just his usual self despite the fact that this expedition was so important to whether they lived or died.

If it was an issue with the atmosphere, they'd all be puffing and panting. They weren't making any noise, *just him.* Becker was so out of shape it wasn't even funny. Walking, so easy for most, was a real chore for him, and he was doing it at a strange angle as though both his knees were shot and he was trying to reduce pressure on them.

'Jesus Christ...are you okay?' She said quietly but forcefully, her annoyance partly disguised by the helium's effect on her vocal folds. She was irritated, but instead of conveying that, she sounded like she'd just swallowed a canary. Becker stood stationery with one hand on his back and continued puffing. He didn't know whether to laugh or be offended.

'I....um...think so, and...well, it depends,' he said quite seriously. 'How far are we going? He asked looking into the distance and gulping. There was *plenty* of landscape ahead. Becker felt cold but guessed he'd warm up fairly quickly, especially walking that far.

'To the water's edge if we need to,' Connie said, with a curt nod, 'we have to find food Becker, or we're done. That might be twenty kays or so, if we have to go all the way, double it to get back.'

Connie heard grunts and groans from Becker, as he realised exactly what might be in front of him. No matter what happened, it would be a *long* walk. He would struggle to do it – and it showed in his demeanour. Becker knew it was important but had seriously walked enough already. His shoulders slumped as he looked angrily into the distance. *'Fuck,'* Becker spat in irritation.

Emma clutched an arm to her chest, and Dimitri said something harsh in Russian, under his breath. *"Schas po ebalu poluchish, suka, blyad!"* Whatever those words meant, they were delivered with the greatest of feeling. Russian cussing, so Dimitri said. Apparently, he was really good at it. No one bothered to ask what he meant, clearly, walking that far was very unpopular with everyone.

'Well, if you're all going, so am I,' Becker said, giving a curt nod to all of them. He hated walking, but he wouldn't be left behind either.

'Okay...but *don't* slow us down Becker,' Connie said, frowning and shaking her head at him. She said something more severe to Becker under her breath that was unintelligible to the group. Becker heard it though and he straightened up slightly.

He saluted and quick marched a few paces, much to the amusement of Dimitri who tried to hide his laughter but failed. He threw his head back and laughed loudly. Everyone heard it – the high-pitched human laughter echoed over the flat alien plain.

*   *   *

Dimitri knew otherwise, but he reckoned Connie and Becker acted like the classic American couple. He realised they were just friends, but still, they acted like they were "together" and had been so for many years. He told Becker as much and received a mouthful in return.

Dimitri eyed Becker, then looked directly at Connie and smiled knowingly. He got nothing back from either of them. If he was looking for agreement, keep trying, Becker thought, maddeningly. Surely, there were more important things to consider, Connie reckoned.

'*Oh whatever,*' Connie said, setting her jaw and striding away. She got the drift. Proxima Centauri was pretty much right above them, there were a few white and grey clouds and the purply sky was everywhere the clouds weren't.

Connie felt certain there'd be edible vegetation on this rock *somewhere*, but to date, all they'd seen was ice, rock, sand and water. The sand and the soil looked really dry. Maybe it had retreated underground. Which led to further ponderings on moisture – did it rain here? It didn't look like it did, the water vapour must go somewhere though and there were clouds in the atmosphere, although not necessarily rain clouds. They needed a meteorologist and a geomorphologist to work it all out and give them a more considered view. To her, it just seemed odd.

The only river or stream they'd seen was the huge waterway that encircled the edge of the ice. Apart from that, they had seen nothing, not even evidence of dry water-flows. The eyeball itself was free of water-flow, at least any surficial evidence of it. That seemed strange – maybe water went through the soil. Was there a subsurface flow perhaps?

She was no specialist, but it all seemed pretty different from Earth. Maybe it was normal for desert regions – who frigging knew, she was no expert. As far as *she* knew, water created streams, wet or dry. But here there was nothing. From what they had seen, the waterway was fed by melting glaciers.

They were walking slowly across a very flat plain that was a light chocolate brown in colour and strewn with very small rocks, a bit like gravel. In the distance was a small elevation, a bluff of sorts, slightly to the east of where they were walking. On the other side of that, just before the very Earthly horizon, were huge ice cliffs and the circumferential waterway they had first spied from orbit. It was truly an eyeball planet *en evidence.* Wherever they looked.

Becker was now about ten metres behind the group. They could literally go no slower for him and still make claim to be moving forward. The poor sod was really struggling. He'd eaten all the lolly snakes he had and had drunk plenty of water so the issue wasn't hydration or calories. It was simply Becker. He was just tired and unfit.

Becker's problem was two-fold. Like Connie had said, sort of, he was fat and out of shape, and his legs hurt like the *beJesus.* Poor old Becker was just totally ill-suited to walking. Much more suited to lying on a sofa than moving his body parts.

'I ain't carrying him,' Dimitri said, and Emma nodded furiously. He must have weighed well north of 200 pounds. Way too much to be carried. Dimitri chuckled to himself, maybe they could roll him, he knew they'd even struggle to do that.

'No frigging way,' Emma agreed, grimacing and looking into the distance. It looked arid, like Mars, she reckoned, although it was a slightly different colour. It had all the requisite rocks on the surface. She looked up and wondered if it rained around here, it didn't look like it – the landscape appeared very dry and it was almost warm, courtesy of the large star and walking a bit. It might have been small, but this rock was very close to its star, despite its new, deeper orbit. It was still very close indeed.

'If you hear a thump, that'll be me going down for the count,' Becker said, from ten metres to the rear. His legs were creaking and clicking like an old Chevy's steering wheel, and they could hear the noise quite distinctly. They all wondered if the poor old bugger had any cartilage in his knees at all or whether it was simply bone scraping on bone.

'Okay...thanks Becker, I'll be sure to listen out,' Connie said, smiling benignly at Dimitri and rolling her eyes, as if dealing with him was like negotiating with a temperamental child.

Becker ambled on, eyes downcast, as he tried to ignore the pain and walk through it...which wasn't easy. Becker desperately needed Paracetamol or some other pain relief. And some food, according to him. *Desperately.*

Connie tried to stop the group by inspecting some of the rocks they came across, for Becker's sake. She knelt down by the side of the nearest decent-sized rock on the surface and pretended to inspect it. Connie was surprised by the size of the vesicles therein. That meant slow cooling and fairly stable conditions. How fucking interesting, she thought, gladdened by seeing Becker slowly grinding his way up to her. The old bugger was clearly stuffed.

Connie saw old father-time from the corner of her eye, as he came up to them, panting and gasping with hands on hips, bent over like he had scoliosis of the spine. At least they were finally one group again, instead of Becker being perennially twenty steps behind them. The rock she was looking at was a chunk of basalt and next to it were thin sheets of something flat like shale or mudstone, leading Connie to wonder if this place used to be an ocean or lake. She knew mudstone was made of clay particles and formed in water, so it seemed very likely. They needed a hydrologist and a geologist as well. Just a suite of physical scientists, Connie thought, that's all we need.

Emma gawked at Becker's face and was worried that he might collapse or start dying or something, he was red as a beet. Good luck getting emergency care around here, she reckoned, surveying Becker's face closely. It'd be up to her or one of the others to do something. It was that "something" that worried her.

What the fuck would she do for someone who fell down and started foaming at the goddamn mouth? Mouth to mouth – *I don't think so.* The best she would be able to offer was wishing him God's speed with his illness. Which would help him nought.

After a brief respite, they started off again and the closer they got to the bluff, the less substantial it looked. Before, from further away, it appeared as quite a large and high landform near the horizon, now it seemed quite small, composed of loose rocks, rather than being a firm landform. It was probably because everything else around them was so goddamn flat that made it stand out.

Approaching the bluff from the east, Connie could see the northern extremity of the "eyeball" pretty well. Ice wrapped around this world from pole to probably pole, with a wide waterway and this piece of "desert" they had just journeyed across. She could see no other body of water anywhere.

Connie squinted at Becker who was now sitting comfortably on a rock, not far off the ground and quite near. He was pointing, with his whole body it seemed, at the bluff. '*Look, look,*' Becker was yelling urgently, with his helium effected voice. He repeated it over and over. Normally, Becker avoided talking because he sounded like a fool, but he was standing and pointing with both hands and his head now, yelling and sounding like a canary on steroids.

The fact that he was standing made her take notice of Becker. If he was stationery, he was normally sitting down and relaxing, trying desperately to recuperate. Otherwise, she would have turned very slowly. The mere fact that he was standing erect and excited made Connie snap her head around. He had clearly found something important that had tickled his interest.

She was stunned by what she saw. *'J-Jesus holy Christ,'* she spouted, having looked and having seen the object of Becker's attention. So that's why he was standing - had to be a good reason for it. And there was.

Nestled among the rocks, sitting like a school kid on one of the larger, flatter rocks was the *kid,* doing nothing in particular. Becker continued to point with his entire body, thankful that someone else had seen him. He'd initially thought he was freaking out and hallucinating. But incredibly, it was *'him'*. Connie and Becker didn't expect it...yet, here he was. In the flesh, so to speak.

His ultra-blue eyes were fixed on Connie like twin blue lasers. He looked exactly like he did the first time she laid eyes on him in Penang. Minan appeared like a High-Schooler, maybe fourteen or fifteen, a man-child, and he wore the same or very similar black clothing that moved with him like a very flexible glove and never seemed to scrunch or bunch up.

He looked very mischievous, but that was probably just her. It was really hard to believe he was here, on Proxima B. It was almost the same as seeing him in Penang, very surreal indeed. *Ridiculously out-of-place* was a good phrase for it. 'Him', nonchalantly sitting on a rock, was something none of them expected.

'Fucking hell, holy shit,' Becker yelled, sounding like a wounded animal. *'What the fuck...is he doing here?'* Becker was staring fixedly at him. Becker swung his gaze to Connie and then back to the boy. Connie virtually mirrored Becker's reaction. The kid's presence was absolutely *not* expected on this rock...or anywhere really. Becker continued to stare at him inquisitively. The kid wasn't saying anything...like why the hell was he here, of all places?

'Is he from one of the other emergency craft,' Dimitri asked, trailing off a bit, realising immediately he was way too young for that.

NASA didn't let anyone so young near the craft, let alone on it. NASA didn't like children. Anyone under the age of eighteen years – *forget it.* Dimitri and Emma gaped at him, totally confused and bemused.

'*What the fuck* is he doing here?' Dimitri said, staring apprehensively at Connie, 'amid the rocks of an alien planet? And better or worse still, you seem to know him, right?' Dimitri scratched his beard - everything added up to shit. *Nothing* made sense to Emma or Dimitri. Who the hell was he?

Where in God's name did the boy come from? Dimitri repeated to himself. He tried to put his brain in neutral, but it didn't work. Twenty steps away was a child who apparently didn't arrive with them. *WTF?* It sounded like abject lunacy; he could tell Emma thought the same. If he didn't come with us...how on Earth did he get here? Was he already here? Her brain spun with crazy, stupid ideas. He couldn't be indigenous to this planet, could he? Dimitri didn't know what to think.

Emma's face and eyes were total bewilderment. Her mouth opened but nothing came out. She was grimacing, frowning, and thinking hard, tapping her lips with a fist but Connie similarly offered nothing. The man-child looked human enough, so what was the answer? It was obvious to anyone with eyes or ears that Becker and Connie had seen him before. Emma's brain was ready to implode under the weight of a so many unanswerable thoughts.

Becker watched the kid closely and felt anger and his temperature rising. The desire to hit him hadn't gone far. The kid had done some monstrous things on the largest scale imaginable. He had so much to answer for. And there he was, only a few steps away.

Minan stood like a typical human and walked over the top of the bluff and disappeared from view down the other side. His black clothing flowed and ran and was seamless, similar to what it looked like the last time they'd seen him. Why did the little shit always wear the same outfit? He was seemingly always dressed in the same suit. Becker assumed it only looked that way, although, he admitted, he didn't have a clue.

His wardrobe must be boring to say the least, like a super-hero wearing a single costume. Maybe it was always the same one – who knew. Discovering the inanities of his existence, was unlikely indeed.

Minan came back from the top of the hill and sat on the same rock. His appearance, *here*, was definitely something they weren't imagining. Becker wondered if the little shit had somehow been watching them remotely. There was no doubt, he could if he wanted to.

They assumed, rightly or wrongly, that he could do pretty much what he liked, within the laws of physics of course. Unnervingly, he seemed to be staring at all of them, or at the very least taking a great deal of interest in what they were doing. When he had focussed on them like that, previously, it had very bad consequences for whoever he happened to be paying attention to.

'Failure for your race is a repeating theme,' the words appeared in their heads, between their ears...*reverberating and loud*. Becker and Connie weren't surprised, with either the words themselves, or how they ended up in their heads. That was the way the kid rolled.

Emma and Dimitri appeared thoroughly overcome...they were expecting *something*, but not that. They'd expected him to talk with his mouth, something they had no chance of understanding. Something that sounded like utter gobbledegook. Instead, they got English...directly.

Dimitri felt nauseous and dizzy, thoughts swirling and churning while he tried to process them. Emma was faint and wobbly on her feet. Both wondered what the hell was happening. They gawked at Connie apprehensively, contemplating what was rattling around in their heads.

'*In m-m-my h-head*,' Emma stammered and Dimitri nodded hard, taking her by the hand and gritting his teeth. Becker considered telling them the whole story right then and there, but that would happen at a different time when they were ready. Connie was of the same mind. *Later*. When they had assimilated this little episode. Connie knew they'd never, *ever* be ready for a story like his.

'He is communicating in English, by,' she glanced quickly at Becker and immediately wondered why she had, 'by direct-injection,' Connie said, lifting her chin and gazing directly at Dimitri. 'No vocal cords required. His name is Minan; we have, encountered him before.'

'*...Encountered...you're serious, aren't you*? Where, how?' Dimitri was completely befuddled. Emma just stared fixedly at the boy - eyes as wide as they could go.

'Just know that Connie and I have had the pleasure of his company before,' Becker said, hoping Dimitri would be satisfied, and leave well enough alone. He couldn't be bothered explaining it – the whole thing was a long story indeed. By the look of Connie, she wasn't interested either, yet. These two didn't need more distress right now. Becker was happy doing nothing at all - expending calories and effort on long winded explanations and a heated Q&A session, didn't appeal to him at all.

Becker studied Dimitri's eyes and could tell the Russian wanted more - much more. The explanation Becker had given him just wasn't going to cut it. All it did was whet Dimitri's curiosity. Becker could see it in his wide, hungry eyes.

'Look, he's an alien, okay.' He knew that'd get him, Becker eyed Dimitri closely. 'That's all we're gonna say...he's a fucking alien. That's it.'

Dimitri sort of assumed that had to be the case, but for it to be confirmed, here and now, blew his mind into tiny little uneven pieces. '*Shit, fuck,*' he spat, moving backward, away from Becker, wringing his hands so hard, his knuckles whitened. 'Okay, okay,' he said to Emma, who was staring into the distance, as though she was in a trance of some sort. '*Holy shit,*' he finished on, staring at the kid closely.

Dimitri felt a strange looseness in his bowels and a heaviness in his head. He was gawking at Minan and thinking about what he might be, and where he might be from, peering closely. 'There is the answer to the Fermi Paradox, not thirty steps away,' he thought.

Dimitri look crushed, as he stared at Minan blankly and wide-eyed. 'And you've met-him before?'

'Where's he f-from?' Emma was staring at him too.

'*Jesus holy fuck,*' Dimitri spluttered, genuinely taken aback. Minan looked human which was a surprise...mind you, if he had tentacles and a boneless body, it would be a surprise too. *Anything* would be a surprise. Dimitri had expected it, but to have it confirmed was stunning. *Alien*. Here, now.

What was under that black suit he wondered...was Minan truly *like* humans? He sure as hell looked like he was. He looked exactly like a human. What did that mean? Something or nothing. Were *we* the shape of intelligence in the Universe?

Dimitri understood that nothing else would be forthcoming from Becker or Connie, quite yet. Both of them looked at the ground. Emma looked haunted and harrowed, poor girl. She had what looked like bruises under her eyes, he'd never seen that before.

Dimitri had so many questions, but he understood "later" as well as the next guy - even though neither of them had said the word, he wasn't an idiot. He got the drift. Anything further about Minan wouldn't be revealed until "later".

The Russian couldn't help himself. His mind was sent into overdrive - how on Earth did this being get here – was his ship parked on the other side of the hill, maybe? There was something very wrong with this picture. Just turning up on a planet was odd behaviour, wasn't it? He had zero experience with off-world intelligences, obviously, but it seemed strange, to just turn up with no apparent means of getting there on show.

The Russian gawked further at Minan, as they all did – waiting for him to do or say something that had meaning. Becker along with everyone else wondered why Minan was *here*, of all places, but knew it was no accident. Minan was on this planet for a good reason and Connie knew that too. What they didn't know, was what that reason was? There were trillions of worlds to choose from. And he was *here* on Proxima B, with them. She struggled to view it in a positive light, given his history.

Connie couldn't help but guess what Murphy or Occam would say about it. She was certain he wasn't here for anything they would consider good. It seemed that it was always a negative for the planet, wherever that planet might be, and or the civilisation, if there was one, which didn't auger well for his visit here.

5

Minan

"Coincidence is God's way of remaining anonymous."
– Albert Einstein

'Failure,' Minan repeated, direct to them...again. That was his message. Again. Same calling-card as usual. Mr negativity, call him what you like, she thought. It was never, *ever*, positive. It seemed he always had something bad to say. Minan was the harbinger of doom, although last time he seemed to help Becker and her.

'If you have nothing nice to say, best you don't say anything at all,' Becker spat at the kid, with bulging eyes and white knuckles. He already felt like belting something, him preferably, forgetting what sort of effect the kid had on him. He was so annoying and exasperating, not to mention chronically negative. The latter was the reason for the former, or that's what he thought anyway.

Connie watched him sitting on the rock, very much doubting that he was here, on this planet, *in person,* if there was such a thing. Hopefully, Becker still remembered the last time he took a swing at him and ended up on his arse. The last thing she wanted was a repeat of that unfortunate debacle. The incident was very embarrassing and awkward, Becker should have known better. Did he know better now? Connie doubted it.

Of course, he *wasn't* here in person. Did "in person" have any meaning at all, she wondered? After all, we were all simulations, weren't we? She realised it didn't work like that, but the question seemed reasonable and appropriate.

Becker stood up very slowly and approached the boy in a wide circle, cracking his knuckles and puffing loudly as he went. He was ready to rumble if that's what it took. She was afraid that was exactly what he was going to do. "Thinking" definitely wasn't his strong point. Connie immediately wondered if he had a strong point, followed by her own muffled gurgles of laughter.

'*Oh fuck,*' Connie exclaimed, seeing Becker make a beeline for Minan. '*This'll be good.*' Connie covered her eyes with a hand.

'Great to see you kid,' Becker said effusively as he came closer to him. 'What are you doing here? Welcoming committee, honoured guest...or what?' Becker swallowed hard and boldly met his laser-like stare. He thought confidence and friendliness might be a better approach. Nothing else had worked.

Creature, not surprisingly, didn't respond, he looked straight through Becker as though the big lug hadn't spoken or had even approached, and now stood right in front of him.

Alien, Emma and Dimitri hadn't forgotten that shocking fact. The questions Dimitri had, were unbricking him slowly, piece by piece. He was going to explode if he didn't get some answers, but he knew getting response from anybody was unlikely in the extreme.

"He's an alien", how the good-fuck was he supposed to leave that one alone? He couldn't, but he already realised if he asked anything, he would get nothing back. He'd get nothing but crickets. Just like Becker.

Becker meandered back from the bluff, very unsurprised by Creature's lack of reaction to his rather pointed question. He had expected no reaction, and that's exactly what he got, zero response and no reaction from him at all. Just brilliant blue eyes that bored into them all. Becker spoke directly to him and got absolutely nought in return, although what he said was largely banter and bullshit. So, it was hardly a surprise he got zero back. Minan didn't respond to anything he considered small-talk or irrelevant.

`Becker sat or more accurately, collapsed, in the same spot. Minan had not moved. He was on the same rock, in the same place, staring at all of them with the brightest blue eyes imaginable, but mainly at Connie.

'You cannot survive on this planet.' Minan said intercranially and loudly. Connie knew there was no point questioning him or adding anything – she'd receive nothing back. They already sort of knew what he was saying. There was nothing biological, anywhere on the planet to sustain them.

Minan was a talker but definitely not a listener or at least not a responder. No doubt he had a definite plan and anything beyond that, he didn't want to know about. He was empirical, factual and very serious.

'Does that mean there's no food in this place... on the entire planet?' Dimitri asked, breathing audibly through his nose. He said, 'we can't survive on this planet, so does that mean-there's no l-life at all, in the sea or on the land?' He almost ran out of breath talking, he was so nervous.

They were stuck on a planet that contained nothing organic...at all. He may as well have said they were *fucked*. Dimitri searched for and his eyes eventually found their ship, glinting in the starshine. There was no way they were getting that thing off the ground – it was here for good. That was its final resting place.

'Um...sounds like it,' Emma said. Connie nodded at her, she agreed with the sentiment, Minan had basically confirmed this world was devoid of anything they could consume. She was happy with the fact that Emma had finally bought into a conversation. She'd spoken up and proffered an opinion on something, albeit small, but it probably meant she was getting a bit more comfortable with the group. That was good, Connie thought, *hoped*. They needed everyone's full buy-in on every action they took. Because theoretically, it could be their last.

'It's probably time you told us how you met our friend there,' Dimitri pointed with a flourish at Minan who was still sitting like a school kid on the same rock. He gawked at Emma, then glanced back at Connie. 'We both want to know, y'know...as a first step.'

'I'm not sure you're ready for it,' Becker said seriously, clearing his throat. 'I know I wasn't ready for it, *nuh-uh...oh nooo...nup, no way.'* Running his hands through his sparse hair, he made eye- contact with Dimitri, remembering when and where he got the information.

'It'll seriously blow your mind,' Becker said, rubbing his eyes vigorously. 'I still don't think I've come to terms with it. How on Earth *do you* come to terms with something like that?' Becker asked rhetorically, eyeing Connie with a faint smirk. 'All of it was a monumental head-fuck.' He spoke the last sentence looking down at the ground, sounding very emotional.

Connie stepped back and then finally came forward and eyed Becker seriously. 'They are ready...as ready as they'll ever be Becker.' Looking at Dimitri square in the eyes, she said, 'you asked for it, you may as well get it...all.

Where the hell should she start? *Big*, Connie supposed, keep their interest, she thought. Dimitri had already shown he was a bit like Becker, and had a tendency to drift off unless he was poked like a bear. Any information needed to be big - which this was. It didn't come any bigger.

Connie looked at Becker seriously and nodded crisply, telling him that she'd handle it. She didn't want Becker doing this – it was important that they got all the facts right. Becker would quite simply fuck it up.

Connie walked back a bit, did a small circle and then walked forward, past Becker. She looked toward Emma and Dimitri and made sure they were paying attention. In the background she saw Minan, stationery as a dead-man, occupying the same piece of strata, looking very out of place on the rock pile of this odd planet. He remained very still, inspecting all the humans closely. No one could miss his presence – he stood out, even though he was sitting down.

'Minan is the creator of our Universe,' Connie said, pointing at him, over the exhortations of Dimitri and Emma. But believe it or not, that's not the best bit.'

'*Come the fuck on,*' Dimitri said loudly, '*is that e-even possible*? He said loudly. 'Can he be that advanced? For God's sake, and there's *more?*' The Russian gaped at the sky and the planet itself. 'Yeah, right,' he burbled suspiciously. 'And my mother is the Queen of England, right?' He proceeded to chortle and chuckle, until he realised that Connie was staring at him, seriously, and very unimpressed.

Dimitri lost the laughing and stared fixedly in wonder at Connie. He gaped at her and realised she was deadly serious. Emma got it too. Both of them looked like they'd been smacked in the face with a shovel, as they stared at each other wide eyed. It was shock in its basest form. They both appeared way beyond stunned. Both were dazed, confused and bewildered by the information they hadn't expected. They felt like refusing to believe it, but on seeing Minan and the faces worn by Becker and Connie, they believed them unambiguously. But they had a whack of questions.

'Just take what we say as fact, it'll be far easier that way, trust me. Don't ask questions, there's too many of them to answer. The how's and why's...*forget it.* We don't have a clue.'

'How can we just a-accept it, *Jesus Christ*, th-'

'*Stop talking,*' Becker boomed. 'Connie hasn't finished yet. He flourished to her with his arm. 'Proceed...'

'Uh, yeah, thanks-Becker...the biggest head-fuck of all this, is that we're digital beings...*and all this*,' she swept her hand across the entire sky, 'is digital only...created by algorithms that he and his Genesis Directorate developed.' She shifted her position, '*Holy shit*,' Connie breathed quietly to herself. Listening to her own voice, it sounded genuinely insane. Abjectly impossible...the stuff of lunacy.

Emma let out an uncontrolled sob and Dimitri was mumbling and muttering something unintelligible in his native Baltic tongue. It all sounded like twisted, jumbled nonsense and summed to nothing. Both of them were stunned and shaken to the core.

'So what are we then? And... what we see, our memories and recollections are all made up of *what*...fake pictures...like a digital movie?' Emma appeared totally and utterly devastated and continued to rant incoherently. What Connie was saying, sounded like pure drivel, the bluster of a crazy person.

Dimitri was doing no better than Emma, as he almost hyperventilated, inspecting his skin closely. He held his arm up to Connie. 'It sure as hell looks real, feels real,' he said as he massaged his skin and rubbed it, eyeing it minutely. I guess that's how smart he is...how advanced his species is.'

'Yep,' Connie said, 'he can do damn near anything he wants, whenever he wants...such is their grasp of nature. Essentially, Minan *is* nature by way of supreme understanding.'

'We're all living, breathing, reproducing...but most importantly, we're *digital beings*,' Connie said, 'us and the remainder of Earth, the entire Universe, anything and everything that's in it, are built on a digital algorithm that Minan over there, designed. Evolution still occurred like we thought but Minan set the fundamental groundwork.' She pointed at him with her eyes, 'and his people from the Genesis Directorate are at the base of everything we know and everything we remember. *Everything*.' Connie stopped, to let it sink in.

Connie thought, they'd end up like her, forever watching people and thinking how real they looked, even though they weren't. Testament to Minan and the GD, she supposed.

'Minan is essentially God,' Connie continued, 'he created our home planet and our Universe. And millions of others in a multiverse of incalculable proportions. The GD is responsible for trillions of universes inside an area humans know as cyberspace.'

'*Jesus, holy...Christ*,' Dimitri squeaked slowly, 'I don't know what to s-say. It's just not something I was expecting to hear, uh...*ever*.' Dimitri could feel his heart thud against his breastbone, pretty good response he reckoned, for a being such as he apparently was. That is, a fucking *simulation* of a real being. A fake, a copy...an ethereal something feeding off math that the kid produced. What a massive, *gargantuan* brain-stunner, he thought.

Dimitri contemplated it more. Being a man of the Christian Bible, he wondered how it all sat with that. It didn't sit well, no doubt about it. If it was true, the Bible was shredded, *gone*, a storybook at best. Without doubt, the creature sitting on that rock not thirty paces away was the real God. The Good Book was no more than a work of fiction. Minan made it so.

Both Dimitri and Emma gawked in Minan's direction. The last thing they wanted to do was to upset him, even though they had nothing to worry about. They felt like prostrating before him or lighting an earthen lamp in front of the great creature. *He had created the Universe!*

Becker saw the familiar look of reverence in their eyes. 'Oh, *for God's sake*...lighten up would you...he's more of a naughty kid than a God.' Becker ambled up to Minan and said something inaudible to Dimitri on his way. Becker walked back to where he started, 'he's not much of a talker...only when he wants to be.'

'Why are "we" a failure, Emma asked, staring at Becker as if in a trance. 'I mean what have we done or not done. I assume "we" means humanity?'

'Correct, yes, "we" is humanity,' Becker said. 'Why are *we* a failure? Well, that's a whole other question. Humanity apparently went outside its algorithm and behaved in an overly *non*-scientific fashion – rather than being solely science-based per Minan's original algorithmic design. How did that happen? Even Minan didn't know. If the Creator doesn't know, then no-one knows, right?'

'It shouldn't have happened, according to Minan,' Connie said, gawking at Creature uncomprehendingly, 'we were supposed to be far more focussed on science than we were, like the other races, *better*, apparently.

'We were designed to surpass anything that had gone before us...but we were very *disappointing*, he said. Rather than being an improvement on the last iteration, we were "failures", according to Minan. Of course, we disagree vehemently with him, but he judges us and everyone else relatively. As a race, we think we've done pretty well, but relative to other races, not so. Hence, we are failures - in his eyes. In God's eyes if you will.'

'Why is he here then? Dimitri asked, with a darting gaze that settled on Connie. It couldn't be good, surely. An audience with God and we were "failures" in his words. It all added up to trouble.

Becker again ran his hand through his thinning hair. '*Fucked* if I know why he's here,' he said, '...who would know?' Becker ground his teeth and wondered about Dimitri's question. Only Minan would know, Becker thought. He had no idea why he was here, nor did he care much.

Their own situation was dire whichever way you looked at it. Add him into the mix, with his negativity bullshit, and things were really grim.

'What this oaf means is, we'd have to ask Minan, and then decipher his answer...*if* we get an answer which we probably wouldn't,' Connie said, rolling her eyes, then watching Becker's every move closely, daring him to disagree.

'Yeah, *if we get one*,' Becker agreed loudly, nodding and releasing a deep sigh. He knew how unlikely any response would be. Connie walked slowly up to Minan. Amazingly, he looked exactly as he used to, deep blue eyes, black hair and clothes and the skin of a porcelain doll. He hadn't aged a zac since she saw him for the first time in Penang. The kid looked *exactly* the same. Young and very healthy. The kid still had the rosy cheeks of youth.

'Why are you here, on this planet,' she asked? 'It can't be a coincidence...are you stalking humanity?' Connie widened her stance but didn't break eye contact with him. Minan examined her closely at the same time as she was looking at him. His blue eyes never left her. They were probing, cold and analytical.

Minan stood up but didn't break eye contact with Connie. 'I must end your Programs, Fyoderov knows about you and knows about your Universe.' Minan spoke loudly enough, so everyone could hear, and was wiping his boyish face as he spoke by direct brain communication. She understood it easily. As usual, despite what it meant for them, he didn't sound nervous or unsure at all. Minan knew what he wanted to say and got on and said it.

'What the hell does that mean?' Dimitri asked, gazing at Minan, then Connie. It was a specific threat but it was so big...so encompassing, that he didn't really get it. He was certain it was nothing good though. The way it was delivered sounded really bad. He saw Becker and Connie both staring at Minan, looking horrified. Their faces were creased with the blackest of scowls.

'Minan means he will discontinue us, he wil...' Connie started.

'You mean kill, right?' Dimitri wanted language he could better understand. 'You mean kill?' Dimitri said louder and more directly, staring morosely at Connie. He knew.

'Yes, kill, discontinue, terminate, call it what you like,' Connie whined, gaping at Minan and glancing at Dimitri. Connie's eyes looked distant and dull. The writing was on the wall. If he wanted them gone, they would be just that. *Gone*. For a second time.

'What about the Universe?' Connie said, clearing her throat, blinking rapidly, waiting desperately for the answer, if she got one. Connie was close to him and drenched him in a loud voice, so she was hopeful.

'Redemption of the Universe was required by the Code.' Minan said, 'and I concurred,' scanning left and right and then glaring straight at Connie. 'Fyoderov demanded termination of this Universe, also by the authority held within the minutia of the Code,' Minan said, not moving his piercing electric blue eyes from Connie as he spoke. 'Both demands will be met by permanent termination of this peculiar Universe. I have brought it back temporarily, but Fyoderov must be in agreeance to make it permanent. If he does not, he will eventually become aware of its existence and termination of your Universe will be very swift, with no notice provided to anyone, as decreed by the Code.'

Emma had stepped slightly closer. She'd heard every word Minan had said. The whole lot was echoing in her head. It all sounded ludicrous. 'What about the *others*?' she asked. By "others", Emma meant other societies. She assumed there must be others, *somewhere out there*. There had to be, especially now.

In any event, the Universe was so bloody big. Emma had always reckoned it was larger than humans thought. And that by itself probably invoked *others*, simply through the laws of probability - didn't it? Minan had to compare us with others, so other intelligences definitely existed. It was high time the Fermi Paradox was put to bed. Emma was sure it had been, Minan had essentially said it. If what Connie and Becker said was true, then the paradox was solved and the answer was sitting only a few metres away. Many others existed too.

*   *   *

'I thought our tech development was pretty good...pretty rapid,' Emma said, somewhat affronted by the accusation that it wasn't as quick as she thought. Of course, if they were assessed relatively, which Minan apparently did, the answer could have been anything, she supposed.

'You were below the median curve for scientific achievements,' Minan said, piercing them all with his sapphire-like eyes. He was sitting again on the same flat rock. That seemed to be his home on this planet.

Dimitri was grimacing and frowning, mainly in disbelief, concentrating on Minan intently. He was tapping a fist against his lips and thinking hard.

'But you said we were the only ones in the Universe? That doesn't make sense.' Dimitri was tightening in the chest and held his knuckles to his lips. To him it was all nonsense. What was going on here? He wondered, none of it appeared to be rational, no matter which way he looked at it? Who the hell have we been compared to?

Emma was totally and utterly muddled, turning away and pulling an earlobe. She had no idea what was going on, or how it possibly worked, she rubbed her chin, shaking her head to complete the picture of abject confusion. She barely knew which way was up.

Connie stared at Emma. 'We are compared to other similar societies in *different universes*', Connie said, trying desperately to keep her voice as deep as possible, in this helium-rich environment. 'He has many under his control, *universes* that he himself has created from algorithms. These were all formed within the auspices of the Genesis Directorate in what we would term cyberspace.' She eyed Emma and knew what was coming next. Connie smiled warmly. 'Don't even ask what is outside cyberspace, because we have lived this question for years and still don't have a decent answer or idea. Minan won't tell us or even speak about it – but we assume it's where they come from, Minan and his people, including the GC. Yes, and his universe whatever that might look like.'

Becker looked at Minan and narrowed his eyes. 'So...you intend to once again terminate our Universe?' He said, thinking of the world full of people back home and this little prick, here in all his glory, about to off them all...again, kill everyone and everything Becker and any of them had ever known.

'If you were actually here, I would off *you*, or at the least do you some proper damage, but you're not here in person, are you Minan?' Becker looked at his stupid porcelain face and brilliant blue eyes, clenching and unclenching his fists, grunting and muttering with rage. 'You're somewhere nice and safe, about to do your evil work remotely, right?'

Becker gaped at Connie and she at him. A faint smile, barren of any amusement at all, was shared. She could tell Becker was pissed to the max, but there was little anyone could do. She was sure Becker wouldn't repeat mistakes of the past...well, fairly sure. The odds of him doing something stupid were reducing, she was sure.

'Actually,' Minan said, standing very straight, 'I came here to *save* you,' his voice was loud in their heads and had an echoing quality, and he actually emphasised a word rather than talking in continual monotone. Becker looked confused, tapping a fist against his lips and nervously smiling. He'd heard it all now. The little shit who promised death to everything and everyone, now offered what...*life? Give me a break*, he said to himself harshly. It was something way beyond the normal.

'*What?*' Becker yelled, knowing there was no way Minan was going to repeat himself. He couldn't believe what he'd just heard.

'*Jesus Christ,*' Connie blurted, ping-ponging her gaze between Becker and Minan. 'How a-are you going to do that? Save us from what?' She knew she had to keep enquiries simple and short. Otherwise Minan would look straight through her, ignoring her completely.

Simply by telling Fyoderov it has been done and hoping he doesn't check with GD.'

'Is that likely to work?' Connie asked.

'It will work for a period of time, but it will not work permanently,' Minan said, injecting the words straight into them without emphasis and without accent. 'I need to return to GD and get direct access to the Terbium data processors. Only then can I make it permanent. Access via GUI is not sufficient to do what I require. I need to get close to the processors.'

'*Holy fuck,*' Becker boomed...so you *are* trying to help us, I'd never thought that would happen, thank you.' Becker's eyes were glossy and bright and he had a smile that cut his face in half. He was genuinely taken aback. Minan was here to help humanity...and Earth, or so it seemed anyway. Becker was frankly stunned.

Minan watched Becker closely but made no attempt to respond, which led to an uncomfortable silence that descended on them all. Even the wind which had been fairly consistent for as long as he could remember, didn't blow at all. All of them were alone with their thoughts. The silence was deafening.

'What should we do then?' Becker eventually moaned. I mean, we can't stay here, right? You said yourself we can't survive here...once our onboard food is gone, that's it.' Becker shrugged his shoulders at Minan and the rest of the group – he had no idea what they should and could do next. All he knew was they couldn't stay here.

Water was okay because they produced it through electrolysis, but food, once the onboard supplies dwindled to zero, was a major issue they'd have to deal with. There was nothing on the planet that could be termed organic and hence there was no way to replenish stocks. So, once the on-board food was gone, they'd be gone soon after. They were all very aware they could not sustain themselves on dirt and ice or cyanobacteria. And once the ship's batteries were flat, water to drink would quickly be gone. The likely story wasn't a good one.

The kid had gone, presumably to interact with GD and do what he needed to do, to ensure his senior, Fyoderov, was kept in the dark about anything human. Thank God the kid appeared to be on their side, because without him they were all apparently irresolvably doomed to disconnection and permanent death. That's what Minan had promised them.

They really hoped he was conveying the truth and he was truly on their side. If he was "just saying it" they were all in a world of trouble, with several questions immediately posed. The first and probably most significant was *why* he was really here? Was he here only to save them? Becker doubted it. His vengeance and abilities were pretty much unlimited. Minan had proved that.

Becker looked around and couldn't see Connie anywhere. She had been standing quite close to him. Now they were both gone. Minan and Connie.

Becker spun around but couldn't see her anywhere. 'I...uh, don't want to alarm anyone, but he's seems to have kidnapped Connie and taken her with him.' Becker said, jerking his head around like a whip, seeing her nowhere. Dimitri and Emma did the same. Connie had indeed gone. Here one second, gone the next. Becker felt the first needles of panic on his skin. With her, they were in major trouble – without her they'd have no hope at all.

*   *   *

She was within Minan's vessel which seemed virtually empty, apart from some toyish controls near a window that stretched around part of the small grey cabin. Outside was black space but there were no stars that she could see. The green plasticky controls were strobing and blinking in white light, the patterns sometimes recognisable as the same, sometimes different. None of it meant a thing to Connie.

Minan pressed a strangely coloured and oddly textured button and they pretty much immediately came upon a huge light-blue sphere that had many long, thin protuberances near its top.

They entered an open panel or port near its centre which was free of the spines, without slowing down a zac. Connie felt like closing her eyes, but once inside the spherical structure, the urge diminished and went away. She couldn't open her eyes wide enough - it was a wonderland of incredible beauty and diversity.

Inside the craft, Connie eyed the light greenish controls and noticed with a brief snort, how much they resembled her little nephew's phone and office set up, which was just a toy. *Incredible*, she reckoned. The damned thing looked scarcely able to navigate or drive anything. Apparently, it could move *between* universes.

'Dimensional drive,' Minan hoisted between her ears. 'We are at one of the homes of the Collective, he said, his azure blue eyes looking forward and seemingly ignoring her entirely. This is where I spend some of my time. His eyes were very blue and shining with what Connie thought was excitement but could have been any Godforsaken emotion. Probably something not on the human palette, she thought. They were inside the polopy sphere, but God knows where the sphere itself was located. It looked like it was in space somewhere, so she'd go with that. She tried not to think about it too much because it really didn't matter. It was what it was.

Connie saw a structure that was centred above a huge floor, below which, she assumed, were the mighty terbium processors of the GD.

The floor seemed to cover the entire base of the sphere, about halfway up, and the structure they were approaching was fairly much in the centre of it, looking very out-of-place and dwarfed by the Sphere itself.

The building had three levels, all of them quite low and substantial only in the horizontal direction. The entire thing was quite low in terms of the space available. The first level was quite large and maybe ten feet high. The second floor was set back from the first, and was smaller, but otherwise identical.

Like the conning tower of a submarine, the third floor was set well above the two lower floors on a high neck of material that made it appear to look over the rest of the structure. The whole thing looked to be made of a silvery metal, she could see no joins or seams anywhere – hardly a surprise. Same as the clothing, she reckoned, all one-piece.

They landed near the structure and did so without Minan's attention. It was clearly directed to its endpoint, and that's where it went. The craft set down without the smallest suggestion of an inertial change – no surprise there either. No other buildings were evident anywhere inside the sphere, this was it. Compared to the size of the sphere, the craft was tiny but no doubt it was very powerful indeed.

The doors on the ship were already open and Minan exited the craft and Connie followed suit. The entire side of the craft disappeared. Together, they stood at the foot of the GD. Staring upward, she could only see a light grey finish to the entire structure. There was Earth-like gravity, which might have been just for her, or maybe it was what Fyoderov and Minan were used to – who knows? The source of the gravity was unknown, but the Sphere didn't look like it was rotating. Connie shrugged her shoulders and put it out of her mind and just accepted it. Fair enough, she thought.

'So...this is where we all came from?' Connie said, her neck tipping back to take in the soaring third floor of the place. She couldn't help wonder why Minan had brought her here. What value could she possibly add? The sheer knowledge in residence must have been stunning. And then there was her. The shortfall in sheer mental aptitude was spectacular.

Connie was dazzled to be in the same place where universes were created. The whole thing seemed quite unbelievable. She realised, with some trepidation, that she was the first human to be brought here. The first human to observe its contours. Well...the first one she knew about anyway. And the God-machine lay beneath them. Connie wobbled and almost collapsed. Minan did something with a ring-thing he wore on his third finger, which was a complete mystery to her. Connie looked at him questioningly.

'Come,' was the only response she received between her ears. Connie eyed him and ambled forward with him as he walked freely through what appeared to be a solid wall.

Against all her instincts, she did the same, following Minan and ending up on the other side of it with him. The feeling of walking through a wall was incredible, although, she supposed if you did it enough times, the wonder would recede a tad.

'Despite all of you being simulated - wave-function and tunnelling are still required to be modified to achieve it,' Minan said, in response to the thought of "how" by Connie which Minan clearly took as reasonable.

Connie took that in her stride. 'So...wherever you want to get in, you can?' Beats having doors and hallways she supposed. Great space-saver as well as money-saver, she thought...no doors or hallways required.

'Yes,' Minan said, between her ears. They could easily move from room to room.

We have come here to see Fyoderov in person,' Minan said, in the same toneless voice.

'Okay,' Connie said, she was hardly going to disagree with him, being on his home turf and all, 'but why take me along?' She really wondered. *WTF?* Again, what was she here for? Connie pondered but could not work it out. She would surely be of no use. And add no value at all. She was smart enough to realize she wasn't here for no reason though - Connie knew that much.

She waited and waited. Then waited some more. There was no response from Minan. He just stared at her blank-eyed and unblinking, piercing her with his shining azure eyes. It was as if he didn't know why she was here either. He just stood there, as if in a trance. Fair enough, she reckoned, wrinkling her nose and bugging her eyes out.

'We will move to the tube,' Minan said crisply, after emerging from whatever trance or coma he was in. Walking ahead, Connie struggled to keep up with Minan, walking and partially running over a grey floor which matched the wall in colour and texture.

The floor seemed hard but she left indents behind her which rapidly smoothed to nothing. So, it was hard *and* soft – that really didn't make a lot of sense. Still, it felt good to run across.

Minan wouldn't tell her what it was, which came as no surprise. Having touched the wall, all she could tell was that it was soft. The floor was firm to walk over but stamping your foot made it soft. *Go figure.* The ultimate in safe building componentry, she assumed.

Soon they were standing beside the tube, which was like an elevator but quite a bit smaller. Minan and Connie hopped in and she saw odd numbers and shapes that were indented. He pressed something and she started feeling the inertia of movement, and then they stopped and the tube opened, the reverse of the way it closed. It turned outward to open itself. There were no doors which wasn't a huge shock.

'Minan, welcome back,' said the figure hunched over the bench in the near distance.

The room sort of looked like a lab back on Earth, it was very white and very bright. There were machines that looked entirely unfamiliar, though again, it was hardly a surprise. Instead of centrifuges and test tubes full of anomalous liquids, there were screens that disappeared into the benchtop and square looking things with bumps and thin spikes all over them. They were lined up one after the other on the benchtop. Connie couldn't even guess what they did. Overall, it looked like a lab, but a very strange one indeed. Interestingly, there was no smell at all.

'Thank you,' Minan replied to Fyoderov, using his mouth and vocal cords for the first time since she'd seen him. Apparently, that was the only way they were supposed to communicate in GD, to actually speak out loud. Fyoderov, if that was who it was, looked very young but his voice was mature and a lot deeper than she expected. She tried to put expectation out of her mind.

Connie whispered to Minan, 'This is Fyoderov, right?'

Correct.' He spoke in a hushed tone, without looking at her. 'Anton, this is Connie Lennox, one of the Programs in one of my portfolios, a human being from Earth,' Minan said, in English, for her benefit, she assumed. He bent upward, and turned fully around to look at her, moving in a very strange, fluid manner.

'Hello, Connie Lennox. Minan, this is the first time...what have I said about bringing Programs here?' He looked her over carefully and quite closely, seemingly impressed with Connie. He made various murmuring and mumbling sounds that ended in a strange whine.

'Sorry Director-General, but I thought on this occasion, it was important to show you.'

Fyoderov harumphed and grunted, mumbling something incoherent under his breath. He gawked closely at Connie again. He mumbled something once again. A long, slow grin was her reward, which had to be good, didn't it? He quickly resumed whatever it was he was doing.

'I want to add the human Universe to your list, because I believe in them,' he said dramatically, licking his lips, an act she'd never seen from Minan before.

Fyoderov gestured Minan over with his right arm and they had a conversation Connie was shielded from. Minan and Fyoderov looked carefully at Connie and then resumed talking. After a few minutes they were finished and Minan returned to her.

'Um...anything you can share?' She asked, eyeing him and gently biting her lip. She would be very surprised indeed if Minan gave her any answer at all. They definitely talked though, but apparently it wasn't to be shared with her. It was obviously a secret between them only. Definitely *no* sharing.

There was no response from Minan as she expected, and an uncomfortable silence ensued for an eternity until Minan said to her directly that they should return.

But return to what? Connie thought immediately, to Proxima B? To a no-food, certain death prison? Why would we return to a planet that could kill us? Which they had no hope of escaping?' Connie struggled to see why? Again, it made no sense to return somewhere that would ultimately be lethal.

'That planet, *um...why?*' She asked. There was no answer to any of the questions she had. She knew Minan could read her mind. Maybe she was asking too many questions. Clearly, she was also asking the wrong ones. Or perhaps he didn't feel like responding, or Fyoderov had instructed him not to. Of course, it could be a combination of more than one. Wherever she looked, there were mysteries that couldn't' be solved.

She also asked Minan about the language they used. Why the hell did they use English to communicate? Language Connie could understand. He didn't reply at all to her semi-constant questions, which left her thinking deeply about it. Connie thought it was because she was there, but Fyoderov used it before he knew she was there. So, what was the answer? In the absence of Minan saying anything, she could only guess. And her best guess was that English was used by Fyoderov whenever he was dealing with Minan. Why – Connie didn't have a clue. Minan turned and eyed Connie squarely with his bright blue eyes boring into her.

'Fyoderov wants humans to complete a series of cognitive and physico-intellectual tasks before induction takes place. If you achieve the right outcome, the planet and your species will be brought into the GC and will be recipients of all its sharable intelligence.' Minan's blue eyes burnt even brighter and she felt compelled to look into them. His eyes seemed to be swirling.

'I believed humanity had already qualified for induction through its unique qualities that went well beyond the algorithm I set for them. They, you, were so different from other races, and we still do not know why. Any non-science outcome shouldn't have happened – yet somehow it did. Fyoderov, however, wants this challenge successfully completed first. He was quite adamant about it.'

Connie shrugged her shoulders and stared at him sceptically. What exactly did he mean by "challenge"? Minan wouldn't answer any questions, but who would be involved with that "challenge", presumably the whole world? She'd worry about that later. Connie had plenty to contemplate right now.

*   *   *

Something else had replaced the boy as an item of interest on the pile of rocks they called the bluff. In the almost-warmth of Proxima B, in the eyeball, it twisted and warped in the strong wind and it looked like a shimmering, golden, desert mirage near the top of the bluff. The thing looked alive, but Becker was sure it only looked that way. The object billowed and wafted in the wind and seemed to beckon, almost summon them, when they looked into it.

Becker thought he had seen it before, it looked like something he'd seen earlier but he couldn't quite place it. He racked his brain and tried to remember. It danced and moved like it was really alive. He wished Connie was here to see it.

Becker felt quite comfortable that she was safe with Minan – after all he was the great creator, he could surely look after one human girl, although some forewarning would have been nice.

Last time he saw something like this, Becker recalled, Nate came wandering out of it, but this time it seemed a lot different. This time it seemed to move a lot more, along the ground and in the air. It was the damnedest feeling that this thing was putting out if you dared look at its mid regions. It wanted you to enter and had something like a Siren's call, it was very compelling indeed.

Becker stared wordlessly at it, almost like he was in a trance, heart pounding. 'I feel like the bloody thing wants me to enter it.' His eyebrows furrowed as he eyed it, surveying it closely. Emma could see the big lug was intrigued. In fact, they all were.

'When I look straight at it, I feel the same,' Emma said, scratching the back of her neck. 'It's a strange compulsion indeed.' She took a step forward.

They all stood together at the base of the bluff. Connie was at their side. She'd appeared from out of nowhere.

'*Jesus shit*,' Connie blurted and jumped back a few steps, gawking at her new surroundings. Connie had appeared from nowhere, and as far as she was concerned, she emerged from thin air. One second, she was in the GD, the next she was with Becker on Proxima.

Becker pretty much repeated her sentiment, almost double-taking when Connie appeared out of thin air. He reared back and was speechless, gasping violently, his feet almost leaving the ground in shock.

From there to this, Connie thought, trying to figure out if she was better or worse off. She honestly had no idea. She was looking at Minan in the GD and back with the group the next second. Her mouth fell open and her eyes bulged. She was staring at a deeply disturbed Becker. *Incredible*, Connie thought, wondering why Minan bothered with a spacecraft at all. Was it for her benefit, or GD's maybe? She really had no clue.

Presumably, Minan had made movement very easy indeed. Apparently, he could do pretty much what he wanted, so it should come as no surprise, really. He was still bound by regular physical rules though, of that she was pretty sure. Had to be. Minan and Fyoderov stretched those rules to the limit and even bent them a bit. Got around them, definitely, but break them – *no* – but it still gave them a hell of a lot of elbow-room to work with.

*   *   *

Strangely, the thing that danced and weaved in front of them was a brilliant, glittering golden in colour and sparkled in the light from its very adjacent star. It disturbed the dust on the rocks like a twisting whirlwind, whipping dust upward to be then caught by the very mild wind and distributed over Proxima B.

Dimitri and Emma agreed, it wanted them to enter. When they ogled it, there was an inertia that pulled and picked at them. It billowed and danced in the exact same spot that Minan had occupied, which begged the question, did he leave through that thing, or what seemed just as likely, did he leave it for *them* to use...as a way out? Minan said they couldn't survive where they were. Straight after that, those objects appeared. Or, was he reading it all wrong? Becker thumbed his chin and nose in bewildered thought. It was one or the other. *Brilliant*, he reckoned. It was like saying he'd narrowed it down to yes or no. In truth, he'd made no progress at all. It was all a complete and utter unknown. It seemed to want them to enter though.

Connie stood beside Becker as Emma and Dimitri ambled over. 'We can't stay here, we know it and Minan certainly knows it, and he has told us as much. So, I say we -go in,' Connie said uncertainly, her face white as a sheet. She didn't want to do it or say it. But they couldn't live here – she was desperate. They were desperate.

'I'm with you Connie,' Becker said, his rapid blinking and hissingly, loud breath heard clearly by Emma and Dimitri, whom he stood uncomfortably near. If they didn't go, nor would he. No way he'd go if they didn't do it as well. They were a team. He couldn't leave them here alone. Team first, Becker reckoned, but he wasn't entirely sure. Maybe talking them around is the thing to do. He wasn't sure about that either. The idea of staying in a place free of edible organics didn't impress him at all – that meant no food.

The thought of splitting up the team was anathema too. Normally, Becker didn't do too well in teams and he didn't like them much, but their little team had been through so much. There was a bond there, no doubt about it.

Becker stood quite still, staring at Emma and Dimitri gravely. 'Well...*stay and die of starvation, or enter that stupid thing*,' Becker pointed to the object that was moving this way and that on the bluff, 'and, well ... who knows. We need food, and we aren't going to be finding it here. There is no choice really. Minan wouldn't off us here.' As soon as he said it, he second-guessed himself. Becker admitted to himself that he nor anybody else, had absolutely any idea about anything. All they had was Occam's Razor. And that said "go into the light". 'If we use it, we have a chance of survival. Like Minan said, if we stay here...we're gone.'

'Sold like a champion car salesman Becker,' Connie said, giggling. You complete and utter twat, she whispered.' Connie turned and covered her mouth with her hand. He really was quite the goose, she reckoned, still chuckling to herself. Making a decent argument for anything, was well beyond him, but he'd done okay, not that she'd ever tell him that.

'*Anyway*', Connie eventually said, 'you've heard from us,' she glanced quickly at Becker and raised her eyebrows, 'what's *your* decision?'

Emma looked at Dimitri and offered him a small, shy smile. 'I agree, we can't survive here, we may as well spin the chocolate wheel

I suppose.' As soon as she finished, she broke off all eye contact and looked down at the steeply pebbled ground. She wasn't sure what to do. Emma was scared to make a decision. She was ambivalent about just about everything...so any decision she made, had to be respected.

'I'm with her,' Dimitri said quickly. 'There's no choice. We have to go. There's nothing here for us,' He gawked in Emma's direction but she was still focussed doggedly on the ground. He wanted to show solidarity, Emma really didn't want to make *any* decisions about anything. Unless she violently disagreed, she was happy to go with their choices.

With nearly everyone in favour of going, Becker ambled up the hill, stepping over rocks, and standing near the anomaly which was twisting and curling in front of him. The others joined him and pondered what might be on the other side. *If* there was another side. Might be just more rocks.

Becker spun around and locked eyes on Connie. 'What about an E-suit, I feel like it's not needed?' He eyed her with interest, waiting for her opinion.

'I feel the same, but yes, it's a huge risk.'

'We're going to a destination chosen by Minan,' he said, so I feel like we'll be fine as we are. Becker twisted his neck, and rubbed it as if it was sore, revealing his anxiety, to Connie at least - it was a graphic tell-sign.

'Let's do it then,' Dimitri said firmly, looking softly at Emma. He smiled shyly at her. 'And hurry up about it.'

They took each other's hands, which was fine for Dimitri, he'd been thinking about a way to hold Emma's hand – he had the strange, overwhelming desire to look after her...but seriously, he thought, here...*now?* It was a very strange, even dangerous place to start anything, let alone something really crazy like a relationship.

Becker led them into the object which continued to duck and weave in front of them. The object acted like a vacuum-cleaner getting rid of the dirt and dust as it made its way over the rocks. Taking some of it, *where*, he had no idea?

After they went through and effectively vanished, the object on Proxima B disappeared into the ether. What had been a golden object shimmering above the landscape and rocks of Proxima B, was now gone. The landform and the planet was now free of anything approaching intelligence, the same as it had been for billions of Earth-years previous.

6

Other Side

"The difference between stupidity and genius is that genius has its limits."
- *Albert Einstein*

They found themselves, all four of them, standing in the middle of a featureless circle; it was quite dim and crackled with dirt and dust underfoot. The circle itself was hundreds of metres in diameter and around it were endless rows and columns of cylinders, Connie and Becker at least, were fairly familiar with this kind of scenario from an encounter with Minan before.

'*Fuck...again,*' Connie yelled, happy to be safe and to be somewhere familiar...but *here*...seriously?

They were looking at the vagaries of a useless planet, now they were in a place gaping at innumerable artificial cylinders. Which was probably free of anything organic. The last thing they expected was to be taken to this world which they'd already seen.

For Emma and Dimitri though, it was all brand new. They craned their necks around and up like Meercats at a place that was quite stunning, although the light was fairly dim. Both of them were shocked by the sheer number of cylinders that seemed to form the basis of everything. Everywhere they turned were impossibly tall mountains made of odd-looking cylinders.

Where in the good fuck were they now? Emma pondered to herself as she took in the view. She assumed they were somewhere important. What were these cylinders and what was inside them?

Why in God's name were there so many of them, Dimitri wondered? So many cylinders, so few answers. He glanced at Connie, hopefully, she'd know. Becker had said they'd been here before.

Emma brought a shaky hand to her forehead and took a few uncertain steps forward as she continued looking at their mountainous surrounds.

They had so many questions but zero answers, or even clues, only pure guesswork and outright conjecture. Becker and Connie had answers to most of their questions, but they weren't telling anyone anything...yet.

They had gravity here, which generally meant they would have to be spinning to obtain mass from the centrifugal force. Gravity would then arise from the Equivalence Principle, *if* they were within the same Sphere as they were before. It certainly looked the same...so far.

There were millions, perhaps more, cylinders from floor to near the ceiling of this dauting place. There were cylinders *everywhere*. The higher ones, they could barely see, they were sparkling in the dim light of this place, the source of which was completely concealed. It was definitely dimmer than last time. Apart from the cylinders and the Sphere itself, the environmental factors were all Earth like.

Temperature, pressure, atmosphere – all pretty much like home. It made them all think, it was all perfect for humans. Dimitri wondered if it was perfect for something else. He couldn't understand why it was like it was. Was it all really for humans? Because it was near perfect – although perhaps just a little dim.

They could see pretty quickly they were right in the centre of a circle, with rows of cylinders radiating outward and upward like spokes from a huge 3-D cogwheel. That's where they were, central to a mighty cogwheel, standing in what they took to be the bullseye of an entire, overwhelmingly large structure. Surrounded by countless numbers of cylinders. *There were so many*. They were truly countless.

'*What the hell?*' Dimitri said loudly, after looking closely at where they were. He looked up and around and then up again. 'What the Hairy fuck is this place? There's no echo...it must be...gigantic, and very full of cylinders.

'*Duh*' Becker said drolly, Connie hit him with a dark, angry expression. He was about to thank Dimitri for "the obvious" but stopped dead on Connie's intervention.

Dimitri ignored Becker completely. 'So...where the hell are we?' He asked in his deeply Slavic voice, snapping his head around to try and take it all in. The poor Russian was totally overwhelmed by the sheer scope of the place, and by the out-and-out number of cylinders that surrounded him. The inside of this Sphere was truly stunning – from the outside you'd never know.

'Connie and I have been here before...although it looks, bigger and darker than last time.' Becker glanced at Connie as she nodded and then raised her eyes, resuming an owlish upward stare. 'Each of these cylinders represents a universe created by Minan...apparently.' Silence descended on them.

'A universe...*Jesus shit, holy c-crap,*' Dimitri spluttered, '*Each and Every one?*' He and Emma gawked skyward, taken aback by what he and Emma now knew to be something astonishing. 'I would normally ask "how" to such an unknown but not here, no way, *nu-uh,* any answer will be utter gibberish,' the Russian said with the faintest of grins. 'Complete and utter hoo-hah,' Dimitri repeated, mumbling and muttering something inaudible in Russian.

'There are more cylinders than last time and it's a bit dimmer too,' Connie said. 'Most are black, but some are white and a few are Becker's favourite colour, *gold.*' She could see the idiot smiling and hamming it up in the corner of her eye. He was being quite the blockhead, Connie reckoned. Where to start, she wondered dismally. She supposed she did lead him on a bit. Connie looked at him, snorted, and shook her head in dismay. He was still holding both thumbs up, in a display of arrogance that really annoyed her.

'Oh dear,' Connie said to herself. He was getting worse and she knew it. Perhaps he had early onset 'Idiocy,' she said to herself, chuckling.

'There's uh...no food here,' Dimitri spat, so while Minan does his thing, whatever that is, what the fuck do we do...*die?*' He glared at Becker wordlessly, who agreed wholeheartedly by rubbing his stomach. They had to get sustenance from somewhere. This place looked totally sterile.

Becker looked genuinely mortified, expelling air slowly but forcibly as he did his best to process what was going on. Someone had said it *before* him. If he mentioned "food", Connie would just tell him to suck it up, so that wasn't an option. He did think about steak and chips a lot. Dimitri wasn't making it easy to keep quiet.

The Russian somehow got away with it, without being belittled, or worse. *Amazing,* Becker thought. There was benefit to being new and unknown that worked in your favour. Just wait until Connie knew him longer. He'd never get away with anything, especially talking about anything as inane and off-mission as food.

This place had death written all over it. No way there was any sustenance here. This place was entirely devoid of anything living, one look would tell you that. It had a distinctly metallic look to it – very, very inorganic, the whole place.

They needed to find something to eat and it wasn't going to happen in this place. This metal cocoon was as sterile as it got. Maybe there was a McDonalds further up, Becker said to himself, feeling the humourless laughter welling up inside him. *Cosmic branch*, he thought, with an ironic snort. He really felt like a burger...or three, although he'd eat anything at the moment...anything that was more or less organic.

Then he remembered the mummified Soviet astronauts, and he quickly swallowed down bile juices that bled into his mouth from a bubbling stomach. That was a truly awful event in his life, and one that he struggled to forget. They often appeared in his darker dreams. Dark brown flesh, dried with ragged bites everywhere – it scared him to death. What a rotten way to go.

They looked horrible and dark, like aged pieces of meat that should have been hanging in someone's shed. And they wore suits that had become loose torn space wear and their skin had wrinkles on wrinkles. Worst of all, there was signs of cannibalism. Whichever way you looked at it, it was a dreadful mess and a scene to be avoided at all costs.

Becker didn't think that would happen to them, but he wasn't absolutely certain. Hunger did strange things to people - that he knew was a definite fact. He remembered when he was stuck in a cave for two days when their escape route filled with water in Bali. They had no food but lots and lots of water.

Becker was famished and developed a huge headache and couldn't think straight. He couldn't sleep and could barely stand up. When he was trying to sleep in the cave with his stomach doing cartwheels, he thought about a film he'd seen where the survivors of a plane crash eventually resorted to cannibalism. Even though he wasn't close to it, given a few weeks, rather than a couple of days, *anything* would have been fair game, given his state-of-mind after only two days.

We were taken from Proxima B,' Emma said, 'presumably because there was no way we could survive...to come here where there's no food to survive on, and equally therefore, no way to live. Doesn't that seem odd?' The poor girl was very confused but she was right. 'It just makes no sense. *Why?*' She yelled. 'What is the point of shifting from one spot to the other if the same problem exists?' Emma turned away from everyone. 'Maybe we came here for a different reason,' she added.

Becker flinched and goggled his eyes. '*Oh...you think?*'

Well, it's an improvement on "duh" Connie thought.

'Don't you find it all a tad ironic?' Emma asked, with eyes boring into Connie's. Now *there's* a question, Dimitri thought. Beauty and intellect, he reckoned, a great pairing. The Russian had it bad.

Dimitri looked angrily at Connie, '*forget why, but where the hell are we...really?*' he said, believing she knew a lot more than she was passing on.

Connie knew "where" they were but had no real idea where the sphere itself was. Guesses were difficult. She didn't even know if this was their Universe. Nothing looked familiar. Where the hell was Sirius or Canopus or Rigel or any of the familiar galaxies like the Whirlpool, Andromeda or M87? Out the window, Connie could see nothing she'd ever seen before. It was a truly alien cosmos.

'Jesus, okay...I get it...you want answers.' She looked at all of them and made sure she had their attention. *'So do I,'* she screamed. 'As for "where we are", we are inside a huge sphere, in space, location *fuck knows*. In fact, I and you lot, know just about nothing about where we truly are. *How's that?'* Connie said loudly. A heavy silence ensued for a few moments.

I don't think we are within our Universe,' Connie continued in a more controlled voice. 'I have no evidence to back that up of course...it's just what I think. I know what they're capable of.' Connie narrowed her eyes and looked straight ahead. She reckoned she'd said enough.

'Okay Connie, so, what do we do then?' Emma said, 'we can't just sit here and do nothing? If we wait in this sphere thingy, we die, apparently, according to Minan. Food, onboard our ship on Proxima B, will last four weeks or thereabouts...here, we have nothing, or so it seems. How the hell are we better off?' Emma looked at Connie with a withering stare, hands on hips, demanding something meaningful in return.

Connie sighed and hung her head, '...who says we have to be better off?' She shot Emma a penetrating look. 'No one made that claim, or even assured us...it's just something we *assumed* would be the case. Minan certainly didn't say it. We need to try and find something we can eat and keep assuming we're here for a reason. If we are, we need to find that reason. We haven't been sent back to Earth like I thought we might be, and Minan does everything for a reason...so we start walking and look for anything that might fit the bill. We try and find out why the hell we are here.'

'Oh fuck,' Becker spat, 'more walking,' he said predictably, 'just what I don't need.' He surveyed Connie cautiously. *Please, no,* he may as well have begged, there was nothing that could be done to avoid it. There was no other means of locomotion. The mission demanded it. Becker didn't want to walk anywhere, but there was little choice, unless they happened to find some automotion along the way. Maybe a bicycle or a trike lying innocuously on the ground somewhere. *Very unlikely.*

You'll be fine Becker, we'll go slow, one foot in front of the other, right?'

Becker offered Connie a one-finger salute and took up his nominal position at the rear of the group.

So, off they went, walking to find something. This place reminded Becker of the tunnels they were in – searching for anything that might tell them why they were here. They just didn't even know what it was they were looking for!

'*Shit*', Connie thought, '*something*', she assumed they'd know it when they saw it. They needed to be on the lookout for something that truly didn't belong in this odd world. Christ all-fucking-mighty, she mouthed to herself, as she started walking forward, knowing how difficult it was probably going to be.

They were ambling along between the outer wall of the structure and the first line of cylinders, where there was a path of sorts that they followed.

'What exactly are we looking for?' Becker asked. He gulped hard, as if he could swallow down his rising uneasiness. Becker felt like an ant peering up at a skyscraper. The walls of the sphere to the left were made of millions of individual cylinders and towered above him like a majestic mountain range. He felt like a tiny sugar ant. To the right were the silvery-white walls of the Sphere itself.

'Look for anything that appears abnormal.' Connie replied. 'Like it isn't part of the cylinders. Doesn't belong, sticks out as really different y'know.'

'This entire place looks like it doesn't belong, the cylinders, the size of this place...the fact that we're here. It's all *abnormal*, the whole lot of it,' Becker spat, peering at Connie's back, fixedly and indignantly.

'Fair enough,' she replied, turning around. 'How about anything that looks like it really doesn't belong.'

'Better,' he said, grinning faintly. He was just yanking her chain.

'The first thing I would ask,' Connie said firmly, 'is why is this huge space pressurised with something we can breathe? And gravity feels about the same as it is on Earth. I assume Minan's done all that for us – like last time. It should be unpressurised with no gravity, shouldn't it?'

'Yep,' Becker said offhandedly, 'he'd hardly send us here to suffocate or float around like a bunch of fools. We're here, nicely under control, while he does his thing with Fyoderov. Whatever that is. Let's just keep walking,' he said grimly. He realised there was no choice.

'Look at you Becker, all keen to walk,' Connie said, giving a slow smile that ended in a bug-eyed grimace. She found it hard to believe he was ready to go.

'I'm *not* keen to walk, I'm just keen to get this stupid side- show on the road,' he said, snorting and shaking his head a little, still nervous about what was to come. Becker wondered where the endpoint was and felt immediately worried. They had to stop walking sometime...didn't they? Walking was only a means to an end, right?

There was extended silence inside the Sphere as each of them focussed on walking, and contemplated their own situation and, ultimately, where they were heading.

Becker and Connie had spoken about her recent trip with Minan. 'Why did Minan bother to take you to see Fyoderov?' Becker asked curiously, 'it seems like there wasn't much of a reason to take you along,' he said to Connie while he plodded on, breathing in gasps.

'You'd think that wouldn't you...Fyoderov only looked at me and then I came back here, but Minan never, I repeat *never*, does anything without a reason. We just have no idea what that reason is. He introduced me to Fyoderov...and that was it. Apart from that, I was just extra baggage.'

All of them walked onward, single file with Connie at the front and Becker, the rear, with Emma and Dimitri in the middle. Becker was grunting and groaning, not loudly, but audibly. Everyone could hear him. And he'd just started walking – Emma wondered what Becker would be like in an hour. He was annoying already. *Just walk, and shut up,* she felt like screaming at him.

They saw several gold and white cylinders up as high as they could see but they saw nothing that was materially out of place. Everything looked the same as last time. Black cylinders with a rare splash of colour.

Suddenly, from nowhere, they were all entirely weightless, Becker noticed his insides feel strange and his lips and eyelids feel like they'd vanished, then his stomach felt like it did after he'd dropped on a roller coaster or in a lift. They all felt like they were in space and totally, utterly weightless.

'*Shi-iiiit,*' Becker screamed, now entirely off the ground. Not by much, but enough. They were all off the floor slightly.

'*Fuck me,*' Dimitri said, so much for rotation and centrifugal force. Clearly, it's stopped doing whatever it was doing, he screamed at himself, watching Emma waving her arms around, trying to right herself. She was doing her best to stay on the ground but losing the fight, slowly rising into the air, arms still flailing around. She had no idea what she was doing.

Connie looked up - it was a long, long way to the top, but she was stable. 'Yeah, it's stopped turning,' she said, 'no more gravity I'm afraid...has the Sphere broken somehow?' Everyone gawked at Connie, hoping like hell she could shed some light on it. She immediately doubted whether anything had gone wrong with the Sphere.

She was supposed to know everything, but in reality, only Minan would have the answers. All Connie could do was add semi-educated guesses that were probably wrong.

Connie thought about it long and hard before speaking, but really, she still had nothing. 'The gravity is either from rotation, y'know $g = r \times w^2$ or it's something we don't understand at all, like gravity plating or dark energy. How the hell could I have any more idea than you lot? All I'd say with any certainty is, if Minan's got anything to do with it, a mechanical problem is very unlikely indeed.'

Becker's eyes glazed over at the description of an equation and the use of "y'know" made him grunt with severe displeasure. He really disliked math and anything related to it. The term "y'know" really made his blood boil. It added nicely to Becker's personal torment. He felt dumb as shit.

Becker gave some force to the floor with a foot and he sailed freely into the ether, keen to leave the vicinity, and gawk at a cylinder really close up. Before anything else happened, he was keen to check out one of these things that were so populous around them.

Becker kept thinking of the Soviets, having encountered their dead bodies when he was in this place before. Was that how they would die? He kept wondering. Would sheer hunger gradually take them down? One by one. Until they were all dead? *Christ,* it was a horrifying thought. Maybe that's why the Soviets died, brought into this place, against their wish, only to find a world devoid of anything organic to eat. And that was the end of the story. Dead, partly eaten, partly mummified Russians. Clearly, they found nothing to eat. Becker thought about them and visualised their horrible brown skin and the rotten, baggy Soviet pressure-suits - it was hardly motivating.

Still, all that aside, Becker wanted to see a damned cylinder up really close. He grabbed a cylinder, stood back on the ground, then jumped for all he was worth, waving his arms around like a madman, trying to change course through the air, and realised that was useless. He grabbed hold of any cylinder to look closely at it. Becker grabbed one and with a decent grip, nulled his momentum and held on until he came to a complete stop in the air. As he expected, there were two lines of figures on each object.

Becker knew from before, that's how it would be. The last time they were here, each cylinder had two lines of figures, one that made no sense at all, and one that made a little sense.

One line, as expected, was totally unrecognisable as a language and looked more like hieroglyphics, consisting of lines, vertical, horizontal, cris-crossing, oblique dashes dots of various sizes...the whole lot meaning absolutely zero to Becker. Probably meant nothing to the rest of the group too.

He thought it might make more sense seen up close, but he was wrong. It still meant less than nothing. It was probably Minan's own language. To Becker, it was just pure gibberish.

The writing above it, however, did thankfully mean something. It was binary, like before, and the number, unsurprisingly, was very large indeed. It had ones in the first and last four columns, and ones when the number of digits was big, based on what Joe had said, meant the actual number was likely huge.

In front of Becker was a black cylinder which he realised, was supposed to represent a universe created by Minan, one on which a decision on its future was still to be made by the GD. In other words, it was probably still developing, like ours was.

Becker stared fixedly at the cylinder, both ends were closed, no surprise there. According to Minan, this was simply a representation of his "portfolio" so humans could visualise it, because that's where we lived our lives...in the visual, apparently. *Look, see, believe.*

Nothing in this place actually existed, not Emma, or Connie, or anyone, or anything...except within the Terbium processors of the Genesis Directorate. There, mathematical widgets and a glorious Kardashev algorithm led to a living universe, to them and everything else around them. Earth and every human owed its existence to Minan and the GD. They just didn't know it. It still sounded amazing and incredible...that it was *true* was a real head-fuck of the highest order.

Outside of the GD, there was nothing, except a simulation...of what was in the GD's processors. How it did it and what would exist if it didn't do it were totally beyond the scope of Connie's mind. Sort of like asking what's outside or beyond your photos held on a computer. Cyberspace was just computing power.

One day, it would be asked in detail, and the answer would be provided and the intricacies understood, sort of, but not now. Connie was sure it had something to do with cyberspace.

Now, they should be just thankful GD and the Collective existed at all. Otherwise...well, oblivion came strongly to mind. They, as a civilization, certainly wouldn't exist. Religions could talk about their God, but unless they were talking about Minan, they were all wrong.

Becker found it hard to believe and harder to conceive that the cyber-energy buzzing and fizzing with different electron states within the GD'S processors embodied millions of creation events happening right "now". Big bangs were a dime-a-dozen within the processors – it was the algorithm that was critical. Universes were only created for life to spawn and the GD to watch and take notes.

It was too much for anyone to get their head around. The capacity and nature of the Terbium processors exceeded the ability of the human mind by a fair margin. To think that one day, if we survived as a species, we could be similar "creationists" was a step too far. Yet, that's what Minan believed would happen. And he should know.

Becker pushed away from the cylinder and grabbing another and another, made his way eventually, back to them, "standing" on the ground with the group. More accurately, the others floating near the ground.

Becker joined them in their small group, were they pondering what their next step should be? He too was floating near the floor. No more walking would be a great start. But how would they move in zero-G? Becker wondered. Floating around sounded nice, he thought, but probably wouldn't work. They'd get nowhere...or move very slowly.

As Becker watched them and wondered, gravity returned in an avalanche, making his lips feel heavy and more generally, gifting everyone a very heavy, enervating feeling they could've done without. The rest of them hit the ground soon after, and thankfully they didn't have far to go. All of them were now squarely on the ground feeling very heavy indeed. No-one collapsed to the ground, which was good.

So much for floating, Becker thought, it was off the table, unless things changed. Which begged the question, Becker reckoned, what would have happened if gravity came back while he was up there? High up, above their heads? He craned his head up and saw the object he was gawking at. Becker was horrified by how high it was. Maybe it was the weightless environment, he had no idea, but it didn't seem all that high from up there. At best he would've broken bones and bruised flesh - at worst, he would've killed himself. Broken neck or back probably.

Becker didn't fancy falling all the way to the floor from way up there. He was surprised he didn't think about it at the time, he was so used to putting his life on the line, apparently, he'd gotten used to it. He didn't give it a second thought. *That* would be a massive surprise, if it were true.

*   *   *

Becker considered it - were they being watched or was that just how it seemed? The whole thing appeared way too contrived, Becker decided, something had to be controlling events, dictating what and when things happened. Something wanted them alive and relatively unharmed. That's how it appeared and that's what Becker believed, rightly or wrongly.

If he fell from up there, with Earth-like gravity, at the very least, he would've been incapacitated. His take was that someone saved him from that. It must have been Minan – he was the only *other* he knew of? Becker almost guffawed out loud at the thought of Minan bothering or wanting to save him from anything.

Becker had wanted to *off* the little shit for some of the things he'd done, and he assumed the feeling was mutual, but now he wasn't so sure the feeling was mutual. Minan had done things he didn't really expect. Minan had done things that suggested the exact opposite.

Becker was pondering the massive difference a few minutes could make, when he heard something odd, that sounded like long toenails scraping and grating along the floor. Focusing on the sound, they heard deep, guttural breathing and heavy, irregular and sluggish footsteps that went along with the "toenails". Something was approaching.

Previously, he'd heard sounds that were pedestrian and very human. This noise was different, but still Connie found it a little familiar. Something or someone very large was walking toward them. Getting closer by the step it seemed. Becker strained forward to listen to the source of the unnerving noises. Becker was afraid of this sound. Everyone was acutely still and listened intently to the noise. It was definitely approaching and, in a line, direct with them, or so it seemed.

Heavy dragging footsteps. It didn't try and hide its approach which he took as a good sign. It clearly hadn't detected them yet. Whatever it was, they heard a loud hissing sound which made every hair on Becker's body stand to attention.

Becker herded everyone, who seemed quite content to stay where they were, up a small alley-way, to hide under the first row of cylinders until whatever it was had passed them. The stack of cylinders was huge and very high, but just underneath the first row was a small gap they could all fit in.

They hoped it, whatever it was, would go past without stopping. If it turned out to be friendly, they could easily catch it up and make their presence known. That was the plan anyway.

All of them felt a little embarrassed, hiding under the bottom row of the cylindrical things, waiting for whatever-it-was to come by and hopefully move past them. It was probably someone who needed help, but that posed another question to Becker – how did whatever it was, get in? Were they like us, he wondered? He doubted it, which drew another pointed question which went unanswered as he focused on the unpleasant sound.

Becker was at the end of the group with his index finger pressed firmly against his lips. They could clearly hear the thing still coming, breathing loudly and rapidly, nails, presumably toenails, scraping and grating on the floor, almost at their aisle. The sound of walking stopped but the sound of heavy, labored breathing continued.

By the sound of it, it didn't bode well for the humans. It was very close, and had stopped completely. Becker could hear its breathing and could smell it. Any possibility of it being a long-lost cosmonaut was gone. It was clearly something very unexpected.

Coming slowly into view was a horrible *something,* at least two metres tall, thick muscled arms, four talons that stretched halfway up both arms and there was one on the end of each arm, sparkling like a scimitar - covered by reasonably fresh blood.

It stood erect on two massive legs, heavily veined, with similar shaped claws set into them at various spots. Walking on long toenails, it made a distinctive metallic sound but was now entirely stationery, sniffing the air aggressively. This thing had evolved to hunt and kill.

It smelt the air by tilting its monstrous head to each side and sniffing loudly, certain that food was somewhere close. The creature moved its massive head upward and pulled in massive snorts of air again.

It moved up the alleyway near where they were hiding. Connie could see most of it and recognised it straight away. Especially, its smell, she would never, ever forget the smell. It smelt and looked exactly the same as that terrible thing from the blue planet.

And like its Doppelganger from Mars, its skin was primeval, cris-crossed with oozing sores, pierced by pencil thick hairs and eyes, soulless and spider-like, six of them, fearsome and grey and set in two juxtaposed lines.

The thing was a spectacular red colour, yellow stripes flashing across its bulging stomach and legs, the most repulsive, fearsome thing any of them had ever seen, be it dream, nightmare or screwball work of fiction. Connie, or any of them, were barely breathing, not moving a muscle. Hoping like hell it would go away without attacking or paying them any attention.

They could hear the thing snorting and rasping, and worse, they could all smell it – and it was getting stronger, the longer it stayed in their vicinity. Emma and Dimitri had hands over their mouth, taking shallow, fast breaths as the beast walked noisily by, scraping one of its sabres along the line of cylinders not a foot in front of them, making a blood-curdling screeching sound. The thing was horror incarnate.

Becker and Connie were bewildered and terrified by its presence in the Sphere, almost hyperventilating - breathing through clenched teeth as they held each other tight, their faces buried in each other, hoping like hell, the thing would move on. If the thing bent down and extended its left arm, it would touch Becker, and then it would be all over. The thing would then probably go into attack mode – and then God help them all.

The creature was stationery only a few feet away, dragging air into its body in ragged, shuddering inhalations that sounded tortured but which were probably normal for the species. Its head looked like a spider, complete with an awful, large hairy mouth, replete with horrid bony structures that were always moving, looking like small limbs, on either side of its funnel-like mouth, with needle-like probably venomous fangs therein.

Like the one on Mars, it could paralyse its prey with a single bite if it wanted to. Two of its eyes looked straight ahead and four were always looking sideways to assess its environment.

Connie wasn't sure what stank more – Becker or the creature. She admitted, the creature won by a fair margin. It was truly rank, mainly by virtue of its diet of pure meat, although Connie couldn't help wonder what it found to eat around here. It looked all banged up and cut, some wounds clearly weeping blood, and quite a bit of it. The life of being a predator, Connie assumed.

The thing smelt of rotten meat and sulfur, sour and very, very off, close to vomit inducing. Something was rotting, at least that's what it smelt like. She clenched her teeth, didn't want to breathe or look, but she gasped and panted with terror...as quietly as she could. Connie couldn't let that thing hear them.

Whatever it was, it was truly horrible to look at. It had the eyes of a spider and the body of a therapod. Good luck if you had arachnophobia with this thing. Couple appearance with the horrendous smell – and this creature was truly a horrible monster. It could smell their own odour and, unlike before, it was obvious that *this time*, it wanted them as food. DNA seemingly wouldn't be their saviour.

Last time, left-handed DNA saved them, but clearly, this time around, that didn't apply. Chirality meant nothing for some ungodly, probably Minan-related reason. This creature was sniffing them out as nutrients. Around here, sustenance, *food*, was clearly very rare indeed, for us, probably entirely absent.

When food was found, no doubt, it had to be consumed. Maximum advantage had to be taken, and by expending the least number of calories. Even though this thing was very alien, she felt quite sure, being a predator, that's how it would operate. She tried to forget the "how" question – it was, what it was. It was here and they had to deal with it.

This thing was probably always out for a kill, even in a prey infested location. *Here*, it would be truly ravenous with prey so rare. Connie was certain it would kill anything with a pulse, especially something with the temerity to hide.

'...*still...stay still*,' Becker urged under his breath, repeated as firmly as he could without moving or speaking above a whisper. The beast spun its head toward him and roared an inhuman burst of larynx power and sputum. The creature's breath was all rotting meat and sulfur. It had definitely been eating something, and recently. Everyone was frozen still with fear, desperately hoping it wouldn't see them or otherwise sense their presence.

It loped off with heavy footsteps, up the small alley and turned to its right to resume its journey up the path that separated the external hull of the Sphere from the first line of cylinders. They could hear it snuffling and snorting as it trudged away.

Connie had been trying to speak for some time, but there was no voice there. With everything that had happened she was so distracted by terror - Connie was as good as mute. All she could do was produce saliva but no sound. Becker eyed Connie and saw tears of dread coming from the widest eyes he had ever seen. She gaped at Emma and Dimitri - they were almost the same. Becker grabbed Connie and gave her a grizzly bear hug.

'*We will fucking prevail,*' he said in her ear, listening to the receding plods of the creature. It sounded like a very large and very heavy bear walking on two legs. "Prevail" – he sure as hell hoped so but wasn't nearly as confident as he made out.

Clearly, Connie had expected to be hauled away and eaten alive by the creature. Or covered in digestive juices to dissolve and liquify. And then sucked up and consumed as a pre-digested mess. In fact, it brought back the dreadful memory of meeting this thing in the middle of a blue jungle, where unbeknown to them and to her especially, they were protected by DNA and chirality, and incredibly, the creature didn't seem to regard them as prey.

Here, they were seemingly protected by nothing, apart from a line of cylinders. All of them were officially food for this creature. Forget left-handed DNA being their protector this time around. The entire group was food.

Eventually, they found the power of locomotion and crawled out from behind the cylinders and stood together in a group, breathing in shallow, quick breaths and glancing at each other with wide eyes, mutely attesting to just how close they were to a hideous end.

Careful to listen for any noise and any vibration at all, they slowly and tentatively made their way forward, walking with short, vigilant steps. By their calculations, the beast should be almost half a kilometre behind them and travelling further away with every step, unless of course, it had turned around. *Anything was possible* – they needed to remember that.

This thing didn't evolve on Earth, so its level of intelligence was unknown. It didn't seem overly intelligent but it could still be cunning, which is simply behaviour taught by experience with quarry.

They all agreed or yielded, that DNA in this creature must match theirs, wound in a right-handed fashion. Last time, it refused to touch them. And the small animals Becker and Quincy had killed for food on young Mars gave the humans no calories or sustenance whatsoever. They might have smelt nice, when they cooked, but that was it.

This time, the creature smelt them as food, that was obvious. Strange, though, because it seemed to look the same. Was its DNA somehow different? The answer Connie supposed, would have to be *yes*. It was odd because the smaller animals looked like food to the humans, especially when it came time to cook them. The scent was intoxicating.

It didn't seem to matter to us, whether DNA was left or right-handed, yet to the creature, it somehow knew. It had forewarning of a calorific deficit, that we didn't possess. Very strange, she reckoned...as we saw ourselves as the highest of life-forms. In some ways we were, and in some ways we clearly weren't.

*   *   *

The creature's assumed direction of travel was based solely on what they had seen. Of course, it could have turned around or circled back. Connie admitted they knew *nothing* about its behaviour.

If it had doubled back or turned around, all their calculations were moot. Any noise, *anywhere*, was listened out for very carefully. As long as they did that, they felt like they were safe from the creature. There also might be more than one of them, so listening out for any sound from any direction was critical.

Toenails and footsteps or any part thereof would be their warning. Sound was their friend. Connie worried about stealth and cunning. They knew *of* this creature but nothing about it. How did it hear, how and in what light did it see? For all they knew it may see in infra-red or even gravity-waves. *Anything was possible*, she supposed anxiously. Maybe, despite what they thought, it was further up the food-chain than humans. If that was the case, they were in very serious trouble indeed.

Connie knew they couldn't concern themselves with what they would never know. They had to keep it as simple as possible and at this stage, stick to what they knew. When it moved, the creature made noise, they could *hear* it...that was their weapon. Use their ears. It wasn't much, but it was something.

That would remain their early detection system. Connie hoped like hell it hadn't learnt stealth, which it probably had. She knew if it hadn't, it'd be the first predator she knew of, that hadn't. It didn't bode well for them, Connie knew, but they couldn't base anything on what they didn't know. Or weren't absolutely sure about.

Becker spoke very quietly, 'where did that ugly fucker come from though?' His first words were predictable. He looked behind himself and to the side, eyes as wide as they could go. His eyes were dilated with sheer terror, expecting anything from anywhere to attack and disembowel them.

'It can't live here,' Emma squeaked, she could no longer keep it in, 'it's biological like us...but there's nothing to eat here, right? There are only cylinders...it won't eat *them*. They're made of...metal, or something hard. At best, it's something ceramic. Totally and utterly indigestible – all of it.'

'Emma is right,' Dimitri said, 'that thing is *totally* out of place in here. Like us. It doesn't belong. It doesn't, it can't live-

'*You're all bloody correct – okay?*' Connie broke in, eyeing each of them seriously. 'The creature, *like us*, doesn't belong here,' Connie agreed, 'but it somehow is here. *Best we get used to it*. It must have eaten *something*, but we haven't seen anything organic since we got here. This thing seems much more at home in a forest where there's plenty of prey, but not so much here.' Connie looked around at the group. It wasn't a pretty sight. All of them were looking down at the ground sombrely, expecting the creature to come back for another go at some point. Probably soon.

Like her, none of them had any idea about the creature – after all, it was alien, how could they? Experience with its behaviour was zero. So, all they could realistically do was look and listen and use human intuition to protect themselves. If it had learnt stealth like many predators on Earth, they'd probably be trapped and killed, then eaten. *Great*.

'Maybe it's just arrived,' Connie added, 'Perhaps it's here for the same reason we are – *fuck knows*. We'd be better off just accepting it and figuring out a way to hide from the damned thing.' She stared directly at Emma and nodded at her.

'The better question is *why*?' Connie said. 'Now, that's worth thinking about - *why* is the fucking thing here?' All of them pondered it, extremely confused and without any sort of insight into the beast itself, why it was here, and why in God's name *they* were here. Just minor questions. Apart from it all being Minan-related, they had no clue.

So far there was a sphere, cylinders and a single creature. a complete mystery to all of them. Connie gawked around herself and after doing a complete circle, looking up and around, she agreed it was all a horrible nonsense.

Becker was intermittently grunting and groaning while Connie spoke, apparently close to butting in. Connie kept talking, despite him, 'so, we know *nada, zilch, nothing*, we assume it must be Minan who is orchestrating all this bullshit, it has to be, but why...*why* has the little fucker sent us and that butt-ugly creature here, of all places? '*Why, why, why?*' Connie shrieked. She was beside herself and scowled at Becker long and hard when she had finished.

Becker's mind was racing, searching for answers...there simply had to be some...didn't there? 'It seems ridiculous to bring us here...with that creature running around. It's hardly a safe bloody environment. In fact, it's downright dangerous to be here.'

'If you talk any louder Becker, it might hear you. *Keep it down for fuck's sakes*...it's only about a kay away and the environment is very quiet indeed.' She eyed him, focussing on his stupid face, tapping her foot and shaking her head. 'I'm sure it'd love to hear from you. Trouble is, it'd find us as well.' Connie gaped at him like an insect at a picnic, gawking at him in disbelief. 'Seriously...what is wrong with you?' He smiled faintly in return but didn't say a thing.

'Let's just do what we can do and walk quietly in the opposite direction to that thing,' Connie said, managing a small, bleak smile and eyed Becker who nodded back at her. 'Keep noise to a minimum and listen for *any* noise beyond the group, who knows how many of those creatures are aboard.' Unblinking, her eyes were dilated with fear. Connie was deadly serious - she realised the stakes. For whatever reason, it was life and death.

Emma had assumed, based on nothing but fresh air, that there was only one of those things. Dimitri was of the same mind. The horror of their situation had just magnified significantly. If there was ten or a hundred of the creatures running around, they really were in deep shit. Emma was already worried, now she genuinely feared for her and everyone's lives. She walked a little lighter on her feet and turned her head to look everywhere. Emma did a full 360 to make sure there was nothing anywhere, including behind her.

They'd walked and walked, and then walked a bit more, listening carefully all the time, and they had seen tens of thousands of cylinders go by on the left and untold amounts of the silvery hull go by on the right. In all that time, they hadn't heard a single sound that wasn't Becker's stomach gurgling and begging for anything biological. He needed food and fluid desperately.

Near the outside hull, ahead, Connie saw a dirty smudge come into view as she ambled forward. On the ground, well before the smudge solidified into anything they could recognise, was a golden necklace, strewn untidily over the floor. It was close and shone in the dim light.

She stopped, bent over and picked it up, tossing it from hand to hand. As soon as she was close enough to have a good look at the gold object, she recognized it for what it was, or at least what she suspected. Impossible as it might have been – and "impossible" it was. Yet, physics said it was okay.

The necklace was her own, she could tell that because it had a photograph of her God-daughter in the locket. What the hell was happening now...*how could that possibly be?* Connie stumbled forward and rubbed her chin hard, still gaping at it, giving a short gasp. It was senseless. She was wearing the damned thing around her neck. Add it to the fucking pile, she thought. *This one though was right on top.* Connie was completely stunned and dropped it back on the ground, where it was now sprawled once again.

Short answer was, this was impossible, because she was wearing the stupid thing. Connie looked down and there it was, literally hanging around her neck. Now there were *fucking* two of them. One was in her hand which she'd just picked up again and one was hanging around her neck. *Go figure,* didn't do this event justice. She was thinking deeply and trying like mad to apply logic but kept coming up with absolute nonsense. Schrodinger's thought-experiment was high in her mind.

Connie fingered the gold necklace she'd just picked up. The same one had been hanging around her neck for more than five years. Both necklaces incredibly, and as she suspected, were identical, apart from the fact that one had been spread untidily on the floor of this alien edifice.

So, she had one around her neck and there was one in her palm. They were the same necklace. Both held identical photos. The first question was obvious. *WTF?*

Connie looked straight ahead and viewed what was initially an unfocussed "something" on the portside of their direction of travel but closer, coming into focus, was a truly horrible and quite irrational scene just ahead. Questions of how and why were totally forgotten on first sight of what was a ghastly mess. Schrodinger fairly slapped Connie in the face as she gawked at it.

It looked like the aftermath of a dreadful car accident. Three bodies were slumped against the silver wall, each about a metre apart. Where were the other remains? That was the obvious first question, after the nausea departed...the second question almost defied description.

In front of them was a nightmarish vision that posed so many questions, Connie didn't dare think about them. She already felt dizzy and faint, just looking at it. In front of them were three bloodied and partly eaten, very dead bodies, Becker, well most of him anyway, Dimitri and Emma. There were various chunks of them missing, presumably eaten or ripped away.

The horror story seemed incomplete, though, because where was she? Connie felt like puking, taking short, quick gasps. She would never forget the putrid smell of death. The odour was pungent and genuinely horrible, not unlike rotting fruit. Apart from the necklace, where was she?

Blood was everywhere - sprayed over the walls and pooled on the floor of the facility, and they were huge, deep red puddles. Litres of dark blood had been spilled and it was everywhere. That, and chunks of flesh that floated freely in the blood. Becker reckoned it was unusual for a predator to leave anything behind. Connie firstly told him to shut it, and secondly, told him even animals from another planet would probably find him offensive. To that, he had no response.

'*Oh shit, oh fuck, oh God,*' Connie screamed, gawking at the chaotic and macabre scene. '*Us...why...how,* it can't be us, we can't be, we're here...alive...and they're over their dead and eaten. We can't be dead and alive at the same time...can we?' Connie stared at Becker in terrified despair, thinking about Schrodinger again, and scared to death, with eyes that weren't blinking and were close to bursting. She wanted to speak but there was no voice, only a dry, crackly hiss, so she swallowed a few times and eventually found saliva and the words.

Instead of too much saliva, she had none. Very unlike her. She realised how upset she was and held a hand to her chest and tried to calm down and slow her breathing. Connie took another glance at the mess and knew it wasn't going to happen.

'*This is not happening,*' Connie stuttered loudly. She immediately thought she must be having a nightmare but soon realised this was pretty much as real as it got. She wasn't even part of the horrible group on show. God only knows what happened to her. Had she escaped or was she eaten entirely. Maybe her body was somewhere else? She took deep, slow breaths to avoid passing out. Once more, she felt like vomiting – the smell combined with the horrid, crazy sight was overwhelming.

Connie continued to gasp and pant, trying to right herself, with her back to the mess and her head in her hands. Connie knew she had to stop looking at it. If she didn't, *well*...unconsciousness lay in that direction.

The whole thing sounded and looked insane...completely card-carrying nuts. Connie knew she was alive, and she found it hard to believe she was even asking the insane question. But that said...where the fuck was she, and was she alive or dead? If she was dead, there must be something left, surely? And if she was dead, why was she alive here and breathing with the group, who were also themselves dead just a few paces away? Connie bit her lip and rubbed her chin – none of it made any sense whatsoever. She found it hard to believe she was considering all this insanity without laughing uproariously. The whole episode was truly ridiculous. The rest of the group were similarly dumbfounded and appalled.

Emma gaped, along with Dimitri and Becker. They all stared and wondered how in God's name it could have happened. Dead, yet they were also alive. Killed there, yet not killed here. How in the name of God did that shit happen? Connie thought it invoked elements of time travel or quantum theory, but she really couldn't add much more. None of them could even offer up a guess. In the human book it was too bizarre for words. All of it was absolutely senseless.

Emma was alive and well where she stood, yet dead at the wall. It had to involve superposition, but that only happened in the quantum world over really short distances...didn't it...?

Connie gave up, she didn't know, and probably never would unless she was told or shown. The truth was – no one had a clue why it was like this. The whole dead and alive thing had them stumped, but they assumed it was the work of Minan. If you could make a universe, then this would be a literal walk in the park.

Dead Becker was without legs, and all three of the bodies had copious bite marks, deep slashing cuts and missing limbs, mainly arms. Blood was everywhere, over their broken bodies and over the floor. These were fresh kills, which carried the question of when it happened. Forget how and why, they had no idea about that, but the "when" must have been recently because the blood looked relatively fresh.

There was something up ahead which was probably dead Connie, meaning the thing hadn't eaten her either, just killed her, and left her body slumped against the wall, like the others. That probably meant it was coming back later to gorge on dead Connie. The dead bodies were owned by the creature now.

No doubt the dead, broken body was the work of the creature, the teeth and the sharp, hook-like talons, not to mention the temperament and the teeth. It had the personal weapons that could do untold damage to something soft and delicate like the human body.

Connie walked ahead and paused, strangely drawn to her own remains. They looked ghastly and very, very odd. She struggled with the dizziness and the faintness. Looking at your own dead body was an intensely unpleasant experience, made worse by all the blood and the shocking stench that surrounded it for some distance. The dead, open eyes were ghastly indeed. It was very hard to look at, especially when your body has been eviscerated and partially eaten by a wild, seemingly crazed predator.

Dead Connie was slumped near the wall with an arm simply ripped off and covered in dark blood that also pooled around and partly under her corpse. She hadn't been eaten, *just killed*, like a cat that plays with a mouse, kills it and then leaves it somewhere the master is sure to find it. The worst thing, once again, were the grey and open, dead eyes. The missing arm wasn't much better.

'*Fucking hell,*' she cried, ogling her own dead body that was totally broken and mutilated, putting the back of her hand against her nose and leaving it there. Apart from the horrendous sight, the smell of blood was like bags and bags of wet coins, and was thoroughly overpowering and generally just horrific. Connie turned around and faced the cylinders, she didn't want to see it, but the smell was enough to make her retch whichever way she faced.

Connie felt nothing but rage for the thing that had mauled her and then killed her stone-dead, with nothing but confusion over the way it happened. She was biting her lip and blinking like a madwoman. She had no idea how it might have happened. She certainly had no recollection of it, despite it clearly being her.

Deep in thought about it, all Connie could come up with was good old Minan. He was responsible, rightly or wrongly, for everything that seemed senseless and downright crazy. That was her take on things and to her it seemed logical and right. *"He" did it.*

Connie agreed with Emma – they needed to get out of this place...*right now.* They also wanted to avoid meeting the creature again, *at all costs* - it'd be back soon enough to eat the leftovers, and then look for more. They had to get the hell out of this hellish sphere.

They came together on the far side of dead Connie. None of them took more than one look, and tried not to breathe and swallowed hard, walking faster as they passed a partially eaten corpse that looked so much like it had been involved in a terrifying shark attack.

Connie glared at each of them long and hard. 'We can ignore the elephant...but seriously, how, *why?*' She was totally and utterly dumbfounded by what had happened. It still seemed impossible...yet, apparently, *somehow*, it had happened, the results were right there in front of them. They couldn't be denied.

They were as dead as they were ever going to get. Yet, all four of them were also still alive, somehow observing their dead selves. What they would term truly impossible had somehow been made possible.

Minan would be the only one who could explain it, but he was absent. He must have invoked a time slippage, or superposition maybe, but the mechanics of it, Minan himself would only know. None of them understood it. If this was a game, they were merely the players. There seemed to be a higher force controlling things, like a videogame, but in very real life.

Connie's best guess was that a law from the quantum world was brought into the macro world of gravitation. She felt her head in a tightening vice as she considered it. She felt nauseous and woozy. This was all way beyond human brain comprehension - Connie knew that much.

It wasn't much of a theory, but at this stage, it was all she had. Emma and Dimitri agreed because they had little else to offer. All Becker heard was a monkey banging loudly on a tambourine in his head.

So, it was back to walking, listening and looking *very* carefully indeed. This massive orange sphere, or whatever it happened to be on the outside, was obscenely quiet on the inside. That was a good thing, she guessed, they could hear no toenails scraping on the floor, no *nothing*. It was a very good thing for them – they could literally hear a pin drop so they should be able to detect anything louder...and outside the group. Connie could hear Becker's breathing, it was quite loud and raspy, not to mention extremely annoying. No-one else breathed like him. Apart from him, the silence was very useful.

Connie's ears were wired and twitching, straining to catch any sound that wasn't of them. She could hear or see nothing that was alarming. *Stealth*, once again, raised its head. Were they walking into a trap? Was the creature intelligent enough to employ a trap? Big cats weren't intelligent as we would define it, and on occasion they used stealth, in fact many meat-eaters relied on it didn't they? Like lions, crocs and bears. They lived by ambushing their prey. Images filled Connie's mind that were concerning to say the least. Thoughts of being caught in a net like butterflies didn't do anything for her state-of-mind. Advanced instinct brought it, forget intelligence, it wasn't needed. All that was required apparently, was an over-arching need to eat and stay alive.

She was too scared to bring it up with the group. If indeed the creature used stealth and ambush, and trapped them or managed to sneak up on them, forewarning helped little. It would be too late. They probably realised it too, if they didn't, they should have. Connie wouldn't be bringing it up – it wouldn't help, it'd be a hindrance, certainly to their state-of-mind.

Connie started walking with the group, expecting to see anything, listening and searching ahead and to the left, on and under the cylindrical peaks, carefully, *everywhere*. Looking for any movement at all, no matter how slight or anything that looked odd or out of place. Nothing was heard or seen. The entire area, apart from their own footfalls, was as quiet as a church in prayer. There was zero movement or sound that they could see or hear. Nothing to raise fears.

They had little choice. Onward they continued, more torturous walking, ambling along in single file, with Becker still at the back and Connie still at the front. After about an hour of relentless walking, Becker was almost on his knees.

Becker's feet and his thighs were on fire and his knees weren't much better. Connie too, was sitting on the ground with her back against the wall of the structure, rubbing her feet, with her Baffin's beside her untidily.

'That's no way to treat your *come fuck-me* shoes Con,' he said with a brief, very tired, guffaw.

'Fuck *you*...how's that?' Connie was in no mood for his irritating Beckerisms. She too, was tired. Her feet felt like she'd been walking on hot coals. God knows how Becker was. The entire group was spent big time.

Connie looked closely at the substance that formed the material holding back the vacuum of space. She was aware that this place was only created by algorithm, but what the hell, she thought. This Sphere and the stuff inside it was as real as anything else in the Universe. From her seated position with her back against it, the wall was very warm, almost hot, and using her finger, it felt like a liquid, but when she withdrew her digit, it was bone dry. Strange substance, that's all she knew.

Connie pushed her finger deeper this time and right at finger length, was an unyielding surface. She didn't know how hard it was, that would involve putting her hand into it and really pushing, which she preferred not to do. Safe to say it wasn't your standard wall. Made of what and called what, she didn't have a clue? Kneeling down, the floor itself seemed very standard indeed, being hard to the touch and easy to walk over. Although if you jumped on it, the floor became soft. To call it intelligent might be over-selling it, but it made you wonder, she thought, surveying the whole place closely. It was definitely a "smart" floor. The walls -who knows?

All of them were famished and had run dry of the water they brought with them, from the craft back on Proxima B. Everything was gone – liquid and certainly any form of sustenance. They desperately needed to eat and drink, especially Becker who licked his lips at her and made her feel quite uncomfortable. The big lug needed any form of consumption desperately.

Connie was certain none of them were or would be regarded as food by Becker, but it was pretty clear that he'd eat most anything. None of them, not even Becker, thought they were near critical, but they all felt mightily scratchy.

Connie, being the eagle-eye of the group, saw movement between the cylinders, the creature *was* coming back, and even though she couldn't see its massive head, she could see it was drooling, massive gobs of thick saliva dropping over itself and the floor. It was clearly on the hunt for food.

The thing was hungry and thinking about food and probably a new kill. It was coming back around to hopefully meet up with some poor stragglers like us, and if not, eat the leftovers from its first kill. It had done a complete loop of this place and wasn't far from coming face-to-face with them. It was time to move off the main drag, or panic or at least do *something different* from what they were doing.

Emma wondered how in God's name she went from being one of the first colonists on Proxima B to this – battling some sort of predator in a very strange land, location...*fuck knows*. It was more bizarre than a dreadful, horrid nightmare. She really meant it; the whole episode was more fantastical than even the most drug-induced hallucination.

The creature was slowly making its way down a narrow path in front of them and they were fairly much shielded from its view. But that wouldn't last. Soon enough, it would see them and break into a death-sprint from which they had no hope of avoiding. It would catch the humans quite quickly and kill them, Becker would be the first to go, because he was the slowest.

Clearly, the creature enjoyed killing, like any predator, Connie reckoned. She thought about her cat and how it treated mice it caught and she shuddered. Connie couldn't count the number of dead, headless mice and rats left on her doorstep or bed by her cat. It did that by instinct, because these things were identified as prey, and had the temerity to move.

If the creature saw their group, it was goodnight. They would be caught by this thing, no doubt, run down, captured and killed. It had heavily muscled legs and could no doubt, sprint really fast if it wanted to – to catch prey. Then kill it, really unpleasantly.

'*Under, under, for fuck's sake get under,*' Connie whispered to them, as forcefully as she could, without speaking too loudly. Last thing they wanted was to alert the stupid thing. 'Put your butt all the way in Becker, not just your frigging *head.*' God, he was such a fool, Connie thought hatefully. He was just like a fucking fat Ostrich, she reckoned.

They were a little further away from the main thoroughfare on this place than the last time, so hopefully Becker's polar bear smell wouldn't reach that far.

Emma and Dimitri seemed none the wiser or were too polite to say anything. Maybe they assumed it was the left-over odour from the creature. Connie knew better. Unfortunately, she knew what an unwashed Becker smelt like.

The toenails-on-the-floor noise was palpable in the silent conditions. If they, and by "they" she meant Minan, had wanted to choose a fearsome, odious, repulsive and lethal creature, they'd selected very well indeed. If there was no "choosing" involved, she'd be very, very surprised. To think that this thing dropped into this place through some random process was a bridge too far – that would be truly unbelievable. Murphy's law would be cracked open and broken forever.

This creature was a made-to-order killer. Any creature would be out of place here, but such a killer was very ironic indeed. Connie reckoned the whole lot was very suspicious, and she was sceptical about its sudden appearance here in the land of cylinders. Connie was pretty sure the creature had been chosen for them. The real question was *"why"* it had been chosen. Why such a vicious, horrible, efficient killer?

The thing slowed and stopped at their alley-way and shrieked a sputum-filled cry of insane hunger and deprivation. The creature's frustrated and hideous scream was so loud as to make their ears ring and reverberate with a blood-freezing noise that kept giving and giving. Connie wondered if the dreadful noise would ever stop. It was truly awful.

Becker's hair, such as it was, almost stood on end, both Dimitri and Emma held each other tightly and prayed silently. They all imagined how it would feel to get caught by this thing. Connie hoped they all realised that their ability to be quiet was front and centre in staying alive. She especially worried about Becker who wasn't known for doing much right. If he did anything wrong here, it was a rapid and unpleasant goodnight and he would lead the creature to the rest of the group. That was very bad.

Becker, in his mind's-eye, saw himself grabbed by the sickle-and-barb claws and ripped under the bottom cylinder and gorged on alive. He did his best to put that image out of his mind. Becker pulled his butt further in and tried desperately to hold his breath. He wisely equated making noise with certain death. Connie could breathe a little easier. At least the clod was making an effort.

The creature looked down the alley with its multi-panelled eyes, drooled and panted, wheezed and snuffled, swivelling its head like a dog, and smelt dead Connie's remains, which lay in the distance nearby.

It smelt Becker, but the remains of dead Connie were just too appealing to its primal senses. It needed to eat desperately – it'd been a long time between meals.

It stood to its full height, which must have been seven feet, and shook its head and body like a wet dog. At the same time, it made a strange whining-growling noise. The creature had a final sniff above the group. It seemed to know they were there but couldn't find them, so it gave up and moved on. It wanted the dead remains of Connie to feast on which it knew from experience, would offer no resistance.

The thing made its way swaggeringly up the main path, drooling all the way and rubbing its sabres together as though it was sharpening them for an assault. It sounded like clanging two large swords together. The sound of toenails scraping and grating on the floor commenced again and gradually receded as the creature made its way back down the corridor toward the alluring scent of dead Connie.

After a few minutes of downtime, re-gaining the power of locomotion, they withdrew from the shielding cylinders and stood up as quietly as they could, trying not to hit anything or make *any* noise to alert the creature that they were emerging back on the track.

Connie had a single finger plastered over mouth, imploring them all to be quiet, if they didn't know that already. If they didn't work that one out by themselves, there was a massive problem.

Otherwise, the creature might turn around and then God help them all. Like any predator, the creature sought sustenance by expending the least amount of energy. Therefore, it was their job to make their detection as difficult as possible.

'Christ, it stunk of meat, and I don't know what,' Becker said, puffing and wiping his nose, deeply affected by its scent and sound. 'Not to mention the way it looked,' he said, while holding his nose.

'Yes, it did stink of meat and *"I don't know what"*, under the cylinders, and then that creature arrived,' Connie said, giggling uncontrollably like a schoolgirl. Emma and Dimitri were grinning too. It broke the awful tension of life and death and blood.

Becker looked at them, darting his gaze to everyone, offering a fake smile and a goofy face, and then he whispered something under his breath. He wasn't happy, that was obvious. Becker didn't like being the butt of a joke, although if it was someone else, *no worries*. He was fully in.

*   *   *

'*Whatever*,' Becker said quietly and petulantly. 'We need to walk, so let's get about doing it,' he said firmly. That was something he never thought he'd say, but there it was. They could still hear the noise of the creature receding into the background, closing in on human remains presumably. All they wanted was to move slowly and noiselessly in the opposite direction. Attracting no attention, hopefully.

All of them had their shoes tied together and all but Emma had the items hanging around their necks, she said it hurt there and had them hanging from a wrist. It didn't matter where the shoes were, as long as their way forward was quiet. Think "mouse", Connie said over and over. She knew noise was their enemy.

After some minutes of trudging along silently, they heard a bloodcurdling scream of utter guttural pleasure. As the creature presumably hooked into dead Connie who was spread over the ground on the main pathway some distance behind them.

The creature ate at least some of dead Connie's body, in a violent orgasm of tearing and chewing. Her remains might be all gone, they didn't know. Didn't wanna know. The roaring was very loud indeed.

'*I don't wanna meet that fucker ever again*,' Becker spat, turning away from where the scream came, covering his mouth.

'*Duh*,' Connie spouted, of course you don't want to meet that fucking thing again, goes without saying.' She tried and failed to put the horrible visions out of her mind. Her recollections were death-filled and macabre. Full of blood and deeply cut flesh. Connie also remembered when she first saw the horrible thing in the dimness under Sydney. How in the good fuck did the damn thing get *there*? And how did it get from there to *here*. There were a lot of things that needed an answer. But they weren't getting a thing. Guesses were useless and inevitably came back to Minan, which did them no good at all.

Resuming their trudging and slogging, Becker wondered if there was a way out of this place or whether they were doomed to be doing this forever, well, until the lack of liquid and sustenance bit too deeply. It would be the worst Groundhog Day imaginable. They could potentially keep walking until they were *totally* done – no food, no water – just dead.

Or until the fucking creature caught up with them or trapped them, anyway. They wouldn't and couldn't evade it forever. One day soon, they would end up on its dinner plate. Becker reckoned they'd end up like the Russian cosmonauts or their dead versions anyway, that was the future. Partly eaten, dead and mummified.

Their only options to avoiding a very bloody death, was to kill it, or befriend it, and the chances of either were close to zero.

*   *   *

They walked as a group until they could go no further. Becker's legs had seized up like an old clunker that had consumed its last drop of oil. He cried out in pain and collapsed to the ground...sore, exhausted, hungry, and desperately needing to drink fluid. Becker had a massive headache, stomach-ache and was fatigued almost to the point of unconsciousness.

Normally, Becker would down a few Advil or have a couple of glasses of scotch to cure a headache. Here, he had no such option. All he could do was put up with it. Same as his knees and thighs, they ached and throbbed and were close to unbearable and he had nothing to treat them with apart from his hands, and a masseuse he wasn't. Despite his manipulation, his legs still hurt like the *bejesus*.

Connie looked at Becker and clenched her jaw. She understood that his legs hurt, but *seriously,* all their legs hurt, not just his. His pain threshold was so low, it made her look super-strong. Connie watched Becker rub both legs furiously and she shook her head, feeling sorry for the old bugger – this was no place for him. He was way too soft.

If the creature heard him, Becker didn't care...actually he did, but they were far enough away, and he was pretty sure they wouldn't be heard. Becker was about twenty metres behind the main group and they too were sitting on the floor and attending to sore muscles by variously rubbing and working on their legs.

Thirst pervaded the group and it, as much as anything else, was making the group feel like hell. Hunger went without saying. Becker could easily murder several pizzas.

'We *get* it Becker...you're hungry. We all have to suck it up – *even you.*' Connie scrutinised his face closely. This time, she felt like saying *"oh poor bugger"* but didn't. In truth, she was too tired to deal with the bullshit that would follow.

'Not a step more. Please,' Becker sobbed, 'I feel like I've already walked a fucking marathon.' The old sod had clearly reached a state of physical ruin. It was hardly surprising, Connie thought, which brought with it the familiar old chestnut – how fucking big was this place? Seeing it from the outside, it clearly had dimensions – so, what were they? From the inside, it was monstrous.

Connie remembered what the damn thing looked like from outside, it was covered with acicular spikes and was the size of a Goddamn moon, so the space inside was hardly a surprise. The Sphere itself was gargantuan. From outside, it appeared truly huge. So, the inside "room" was fair enough.

'*Jesus*, toughen up Becker, the curve is not far ahead...see?' Connie stabbed the air vigorously with her finger, gawking ahead to see the start of a wide U-turn at the end of what was a very long, straightish pathway that existed between the cylinders and the side of the Sphere. *Thank fuck for that*, she reckoned. Something a little different. That's what they all needed. Becker especially.

Becker gawked at it and knew the same never-ending path existed on the other side of this place, same as the one they were on. *Never-ending torture.* 'I honestly can't go on,' Becker moaned, in a pitch designed for maximum pity. Emma and Dimitri went to his aid. They actually entertained his bullshit. Despite being tired themselves, they went to Becker's aid. Connie just stood there, tapping her foot. She'd seen it all before. '*Oh Christ,*' Connie whispered under breath, seeing them going to his aid.

Becker kept trying to get up, but each time, he fell back down to the floor. They both grabbed him under the arm-pits and pulled him upright. He was like jelly as he tried his best to remain upright, wobbling to and fro, like someone with a serious vertigo issue. Connie eyed him harshly and shook her head, snorting.

Connie bared her teeth, before drawing a breath loudly, 'Seriously Becker, we need you to suck it up, like we have. No-one feels like walking right now...but there is *no* choice. Until we find what we're looking for, if we do, and whatever that might be, we *have to* walk. Understand that there is zero choice here. If we stay in one spot, we die.'

'We're not carrying you Becker, you'll have to do this yourself,' Dimitri said, and Emma nodded forcefully. 'You weigh a bloody ton,' the Russian said, wiping his brow and looking around, listening for sound. He thought he heard something but it was just his own stomach gurgling, which desperately needed food.

'Thanks a lot,' Becker said downcast, looking at Dimitri and sighing heavily, 'you're no twiggy yourself.'

'I ain't needing to be carried,' he replied.

'Either am I,' Becker said, and he meant it. He wouldn't be carried, *period*. He'd walk himself. Somehow.

If he moved at all, it would be under his own steam, he had *some* goddamn dignity. 'Anyway, we should join Connie.' He was keen to change the subject. Becker was pushed on, mainly by pride, ignoring his screaming leg muscles and knees. All of them re-joined Connie as a group. He immediately sat down or more accurately, fell down, while they contemplated their next move. Becker hoped it was to stay still but knew it wouldn't be.

Connie's brain was in overdrive, her head hammering with thought, despite its calorie and fluid deprived condition. She knew how important their next move could be. She knew everyone was exhausted and could barely move. Becker was a fucking disaster. Connie rubbed her chin and stroked her forehead. Why would Minan put them in such a monstrous situation?

None of it made sense – she remembered Harry, and his ability to simplify things, cut through the bullshit, even if it was only to add William of Occam to the brew. What was the simplest answer, irrespective of what humans thought or wanted?

She'd thought about it deeply and come up with zero. *Great.* Connie needed Harry here in person to think this situation through. He'd come up with something. Even if it was just crap that they could instantly discard. Or possibly it may have led to something a little better.

Perhaps something significant would crystallize in her brain as they walked around the bend where the straight path came near the other extremity of the sphere. Connie flourished her arms up and forward and came to her feet. All of them stood accordingly. Becker got to his feet very slowly, grunting and groaning all the way until he was sort of upright.

'Now I know how they felt on that river thing, all those years ago…Kwai wasn't it?' Becker had trouble even pushing air out.

'You honestly have no idea, do you?' Connie snapped, looking daggers at him. She snorted loudly and narrowed her eyes as she gaped at Becker and really looked closely. Connie could see the duress the poor old blighter was under and her glare softened as she inspected her own hands. She could see he wasn't just bullshitting - he was really and truly struggling to stand up.

'We go slowly and listen *very* carefully - with four sets of ears we should have reasonable forewarning of any trouble,' Connie made direct eye contact with everyone, lingering on Becker. He nodded back, even he seemed to understand. 'If we hear anything, we hide as a group, like before,' she said, surveying them all grimly. 'Under the, bottom-most cylinders,' she finished.

'What if that thing can hear like cats and dogs can,' Becker said, gawking around and pulling the back of his hair, generally looking nervous and fidgety.

'Well...we can't do anything about that,' Connie said, nodding. 'Now, we walk...slowly, quietly and listen and look for *anything*.'

The group set off and started walking, seeing the curve a few hundred metres ahead.

'*Hey*,' Becker quietly boomed from behind, making them come to a halt ahead of him.

'Keep your stupid voice down Becker,' Dimitri said,' pointing aggressively at him.

'Fine...I was trying to...I was just going to say, *boss-lady* said walk slowly and listen carefully, when does the first part start?'

Connie shook her head and stared at him vacantly. 'We *are* going slow, brainiac. *Jesus Christ*. Seriously, what a stooge,' she muttered quietly to herself. Connie gazed at Emma and Dimitri, 'just walk...he'll start soon enough.'

*   *   *

Still walking toward the bend, everything at "the end" of the straightish path came very slowly into view. Connie saw Minan and four, what would you call them, she wondered, searching her mind? Golden tornadoes sounded wrong. They were *totally unexpected* - she knew that much.

They were similar to what brought them here, all pretty much the same, but slightly different to the one's on Proxima B. They definitely moved less. The one's on the planet moved a lot, sucking up dust and dirt all over the place. These were quite still and barely moved on the ground at all. But they were still golden and strikingly beautiful.

Apart from that, they were almost identical to the one's on the planet that brought them here. These, like the others were golden and very strange...ethereal...very otherworldly. Becker's hair and in fact all the hair on everybody's body, had a strong magnetic-static reaction to the anomalies in front of them. All the hair on their bodies was pulled in the direction of the anomalies and stood up proudly on their skin. Becker and Emma went deeply red in the face when they gazed at them; and returned to normal when they didn't. The effect on the body was very odd indeed.

'That is another hurdle achieved,' Minan said, in his usual emotion-less, mouthless intonation. Connie was certain he only spoke English to accommodate humans. Because we had no hope of understanding anything unless it was in one of our home languages.

Just the nature of the beast. Minan could probably speak anything if he had to.

'Two to go,' he said, eyeing all of them with brilliant blue eyes. They were clearly getting brighter.

Connie glared directly back at him, "two to go" she repeated? Until what,' she asked? 'What the hell does "two to go" mean,' she asked herself, staring mindlessly at Minan?

Minan watched her silently with his laser-blue eyes and held his head very still. No doubt he heard her. Minan made no attempt to answer the question and simply stared back, vacantly, as if he'd entered some sort of off-line mode. His eyes were still blue and staring though - just less bright. He didn't move a muscle, looking like a statue.

'*Hello?*' She questioned loudly. Nothing. Just silence and nothing. Connie glared at him curiously. 'How was it that there were copies of us running around this place?'

His bright blue eyes were back and alert. 'They weren't copies and they weren't running around anywhere,' Minan said mechanically, moving his vision to Connie, still staring with very bright blue eyes now. 'Time was reversed using something similar to Lagrangian t-symmetry which allowed it to run backward as far as I needed.' Minan suddenly turned around and faced the hull of the ship, which left Connie peering at his back, which she didn't like. He'd finished talking or taking questions. Conversation over, apparently.

'Why the hell did he keep reversing time, and don't say because he could,' Becker asked? And if we-'

Minan turned back to them and instantly started talking over Becker by direct vocal injection. 'Because you kept failing,' Minan said, 'hardly surprising, given your history,' he nonchalantly added. 'It took you five attempts to get this far,' the boy finished, turning back around to face the hull. 'You are only here because I intervened,' he said inside them.

Emma and Dimitri both looked at Minan in wide-eyed astonishment. They knew he said something important, but they had no idea what. They really didn't understand him. Both continued to stare at Minan with their mouths open, waiting for more, but nothing came. Dimitri shook his head like a dog.

Minan didn't move or make any further sound. The answer was pretty obvious, he thought. Nothing further required answering. So, Minan ignored further questions.

Connie eyed the kid who was still facing away from them, and realised he wasn't going to answer *any* questions. She was Connie iteration #5, and so was everybody else - iteration #5. The other four had been killed and partially eaten by the creature or creatures that roamed around this Godawful place. Connie eyed the place they were in and realised for the first time, what it was...this was a fucking killing-field. There was no apparent means of escape. Four versions of themselves had died trying.

Except that they kept coming back, thanks to Minan. Connie supposed she should thank Minan, after all, she had no memory of being killed at all. That made sense because it wouldn't work if she did. It'd be ridiculous...not to mention horrible to the max. Connie remembered only one continuous timeline, so how it was done, was a complete mystery to her.

Minan wasn't saying a thing, so as a source of information about all this, he was useless, and was still facing the hull. He was silent on everything.

'So, which of these things should we use?' Connie spoke loudly, pointing with her hand, hoping against hope that Minan would turn around and answer the question. There were four golden objects in front of them – each looked identical to the other. If we were expected to choose, we'd have nothing better than eenie, meeney, miney, moe to choose. And that was no good for anyone.

Minan eventually did turn around and addressed them with eyes as brightly blue as they remember them ever being. His eyes now looked as though they were blazing with knowledge and memory and awareness, perhaps memories of the future. To what extent he was artificially augmented, if at all, they had no idea. Thinking "anything was possible" seemed a bit overused but it definitely related well to Minan. They knew next to nothing about him. Just that he was mega-advanced and was the birth mother and father of both humanity and the Universe.

Minan stared at Connie, no blinking and eyes a pale blue now, a colour that didn't vary, and they bored sharply into her. She waited for the voice, there was static between her ears. He said, 'you must choose the galactic coordinates for Earth and go through that object and that object only. I will not be repeating,' Minan said, still staring fixedly at Connie. 'The others will take you to places where it will be difficult to survive.' Minan walked closer. 'Choose one wisely and move through it, the numerals are thus.' Minan flourished with an arm. 'No environment suits are necessary for any of the objects.' He definitely considered Connie to be the leader, he still stared at her indignantly.

With a sweep of his arm, numbers appeared horizontally on each object. They were binary and looked like so-much gobbledegook.

Becker saw the numbers and let out a huge, exasperated splutter. '*Oh shit,*' he said on first sight of them. He wasn't happy at all. Becker watched in horror and agitation as the dark symbols fell downward from each golden anomaly.

'What the fuck does stupid math have to do with it?' He shook his head and let out another huge snort. *'It's a joke, right?'* Becker instantly knew it wasn't, Minan definitely wasn't the joking or fun kind. Quite the opposite really. They were the same number-format as before, Becker thought, feeling totally useless. He looked closely but nothing specific came to him. Becker needed Joe or Harry by his side.

He was unable to read binary for shit. That sort of stuff was left to other people with thicker glasses. Becker equated binary numbers with math and nerds for some reason. Math lay at its base certainly, as it did for decimal numbers, but it wasn't math per se. No one bothered to try and change his mind though.

```
#1 was 000111011110110101011001111010010100
#2     000111011110110101011001001011101000
#3     000111011110110101011001001010010110
#4     100111011110101011001001111010111001
```

'*Seriously, what does he take us for?* Becker spat. If he wants to help us, can't he just do it? I mean, is this supposed to help us make a decision or *not* to make it? *Jesus shit,*' he breathed noisily and cracked his knuckles, looking murderously at the boy. 'How the hell can that crap be an answer to anything.' He shook his head in dismay. 'I've seen binary before, but that doesn't mean I *get* it,' Becker said ruefully. 'Like before, I hope *someone* can answer that, because I sure as shit can't.' Becker gazed hopefully at the group and didn't much like the faces he saw. '*Fuck,*' he finished and looked downward, believing they were done and dusted.

*   *   *

Becker was fidgeting and squirming and holding his breath, wondering what Connie would say this time. Last time, they had Joe and Quincy and Vic to lean on. In any event, he thought, she knew this crap relatively well. Certainly, better than he did, which wasn't hard. It was computer language, that's all he knew. "

Connie looked at the back of the kid and really thought about it. 'Is this in degrees and minutes and seconds Minan? You did say *galactic coordinates*, right?' Connie stared directly at his back.

He turned around and a loud "yes" reverberated in her head. She thumbed her chin and gazed calmly at the numbers. Emma, Dimitri and Becker had no idea at all – it may as well have been written in a foreign language they didn't understand at all. Hebrew maybe. The numbers meant absolutely nothing to any of them. Nor did they know the answer to the question. Nought out of two was very bad indeed. A terrific way to start, Emma thought. She prayed that Connie herself could work it out.

Thankfully, the numerals seemed to mean something to Connie. She gazed at all of them, one by one and repeated the same process several times.

'Be aware that no further time reversal will occur,' Minan trumpeted, in his pitch-less intonation that they received directly, without any imposition on his craniofacial muscles. 'I am now unable to do it. We do not have enough surplus time assembled.'

Becker squirmed, 'So, no pressure, right?' Minan didn't bother looking at Becker, during or after he spoke.

Connie glanced at Becker and then focussed on the numbers, and then stared at the group for an extended period. She was clearly thinking about it hard. 'I remember Vic talking about it and Harry arguing the point...yes, not surprising, right? Anyway, that's not the point, what is important is that the orbit of Earth is fairly circular and the initial longitude and latitude of the orbit wasn't anywhere near zero.' She rubbed her chin and gawked at the daunting numerals.
Connie spoke more to herself than the group. 'But I don't really fully understand binary numbers.' She wrinkled her brow and bit her lip as she continued to assess the numbers. 'Please, add something if you know something...*anything*.' Connie eyed Emma and Dimitri in particular, but both remained silent. Becker was visibly sweating and crossed his arms across his chest. He saw what was happening and wasn't happy. He knew next to nothing about binary numbers, but he seriously objected to not being asked.

'*Heeeeyyyy, what about me?*' Becker spat at them. He was totally left out and considered pretty much superfluous to the discussion. As soon as he'd said something, he wished he hadn't been asked, and left it at that.

'Okay, go Becker, what do you know about binary and all that?' Connie asked, flourishing her arm, and offering Becker a tight smile and a nod, which in this case meant *go for it.* Everyone looked at him. He was still visibly sweating.

'I actually can't add anything on this occasion, but that doesn't mean I don't want to be asked,' Becker said, clenching and unclenching his fingers. Becker nodded as though he'd added something useful.

Emma and Dimitri eyed Connie, who looked sideways at Becker and found him hard to believe, 'You are joking surely, *"on this occasion?"*, yeah okay, fine, whatever you say.' Connie turned away from him roughly, muttering disparaging comments under her breath.

Connie looked at all of them, steeling herself, putting her hands on her hips, realising how important this decision was to them all. 'If it's in degrees, using the galactic coordinate system I've heard of, it's around forty degrees, it certainly *isn't* zero. So, I go for number four,' Connie said, peering down and hugging herself with both arms, wondering, *hoping* she was right. She wasn't sure at all, and she didn't know binary numbers for shit. She relied on Joe or Harry for that, but clearly, they weren't here, so it was up to her.

Dimitri and Emma had never seen binary before and could add nothing. She felt like she was forgetting something significant though but couldn't quite put her finger on it. Connie desperately needed her old friend Joe with her. He'd know, she felt sure. Joe would know exactly what each numeral meant and he'd know the GCS for Earth.

In short, he'd know the answer to the question that was posed by Minan. What he wouldn't know and what no one knew, was why we had to answer the inane question in the first place. *And in binary*, a numbering system they weren't really familiar with. It was just like under the ice in Antarctica – it was all so inane and ridiculous. Connie didn't even wonder "why", it seemed this was how their civilisation rolled.

'So, we enter number four, Connie said as emphatically as she could, which in reality, was little more than a croak in the back of her throat.'

'That's all fine,' Emma agreed, 'but we're acting on the say-so of him.' She pointed at the black suited young creature with her eyes. 'Minan...I mean...who the hell is he? You tell me he's a virtual God, and has created everything around us...*everything*...how do we know you haven't been infected with some sort of hypnosis *something or other*?' She stared directly at Connie and was deadly serious and continued 'So, that you only think these things, you and Becker, but they aren't true, and Minan is not who you think he is. Alien okay, but is he just a naughty little boy?' Emma eyed Connie, scrutinising her face closely, waiting for her serious expression to break, but it didn't. Emma was very serious and almost accusatory.

Connie swallowed, wet her lips and furrowed her brow. 'I have to concede that it's a possibility, but everything Becker and I have been witness to suggests that was how it was...that what Minan says is real, or at least as real as things got. He's done things, shown us things and been in places we would consider impossible. Remember, he turned up at Proxima B. How did he get there? It certainly wasn't with us. Minan was just there. And there's a lot of evidence from our venture to Antarctica, which I can go into later, if indeed I choose the right code.'

'Okay,' Emma said, scrubbing a hand over her face, peeping furtively at everyone. 'I feel better having asked the question.' Emma lied. She still wasn't sure. Dimitri gawked at her with round eyes, 'you go girl.' He was a misogynist idiot like Becker.

Make your choice and enter, the creature you have evaded is not far away,' Minan said. He'd already turned around to face the hull. No one wanted to face that ugly, ferocious thing again. And this time, if the worst did happen, there would be no coming back, apparently. Dead would be dead for keeps.

'I say four,' Connie muttered. 'Everything points to it being the correct one.'

'Four,' Dimitri said.

'Four,' Emma said.

Becker looked from one to the other of them. 'Same,' he said. 'Make it so Connie.' He mumbled incoherently as he turned away from the group, suggesting he wasn't as confident as he sounded about entering number four. *Whatever,* he told himself. Becker didn't trust much, but he trusted Connie. And he didn't want to face that thing again.

Seeing the creature moving speedily down the path toward them was enough to get them moving quickly toward the line of billowing anomalies. They preferred *not* to make the creature's acquaintance again.

Connie remembered in a flash what happened the last time they were attempting this. In the wall, it was a disconformity of a strange blackness, this time, instead of sump oil and black, it was deep golden in colour. She just hoped like hell, she, *they*, had chosen correctly. If not, they'd probably end up back at Proxima B. In a place where medium-term survival was very unlikely indeed.

They all entered the anomaly they'd chosen and promptly disappeared from the Sphere. After she entered, Connie realised, *remembered actually*, that binary numbers were largest on the left and should be read right to left. *Shit, shit, fuck,* she thought and then they were there, wherever *there* was. It was way too late to change destinations now. Left to right, right to left, *whatever...*they were wherever they were.

'*Oh...you're not fucking serious,*' Becker said, gawking at the view of their new surrounds. He could see Proxima B and the emergency craft they arrived on and they weren't far away at all. Connie, Dimitri and Emma were by his side, all of them, gasping and panting in terror, staring anxiously at the ship and the planet.

Connie ran to the ship and opened the hatch by rotating the yoke anti-clockwise and punching the open-hatch button and pulling the lever. Connie was inside, followed by the rest of them. She went straight to the huge containers of water and upended the first one all over herself.

Emma grabbed it after Connie was finished and did exactly the same thing. Dimitri and Becker followed, after seeing the girls completely saturated. After what they'd been through, they reckoned they deserved it. Waste of water be damned. They had a good supply onboard and they all knew it.

From a similar multi-gallon container, they all drank deeply, straight from the container. The macaroni-cheese got a huge thumping as well. All of them needed that as well. Food was missed critically, especially by Becker who did his best to make up for lost time. It wasn't a steak but what the hell. Both their thirst and hunger were taken care of for the first time in a long time.

*   *   *

Sleeping well had been a massive problem since they awoke from their extended slumber, but not last night. With a full stomach and thirst extinguished, they slept long and well. Their brains were given a well-earned rest from deprivation and denial. Even though the seats weren't designed for sleep, it didn't matter. They would have slept on nails if need be. And slept well.

Extreme tiredness and nutritional satisfaction made them very comfortable - they all slept in a dreamless slumber. The future, as grim as it looked, could wait until they woke up.

Next morning, the avalanche began.

'Well...what the hell do we do now?' Dimitri asked the obvious question as he stretched high and hard with both arms. 'What should we, um...do now?' he said, in a weirdly high-pitched voice that they had all become fairly much accustomed to on Proxima B.

He peered at Connie through sleep thickened eyes. Emma eyed Connie while Becker continued to snore with his head back on the chair, totally oblivious to everything and everyone around him.

'Very fucking nice,' she said, gawking at him and shaking her head. 'Anyone want to try and wake him...I've tried and I thought he was waking, but it only made him snore louder.' Everyone gurgled with laughter. 'Anyway, when he wakes, I reckon we should finish the trek we were on, which ended when we ran into our friend, Minan.'

Dimitri eyed Emma and they both looked at Connie in agreement.

'It's a long walk, but were in,' Dimitri said. Emma nodded reluctantly, suggesting she knew they had little choice even if she didn't want to do it. She peered at Dimitri. They all agreed – they had to walk.

'Don't know about Becker though, he won't wanna walk.' Emma glance at Becker that back at Connie.

'Okay, good, and don't worry about him. Let him snore for a bit longer. If we wake him, all he'll do is moan and groan and complain of sore legs and a tender back...he'll be impossible. I'll tell him what's happening. There'll be no asking, just telling.'

*   *   *

Becker walked reluctantly forward. His knees hurt, his legs were heavy, his back was sore, and as a whole, he was dog-tired. All things considered, he was a complete wreck and ready to lie down again, and very unprepared to move. But it seemed, he had little choice. Forward he had to go. The captain said so. He was fourth in line, walking maybe ten metres behind Emma, who was third in line. From where they were, he could see the outcrop of rocks where they first saw Minan. There were granules, pebbles, cobbles and boulders, covered with dust, showing the results of volcanism and subsequent weathering on this far off rock, which all happened under beautiful violet skies. At least there was no creature here - they could if they decided, make as much noise as they wanted to, and nothing would be the wiser. It was nice to have at least that little freedom.

No one was keen to walk though because they'd all had enough of it, but they rightly realised there was no other means of getting around. Nor did they want to talk, mainly because of the effect of helium on the vocal cords. That applied especially to Becker and Dimitri who sounded nye on ridiculous, Emma and Connie just sounded cute, like two teddy-bears. The two men were tiring of the unrelenting ridicule.

No-one said a thing for a long time. Silence dominated as they walked. All they could hear was the tromping of their own feet on the hard ground.

'How-far to go?' Becker asked, dragging in a hissing breath, watching from a fair distance behind the group. His legs and back had warmed up a bit but they still hurt like hell, which would only get more severe, he was sure.

'Let me guess...you've had enough of this walking thing, right?' Connie didn't bother to turn around. She kept walking and looking straight ahead. The answer was clear. Except, this time, they were all tired, not just him.

'Well, a rest *would* be nice,' Becker said, holding his back like he could collapse at any time. It hurt like hell, on the verge of spasm, he was sure. Mind you, it had been like that since he left Earth-orbit.

'Oh, *poor bubbie*,' she offered, giving him a condescendingly, disdainful smile. She glanced at the others. 'What do you reckon guys...rest time?' Both of them nodded in agreement. They too, had enough walking for the time being.

'You have your wish, Becker...it is indeed rest time.'

Everyone downed their backpacks and collapsed on the ground next to them. Becker ambled up to the group and did the same. Under the violet sky with a few high clouds, it was just them, in a cluster on the ground. With their heads on backpacks as pillows, they rested, and stared upward at the oddly coloured sky.

Becker looked at Connie, keeping out the glare of Proxima Centauri with a hand. He asked the obvious question. 'Why is the sky violet?' He said curiously.

'I've been wondering the same thing Becker. I'm really not sure, but I do know that a thick atmosphere will scatter shorter wavelengths of light. Then there's nitrogen and the helium together...and *wallah* I suppose, we have purply skies, very different from our blue skies of home. Violet is probably an interplay of all of them.'

They all looked thoughtful and nodded in agreement. 'Sounds good to me,' Becker said, quietly observing her from his position on the ground. 'Probably doesn't matter too much.'

Across from where they were currently lying with their backpacks for pillows, was the outcrop they'd first found Minan on. Now it was empty of everything except rocks, dirt, exposed strata and dust. It was a low surface gossan, a landform that was devoid of any interesting secondary staining and was maybe twenty metres above the plains that surrounded it.

It was small but appeared more significant because everything else around here was flat as a pancake. Was there an orebody below it, like there might be on Earth? An oxidised or secondary zone of deeper primary mineralization? Based on the mineralization within it, or significantly, the lack of it, probably not. But who knew how it worked on an alien planet? Probably the same as Earth, but...maybe not. Until they could get some specialists here, they wouldn't know for sure.

Becker lay back, using his backpack as a pillow, enjoying the heat of the star on his face and *not* walking. He saw Connie, then Emma, transfixed by something, so he turned around to gander in the same direction. What was so damn interesting over there? He craned his neck, stretching to see, still lying down.

'*Oh shit...fuck!* Becker thought, sitting up immediately and peering closely at him, swallowing several times. It can't be him...surely. 'Not again...*Jesus*, enough already, why is he here *again*? 'You gotta be fucking *kidding*,' he said gruffly, wondering why he had followed them to Proxima B *again*. He thought they were done with Minan... at least for a while anyway. Becker, and in fact all of them, had seen quite enough of him.

Connie saw him and knew he was their only means of escaping this rock. She wondered how they could possibly use *him* to their advantage. Minan had his own inflexible agenda and getting him to depart from it was probably impossible. In her mind's-eye she was thinking human versus mouse.

Becker knew Minan wasn't back this time for a "constructive" reason. He was here for a second time and they firmly believed he wasn't there to wish them a good trip. It had to be bad, Becker thought. Everything that came out of his gob tended to be a negative.

Connie and the rest of them were staring at him and at the golden objects that were sucking at the ground around him. She thought they'd gotten rid of them. But, like before, there were four of them, mirage-like, shimmering *somethings* that appeared at least partially see-through, very much like the others. They were lustrous and translucent and he noticed he could see rocks and in fact the entire landscape behind them. They were very pretty to the eye as they danced and twisted in front of him, cleaning rocks of dust as they moved. She'd seen it all before.

The wind and the atmosphere appeared to have no effect on the objects – that was clear. They were far from a natural phenomenon. They moved under their own power and made movements that were nothing to do with air pressure. Wind and its vagaries made no difference to these things at all. Their movement was controlled by something else entirely.

The fact that there were four objects made Connie immediately suspicious. They previously had four objects. Did they get the last answer right or wrong? Only time would tell, she assumed. Minan wouldn't say boo, unless it was something he initiated or it was important to whatever he was considering. So, they had no hope of getting more information. They just had to accept it.

Becker watched them all, and it was fairly obvious what was happening. Connie and the rest of them were waiting for Minan to speak to them. They ping-ponged their gaze between themselves and the kid, trying to anticipate the landing of the words. He looked like he was preparing to speak. Whenever he looked directly at one of them or the group, he spoke. He was doing that now. They were fairly sure it'd be brain-to-brain stuff, and no doubt it would be negative...or somehow bad for the group or the planet.

Minan was staring blankly at Connie without blinking. 'You cannot survive on this planet,' came the expected voice between her ears. *Big surprise*, Becker thought, a negative for us all to share. 'The only way to live is by selecting the correct object. The incorrect object will take you back near your ship again. I then rely on my initial statement.'

Again, she thought grimly. Connie hated the sight of these things...even though they were pretty to the eye, they offered potential death by slow starvation if they weren't used right.

'OOO-kayyy,' Connie said, 'but how do we know which of those things is the right one? It can't be just luck? Connie was pretty sure it'd be like last time. There would be some manner of intuition required. Some brain power involved - she was sure.

'How old is your planet,' Minan then took a deep breath, which was the first time he'd ever done that, it wasn't a sigh but it was an audible breath. Maybe it was his version of a sigh. 'The age of the Earth is the answer you seek, to choose the correct object. It is quite a simple question that Fyoderov wanted answered.'
Minan then walked back to the top of the bluff, making various hand movements that meant nothing to the humans. Long sets of numerals appeared on each object, flowing downward. All of them wondered what it had to do with Fyoderov. The plot thickened, Connie thought. She remembered Minan having discussions with his boss when she mysteriously accompanied Minan to the GD.

Connie wondered what Fyoderov's role in all this was. Why did he have a question for them – what in God's name was he trying to achieve? There was clearly something they were missing. She racked her brain but predictably came up with nothing.

He focussed on Connie. 'Choose one and enter that object. You will know the result without delay. You have one chance.' Minan said.

Connie looked at the group, 'He means,' Connie said, 'if we end up near the ship, on this planet, groundhog-day style, we've failed. And on this fucking planet, we can't live, apparently, according to Minan. From that we can assume that there is nothing to consume on the eyeball part of the planet and probably only ice on the rest of it. We can't eat cyanobacteria. *Christ.*' Connie gawked at the binary figures that flowed downward on the objects, toward the ground.

```
#1     101010011010011001010100000100000000
#2     110011101110011100010010010100000000
#3     111101000010011111010000100100000000
#4     100001000110010110010101110100000000
```

'*Oh shit,*' Becker blurted, '*here we fucking go again*...how the hell are we supposed to read that lot? Makes about as much sense as the last lot.' He walked a little closer to the numerical messes and squinted angrily at each of them - unsurprisingly, proximity made no difference. It still meant zero to him. *Absolutely nothing.* If the kid was trying to destroy his self-worth, job done, Becker reckoned. *Good one, Minan.*

Connie thought again, where was Joe when you needed him...or Vic or Harry? They were all over binary. Now that she had remembered the really big numbers were on the left of a large "one" that filled the sequence of digits, a little was brought back...but only a little. But firstly, what was the answer to the question?

By the look of the others in the group, they had no idea about any of it...or maybe it was just the binary numerals that had them flummoxed. In any event, the question seemed way too much for them. All Connie could see were shaking heads and screwed-up faces. They were all seriously out of their depths with this stuff.

'The age of the Earth...anyone know? Connie studied all three of them narrowly. As she thought, no one had a clue how old their own planet was – all she got were wide eyes that said nada. Connie knew it was older than four billion years and younger than five billion. But she really couldn't narrow it down any further. Was it closer to four or five, she racked her brain, but just didn't know? No-one else could add anything useful.

When it was spoken in an environment like this, and the words came from Minan, the information seemed so basic. But few humans actually knew it. *Clearly, they should know it.* After all, they lived on the damn thing. And called it home. But the age of the planet was a mystery to most.

The exact number of years as an age eluded her too. So, given that no-one had any bright ideas, she'd have no choice but to search for one around the four-billion-year mark. Wasn't foolproof by any means but it was all she had. If there were multiples that had a four, then she was in real trouble. In Becker-speak, they were *fucked and gone*. They'd probably end up relying on pure luck.

Connie gazed at each binary number carefully. They had come a long way, it'd be horrible to make a mistake now and be damned to this planet forever, until their sustenance gave out and they suffered very ugly deaths indeed.

Connie had no doubt that Minan would simply disappear with his golden shifts if they got the answer wrong. They'd be totally on their own. It would be us versus the planet and Connie was sure we would soon join it, given not much time at all. They'd all be dead.

There was only one bunch of binary numerals which said four billion and that was number one. The rest were substantially larger or smaller than four, so it wasn't those, *if* her memory and understanding of binary was correct. She felt like wiping her brow, this decision was a big one. If she was wrong, they would all eventually be dead. *No pressure...like shelling peas.* Connie felt ill at the prospect. Being a leader was hard work even under the best of circumstances. Here, it was nigh on impossible because lives quite literally hung on every decision you made. Made especially hard when you're only leader by default. Connie knew she was never supposed to lead anything. Looking at everyone else, there wasn't much choice. No-one else could or would do it.

They all entered anomaly number one. It looked like they were part of a death-march, single file, very slow. Touching the object of choice, they vanished from the Sphere. The creature wasn't far from sighting them, almost entering the curve, and only blocked from seeing them by a final skyscraper of cylinders that sat between it and them. Another few minutes and it would have started a death-charge from which there would have been no escape. Of course, Minan could have controlled the creature if he chose too.

7

Rinse, repeat

"Intellectuals solve problems, geniuses prevent them."
Albert Einstein

It was clearly a dim tunnel of sorts.

'*Oh fuck...again*,' Becker moaned after looking around, white as a sheet, eyeing his new location, that looked eerily familiar. It looked awfully like a tunnel, albeit a very different one. He was stoked to be alive and on solid ground and not on Proxima B, *but* they were seemingly back in a fucking tunnel.

'*Jesus Christ*...similar, but very different by the looks,' Connie agreed, turning around, and trying to take it all in. She then stared at Becker, goggling her eyes. 'It's *good news* though, it means we've chosen correctly...we aren't near our ship on the surface of Proxima B.' Connie grinned feebly. She was happy to be off-planet but felt like there was an awful lot in front of her. Saying it was "good news" was a bit premature. Connie realised that as soon as she said it. They could still be literally anywhere.

'Where are we now?' Emma asked and Dimitri looked questioningly along with her. He and Emma gawked around – nothing looked familiar. Maybe they weren't off planet at all, perhaps they were *under* it. Although that didn't make sense either. But really, nothing had made sense since they left the Moon, all that time ago.

'These tunnels or whatever they are look artificial,' Emma said with a slight headshake, blowing out her cheeks. She was seriously confused. She had no idea about why, who, or where?

'Just take this as fact – I can't answer *any* questions,' Connie said seriously. She stared at Becker and Dimitri sternly, hoping Emma would hear too, it was meant mainly for her. 'We started out in a tunnel similar to this one, and it turned out to be under Sydney in Australia...on *Earth*. Although gravity and air seem similar, there appears to be no helium here. Our voices are the same as on the Sphere, *not* Proxima B. That said, we should take nothing for granted.' She stared them all down. Emma continued to gaze at Connie long after she finished talking. To say she was baffled and puzzled was a huge understatement.

Whatever this place was, they'd probably never been here before. To hammer that home, it smelt of something feral, an odour she'd never smelt before. It was a tunnel definitely, but it was very different from the first one. It certainly smelt differently and it looked very different. The question of *why* they were here was high in Connie's mind. She refused to repeat herself by asking it – she'd leave that to Emma.

*   *   *

Thankfully but very suspiciously, there were four bottles of clear liquid not far away that they all demolished straight away after Connie sniffed it and was convinced it was clean water only. It was absolutely life-saving – for all of them, or so they thought. They were all enormously thirsty again, having drunk deeply on Proxima B, not sure when the next drink was.

How did the bottles of water get there? Becker just took it in his stride, with minimal thinking about how the bottles got there. For him it was see water – consume water, without thought. He would be so easy to poison if you were that way inclined. Becker didn't even give it a smell. Just straight into it.

The rest of them were highly suspicious, wondering what role Minan played in it. Connie couldn't help seeing him as a puppeteer of sorts...the mental images were disturbing.

'*What about food,*' Becker yelled? 'Water is great, no doubt we need it, but it's only part of the story...am I right?' Becker glared at everyone. He was starving and yearned desperately for anything edible, but especially wanted a nice plump steak. Becker would have it raw if he had to. The rest of them were just glad to be on solid ground, in decent conditions. Clearly, Becker wanted it all. Sustenance, terra firma and general conditions – *the lot,* including no walking. This definitely wasn't the life for him.

'Food is just a state-of-mind Becker, you'll be fine,' Connie said, smiling faintly. 'Humans can go *at least* a fortnight with no food. For you, maybe a month.' She gazed at his midriff and nodded knowingly.

'Gee, thanks Con...state-of-mind 'ayyy, tell that to my stomach.' The water only made him hungrier. He needed real food, desperately. His dreams of a thick steak were getting more and more vivid. Becker knew things were grim.

Connie eyed their surrounds closely. It was even mustier in here than the last place. Actually, it stunk of something very feral, and there were hundreds, maybe thousands of old shoes, *human shoes*, seemingly discarded, in a mound on one side of the walls. Why they were there, she had no idea? She noted that they looked like human shoes though. So did everyone else. Nothing was said out loud, but everyone hoped it meant something positive. Connie assumed the shoes were of human origin, but *were they?* Minan probably had feet like us. She wasn't sure...shades of grey obscured everything. Connie didn't know what to think.

Rusty railway tracks were fixed to old wooden sleepers that disappeared into the distance. It also suggested an Earthly origin because tracks like that meant trains or something very similar. Maybe other worlds and races had them too, but she doubted it. Connie felt sure they were a home technology, but she wasn't entirely certain. They were quite a basic tech on Earth so maybe they were on other worlds too. In other universes.

The tracks were right in the middle of the tunnel and she could see wooden sleepers, very old and well worn, peeking above the fine alluvium. Along with the shoes, the tracks were an important tell-sign of location. Nothing was a given though.

Everything they could see was orangey-brown with large oblong bricks covering the walls and the curved amphitheatre-like roof. On the bottom where the train tracks were, they were discoloured and rusty all over, meaning a locomotive had not used the tracks for many years.

'I'll say it...if no one else will,' Becker eyed everyone closely, his gaze settling on Connie.

'Okay genius let's have it,' Connie said, rolling her eyes at Emma and Dimitri. 'This'll be good...proceed Becker please...we would love your wisdom.' She gestured with her hand for him to continue, that the floor was his. Connie knew what he was going to say – if there was one thing, he was good at, jumping the gun was one of them.

'*Whatever Connie*, but all clues lead to this being on Earth, the shoes, the railway tracks, the lack of helium...all Earth.' Becker stared at them, wide-eyed with a huge smile on his face and thumbs in the air.

'It's hardly empirical Becker...just temper that enthusiasm until we know for sure. Because quite frankly, we don't.'

'Okay, but it looks hopeful anyway.' His face dropped and his shoulders slumped a bit.

All of them nodded and smiled. Emma and Dimitri agreed with Connie, things definitely looked hopeful, but two pieces of evidence did not mean it was a done deal.

*　　　*　　　*

Some sort of light bulbs were illuminating the path for as far as they could see inside this arrow-straight tunnel. It looked like it narrowed alarmingly as she peered down it, but she was sure it was just the nature of vision.

Every fifty, or a hundred and occasionally, every two hundred metres, there was a tunnel that went off to their left. It was exactly the same in appearance to the tunnel they were in, but there were no train tracks on the flat bottom. A nest of five pipes ran along the roof of the main tunnel and they also deviated into the side tunnels.

One of the pipes was clearly for power because the lights were on, but the rest, who knew? An obvious question was – *why* were the lights on? Ordinarily, it would be pitch dark in this place, Connie supposed, picking at her chin, wondering. What the hell were they on? This was an old, disused tunnel presumably. She tried to remember the first tunnel - was it the same?

No, she was fairly sure it was different. There certainly weren't any lights. But interestingly, the first tunnel wasn't dark either, she was sure she would've remembered if there were lights or not.

Connie tried desperately to recall the first tunnel they appeared in, maybe this one was an extension to that one? Both tunnels looked different which made her wonder more. She strained her eyes into the distance – was it actually possible?

Of course, it was possible, she decided, anything was. This tunnel could conceivably be very different indeed, but still be "joined". In other words, she didn't know shit. Anything *was* possible.

What really mattered was where it led, if anywhere. Connie hoped it went *somewhere*, so they knew where the hell they were. If they were still on Proxima B, which she doubted because of the lack of helium, she wanted to know about it. She assumed, rightly or wrongly, that it opened at the surface *somewhere*. She had fingers crossed on both hands.

*　　　*　　　*

'Don't tell me, more walking, right?' Becker rubbed his chest and appeared to go a little pale. 'Just what I feel like doing on an empty stomach with sore legs,' he said, grinning sourly to paper over the real horror he was feeling.

'Good to hear you're excited, Becker,' Connie said without turning around. 'I thought I heard something moving and echoing in the distance...but I couldn't see anything, and the sound's gone now.' Connie shook her head, goggled her eyes and turned around to face the group.

'It's time to walk, so best we get about doing it,' she said nervously, looking closely to make sure they were all ready. She wondered, as they all did, where the hell they'd been sent? Connie hoped Becker was right, but she had major doubts, not the least being the nature of Minan.

Behind Becker, maybe three hundred metres distant, was a *thing,* quite low to the ground, all its eyes and the yellow stripes shining in the light from above, seemingly as surprised to see them gawking at it as they were to see it.

The humans were horrified to see the ghastly thing behind them, seemingly tracking them, while they walked nonchalantly ahead. The thing took huge sniffs of the atmosphere low to the ground despite being able to see them quite easily. The frightening thing had somehow followed them into the tunnel and was stalking them like a lion does an antelope.

Now, it was moving very slowly, watching them intently. The group were walking slowly forward and their odour formed a sheath that extended behind them in the motionless atmosphere – and the creature was within that sheath about ninety metres distant.
Connie could just make out its talons and shark-like teeth, and could see it drooling, with the saliva running down its own leg. It was gnashing its teeth by moving its jaw repeatedly up and down on a muscular hinge. It wanted to kill and eat.

'*...the fuck is wrong Con,*' Becker snapped, knowing Connie only stood and looked like that for a couple of reasons, none of them good. In fact, all of them really *bad*. She appeared genuinely horrified, her swollen eyes and open, frozen mouth said it all. Connie was obviously looking at something terrible – that posed an imminent danger to them all. He knew that likely only meant one thing.

They were all focussed where Connie was looking and they saw it. They could see clearly that the fucking thing had learnt stealth. She would always remember what Quincy told her to do, but this was no dinosaur with questionable eyesight, it was a goddamn killing machine that could probably see in infra-red if it wanted to. DNA would obviously be no saviour this time. They were food for this thing - it wasn't tracking and smelling them for no reason.

They only had one option. And it wasn't to stand still and hope it didn't see them. Clearly, this creature was from a whole other planet. Different planets, different eco-systems, different origins - different behaviours, Connie assumed. But in essence, same machine. In fact, it was way worse, this one no doubt, had the same DNA as them. Which meant, it wanted them as sustenance.

'*Fucking run*,' Connie screamed. This was no time for silence. Their presence in this tunnel was a known fact to it. She sprinted up the left side of the tunnel, avoiding the tracks and the sleepers and running as fast as she could go. Connie could hear them - she knew the rest of the group was right behind her, as she put all her energy into running.

Being eaten alive was a good incentive for sprinting as fast as you possibly could. Emma pretty much kept up with her and Dimitri was close behind.

Becker was a full ten metres behind the Russian and falling further behind, although he was clearly trying as hard as he could. She knew to avoid attack, she only needed to run faster than the slowest runner. That put Becker in serious trouble indeed.

Connie hoped against hope that she would spy a ladder leading to a porthole on the surface. So far, she saw nothing, neither ladder nor hole. All she saw was more tunnel. This place was never-ending. If it turned out to be a loop they were done. They couldn't outrun the damn thing forever.

Turning around, she saw Becker at the rear, running as fast as he could, which wasn't really fast at all, foaming at the mouth and nose, or that's what it looked like, he was trying so hard. The creature too, was drooling, although for a whole different reason, in thick wads from the mouth, and was maybe fifty metres behind him and closing quite quickly for a kill.

Becker couldn't run any faster but was lagging well behind the group. If the fool fell, it was game over.

Ahead, the tunnel ended in a flattish wall. There appeared to be no escape this time. Connie initially thought they could double back and evade the creature like a football player faking the opposition, but then she realised the agility of the creature and its large, multiple talons on each arm. It gave them no hope of evading it and surviving.

They'd be easily caught and then killed and dismembered. Which deterred her from that course of action a tad. Perhaps they should have followed Quincy's advice and not moved...hoping like hell they wouldn't be seen? But everyone knew that wouldn't work. This thing had six eyes, likely binocular vision, and an overall visual acuity that was probably superior to humans. If anything moved or didn't move, this thing would see it and kill it.

As it was, they were all lined up on the wall like a fucking buffet, with the creature not far away to do the choosing. Becker was finally with them, having eventually made it, puffing and breathless and himself drooling everywhere. The poor old sod was totally spent as he turned around on the wall to face his horrid fate. He well realised he couldn't bash his way through solid rock. And his chances of getting past the creature were effectively zero.

The most repulsive, fearsome and odorous thing any of them had ever seen or smelt came furtively up to them, apparently expecting anything from anywhere. The creature nervously approached Connie slowly and stealthily, its huge head looking left and right like a large dog. And she was right, it was exactly the same one she came across in the blue forest on Mars.

She could tell that because it still had a large x-shaped scar on its shoulder. So much for a different planet. So much for different DNA protecting them from being eaten, she thought. It totally defied any form of logic you wanted to throw at it.

If it was the same creature, *why* didn't the chirality of DNA save them? Because so far, it was doing a piss-poor job of doing that. Connie immediately thought of Minan and wondered what impact he had? Anything that was illogical and thoroughly counter-intuitive – cue Minan.

The creature was on Connie first, smelling the air around her, snorting and sniffing her like a dog set loose on dog food. Except there was no eating...just sniffing. It went from top to bottom – very Einsteinian.

Despite looking and sounding ferocious, it did nothing. Every hair on Connie's body stood up as she breathed in small, sharp bursts – expecting to die agonisingly at any moment. The creature's barbs were barely centimetres away from her flesh. Connie breathed and heaved and felt like vomiting – smelling horrible, acrid bile everywhere. Like the first time though, it moved off her without inflicting any harm at all, all she got was a shower of spittle. It had a good sniff, but did no physical damage at all. Maybe it *was* like the first time, Connie thought, perhaps it even remembered, who knew? Why then, did it eviscerate four other versions of her? Nothing seemed to make a whole lot of sense.

Did this thing have the ability to remember or to think? Connie doubted it, maybe it had advanced instinct. They needed a zoologist to work this ugly thing out.

Having looked it in its eyes, even though it had six of them and resembled a spider, there was an intelligence and aptitude that was palpable, she thought. It possessed more than just instinct, she was sure, having looked at the thing closely. Humans equated spiders with insect-like stupidity – but not this one, Connie reckoned. It was smart. Next, the creature shuffled over to Dimitri and took a huge sniff and seemed to like what it smelt. The creature's hidden crest came fully out and its eyes all changed from naval grey to a much lighter colour, perhaps light grey or cream. The crest was a brilliant, vivid crimson-red and was fully erect atop its head, like a massive, horrid, predatorial cockatoo.

Despite the peril of the situation, Becker couldn't help but think "smorgasbord". Here we were, all in a single line...just waiting for the creature to arrive and select. Becker was fairly sure the brute was displaying pleasure, although it was hard to tell.

The crest seemed to suggest it, but he really had no idea. If the damned thing moved onto him, Becker had decided to run. No way he'd let that ugly fucker do the sniff-thing on him...*no way*.

With the crest still fully upright, it stuck its second arm-barb into Dimitri's chest having retracted the first one fully. The Russian screamed in pain and was forced forward toward the creature who immediately went for the kill stroke and cut Dimitri's throat with the first barb from the other arm, showering Emma with warm blood. She squealed and squashed herself further backward against the wall and closed her eyes. Dimitri was as good as dead. He bled out in seconds from a massive, deep jugular wound that flooded the ground with blood.

The creature pulled Dimitri away from the wall and ambled backward and then forward, dragging him along the ground with one muscled arm. He dropped Dimitri about a hundred metres away and proceeded to enjoy his meal.

The creature stood tall after it took a bite with its head craned back to allow gravity to help drag bits of meat down its very wide throat, which was more of a funnel, ringed with massive, sharp, shark-like teeth.

'*Fuck...sh-sh-shit*,' Emma said, shaking her head and muttering more profanities, wiping the red stains from her face, trying desperately to get rid of some of the blood on her. It was literally everywhere. On her, around her, in horrible, stench-ridden black puddles under her.

Dimitri was taken down by something that was very familiar with killing. She heard the cracking of bones as the creature searched for the precious marrow which was especially nutritious and probably tasted really good to the creature. Emma didn't want to look, deliberately focussing closely on the ground right in front of her.

'*We have to move or-that's us*,' Connie said, gawking at the mess not far away, with as much strength as she could muster. She could smell the creature and the kill that used to be Dimitri and felt light-headed and dizzy. To think, that mess and that stench used to be a living, breathing person. It was a fucking nightmare.

At these times, it was really hard not to think of yourself. None of them wanted to end up like that. *No-siree!* If she wasn't hard up against the wall, she was sure she would have crumpled to the ground in a heap. She was dizzy and wobbly, even up against the wall.

Emma cocked her head and closed her eyes, conscious of a low pitched, low volume but fairly continuous sound, somewhere behind her, she ogled sideways at Connie, '*I-hear talking, people...crowds maybe*,' Emma yelled, the first tendrils of excitement hitting her voice. She turned her head and looked behind herself, pointing at the wall.

'*There*,' she yelled again, turning around a bit and squashing her ear on the wall. 'The noise...behind that wall. '*There...there*,' she repeated again, louder. Emma stared at Connie maniacally, her eyes bulging. The question was palpable.

Connie could hear noises too, talking. A lot of people. Maybe a crowd. Whatever it was, it was *people*. Emma had her ear on the rock, listening intently. She was certain there were a lot of "people" somewhere beyond that wall. Emma pulled her ear away and gazed at them all in wonder. How the hell do we get to them? Emma wondered.

Connie firmly believed there was no way to avoid the thing which was blocking the tunnel only ten or so metres in front of them. As it was, if things stayed the same, they were simply waiting to die. Their only option was to escape this tunnel. Of course, the big question was how?

Connie gawked at the wall and hit it with her palm. Hearing it, hitting it, was one thing, but how the fuck do we get through the *Goddamn wall*, she yelled silently to herself. Time was nearly gone, the bone crunching would only go on for so long, then *it* would want more. More of them. The creature continued to eat, unceremoniously.

Panic wasn't far away, she felt it picking at her and growing. Connie's legs were shaking and wobbling under her, she wanted to run, but run where? Somehow, she implored herself to stay still. They had to get through the wall, preferably in one piece. The thing had already nailed Dimitri and would soon return for more.

The creature's behaviour was hardly surprising given that there appeared to be no other source of calories in the tunnel, not animal nor anything else. It had to have food or it would die. But how in God's name did something from a different planet get into this tunnel, she wondered? She couldn't stop dwelling on it.

Her mind kept springing back to Minan. After all, he sent them to blue Mars in the first place. Once again, she thought it had to be Minan and his handiwork. Surely, they weren't on or under blue Mars, were they? The answer, *fuck knows*, was getting old and tiresome - and she knew it. But it seemed apt.

Connie spied a narrow gap between the wall of the tunnel and the flattish back wall. That had to be their only chance for life. Stay here and probably die or get through that gap and live a bit longer. There was no way on God's green Earth the creature was getting through there. With a massive chest like that, no way it was getting through.

With a lot of pushing and prying they'd get Becker through and they would easily follow. It would be a challenge forcing Becker through, but everyone was confident they could do it. That would have to be the plan anyway. If they couldn't...well, he'd die. Simple as that. Connie swallowed and could taste sourness and heat as she visualised it in her mind.

Connie pointed at the rock and Emma and Becker soon caught on. Becker was doubtful, Emma was excited. With a bit of jimmying and scraping, Connie and Emma got through. The creature stood up above the Dimitri leftovers and uttered a bloodcurdling, inhuman roar, which rang in their ears. The creature could see that Emma and Connie had gone. *Prey escaping was bad.* Only Becker remained as the single remaining occupant of the tunnel.

Becker was determined to get through the gap. He scraped and grinded and pushed until he was totally and firmly stuck. The creature was almost on him and could smell the blood left on the rock by Becker's scratches.

'*Come on porky,*' Connie yelled at the top of her voice, hoping to motivate him to bloody well move. 'Suck it in and come join us on this side.' She looked at Becker with feverish eyes. *Don't let it happen to you*, she shouted in her head, still staring desperately at him.

'*Move, for fuck's sake,*' she screamed, staring at him full in the eye. She started crying and Becker saw it.

'It's close Becker...really, really close,' she said, trailing off and fearing the worst. His gut was preventing passage. She sniffed back the tears, or at least tried to. Being an emotional wreck wouldn't help him any.

He was beyond terrified, poor guy, Connie could see it in his eyes, Becker was taken with raw panic, to get through the gap and away from the razor-sharp claws of the scrabbling creature.

'Aarrgghh, umph,' Becker was jiggling his body, trying his very best to force his way through. '*Pull my arm...pull... pull...help me,*' he puffed and gasped loudly. He was looking closely at Connie.

Becker could see the creature getting really close with his peripheral vision, just like Connie had said. She sounded and looked drop-dead scared. Claws and razor-sharp barbs were scraping over hard rock only centimetres from his torso and he could see the damn things digging into the rock. They were very, very sharp. The creature was driven to get him.

'*The fucking thing is nearly on me,*' he shrieked in utter terror. Panic was consuming him – he could see Connie's wet, bulging eyes, ping-ponging between him and the creature, and she looked wide-eyed and horrified, and he could see the maniacal creature reflected in them. Becker knew he had to try harder, he couldn't leave her now. Not now.

With one last Herculean effort, he sucked in his gut until there was no more to suck in and then pushed and scraped his way through and popped out on the other side, falling squarely on Emma who was closely watching his progress, rooting for him, giving Connie support. He ended up right on top of her, pinning her to the granite-laden ground.

The creature tried its best to follow Becker but quickly realised it couldn't and gave up. Hard rock was a difficult enemy at the best of times, most times it couldn't be beaten. The thing made plenty of noise trying to get past it, ending in what they took to be a loud growl of frustration and surrender. It slowly backed-off from the rock and turned around, returning to the tunnel and its recent kill. It would take out its annoyance on the dead Russian. Dimitri was dead permanently this time. In this case, dead meant forever.

All of them, clearly ecstatic to be alive, smiled widely at their dim new surroundings. Becker wondered where the fuck they were this time, although anything had to be an improvement on being in there with *that* creature thing. He brushed himself down and with a knowing grin, looked at Connie.

There was no imminent danger of being eaten alive or slaughtered by sharp teeth and sabres – so that was the good news, he supposed.

They had ventured into yet another broader tunnel but at the end, it seemed quite well lit and ended in a much larger tunnel, that seemed better kept, with newer silvery train track up the left-hand side. Reasonably fresh bright paint was on the bricks of the tunnel, making it look very different than the one in which they encountered the creature.

The voices, the *sound*, must have come from a station of sorts further along, Connie *hoped*. Whatever it was, it just had to be good news, didn't it? In Becker's book, sounds of voices meant people and people meant humans. And that meant Earth. In reality, it didn't mean that, at all. But still Connie thought ...*Hopefully*, it meant that.

Whichever way you looked at it, this place was a huge improvement on the last place they were in. He knew what it meant if the voices were people...*human* people. They all did. Like Connie said though – don't get ahead of yourself, let reality be the arbiter. The voices could be anything...and anyone. *Anything*.

She assumed the crowd noise, whatever it was, would get louder as the mass of individuals got larger, like what usually would happen preceding the arrival of a train or whatever rode the tracks. She hoped like hell that's how it would be. It would be like that back home, or anywhere probably...on any planet, she thought, and snorted loudly, goggling her eyes. The "logic" chestnut thudded into her brain.

Connie, and indeed all of them, knew what finding an abundance of people meant. It meant finding *safety* and *home*. At least that's what they all assumed. If the noise was something other than they hoped, she and they would need to keep thinking, and probably moving without being heard.

*   *   *

They hopped up on the platform with a lot of the crowd focussing on Emma, whose dress was splattered with fresh blood. The huge double-sided sign on the platform said, "Pitt Street".

'Holy f-fuck,' Connie said to herself as she prepared to jump up on the platform, 'Sydney...Earth, *Jesus Christ,'* she whispered, trailing off. So many thoughts hit her at once, she felt totally and utterly off-centre. An avalanche of ecstasy struck all of them, how times had changed. Dizzy, faint, giddy...call it what you like. It was too much, they were home...on Earth. Finally, back *home.* Away from that thing - it felt like the realization of an impossible, absurd dream. From Proxima B back to Earth with zero travel time. It was truly preposterous. The rest clearly felt the same dizzying emotions. Becker and Emma hugged and wished Dimitri had made it. He'd come so far, and to be killed on Earth, *after* he'd returned home, was a fucking travesty.

Minan had really come through for them. Even in the afterglow of happiness and return, Connie wondered why Minan had asked them those obtuse questions that required answering in binary? Very strange, she thought, but he apparently thought these questions and answers were of the utmost significance. *Go figure,* Connie reckoned. She'd never presume to understand his thinking.

Minan had stunning abilities and was of incredible import to their Universe, so whatever he said and did...well, it was good practice to do what he said. Otherwise, it could lead to huge trouble, couldn't it? Again, she'd never presume to comprehend why he did things but concurring with the mind of Earth's real God, was the correct behaviour. Connie felt comfortable with it.

*   *   *

Blood-stained Emma, a bit like fabled Moses, *spread* the large, dense crowd, everyone giving her and the rest of her party a wide as possible berth, as they made their way toward the stairs that led to Sydney proper.

crowd would have guessed that she'd been involved in a rather gruesome killing of some sort and was wanted by the police. Everyone that saw her, stood aside and let her through. No-one in the crowd wanted to confront her. Emma apparently had the scare-factor to cut a swathe through the crowd.

The group, numbering only three now, all ran forward with Emma at the front, going to the city itself. Sydney beckoned above them. Becker and Connie could smell it in front of them, smoggy, oily...and generally funky, and they loved it. It was the smell of Earth. The three of them ran to the escalators that weren't far away, and ascended them, as quickly as they could, jumping from one stair to another. Becker was lagging behind as usual. The three of them went up a second escalator to ground level.

They sat at the nearest bench they could find on the first street they could find which was Bathurst Street and regained whatever small amount of strength they still had.

Becker caught up to them, wiping his mouth with his sleeve, 'beats the hell out of being chased by that creature through an old train tunnel.' He swung his head wonderingly, this way and that, smiling widely, taking in the mall in which they now sat, in the middle of the city. Significantly, to him, he could smell fried food. He inhaled deeply and had a face-splitting smile on his face. Becker gaped at Connie, '*God, it's been a while.*'

'*Hear, hear,*' Connie chimed, and Emma nodded vigorously. Becker was puffing while he was talking, even as he was seated. 'We're back,' Connie said, 'back on Earth...*somehow*. We have to thank Minan I suppose.' She stood up and stretched in the sunshine, enjoying the novel feeling of having heat on her back. The heat of a beautiful, distant Sun. Connie forgot how good it felt. This time, she wasn't underground, or wearing a heavy spacesuit in gravity. Connie was outside, enjoying a small, yellow star that was at just the right distance.

'We can thank Minan, but you got the questions right Con, we had no idea.' Becker looked at Connie, then gazed at Emma and shrugged a shoulder. 'It's uh...not something we're familiar with.' He eyed Connie long and hard.

'Good work Con.' Emma looked at Connie warmly.

'Thanks guys, appreciate it, but it was a team effort. I was trying to save myself as well, so no thanks necessary.' She knew that without her, they were all gone. They might have fluked one answer, but two – *no way.*

Becker and Emma were enjoying watching all manner of people leisurely ambling past their bench, none the wiser. A few gave Emma a second look and then gave her a wide berth, but generally all three of them were invisible. They were pretty much ignored as they perched on the bench, on one side of the mall, and that was nice. It felt good to just watch the world go by and relax.

'I smell food,' Becker said again, smiling contentedly, smelling the alluring scent of fried food. There was a 'Macca's' food joint a bit further down the mall which was shovelling out fries and burgers. The smell was intoxicating and like Becker said, it more than beat the shit out of the smell of the creature.

'We'll eat soon enough,' Connie said, 'you can wait another few minutes, big man.'

Becker gaped around, trying to find the source of the aroma, which he soon enough did. It was his favourite restaurant, along with the delicious steaks of Hog's Breath.

'Oh, you are fucking joking,' Becker spat in a strained voice. Sitting on a bench across the other side of the mall was a young person in a very dark suit indeed. It was Minan. He was in the middle of the bench opposite to them, surrounded on both sides by couples ensconced in talking and not worrying a zac about who they might be sitting next to. Wouldn't they be gob-smacked to know who they were actually sitting next to.

Minan was watching two birds frolicking in a leafless tree nearby. He looked like he didn't have a care in the world. Looking like a kid who had just been to a job interview somewhere in Sydney central Minan didn't look much different from anybody else unless you looked very closely at the way he and his clothes moved.

8

Convocation

"Logic will get you from A to Z; imagination will get you everywhere."
— Albert Einstein

The kid had a very dark suit on which didn't scrunch when he moved – it flowed and glided with him when he moved his muscles. There were no seams or hems or pleats, it was totally one piece of material or whatever it was.

The boy got up and stood tall, stretched, and walked directly toward them, across the mall. He'd ditched his tie and was now sporting an open necked white shirt and looked like any young office worker on a break. Minan was, however, very, very different from a regular office worker. He was the parent of humanity. He was one of the parents of the Universe. Truly one-of-a-kind. His visit to Earth was unheralded.

The person sitting next to Becker got up and started walking down the mall toward the middle of Sydney. Minan took his place and sat right next to Becker, stretching his arms over his head and then resting his hands in his lap, eyes looking straight forward. He seemed quite content to just sit there and enjoy the Sun.

Becker felt compelled to say something. 'So, we meet again.' *Brilliant*, he thought immediately. It made Minan seem like some James Bond villain. Not surprisingly, Minan didn't respond. He just kept looking straight ahead. At what, Becker had no idea. Probably nothing. That was him, he had a strictly no pleasantries offered ever and no answering-banal-questions policy. Minan may have looked like a human being, but he didn't behave like one.

'You have succeeded,' Minan said, not moving a muscle, still gazing straight ahead.

Becker looked straight at Connie, and she at him, raising their eyebrows, both of them stunned. What the hell did that mean? It was the opposite of what he normally said and left them totally gobsmacked. The kid finally said something positive.

Normally, he referred to failure or something similar. He was never encouraging, as they would define it. He was almost always negative. Minan seemed to delight in bringing them down. They reckoned he did save them a few times but say anything like that – *no way.*

'Earth has succeeded,' he repeated in monotone that appeared in their brains loudly via direct infusion.

Confusion and surprise hit them like a sledgehammer after Minan spoke. Minan definitely wasn't one for positive *anythings*. Every time they'd seen him, he had a negative for all of humanity or its Universe...until now.

'Yeah, okay Minan, got it...but *how* did we succeed? *How,*' Connie asked him suspiciously, tilting her head to the left and staring hard at him. She was very wary about what he'd said. Looking down at the brick pavers of the mall, she wondered if she'd get an answer to her query.

She wanted to know what they'd done to "succeed". And what did "succeed" mean? Minan was clearly here to tell them something important, or he wouldn't have bothered to be here at all. That was clear. But what exactly was inside that head of his? Connie puzzled. She knew his intelligence made her seem like an insect in comparison.

He looked strangely animated. Normally, Minan was very subdued indeed. He was silent for a long time, as though he was thinking hard about something before speaking. He was so close, Becker felt like elbowing him for a response, but he refrained. Probably a good decision. It was easy to forget who he was.

Becker needed to remember who the little shit was. He didn't think he was giving him enough credit. Instead of pushing him with his elbow, Becker gazed at him side-on and waited for the answer which sounded like it was coming. He could hear a buzzing between his ears which tended to precede words.

'You are alive,' Minan finally said, '75 percent of you have survived. That was the cut-off that Fyoderov agreed to.' Minan paused for quite a while, and again looked like he was struggling with something.

'Therefore,' Minan continued, staring at Connie, then the rest of them, one at a time, with the bluest eyes, '...Earth now becomes part of the Collective. It is a big occasion for your planet. I wanted you to be inducted immediately, but Fyoderov demanded a trial of sorts. If you passed, you would be inaugurated. If you failed, you would stay as you are.'

'But you r-restarted us four times, doesn't that mean we failed?' Connie said. She stared openly at Minan. 'Dying is a failure, right?' *Surely*, she thought, dying must equal failure. She couldn't imagine anyone arguing against that.

'That was my decision and mine alone, to ensure that failure wasn't the outcome,' Minan said. 'Fyoderov will never know of the time slippage.'

Becker was stunned by his behaviour. For Minan to be here, with this information, was an unusual and in fact as far as he knew, unique occasion.

'Um...er, how will Earth know it's become part of this Collective of yours,' Becker asked. He looked at Connie, shaking his head and tapping an earlobe with his index finger.

'They have no idea about any of this,' Becker said, 'they don't even know there *is* a Collective. They haven't met one alien race yet...they don't even know about *you*. Remember, on Earth, we are still in the age of the Fermi Paradox.' Becker looked squarely at Connie and a questioning gaze passed between them. Connie wasn't sure that was even a question. She was fairly sure Minan wouldn't respond.

'He's right,' Connie said, 'we know others exist, but those on Earth have no idea at all. How will they know they have been inducted into some master race?'

'We will land a regulation craft on your planet,' Minan said.

'*Oh fuck, oh shit*...good luck with that,' Becker said, 'it'll scare everyone to hell and back. DoD will use the damn thing as target practice. Probably start a war or the like.'

'No, that will not happen, because we will immediately offer immortality to everyone on the planet as a genetic vaccine that will render the recipient immortal and subsequent generations the same. Reproduction of cells will be rendered perfect by modifying Binary Fission and Cytokinesis within your cells.'

Minan talked over the muted, garbled sounds of awe and amazement from the humans. 'At the same time, all genetic disease which afflict your DNA, including cancers, will be cured and eliminated forever. Interstellar and intergalactic travel will become easier, with space shortening tech and simple generation of antiparticles and their gravitational isolation, to create a lot of power from very little matter.'

Minan gazed at each of them, full in the eye, eyes stunningly bright and blue. In reality, he *was* mildly curious. He knew all these things were huge advances for humans. They would take millennia to achieve these things by themselves. The understanding from twelve science-based races, was theirs.

'How to manage a global population is also part of the deal. In essence, all these improvements to the human condition will be used as inducements. It has worked many times before and will work on Earth.' He appeared very sure of himself.

Minan shared a playful grin with all of them. None of them had ever seen him do anything like it. Becker wondered if he was finally chilling out a bit. After deliberating for a second, he doubted it, he'd seen way too much of his serious side. Minan had shown himself to be very solemn and grave indeed. This was the first time he'd displayed something different. It seemed that we were now friends rather than "bothersome".

Becker looked unimpressed and worried. "Immediately" won't be quick enough...you need to understand the headspace of our military. It's run by old men in bi-planes...holding enough destructive force to destroy the planet in their palms.'

Minan clearly hadn't finished talking yet but he completely ignored Becker and his histrionics, and Minan had done it many times before so he wasn't going to be taking advice from Becker or even listening to his crazy thoughts.

When Minan had something, he wanted to say, it was *look out*. His contribution to a conversation was normally a short negative. But right now, he was far more, *and unusually*, chatty. Connie thought he looked a bit different too, his eyes were even brighter than normal and there appeared to be more suppleness and movement in his face.

We will also help you to construct a small fusion reactor,' Minan said, 'to allow you to remove unnecessary carbon from your world. And render your planet's biosphere liveable for the long term. We need to move quickly because a fatal tipping point is not far away. Coal burning must be stopped. In short, you will have the technology to make your planet sustainable forever.'

'The reds won't be happy, *oh noooo*,' Becker whispered, smiling widely at the thought of China living without coal, of all things. It underpinned their entire frigging economy. Connie shushed him to allow Minan to continue. This was getting interesting. She wanted to hear everything the kid had to say – not Becker's bullshit.

Minan turned to Connie and Becker for the first time, altering the position of his head so he could see all three of them. His bright azure eyes went emerald green for a moment, as he stared at all three of them. They'd never seen that either. He was showing them a lot of character that was brand new to them.

'You three evaded destruction on the journey to Proxima B. As a quartet and ultimately a trio, you evaded the Paradren (*Parah-drayn*) creature, passed the math test and chose the correct destination on two occasions. You then did the same here, and you are alive and sitting on this bench.'

Connie eyes were stony with suspicion. *Why the tunnels...why, why, why Minan?* Connie thought and hoped there'd be a chance to ask him that, and she hoped to Christ he'd answer her question. If not, it was something she'd be asking herself forever. So, she blurted it out, perhaps louder than she really meant to.

When she had a chance to think, which was rare, it dominated everything. The final episode really cemented it. Either, Minan had a thing for underground tunnels or there was another reason he opted for them. Connie needed to know more. The question of *why* threatened to break her skull. Thankfully, Minan picked up on her intense curiosity.

Minan altered the position of his head slightly so he could stare directly into Connie's eyes. 'It was the only environment in which the Paradren was active, the tunnels were just right as was the sphere with the cylinders, he said. 'Any dimmer and it hibernates, any brighter and the creature is permanently confused and enters a stasis similar to hibernation called estivation or torpor and it can last a very long time. It has evolved to live its life in rainforests on planets orbiting small, dim stars.

'This planet, Earth,' he flourished an arm, 'owes you a great debt of gratitude,' he said, very seriously, still gazing at Connie with large blue eyes. Something important was coming, she was fairly sure. It was the strength of his gaze, boring into her. Minan had something of substance to say. Hopefully, he'd come clean on all the crap that had happened.

'You have qualified the planet to become a member of the Collective,' Minan said. 'Members of the Collective will grow from twelve to thirteen civilisations. The Earth's people will be made immortal and disease-free, and they will all possess the power and the knowledge to fuel anything they choose, in a carbon-free environment.'

Connie admitted it all sounded wonderful. Those that preferred the status-quo would be in the minority, but there would be a few who would protest, she was sure. They wouldn't want anything that was offered by this so-called "Collective". They would be the "anti-techers" as it were.

Connie could see the violent protests in her mind and it wasn't pretty. They'd be on the streets, ready to kill or maim the newcomers and their supporters, or at the very least, reject all their offers.

What would we say to the minority, she wondered...tough luck, majority rules? That wouldn't do it, or even come close to working. Maybe they were right though – it *may* be too good to be true. They'd be suspicious and distrustful and would expect there to be some payback required. A payback that would only be revealed years down the track. After humanity had gotten used to all the benefits.

Those concerns had been put to Minan, and he'd rejected them outright. There was no payback required, not now or in the future. It was free assistance from a group of minds that looked after the multiverse, and civilisations that warranted help.

Immortal populations, all cancer free with unlimited fusion energy. Only those that wanted it, got it, presumably. They would certainly be the majority but not the entirety. She was sure humans would work it out. Whatever they worked out, Earth would be part of the Collective.

But everyone knew there was no such thing as a truly free lunch. Or was there?

Time would tell.